Barbara Delinsky

Looking for Peyton Place

S0-BCI-570

**LARGE
PRINT
PRESS**

Waterville, Maine

Copyright © 2005 by Barbara Delinsky

All rights reserved.

This book is a work of fiction. Names, characters, places, and incidents either are products of the author's imagination or are used fictitiously. Any resemblance to actual events, locales, or persons, living or dead, is entirely coincidental.

Published in 2006 by arrangement with Scribner, an imprint of Simon & Schuster Inc.

The text of this Large Print edition is unabridged.
Other aspects of the book may vary from the original edition.

Set in 16 pt. Plantin by Minnie B. Raven.

Printed in the United States on permanent paper.

The Library of Congress has cataloged the Thorndike Press® edition as follows:

Delinsky, Barbara.
    Looking for Peyton Place / by Barbara Delinsky.
       p. cm.
    "Thorndike Press large print basic series" — T.p. verso
    ISBN 0-7862-7702-5 (lg. print : hc : alk. paper)
    ISBN 1-59413-138-4 (lg. print : sc : alk. paper)
    1. City and town life — Fiction. 2. New England — Fiction. 3. Paper mills — Fiction. 4. Pollution — Fiction. 5. Large type books. 6. Domestic fiction. I. Title.
PS3554.E4427L66 2005
  813'.54—dc22   2005008967

To my family,
with thanks and love

National Association for Visually Handicapped
---------------------------- *serving the partially seeing*

As the Founder/CEO of NAVH, the only national health agency solely devoted to those who, although not totally blind, have an eye disease which could lead to serious visual impairment, I am pleased to recognize Thorndike Press★ as one of the leading publishers in the large print field.

Founded in 1954 in San Francisco to prepare large print textbooks for partially seeing children, NAVH became the pioneer and standard setting agency in the preparation of large type.

Today, those publishers who meet our standards carry the prestigious "Seal of Approval" indicating high quality large print. We are delighted that Thorndike Press is one of the publishers whose titles meet these standards. We are also pleased to recognize the significant contribution Thorndike Press is making in this important and growing field.

Lorraine H. Marchi, L.H.D.
Founder/CEO
NAVH

★ Thorndike Press encompasses the following imprints: Thorndike, Wheeler, Walker and Large Print Press.

Acknowledgments

Gathering information on Grace Metalious was a challenge. So long after her death, precious little about her is in print. Two books, in particular, were a help: *The Girl From "Peyton Place,"* by George Metalious and June O'Shea (Dell Publishing Company, 1965) and *Inside Peyton Place: The Life of Grace Metalious*, by Emily Toth (Doubleday & Company, Inc., 1981). I found additional insight on Grace and her times in Ardis Cameron's introduction to the most recent edition of *Peyton Place* (Northeastern University Press, 1999). Finally, for information on Grace's childhood years in Manchester, New Hampshire, I thank Robert Perrault.

Having absorbed what I could from these sources, I tried to imagine what Grace would think, feel, and say. If my imaginings differ from what those who knew her saw, the fault is mine and mine alone.

For information on the current state of mercury regulation, I thank Stephanie

D'Agostino, Co-Chair of the Mercury Reduction Task Force, New Hampshire Department of Environmental Services. For insight into what mercury poisoning actually *feels* like, I thank Claire Marino. At her behest, I advise readers that the treatment for mercury poisoning outlined in *Looking for Peyton Place* is still considered "alternative medicine." Though individuals do swear by its success, there is, as yet, no scientific study to suggest that it be the treatment of choice.

Thanks to the entire tireless Scribner publishing team. And again, always, I thank my agent, Amy Berkower.

Prologue

I am a writer. My third and most recent novel won critical acclaim and a lengthy stay on the best-seller lists, a fact that nearly a year later I'm still trying to grasp. Rarely does a day pass when I don't feel deep gratitude. I'm only thirty-three. Not many writers attain the success I have in a lifetime, much less at my age, much less with the inauspicious start I had.

By rights, given how my earliest work was ridiculed, I should have given up. That I didn't spoke either of an irrepressible creative drive or of stubbornness. I suspect it was a bit of both.

It was also Grace.

Let me explain.

I am from Middle River. Middle River is a small town in northern New Hampshire that, true to its name, sits on a river midway between two others, the Connecticut and the Androscoggin. I was born and raised there. That meant living not only in the shadow of the White Mountains, but in that of Grace Metalious.

Grace *who?* you ask.

Had I not been from Middle River, I probably wouldn't have known who she was, either. I'm too young. Her provocative best-seller, *Peyton Place*, was published in 1956, sixteen years before I was born. Likewise, I missed the movie and the television show, both of which followed the book in close succession. By the time I arrived in 1972, the movie had been mothballed and the evening TV show canceled. An afternoon show was in the works, but by then Grace had been dead seven years, and her name was largely forgotten.

I am always amazed by how quickly her fame faded. To hear tell, when *Peyton Place* first came out, Grace Metalious made headlines all over the country. She was an unknown who penned an explosive novel, a New Hampshire schoolteacher's wife who wrote about sex, a young woman in sneakers and blue jeans who dared tell the truth about small-town life and — even more unheard-of — about the yearnings of women. Though by today's standards *Peyton Place* is tame, in 1956 the book was a shocker. It was banned in a handful of American counties, in many more libraries than that, and in Canada, Italy, and Australia; Grace was shunned by neighbors and received threatening mail; her husband lost his job, her children were harassed by classmates. And all the while millions of people, men and women alike, were reading *Peyton Place* on the sly. To this day, take any copy from a library shelf, and it falls open to the racy parts.

But memory is as fickle as the woman Grace claimed Indian summer to be in the opening lines of her book. Within a decade of its publication and her own consequent notoriety, people mentioning *Peyton Place* were more apt to think of Mia Farrow and Ryan O'Neal on TV, or of Betty Anderson teasing Rodney Harrington in the backseat of John Pillsbury's car, or of Constance MacKenzie and Tomas Makris petting on the lakeshore at night, than of Grace Metalious. *Peyton Place* had taken on a life of its own, synonymous with small-town secrets, scandals, and sex. Grace had become irrelevant.

Grace was never irrelevant in Middle River, though. Long after *Peyton Place* was eclipsed by more graphic novels, she was alternately adored and reviled — because Middle River knew what the rest of the world did not, and whether the town was right didn't matter. All that mattered was the depth of our conviction. We knew that *Peyton Place* wasn't modeled after Gilmanton or Belmont, as was popularly believed. It's *us*, Middle River said when the book first appeared, and that conviction never died.

This I knew firsthand. Even all those years after *Peyton Place*'s publication, when I was old enough to read, old enough to spend hours in the library, old enough to lock myself in the bathroom to write in my journal and to have the sense that I was following in a famous someone's footsteps, the town talked. There were too many parallels between Peyton Place and Middle River to ignore, starting with the physical layout of the town, proceeding to characters like the wealthy owner of the newspaper, the feisty but good-hearted doctor, the adored spinster teacher and the town drunk, and ending, in a major way, with the paper mill. In *Peyton Place*, the mill was owned and, hence, the town controlled by Leslie Harrington; in Middle River, that family name was Meade. Benjamin Meade was the patriarch then, and he wielded the same arrogant power as Leslie Harrington. And like Leslie's son Rodney, Benjamin's son, Sandy, was cocksure and wild.

Naysayers called these parallels mere coincidence. After all, Middle River sat farther north than the towns in which Grace Metalious had lived. Moreover, we had no proof that Grace had ever actually driven down our Oak Street, seen the red brick of Benjamin Meade's Northwood Mill, or eavesdropped on town gossip from a booth at Omie's Diner.

Mere coincidence, those naysayers repeated.

But *this* much coincidence? Middle River asked.

There were other similarities between the fictitious Peyton Place and our very real Middle River — scandals, notably — some of which I'll recount later. The only one I need to mention now is a personal one. Two major characters in *Peyton Place* were Constance MacKenzie and her daughter, Allison. With frightening accuracy, they corresponded to Middle River's own Connie McCall and her daughter, Alyssa. Like their fictitious counterparts, Connie and Alyssa lived manless in Connie's childhood home. Connie ran a dress shop, as did Constance MacKenzie. Likewise, Connie's Alyssa was born in New York, returned to Middle River with her mother and no father, and grew up an introverted child who always felt different from her peers.

The personal part? Connie McCall was my grandmother, Alyssa my mother.

My name is Annie Barnes. Anne, actually. But Anne was too serious a name for a very serious child, which apparently I was from the start. My mother often said that within days of my birth, she would have named me Joy, Daisy, or Gaye, if she hadn't already registered Anne with the state. Calling me Annie was her attempt to soften that up. It worked particularly well, since my middle initial was *E*. I was Anne E. Annie. The *E* was for Ellen — another serious name — but my sisters considered me lucky. They were named Phoebe and Sabina, after ancient goddesses, something they felt was pretentious, albeit characteristic of our mother, whose whimsy often gravitated toward myth. By the time I was born, though, our father was sick, finances were tight, and Mom was in a down-to-earth stage.

If that sounds critical, I don't mean it to be. I respected my mother tremendously. She was a woman caught between generations, torn between wanting to make a name for herself and wanting to make a family. She had to choose. Middle River wouldn't let her do both.

That's one of the things I resent about

the town. Another is the way my mother and grandmother were treated when *Peyton Place* first appeared. Prior to that time, Middle River had bought into the story that my grandmother was duly married and living in New York with her husband when my mother was conceived, but that the man died shortly thereafter. When *Peyton Place* suggested another scenario, people began snooping into birth and death records, and the truth emerged.

If you're thinking that my grandmother might have sued Grace Metalious for libel, think again. Even if she could prove malicious intent on Grace's part — which she surely couldn't — people didn't jump to litigate in the 1950s the way they do now. Besides, the last thing my grandmother would have wanted was to draw attention to herself. Grace's fictional Constance MacKenzie had it easy; the only person to learn her secret was Tomas Makris, who loved her enough to accept what she had done. My real-life grandmother had no Tomas Makris. Outed to the entire town as an unmarried woman with a bastard child, she was the butt of sly whispers and scornful looks for years to come. This took its toll. No extrovert to begin with, she withdrew into herself all the more. If it hadn't been for the dress shop, which she relied on as her only source of support and ran with quiet dignity — and skill enough to attract even reluctant customers — she would have become a recluse.

So I did hold a grudge against the town. I found Middle River stifling, stagnant, and cruel. I looked at my sisters, and saw intelligent women in their thirties whose lives were wasted in a town that discouraged free expression and honest thought. I looked at my mother, and saw a woman who had died at sixty-five — *too young* — following Middle River rules. I looked at myself and saw someone so hurt by her childhood experiences that she'd had to leave town.

I faulted Middle River for much of that.

Grace Metalious was to blame for the rest. Her book changed all of our lives — mine, perhaps, more than some. Since Middle River considered my mother and grandmother an intricate part of *Peyton Place*, when I took to writing myself, comparisons with Grace were inevitable. Aside from those by a local bookseller — analogous in support to Allison MacKenzie's teacher in *Peyton Place* — the comparisons were always derogatory. I was a homely child with my nose in books, then a lonely teenager writing what I thought to be made-up stories about people in town, and I stepped on a number of toes. I had no idea that I was telling secrets, had no idea that what I said was true. I didn't know what instinctive insight was, much less that I had it.

Too smart for her own good, huffed one peeved subject. *There's a bad seed in that child,* declared another. *If she isn't careful,* warned a third, *she'll end up in the same mess Grace did.*

Intrigued, albeit perversely, I learned all I could about Grace. As I grew, I identified with her on many levels, from the isolation she felt as a child, to her appreciation of strong men, to her approach to being a novelist. She became part of my psyche, my alter ego at times. In my loneliness I talked with her, carried on actual conversations with her right up into my college years. More than once I dreamed we were related — and it wasn't a bad thought at all, because I loved her spirit. She often said she wrote for the money, but my reading suggests it went deeper than that. She was driven to write. She wanted to do it well. And she wanted her work to be taken seriously.

So did I. In that sense alone, Grace was

an inspiration to me, because *Peyton Place* was about far more than sex. Move past titillation, and you have the story of women coming into their own. This was what I wrote about, myself.

But I saw what had happened to Grace. Initial perceptions stick; once seen as a writer of backseat sex, always seen as a writer of backseat sex. So I avoided backseat sex. I chose my publisher with care. Rather than being manipulated by publicity as Grace had been, I manipulated the publicity myself. Image was crucial. My bio didn't mention Middle River, but struck a more sophisticated pose. It helped that I lived in Washington, a hub of urbanity even with its political hot air — helped that Greg Steele, my roommate, was a national correspondent for network television and that I was his date at numerous events of state — helped that I had grown into a passably stylish adult who could wear Armani with an ease that made my dark hair, pale skin, and overly wide-set eyes look exotic.

Unfortunately, Middle River didn't see any of this — because yes, initial perceptions stuck. The town was fixated on my being its own Grace. It didn't matter that I had been gone for fifteen years, during which time I had built a national name for myself. When I showed up there last August, they were convinced I had returned to write about them.

The irony, of course, was that I didn't seriously consider it until they started asking. *They* put the bug in my ear. But I didn't deny it. I was angry enough to let them worry. My mother was dead. I wanted to know why. My sisters were content to say that she died after a fall down the stairs, in turn caused by a loss of balance. I agreed that the fall had killed her, but the balance part bothered me. I wanted to know *why* her balance had been so bad.

Something was going on in Middle River. It wasn't documented — God help us if anything there was forthright — but the *Middle River Times,* which I received weekly, was always reporting about someone or other who was sick. Granted, I was a novelist; if I hadn't been born with a vivid imagination, I would have developed one in the course of my work, which meant that I could dream up scenarios with ease. But wouldn't *you* think something was fishy if people in a small town of five thousand, max, were increasingly, chronically ill?

19

As with any good plot, dreaming it up took a while. I was too numb to do much of anything at first. My sisters hadn't painted a picture anywhere near as bleak as they might have, so my mother's death came at me almost out of the blue. I'd like to say Phoebe and Sabina were sparing me worry — but we three knew better. There was an established protocol. What I didn't ask, they didn't tell. We weren't very close.

The funeral was in June. I was in Middle River for three days, and left with no plans ever to return.

Then the numbness wore off, and a niggling began. It had to do with my sister Phoebe, who was so grief-stricken calling me about Mom's death that she didn't know my voice on the phone, so distracted when I reached Middle River that carrying on a conversation with her was difficult. It was only natural that Mom's death would hit her the hardest, Sabina argued dismissively when I asked her about it. Not only had they lived and worked together, but Phoebe was the one who had found Mom at the foot of the stairs.

Still, I had seen things in Phoebe during those three days in Middle River that, in hindsight and with a clearer mind myself now, were eerily reminiscent of Mom's unsteadiness, and I was haunted. How to explain Mom being sick? How to explain *Phoebe* being sick? Naturally, my imagination kicked into high gear. I thought of recessive genes, of pharmacological complications, of medical incompetency. I thought of the TCE used to clean printing presses down the street from the store. I thought of *poison,* though had no idea why anyone would have cause to poison my mother and sister. Of all the scenarios I dreamed up, the one I liked best had to do with the release of toxicity into the air by Northwood Mill. I detested the Meades. They had been responsible for the greatest humiliation of my life. As villains went, they were ideal.

That said, I had been in enough discussions with Greg and his colleagues about the importance of impartiality to know not to point every finger at Northwood. During those warm July weeks, I divided my time between finishing the revisions of my new book and exploring those other possibilities.

Actually, I spent more time on the latter. It wasn't an obsession. But the more I read, the more into it I was.

I ruled out TCE, because it caused cancer, not the Parkinsonian symptoms

Mom had had. I ruled out pharmacologic complications, because neither Mom nor Phoebe took much beyond vitamins. Mercury poisoning would have been perfect, and the mill did produce mercury. Or it had. Unfortunately for me, state records showed that Northwood had stopped using mercury years before.

I finally came across lead. Mom's store, Miss Lissy's Closet, had been rehabbed four years ago, largely for decorating purposes, but also for the sake of scraping down and removing old layers of paint that contained lead. My research told me that lead poisoning could cause neurological disorders as well as memory lapses and concentration problems. If Mom and Phoebe had been in the store while the work was being done, and ventilation had been poor, they might have inhaled significant amounts of lead-laden dust. Mom was older, hence weakened sooner.

Lead poisoning made sense. The clincher, for me, was that the Meades owned the building, had suggested doing the work, and had hired the man who carried it out. I would like nothing more than to have the Meades found liable for the result.

Facts were needed, of course. I tried to ask Phoebe whether she and Mom had been in the store while the work was being done, what precautions had been taken, whether the date of the work had preceded Mom's first symptoms. But my questions confused her.

Sabina wasn't confused. She said — unequivocally — that I was making things worse.

Worse was the operative word. Phoebe wasn't recovering from Mom's death, and my imagination wouldn't let go.

By the end of July, I made the decision. August promised to be brutal in the nation's capital — hot, humid, and highly deserted. Most of my friends would be gone through Labor Day. Greg had been given a month's leave by the network and was bound for Alaska to climb Mount McKinley, which was a three-week trek even without travel to and from. There was little reason for me to hang around in the District and good reason for me to leave. I had done all I could from afar. I had to be with Phoebe again to see if what I imagined seeing in her were really symptoms. I had to talk with people to learn how much of the paint removed had contained lead and how it had been removed. A phone call wouldn't do it. A *dozen* phone calls wouldn't do it.

I hadn't spent more than a weekend in Middle River in fifteen years. That I was willing to do so now vouched for my concern.

By the way, if you're thinking I never saw my mother and sisters during those years of exile, you're wrong. I saw them. Every winter, we met somewhere warm. The destination varied, but not the deal. I paid for us all, including Phoebe's husband while they were married and Sabina's longer-lasting husband and kids. Same with the summers we met in Bar Harbor. I had the money and was glad to spend it on our annual reunion. Unspoken but understood was my aversion to the tongue-wagging that would take place if I showed up in town.

I was right to expect it. Sure enough, this August, though I pulled up at the house on Willow Street at night, by noon the next day, word of my arrival had spread. During a quick stop at the post office, I was approached by six — *six* — people asking if I had come home to write about them.

I didn't answer, simply smiled, but the question kept coming. It came with such frequency over the next few days that my imagination went into overdrive. Middle River was nervous. I wondered what dirty little secrets the locals had to hide.

But dirty little secrets of the personal variety didn't interest me. I had no intention of being cast in the Grace Metalious role. She and I hadn't talked in years — as "talking" with a dead person went. I had earned my own name. I had my own life, my own friends, my own career. The only reason I was in Middle River was to find an explanation for my family's illness. Could be it was lead. Could be it wasn't. Either way, I had to know.

Then came the photo. Several days before I left Washington, I was at the kitchen table with my laptop, finishing the revisions of my next book. Morning sun burned across the wood floor with the promise of another scorcher. The central air was off, the windows open. I knew that I had barely an hour before that would have to change, but I loved the sound of birds in our lone backyard tree.

I wore denim shorts, a skimpy T-shirt, and my barest Mephisto slides. My hair was in a ponytail, my face without makeup. I hadn't been working fifteen minutes when I kicked off the slides. Even my iced latte was sweating.

Studying the laptop screen, I sat back, put the heels of my feet on the edge of the seat, braced my elbows on my knees and rested my mouth on my fists.

Click.

"The writer at work," Greg declared with a grin as he approached from the door.

Greg was usually the handsome face of the news, not a filmer of it. But he was a digital junkie. He had researched for days before deciding which camera to buy for his trip. "That the new one?" I asked.

"Sure is," he replied, fiddling with buttons. "Eight megapixels, ten times optical zoom, five-area autofocus. It's a beauty." He held out the camera so that I could see the monitor, and the picture he had taken.

My first thought was that I looked very un-Washington-like, very naive, very much the country girl I didn't want to be. My second thought was that I looked a lot like Grace Metalious had in her famed photograph.

Oh, there were differences. I was slim, she was heavier-set. My hair was straight and in a high ponytail, while hers was caught at the nape of her neck and had waves. In the photograph, she wore a plaid flannel shirt, jeans rolled to midcalf, and sneakers; I wore shorts and no shoes. But she sat at her typewriter with her feet up as

I did, with her elbows on her knees and her mouth propped on her hands. Eyes dark as mine, she was focused on the words she had written.

Pandora in Blue Jeans, the shot was called. It was Grace's official author photo, the one that had appeared on the original edition of *Peyton Place* and been reproduced thousands of times since. That Greg had inadvertently taken a similar shot of me so soon before my return home struck me as eerie.

I pushed it out of my mind at the time. Weeks later, though, I would remember. By then, Grace would be driving me nuts.

Her story had no happy ending. As successful as *Peyton Place* was, Grace saw only a small part of the money it made, and that she spent largely on hangers-on who were only too eager to take. Distraught over reviews that reduced *Peyton Place* to trash, she set the bar so high for her subsequent work that she was destined to fail. She turned to booze. She married three times — twice to the same man — and had numerous affairs. Feeling unattractive, untalented, and unloved, she drank herself to death at the age of thirty-nine.

I had no intention of doing that. I had a home; I had friends. I had a successful career, with a new book coming out the next spring and a contract for more. I didn't need money or adulation, as Grace had. I wasn't desperate for a father figure, as she was, and I didn't have a husband to lose his job or children to be taunted by classmates.

All I wanted was the truth about why my sister was sick and my mother was dead.

Chapter 1

I approached Middle River at midnight —
pure cowardice on my part. Had I chosen to,
I might have left Washington at seven in the
morning and reached town in time to cruise
down Oak Street in broad daylight. But then
I would have been seen. My little BMW convertible, bought used but adored, would
have stood out among the pickups and vans,
and my D.C. plates would have clinched it.
Middle River had expected me back in June
for the funeral, but it wasn't expecting me
now. For that reason, my face alone would
have drawn stares.

But I wasn't in the mood to be stared at,
much less to be the night's gossip. As confident as my Washington self was, that confidence had gradually slipped as I had
driven north. I drank Evian; I nibbled a
grilled salmon wrap from Sutton Place and
snacked on milk chocolate Toblerone. I
rolled my white jeans into capris, raised
the collar of my imported knit shirt, caught
my hair up in a careless twist held by

29

bamboo sticks — anything to play up sophistication, to no avail. By the time I reached Middle River, I was feeling like the dorky misfit I had been when I left town fifteen years before.

Focus, I told myself for the umpteenth time since leaving Washington. *You're not dorky anymore. You've found your niche. You're a successful woman, a talented writer. Critics say it; the reading public says it. The opinion of Middle River doesn't matter. You're here for one reason, and one reason alone.*

Indeed, I was. All I had to do was to remember that Mom wouldn't be at the house when I arrived, and my anger was stoked. I wrapped myself in that anger and in the warm night air when, in an act of defiance just south of town, I lowered the convertible top. When Middle River came into view, I was able to see every sleepy inch.

To the naive eye, especially under a clear moon, the setting was quaint. In *Peyton Place*, the main street was Elm. In ours, it was Oak. Running through the center of town, it was wide enough to allow for sidewalks, trees, and diagonal parking. Shops on either side were softly lit for the night in a way that gave a brief inner glimpse of the purpose of each: a lineup of lawn mowers in Farnum Hardware, shelves of magazines in News 'n Chews, vitamin displays at The Apothecary. Around the corner was the local pub, the Sheep Pen, dark except for the frothy stein that hung high outside.

On my left as I crossed the intersection of Oak and Pine, a barbershop pole marked the corner where Jimmy Sacco had cut hair for years before passing his scissors to Jimmy the younger. The pole gleamed in my headlights, tossing an aura of light across the benches on either side of the corner. In good weather those benches were filled, every bit as much the site of gossip-mongering as the nail shop over on Willow. At night they were empty.

Or usually so. Something moved on one of them now, small and low to the seat, and I was instantly taken back. Barnaby? Could it be? He had been just a kitten when I left town. Cats often lived longer than fifteen years.

Unable to resist, I pulled over to the curb and shifted into park. Leaving my door open, I went up the single step and, with care now, across the boardwalk to the bench. I used to love Barnaby. More to the point, Barnaby used to love me.

But this wasn't Barnaby. Up close, I could see that. This cat, sitting up now, was a tabby. It was orange, not gray, and more fuzzy than Barnaby had been. A child of Barnaby's? Possibly. The old coot had sired a slew of babies over the years. My mother, who knew of my fondness for Barnaby, had kept me apprised.

Soothed by the faint whiff of hair tonic that clung to the clapboards behind the bench, I extended a hand to the new guard. The cat sniffed it front and back, then pushed its head against my thumb. Smiling, I scratched its ears until, with a put-put-putter, it began to purr. There is nothing like a cat's purr. I had missed this.

I was straightening when I heard a murmur. *Cats have claws,* it might have said, but when I looked around, there were no shadows, no human forms.

The cat continued to purr.

I listened for a minute, but the only sound here on the barbershop porch was that purr. Again, I looked around. Still, nothing.

Chalking it up to fatigue, I returned to my car and drove on — and again the town's charm hit me. Across the street was the bank and, set back from the sidewalk, the town hall. The Catholic church was behind me and the Congregational church ahead, white spires gently lit. Each was surrounded by its woodsy flock, a generous congregation of trees casting moon shadows on the land. It was a poet's dream.

But I was no poet. Nor was I naive. I knew the ugly little secrets the darkness concealed, and it went far beyond those men who, like Barnaby, sowed their seed about town. I knew that there was a place on the sign between *Farnum* and *Hardware* where *and Son* had been, until that son was arrested for molesting a nine-year-old neighbor and given a lengthy jail term. I knew that a bitter family feud had erupted when old man Harriman died, resulting in the splitting of Harriman's General Store into a grocery and a bakery, two separate entities, each with its own door, its own space, and its own sign, and a solid brick wall between. I knew that there were scorch marks, scrubbed and faded but visible nonetheless, on the stone front of the newspaper office, where Gunnar Szlewitchenz, the onetime town drunk, had lit a fire in anger at the editor for misspelling his name in a piece. I knew that there was a patched part of the curb in front of the bank, a reminder of Karl Holt's attempt to use his truck as a lethal weapon against his cheating wife, who had worked inside.

These things were legend in Middle River, stories that every native knew but was loathe to share with outsiders. Middle River was insular, its face carefully made up to hide warts.

Holding this thought, I managed to avoid nostalgia until I passed the roses at Road's End Inn. Then it hit in a visceral way. Though I couldn't see the blooms in the dark, the smell was as familiar to me as any childhood memory, as evocative of summer in Middle River as the ripe oak, the pungent hemlock, the moist earth.

Succumbing for an instant, I was a child returning with chocolate pennies from News 'n Chews, shopping alone for the first time, using those rosebushes as a marker pointing me home. I could taste the chocolate, could feel the excitement of being alone, the sense of being grown-up but just a tad afraid, could smell the roses — unbelievably fragrant and sweet — and know I was on the right path.

Now as then, I made a left on Cedar, but I had no sooner completed the turn when I stepped on the brake. On the road half a block ahead, spotlit in the dark, was a tangle of bare flesh, one body, no, two bodies entwined a second too long in that telltale way. By the time they were up and streaking for the trees amid gales of laughter, I had my head down, eyes closed, cheeks red. When I looked up, they were gone. My blush lingered.

"Pulling a backabehind," it was called by the kids in town, and it had been a daredevil antic for years. Middle River's answer to the mile-high club, pulling a backabehind entailed making love in the center of town at midnight. This couple would get points off for being on Cedar, rather than on Oak, and points off if the coupling failed to end in, uh, release. Whether they would tell the truth about either was doubtful, but the retelling would perpetuate the rite.

Growing up here, I had thought pulling a backabehind was the epitome of evil. Now, seeing two people clearly enjoying themselves, doing something they would have done elsewhere anyway, I was amused. Grace would have loved this. She would have written it into one of her books. Heck, she would have done it herself, likely with George, the tall, sexy Greek who was her first and third husband and, often, her partner in rebellion.

Still smiling, I approached the river. The air was suddenly warmer and more humid, barely moving past my flushed face as I drove. The sound of night frogs and crickets rose above the hum of my engine, but the river flowed silently, seeming this night unwilling to compete. And yet I knew it was there. It was always there, in both name and fact. Easily 70 percent of the town's workforce drew a weekly paycheck from the Northwood Mill account, and the river was the lifeblood of the mill.

A short block up, I turned right onto Willow. It wasn't the fanciest street in town; that would be Birch, where the elite lived in their grand brick-and-ivy Colonials. But what Willow lacked in grandeur it made up for in charm. The houses here were Victorian, no two exactly alike. The moon picked out assorted gables, crossbars, and decorative trim; my headlights bounced off picket fences of various heights and styles. The front yards were nowhere near as meticulously manicured as those on Birch, but they were lush. Maples rose high and spread wide; rhododendron, mountain laurel, lilac, and forsythia, though well past bloom, were all richly leafed. And the street's namesake willows? They stood on the riverbank, as tall and stately as anything weeping could be, their fountainous forms graceful enough for us to forgive them the mess their leaves made of our lawns.

Quaint downtown, quintessentially New England homes, historic mill — I understood how a visitor could fall in love with Middle River. Its visual appeal was strong. But I wasn't being taken in. This rose had a thorn; I had been pricked too many times to forget it. I wasn't here to be charmed, only to find an answer or two.

Naturally, I was more diplomatic in the voice message I had left earlier for Phoebe. The few questions I had asked since I'd been here last hadn't been well received. Phoebe was unsettled and Sabina defensive. I didn't want to get off on the wrong foot now.

With Mom gone, Phoebe, who was the oldest of us three, lived alone in the house where we grew up. If I still had a home in Middle River, it was here. I didn't consider staying anywhere else.

"Hey, Phoebe," I had said after the beep, "it's me. Believe it or not, I'm on my way up there. Mom's death keeps nagging at me. I think I just need to be with you guys a little. Sabina doesn't know I'm coming. I'll surprise her tomorrow. But I didn't want to frighten you by showing up unannounced in the middle of the night. Don't wait up. I'll see you in the morning."

The house was the fifth on the left,

yellow with white trim that glowed in my headlights as I turned into the driveway. Pulling around Phoebe's van, I parked way back by the garage, where my car wouldn't be seen from the street. I checked the sky; not a cloud. Leaving the top down, I climbed out and took my bags from the trunk. Looping straps over shoulders and juggling the rest, I started up the side stairs, then stopped, burdened not so much by the weight of luggage as by memory. No anger came with it now, only grief. Mom wouldn't be inside. She would never be inside again.

And yet I pictured her there, just beyond the kitchen door, sitting at the table waiting for me to come home. Her face would be scrubbed clean, her short, wavy blonde hair tucked behind her ears, and her eyes concerned. Oh, and she would be wearing pajamas. I smiled at the memory of that. She claimed it was about warmth, and perhaps it was, though I do remember her wearing nightgowns when I was young. The change came when I was a teenager. She would have been in her forties then and slimmer than at any time in her life. With less fat to pad her, she might have been chilled. So maybe it really was about warmth.

I suspect something else, though. My grandmother, who had always worn pajamas, died when I was fourteen. The switch came soon after. Mom became her mother then, and not only in bedtime wear. With Connie gone, Mom became the family's moral watchdog, waiting up until the last of us was home without incident — *without incident,* that was key, because incident led to disgrace. Public drunkenness, lewd behavior, unwanted pregnancy — these were the things Middle River talked about in the tonic-scented cloud that hovered over the barbershop benches, through the lacquer smell in the nail shop, over hash at Omie's. Being the butt of gossip was Mom's greatest fear.

Grace Metalious had hit the nail on the head with that one. As frightened as the fictitious Constance MacKenzie was of her secret leaking out in *Peyton Place,* she was more terrified of being talked about when it did.

Mind you, other than the fiasco with Aidan Meade, I never gave Mom cause for worry. I didn't date. What I did, starting soon after I could drive, was to go down to Plymouth on a Saturday night, stake out a table at a coffee shop, and read. Being alone in a place where I knew no one was better than being alone on a Saturday night in Middle River. And Mom would be waiting up for me when I returned, which eased the loneliness.

Feeling the full weight of that loneliness now, I went on up the stairs, opened the door, and slipped inside. Mom wasn't there, but neither was the kitchen I recalled. It had been totally renovated two years before, with Mom already ill, but determined. I had seen the changes when I was here for the funeral, but, climbing those side steps, my mind's eye still had pictured the old one, with its aged Formica countertops, its vintage appliances and linoleum floor.

In the warm glow of under-cabinet halogens, this new kitchen was vibrant. Its walls were painted burgundy, its counters were beige granite, its floor a brick-hued adobe tile. The appliances were stainless steel, right down to a trash compactor.

I didn't have a trash compactor. Nor did I have an ice dispenser on the refrigerator door. This kitchen was far more modern than mine in Washington. I was duly impressed, as I had been too preoccupied to be in June.

The kitchen table was round, with a maple top, wrought-iron legs, and ladder-back chairs of antique white. Setting my computer bag on one of the latter, I turned off the lights, went through the hall and into the front parlor to turn off its lamp. There I found my sister Phoebe, under a crocheted afghan on the settee. Her eyes were closed; she was very still.

Of the three of us, she resembled Mom the most. She had the same high forehead and bright green eyes, the same wavy blonde hair, the same thin McCall mouth. She looked older than when I had seen her last month, perhaps pale from the strain of carrying on. Totally aside from any physical problems she might be having, I could only begin to imagine what the past month had been like for her. My own loneliness in coming home to a house without Mom was nothing compared to Phoebe's feeling it all the time. Not only had she lived with Mom for all but the short span of her own marriage, but she worked with Mom too. The loss had to be in her face day in and day out.

Lowering my bags, I slipped down onto the edge of the settee and lightly touched the part of her under the afghan that would have been an arm. "Phoebe?" I whispered. When she didn't move, I gave her a little shake.

Her eyes slowly opened. She stared at

me for a blank moment, before blankness became confusion. "Annie?" Her voice was uncharacteristically nasal.

"You got my message, didn't you?"

"Message," she repeated, seeming muddled.

My heart sank. "On your voice mail? Saying I was coming?" I had assumed the lights were left on for me.

"I don't . . . on my voice mail? I think so . . . I must have." Her eyes cleared a little. "I'm just groggy from medicine. I have a cold." That explained the nasal voice. "What time is it?"

I checked my watch. "Twelve-ten." Deciding that grogginess from cold medicine was reasonable, I tried to lighten things with a smile. "The kitchen startled me. I keep expecting to see the old one."

I wasn't sure she even heard my remark. She was frowning. "Why're you here?"

"I felt a need to visit."

After only the briefest pause, she asked, "Why now?"

"It's August. Washington's hot. I finished the revisions of my book. Mom's gone."

Phoebe didn't move, but she grew more awake. "Then it is about Mom. Sabina said it would be."

"You told Sabina I was coming?" I asked in dismay. I would rather have called Sabina myself.

"I was over there for dinner. I couldn't not say."

Fine. I didn't want to fight. Sabina would have found out soon, anyway. "I miss Mom," I said. "I haven't taken the time to mourn. I want to know more about those last days, what was wrong with her, y'know?"

"What about the house?"

I frowned. "What about it?"

"Sabina said you'd want it."

"*This* house?" I asked in surprise. "Why would I want it? I have my own place. This is yours."

"Sabina said you'd want it anyway. She said you'd know all the little legal twists, and that it would be about money."

"Money? Excuse me? I have plenty of money." But I wasn't surprised Sabina would think I wanted more. She was always expecting the worst of me, which was why I would have preferred to phone her myself to let her know I was here. Then I might have nipped her suspicions in the bud.

"Have I asked for anything from Mom's estate?" I asked now.

43

Phoebe didn't reply. She looked like she was trying to remember.

"Mom's been dead barely six weeks," I went on. "Has Sabina been stewing about this the whole time?"

"No. Just . . . just once she found out you were coming, I guess."

That quickly, I was back in the midst of childhood spats. Sabina was the middle child, which should have made her the peacemaker of the family, but that had never been the case. The eleven months between Phoebe and her had left her craving attention, a situation I had aggravated with my arrival when Sabina was barely two.

Now I said, "This is why I called you and not her. I knew she wouldn't be happy about my visit, and that's really sad, Phoebe. Middle River's where I grew up. My family is here. Why does she have to feel threatened?"

Phoebe still hadn't stirred on the settee, but her eyes were as sharp as Mom's could be when she was worried we had done something wrong. "She doesn't know you anymore. I don't either."

"I'm your *sister*."

"You're a writer. You live in the city and you travel all over. You eat out more than you eat in. You know *celebrities*." Her eyes rounded when she recalled something else. "And your *significant other* is on TV all the time."

"He isn't my significant other," I reminded her.

"Roommate, then," she conceded and took a stuffy breath. "But even that's totally different from Middle River. Single women don't buy condos here with single men."

"Greg and I protect each other — but that's getting off the subject. I'm your *sister*, Phoebe," I repeated, pleading now, because the discussion was making me feel even more alone than I had felt entering the kitchen and finding no Mom. "I've tried to *give* in the last few years. Isn't that what our vacations were about? And the money for the new van? And even the new kitchen," I added, though my part was the appliances alone. "Why do you think I would try to take something you have?"

Seeming suddenly groggy again, Phoebe lifted an arm from under the afghan. She squeezed her eyes shut, rubbed them with thumb and forefinger. "I don't know. I don't keep lists."

"Phoebe," I chided.

"I guess not, but Sabina says —"

"Not Sabina," I cut in. "*You*. Do *you* distrust me, too?"

In a reedy voice, she said, "I'm confused sometimes." Her hand fell away. She opened her eyes, looking pitiful, and again, my heart sank. Something was definitely wrong.

"It's your cold," I reasoned, but was suddenly distracted. With the afghan lowered, I could see what she was wearing. Smiling, I teased, "Are those pajamas?"

She was instantly defensive. "What's wrong with pajamas?"

"Nothing. It's just that it was a Mom thing to do."

"She was cold. Now I'm cold."

The room was not cold. If anything, it was hot. I had entered town with my top down, while Phoebe had her windows shut tight. The house had no AC. Even the warmth outside would have stirred the air in here. Surely the moisture of the night would have helped Phoebe's cold.

Again, I thought how wan she looked. "Have you been sick long?" I asked.

She sighed. "I'm not sick. It's just a cold. They're a fact of life. Customers bring them into the shop all the time. It's late. I'd better go to bed."

I rose from the settee and shouldered my

bags, then glanced back. Phoebe was holding the arm of the settee with one hand while she pushed herself up with the other. She reminded me of Mom the last time I had seen her. That wasn't good.

"Seriously, Phoebe, are you okay?"

On her feet now, she held up both hands. "I. Am. Fine. Go on. I'll get the light."

I was in the hall when the parlor went dark, leaving the stair lit by a lamp at the top. I went on up, then down the hall to the room that had always been mine. Dropping my bags inside, I turned back to wait for Phoebe. She walked slowly, seeming a tad unsteady. Middle-of-the-night grogginess? Possibly. But the niggling I had felt after being here last time was now a bona fide burr.

She came alongside, very much Mom's height, which was several inches shy of mine, and said, "Your room's just the same. I haven't touched anything."

"I wasn't worried. What about your room? Are you still sleeping there?"

"Where else would I sleep?"

"Mom's room. It's the biggest. This is your house now. You have a right to that room. Didn't Sabina suggest it last time I was here?"

"I guess," Phoebe said, confused again.

47

"But it'd mean moving all my things, and I've been in my room for so long." Her eyes grew plaintive. "Do I really have the *energy* for that?"

She should have it. She was only thirty-six. Clearly, though, she was depleted both physically and emotionally. I wondered how she managed to handle the store.

Rather than express doubt when she seemed so vulnerable, I said, "So, what time will you be up in the morning?"

"Seven. We open at nine."

"Can you stay home if your cold is worse?"

"It won't be worse."

"Okay then. I'll see you for breakfast?"

She nodded, frowned, added, "Unless I sleep later. I've been exhausted. Maybe it's the cold. Maybe it's missing Mom." With an oddly apologetic smile, she went on past me, down the hall.

"Want me to turn out the lamp?" I asked.

She looked back. "Lamp?"

I indicated the one at the top of the stairs.

She stared in surprise. "No. Leave it on. If it had been on that night, Mom wouldn't have tripped. It was dark. If she'd been able to see, she wouldn't have fallen, and if

48

she hadn't fallen, she'd still be alive."

"She was ill," I reminded her. "It wasn't so much the dark as her balance."

"It was the dark," Phoebe declared and disappeared into her room.

I didn't sleep well. Once I opened the windows, pulled back the covers, and removed every stitch of clothing, I could deal with the heat, but the city girl I had become wasn't used to the noise. Traffic, yes. Sirens, yes. Garbage trucks, yes. Peepers and crickets, no. Naturally, lying awake, I thought about Mom, about whether Phoebe was sick, too, and, if so, whether it was from lead or worse, and each time I woke up, I thought of those things. Dawn came, and the night noises died, which meant that the river emerged. Our house sat on its banks. The waters rushed past, carrying aquatic creatures from upstream, leaves and grasses from its banks, all hurrying past the stones that lined its bank.

Seven came, and I listened for Phoebe, but it wasn't until seven-twenty that I heard signs of life in the house. Wearing a nightshirt now, I was sitting on the edge of the bed, about to stand, when Sabina slipped into the room.

Sabina and I were Barneses, with

49

Daddy's midnight hair, pale skin, and full mouth. When we were kids, these features had come together on her far better than they had on me. Sabina was pretty and popular. I was neither. We were both five-eight, though Sabina had always insisted she was half an inch taller than I was. I didn't fight her on it. There was plenty else to fight about. Even as she approached the bed now, I felt it coming.

I tried to diffuse things with a smile. "Hi. I was going to call you. Is Phoebe awake?"

"No," Sabina replied in a low voice. She folded her arms and held them close. "I wanted to talk with you first. This has been really tough on her, Annie. I don't want you riling her up."

Dismayed by the abruptness of her attack, I said in a conversational tone, "I'm doing okay, thanks for asking. How are you?"

She didn't blink. "We could spend five minutes on niceties, but this is really important. Phoebe is having trouble accepting that Mom's gone. I don't know why you're here, but if you're thinking of doing anything to stir up trouble, please don't."

I was annoyed enough to lash back. "Phoebe is doing more than 'having trouble accepting that Mom's gone.' She looks physically ill. She says it's a cold. I'm wondering if it's something else."

"Oh, it is," Sabina confirmed, "but it's nothing you can fix. The way she's acting — like Mom did? It's a natural thing that sometimes happens when a loved one dies. I talked with Marian Stein about it."

"Who's Marian Stein?"

"A therapist here in town. I'm on top of this, Annie."

"Is Phoebe seeing her?"

"Of course not. Phoebe doesn't need therapy, just time. This'll pass."

"Has she seen her doctor?"

"No need. Colds disappear. Symptoms pass."

I knew not to mention lead. It wouldn't be well received. So I said, "Mom was diagnosed with Parkinson's. It can run in families."

Sabina's eyes hardened. "And *that*," she said, still in a low voice but laced now with venom, "is why you shouldn't be here. She needs encouragement. You're so negative, you'll set her back."

"Oh, come on, Sabina," I scoffed. "I have enough sense not to mention this to her. But I Googled Parkinson's after Mom was diagnosed. If Mom had it, and if

51

Phoebe has it, you or I may stand a greater risk. Aren't *you* worried about that?"

"*If* Mom had it?" Sabina charged. Her arms were knotted across her middle.

"There are other causes for the symptoms she had," I blurted out and regretted it instantly.

"I knew it! I knew you'd stick your nose in! Well, where were you last year or the year before that or the year before that? Fine and dandy for you to criticize us now —"

"I'm not criticizing."

"— but *you* weren't around. We were, Annie. Phoebe and I took Mom to the doctor, got her medicines, made sure she took them when she would have forgotten. Phoebe has been running the store for the last five years —"

"Five?"

"Yes, five. It's been *that* long since Mom was functioning *well*."

Five years put a crimp in the lead theory. It would mean Mom had become ill long before the store was awash in lead-paint dust. There might yet be a connection, certainly with regard to Phoebe, but it would take some looking.

I was annoyed. "Why wasn't I told back then?"

"Because you weren't here!" Sabina shouted and immediately lowered her voice. "And because the symptoms were so mild we thought it was age at first, and because Phoebe was there to cover at work, and because Mom would have been horrified if she'd known we were talking behind her back. You know how she was. She *hated* being talked about. So we didn't tell you — didn't tell *anyone* — until the symptoms made it obvious, and even *then* you stayed away. So don't criticize us, Annie," she warned. "You have no idea what it's been like. We did the best we could."

I was quiet. What could I say to that? Yes, I felt guilty. I had from the moment I learned Mom had died. I kept telling myself I was here on a mission; that was the initial premise. But maybe my mission was broader than I had allowed. So mentally I amended that premise with **TRUTH #1: Yes, I had come to Middle River to learn whether Mom had died of something that was now affecting Phoebe, but I was also here out of guilt.** I owed my sisters something. I wanted to make it up to them that I hadn't helped when Mom was sick.

Not that I could say that to Sabina. The words would positively stick in my throat.

Instead I asked, "How are Lisa and Timmy?" They were Sabina's kids, aged twelve and ten respectively. I actually knew how they were; I had an active e-mail relationship with them, and had been in touch with them a lot in the last month, though I don't think Sabina knew it. Her kids were astute; they knew there was tension between Sabina and me. My relationship with her kids was a little secret we kept. None of us was risking Sabrina's wrath by rubbing her nose in it.

She did relax a bit at mention of the kids. "They're fine. Excited that you're here. They'll probably ride their bikes over later. They want to know how long you're staying."

"They want to know," the devil made me ask, "or you do?"

She didn't deny it. "Me. Phoebe, too. This is her house."

It was a definite reminder. "For the record," I said, "I don't want the house. I don't want the store. I don't want Mom's money. The only thing I want, which I told you in June, is to have this room to use when I come."

Sabina looked dismissive, clearly doubtful I was telling the truth. "How long are you staying?"

"Assuming Phoebe has no problem with it, until Labor Day."

"A whole month?" she asked, seeming alarmed. "What'll you *do* all that time?"

"I have some work. Mostly I want to relax. Give Phoebe a hand. Help her get better. Talk with people around town."

"Who?"

The sharpness of the question put us right back in the boxing ring. "I haven't really thought that far."

"Are you kidding? Annie Barnes hasn't thought that far? I know what you're here for, Annie. You're here to cause trouble. You'll walk innocently around town like you did when we were kids, asking questions you have no business asking, pissing people off right and left, and then you'll go back to Washington, leaving us to mend fences. And then there's the thing about writing. You have some work. What work?"

"Whatever final edits my publisher wants on next spring's book. Written interviews that they'll need. Plotting a new book."

Sabina's mouth tightened. "Are you planning to write about us now that Mom is gone?"

"No."

"I think you are. You'll ask your questions and piss us off, and then when you're back in Washington and we're cleaning up the mess, you'll write something that'll make the mess even worse." She held up her hands, palms out. "I'm asking you. *Begging* you. Please, Annie. Mind your own business." The plea was barely out when she turned, strode to the door, and pulled it open.

Phoebe stood there. Seeming wholly oblivious, simply surprised to see Sabina, she said, "I didn't know you were here. But I'm making, um, I think, what was it I was thinking, well, I think I'll make eggs for breakfast. Should I make enough for three?"

Chapter 2

The Middle River Clinic was on Cedar Street, half a mile from Oak. Like the town itself — in that very euphemistic way — the clinic building was deeper than it appeared from the front, stretching an entire block to School Street over grassy dips and swells that were liberally strewn with, yes, cedars and oaks. Appropriately, the School Street entrance fed directly into a small emergency room that, over the years, had been a staging area for the treatment of countless playground wounds, strep throats, and allergy attacks. The oldest generation of Middle Riverites had been born and given birth here too, back when the clinic was a bona fide hospital. Nowadays, except for the most sudden of cases, childbirth and such took place in Plymouth.

The first floor housed offices for the doctors who serviced the town as part of the Middle River Medical Group. The second floor was rented out to independent practitioners, currently including a large team of physical therapists, a pair of chiropractors, and an acupuncturist. Psychologists were scattered throughout — small towns always had those — along with lawyers, investment counselors, and computer people. Sandy Meade wasn't picky; he owned the building and wanted every space filled. He might have balked at renting to a video store stocking adult entertainment — he did have standards — but he was fine with most else, as long as the rent money arrived in full each month.

The building was a handsome brick structure, two stories high, with white shutters, gutters, and portico. The last time I was inside was to visit the emergency room the Thanksgiving before I left town. Sam Winchell, who owned the newspaper and whose family lived out of state, had been joining us for Thanksgiving dinner since Daddy died; that last year, he cut himself sharpening the turkey knife. I was the person he was closest to and, hence, was his designated driver, while the others stayed home keeping the food warm.

By the time I arrived this August day, I had already dropped Phoebe at work, stopped at the post office and run into all those people who asked if I was going to write about them, visited Harriman's Grocery, and returned to the house to fill the refrigerator with food. It had been pathetically empty. Eggs for three? Phoebe hadn't had eggs enough for one. With Sabina gone — and no arguments there — we two had settled for stale bran flakes. Dry.

I was no fool. While in town, I had also stopped at News 'n Chews for a bag of chocolate pennies. A pack of M&Ms would have satisfied my chocolate craving, but I could get M&Ms anywhere, anytime. Chocolate pennies, hand-dropped by the Walkers for three generations and counting, were something else. They were well worth the risk of my being seen by even more people.

But then, word was already spreading. I suspected my own sisters had told friends, who had told friends, who had told friends. I wasn't about to drive my convertible down Oak Street — that would be a distasteful show on my first day back — but there was no way I could be invisible in a place desperately in need of food for talk.

Thomas Martin, the doctor who had treated my mother, was the director of the Middle River Clinic. He was new to town by Middle River standards, brought in three years ago when old Doc Wessler retired. The *Middle River Times* described Dr. Martin as not only a respected general practitioner, but a man with a business degree that would stand him in good stead for the demands of running a modern clinic.

I didn't call ahead for an appointment; the Middle River Clinic wasn't Memorial Sloan-Kettering. Nor did I tell either of my sisters what I planned to do. I didn't want an audience here, didn't want idle minds speculating. For the record, I simply wanted to thank the doctor for seeing my mother through her final days. Though I had met him after the funeral, I hadn't had the presence of mind to be overly gracious. Granted, my gratitude would be misplaced in the event that he had bungled her case and misdiagnosed her illness. But he was an outsider, like me; for that reason alone, I gave him the benefit of the doubt.

He was with a patient when I arrived, but his secretary knew me. Growing up, we had been classmates, my bookworm to her cheerleader. Her eyes widened and she smiled, which was more than she had ever done in response to me back then.

"You look great, Annie," she said in surprise, then added in immediate sympathy, "I'm sorry about your mom. She was a nice woman, always kind, whether you ended up buying something at the shop or not. And coming in here, she was always respectful. Some aren't, you know. They hate the paperwork and blame us for it. Well, we hate the paperwork too. Wow, Annie, you really *do* look great. Being famous must agree with you."

"I'm not really famous," I said, because success as a writer was different. There was no face recognition, no entourage, no advance man. My name was known in reading circles, but that was it.

Not that I said any of that now. I was socially tongue-tied and defensive, both of which were conditioned reflexes where Middle River and I were concerned.

Graceless, I forged on. "I was hoping to see the doctor to thank him for taking care of my mother. Does he ever take a break?"

"It's coming right up," she replied cheerily, standing. "I'll let him know you're here."

Five minutes later, the man appeared. He wore the obligatory lab coat, over an open-necked blue shirt and khaki slacks. His hair was short and dark, his eyes clear and blue, his body lean. When I stood to meet him, I saw that he was just about my height, perhaps the half inch taller than me that my sister always claimed to have.

An incompetent quack? If so, he showed no guilt, but rather approached with an easy smile and a friendly hand. "You're the lady of the hour."

I was immediately disarmed by his warmth, though, in truth, I might have liked him simply because he wasn't a native of Middle River. Moreover, since he wasn't from here, there was nothing emotional to hinder my speech. With a comfort I had developed in the last fifteen years, I said, "Sounds like you've had your ear twisted by someone other than Linda here."

"Three out of four patients this morning," he confirmed, eyes twinkling.

"Please don't believe what they say. There's a whole other side to me."

"As there is to us all," he remarked and, without ceremony, took my arm. "I'm buying coffee," he said, guiding me out.

The coffee shop was actually a small restaurant run by two of Omie's grandchildren. Younger than the diner by that many generations, it was called Burgers & Beans, the beans meaning the coffee kind, to judge from the rich smell that greeted us when we walked in the door. In addition to burgers, there were sandwiches and salads. We stuck to coffee.

"Want to chance it outside?" Tom asked, darting a glance at the patio, with its round wrought iron tables and umbrellas in the sun.

I smiled appreciatively. The fact that he understood my reluctance to be seen made me like him even more.

But the cat was already out of the bag. It would have been absurd for me to hide now. "Sure," I said lightly. Putting on a courageous face, I led him past several people who were definitely familiar and openly staring, to a table at the patio's edge. Whiskey barrels filled to overflowing with impatiens marked the border between flagstone and grass. I sat in the sun, just beyond the umbrella's shade. It was still early enough in the day for the warmth to feel good.

After settling himself, Tom said, "We have something in common, you and I. I spent ten years in Washington — college, med school, and residency."

"Did you?" I asked, our connection deepening. "Where?"

"Georgetown all the way."

"We're fellow alums. Did you live near Wisconsin?"

"For a while. Then Dupont Circle. It's a

fabulous city. Hot in summer, but fabulous."

"Hot in summer," I confirmed and took a drink of coffee. Middle River could be hot — might well be hot this very afternoon — but not with the relentlessly steamy heat that seared Washington day after day.

"Is that why you're here," Tom asked, "to escape the heat?"

I was amused. "What did your patients say?"

"That you were here to write. That you're Middle River's version of Grace Metalious, and that of *course*," his eyes twinkled again, "I knew the Peyton Place link."

"You did know it," I surmised.

"How not to? It's the basis of tourism here. The inn offers Peyton Place weekends, the town historian gives tours of the 'real' Peyton Place, the newspaper puts out a *Peyton Place Times* issue on April Fools' Day each year. And then there's the bookstore. You can't walk in there without seeing it. *Peyton Place* is still prominently displayed, along with a *Reader's Companion* that outlines the parallels between Peyton Place and us."

"Do you remember *Peyton Place*?"

"I'm forty-two. It came out before I was born, but it was on my mother's nightstand for years after, all dog-eared and worn. I read it when I first came here."

"Did it make you rethink your decision?"

"Nah. *Peyton Place* is fiction. Middle River has its characters, but it isn't a bad place."

I might have argued and said that Middle River was a *vile* place for one who didn't conform to its standards. But that felt like sour grapes on my part. So I simply cleared my throat and said, "Sandy Meade must have made you one sweet offer to get you to leave wherever you were after Washington to come here."

"Atlanta," he said easily, "and I wanted a quieter life. I bought a house over on East Meadow. It's three times the size of anything I could have bought elsewhere, and I had money to spare for renovations."

"Annie?" came a curious voice.

I looked around at a woman I instantly recognized, though I hadn't seen her in years. Her name was Pamela Farrow. She had been a year behind me in school, but her reputation for being fast and loose made the leap to my class and beyond. Back then, she had been a looker with shiny black hair, warm green eyes, and curves in the right places well before the rest of us had any curves at all. Now her hair wasn't as shiny or her eyes as green, and her curves were larger.

She hadn't aged as well as I had.

I'm sorry. That thought was unkind.

I atoned with a smile. "Hi, Pamela. It's been a while."

"You've been busy. We hear about the incredible things that are happening to you. Do you really live with Greg Steele?"

I wouldn't have guessed Pamela knew who Greg was; she didn't strike me as the type to watch the news, evening or otherwise.

And that was another unkind thought, which was why I hated Middle River. It brought out the worst in me. Back here for less than twelve hours, and I was being snide again. It was defensiveness, of course. I was lashing out with words, or in this case thoughts, to compensate for feeling socially inept. Which I wasn't now. At least, not in Washington. Here, I regressed.

I nodded in reply and drank more of my coffee.

"Well, we love hearing news of you," Pamela gushed. "You're our most famous native." She turned to the man with her. Unfamiliar to me, he wore glasses and a shirt and tie, had neatly combed hair, and exuded a style of conservatism. I was floored when Pamela said, "Annie, this is my husband, Hal Healy."

I would never have guessed it. Never. Either Pamela had changed, or this marriage was a mismatch.

I held out a hand; he shook it a bit too firmly.

"Hal was brought to town to be principal of the high school," Pamela said with pride, and here, too, I was surprised. The high school principal in my day was a sexy guy not unlike Tomas Makris in *Peyton Place*. Hal Healy had the look of a marginal nerd. "We've been married six years," Pamela went on. "We have two little girls. You and Greg don't have kids yet, do you?"

Not wanting to explain that Greg and I weren't sexually involved, I simply said, "No. We don't. I assume you both know Tom?"

"Oh yes," Pamela said with barely a glance at the doctor. I might been flattered by her attention to me, if I hadn't thought her profoundly rude to Tom. "So tell me," she went on in something of a confidential

67

tone. "We're all wondering. Are you really here to write about us?"

I smiled, bowed my head, and rubbed my temple. Still smiling, I looked back up. "No. I'm not here to write."

Her face fell. "Why not? I mean, there's still plenty to write about. I could tell you stories . . ." She stopped when her husband gave her shoulder a squeeze.

"Honey, they're having coffee. This isn't the time."

"Well, I could," Pamela insisted, "so if you change your mind, Annie, please call me. You look so different. Very successful. I always knew you'd go places." She grinned, waved, and let her husband steer her away.

Dismayed, I turned to Tom. "She didn't know anything of the sort. I was a pain in the butt back then — a gangly runt with an attitude. And I wrote lousy stories."

"Well, you don't now," the doctor said, suddenly seeming almost shy. "I read *East of Lonely* and liked it so much that I bought and read your two earlier books. You're an amazing writer. You capture emotion with such a sparseness of words." He was actually blushing. "I say your success is well earned. So when it comes to Middle River, you have the last laugh.

People like Pamela, they really are proud of you. For what it's worth, I've never heard anything bad."

"You're too new to town," I said, shaking my head, but his words were a comfort. He reminded me of Greg, not as much in looks as manner. Both were easygoing and could blush. *Honest* was the word that came to my mind.

Yes. I know. I wanted to like him because I needed a friend, and because I needed a friend, I didn't want to consider the fact that Tom might be smooth and glib and not honest at all. My mother was dead. I had to remember that.

But then Tom said the one thing that could most easily make me forget. "What do you know about Grace Metalious?" he asked.

I grinned. "Most everything." I could be smug about this as I wasn't about much else in life. "What do you want to know?"

"Did she really drink herself to death?"

"She drank heavily, some sources say a fifth of vodka a day for five years. And she died of cirrhosis of the liver. *A* plus *B* . . ."

"Gotcha. What was so bad about her life that she had to escape into booze? Was it not being able to write a follow-up to *Peyton Place*?"

"Oh, she did a follow-up. Her publisher insisted on it. But she hadn't wanted to do it, so she dashed it off in a month. They had to hire a ghostwriter to revise it and make it publishable. In any event, it was widely panned. There were two other books after that, one of which was her favorite. Neither book was well received."

Smoothly, he returned to me. "So here you are with a major success, like Grace with her *Peyton Place*. Do you worry about matching the success of *East of Lonely*?"

"Of course I do," I said baldly. "There's ego involved, and professional pride, even survival as a writer. It's a mean world out there. But I do love the process of writing."

"Didn't Grace?"

"Yes. But my success didn't come with the first effort. Hers did. When you score a home run the first time up at bat, it's hard to top yourself the next time. Besides, there were other things that got her down — like her agent. He cheated her out of a lot of money. The little she did get, she spent. She had expensive tastes."

"For a Manchester girl?" Tom asked with a smile, and at my look of surprise said, "Hey, I took the Peyton Place tour. She grew up in Manchester with her mother and grandmother."

"Uh-huh. In a house full of women. Like me."

"Her father left," he cautioned. "Yours died. There's a difference."

"But we were both tenish when it happened, and the end result was the same. There was no father in the house to hold the reins. The women did it. They were strong, because they had to be. Which brings me to the reason I'm here." *About time, Annie.* "I want to talk about my mom."

He grew serious. "I'm sorry about her death. I wish I could have done more."

"The fall killed her. I know that. She broke her neck and died from asphyxiation. But before that — was it really Parkinson's?"

He didn't seem surprised by the question. "Hard to say," he admitted. "She had an assortment of symptoms. The tremor in her hand, the balance issue, the trouble walking — these were consistent with Parkinson's. The memory problem suggested Alzheimer's."

"But you choose Parkinson's."

"No. The most treatable of her symptoms were the ones associated with Parkinson's, so those were the ones I addressed."

"Did you suggest that she see a spe-

71

cialist?" I asked with something of an edge, because Tom Martin was, after all, only a general practitioner, and while I had the utmost respect for GPs and the way they juggled many different things, we weren't talking about a common cold or the flu.

"Yes," he said calmly. "I gave her the name of someone at Dartmouth-Hitchcock, but she never went. She felt it was too much of an effort. And that was okay. I consulted colleagues there and in Boston. They studied her file via computer and agreed with my diagnosis. There's nothing more that an actual trip to Dartmouth-Hitchcock would have accomplished. There are no tests to conclusively diagnose either Parkinson's or Alzheimer's. It's strictly a clinical diagnosis, a judgment call made by the physician. The medication I gave her helped as much as any could."

"There's no history of either disease in our family."

"Neither has to be hereditary."

"Is it possible she had a little bit of both?"

"It's possible."

"What would the likelihood have been of that at her age?"

"Slim."

Layperson that I was, I nonetheless

agreed. "Could her symptoms have come from something else?"

He frowned slightly. "What did you have in mind?"

"I don't know." I was deliberately vague. "Something in the air, y'know?"

"Like acid rain?"

"Could be," I granted. "Air currents being what they are, New England has become a receptacle for toxins from plants in the Midwest. But I was actually thinking about something more local, like lead."

"Lead?"

"From lead paint. All the old paint was sanded off when Miss Lissy's was repainted. The air had to have been loaded with lead." Yes. I know. Sabina said Mom had been symptomatic for five years, and this work was done only four years ago. But what if Mom had been simply *aging* prior to then? Losing interest in daily chores? Experiencing a major postmenopausal funk? What if lead poisoning had taken over where the other had left off?

Tom smiled sadly. "Nope. Sorry. I tested for that at the start. There was no lead in her blood."

I felt a stab of dismay. I had been *sure* it was lead. "Could it have been there and gone?"

He shook his head.

"My sister seems to have some of the same symptoms."

Tom frowned at that. "Sabina?"

"Phoebe."

"I never saw any symptoms. What are they?"

"Poor balance. Bad memory. They're pretty new. I only saw the bare beginnings of them when I was here in June. Sabina says it's part of mourning Mom. Sympathetic symptoms. But what if it isn't?"

"If it isn't, she ought to see me," he advised. "Think you can get her in?"

"I don't know. It might be hard with Sabina standing guard. If Phoebe were to see you, would you be able to tell whether the problem is real or psychosomatic?"

"Possibly. Your mother had no control over the symptoms. Your sister may. That would be significant. Plus, I can test for lead."

I finished my coffee and set down the cup. "Getting back to the other thing. You know, acid rain or whatever. Do you think there's an abnormal amount of illness in this town?"

He drank his own coffee, seeming momentarily lost in thought. Then, with a blink, he put the cup down. "There may be."

"What do you think is the cause?"

"I've been trying to figure that out since I arrived."

"How?"

"Watching. Asking questions."

"And what are your thoughts?"

He was quiet for a minute, turning the cup round and round on the table, watching it turn. Then he stopped, paused, finally raised his eyes. "Acid rain, or whatever. But you didn't hear that from me."

"Why not?"

"Because I have no scientific proof."

"You diagnose Parkinson's and Alzheimer's with no scientific proof," I said.

"The other is something else. It implies a very large problem, one that has become extremely political. I can state my opinion, and even point to a pattern, but there are those who'll say I'm crazy, and they might just be powerful enough to destroy my credibility in this town."

"Would you sacrifice the health of the people for the sake of your credibility?" I asked, edgy again.

He sat forward, more intense now. "I lived in Washington long enough to know people there. I say things — believe me, I do — and maybe my arguments have so far fallen on deaf ears, but to some extent I'm hog-tied. I've had to make a choice — politician or doctor. Yes, I'm worried about my credibility. I think I'm the best doctor this town has, in part because I ask every question I know how to ask and treat my patients accordingly. If I give up my practice to crusade for the cause, who will take care of the people here?"

"A replacement," I said, seeing his point, "but one who might be so beholden to the Meades as to disavow everything you would be down there in Washington trying to do. Have you talked to the Meades about this?"

"About what?"

"Acid rain, or whatever."

Cautiously, he asked, "Why would I talk with the Meades?"

"Because they run the only industry in town."

"I thought we were talking about pollution from the Midwest."

"We were."

Tom was silent. After a minute, he said, "They say I'm barking up the wrong tree."

"About which, acid rain, or whatever?"

His eyes held mine. "Whatever."

"What is whatever?"

"I'm not sure."

"Have you done any research?"

"Some."

"Can you give me a lead?"

"If I did that and certain people found out, I could lose my job."

"Like, you could lose your credibility?"

"You ask a lot of questions," he said with some irritation.

I eased up, actually smiled. "I'm more diplomatic about it back in Washington. Here, I revert to form. I always did ask questions. It didn't go over big when I was little."

"It may not now, either," he cautioned. "There are some who'll say you just need a scapegoat for your mother's death."

"I do. I half wanted it to be you."

"I half wanted it to be me, too. When a patient dies, I agonize over what I might have done differently. But I'm stumped in this case. I charted Alyssa's symptoms, consulted with colleagues, encouraged her to go elsewhere for a second opinion. I asked her every question I knew to ask to determine if she'd been exposed to something bad. Short of sending her off on a wild goose chase for a cure for a nebulous ailment, I did what I could to ease her symptoms."

"I know," I said. And I did. "But now I

have to find someone else."

If he was relieved to be off the hook, he didn't let on. "Be careful, Annie. The Meades own this town. You know that better than me."

I paused. "You heard that story then?"

"The one about you and Aidan Meade?" He nodded.

"Huh." I took a deep breath. "Well, the thing is, I'm a different person now from the one I was then. Middle River power isn't the only power in the world. You may be hog-tied, but I'm not. I know how to get things done. Look," I said calmly, "it could be that Mom's symptoms truly were from Parkinson's or Alzheimer's, but now Phoebe's showing the same symptoms, and you say it's not from lead. I have a month, I have energy, and I have an incentive to use both. So think of it as me doing your dirty work. I don't care about my credibility here, and I certainly don't have a job to worry about. You took care of my mother, so I'm here to thank you for that. That's what I told your secretary. It's probably well on its way around town by now." I leaned over the table toward him and half whispered an urgent, "Point me in the right direction, Tom. I'll be forever in your debt."

He finished his coffee and rose, took my empty cup, and deposited both in a nearby receptacle. I was beginning to think that was the end of it, when he returned, slipped back into his seat, and said with deadly quiet, "I'm wondering about mercury."

I sighed. "It can't be. The mill stopped using mercury long before my mother got sick."

"But mercury is unique," he said. "It enters the body, settles in an organ, and waits. Symptoms may not surface until years after exposure. That's what makes the possibility of mercury poisoning in Middle River an intriguing one."

I was feeling a rush of adrenaline. "Intriguing is an understatement. Are you sure that's what it does?"

"Lies dormant? Very sure. The problem is that I've never been able to connect one of my patients with an incident of actual exposure. Do that, Annie, and you'd top Grace."

Chapter 3

That quickly, I shifted gears. Not lead. Mercury — and not the planet Mercury or the cute winged god of Greek mythology. This mercury was the slinky silver stuff found in thermometers. It was a metal. I was no expert on the subject, having explored it and quickly (if erroneously) dismissed it. But it was virtually impossible to live in Washington and not know of the controversy. Rarely did a week pass without an article on the mercury problem appearing in the *Post*, and a problem it was. Mercury emissions were a serious health hazard, environmentalists said. The other side, whose profits depended on the output of mercury-emitting plants, adamantly fought regulations.

As villains went, mercury would be perfect and, if the mill was the polluter, all the better for me. True, Northwood didn't currently use mercury. That had put me off the track. But Tom put me right back on with his claim that mercury could lie dormant in the human body for years before manifesting itself in symptoms. So what if something had happened way back when? The Meades had to know the potential for harm. If the mill had contaminated the town without the Meades' knowledge, shame on them. If they did know it and had either done nothing or, worse, covered it up, they could be criminally charged.

With deliberate effort, I reined in my thoughts. Mercury was a more explosive issue than lead. For that reason alone, caution was the way to go — not that I would have always taken that route. Once upon a time, I would have barged ahead with accusations. But I was a grown-up now and — I liked to think — responsible. Credibility rested on being cool-headed and deliberate. I knew not to draw conclusions before I had information, because there were, indeed, immediate questions. If mercury was the problem and the mill was its source, it remained to be seen why my mother, and perhaps my sister, was affected. Neither of them worked at the mill. Downriver from it, yes. But not at a place of immediate exposure. And why my mother and sister, and not my grandmother before them? After a life of consistently good health, Connie had died of an aneurysm.

Surely, there were answers to be had. I didn't want to get excited until I made a few connections. That meant going back to the drawing board to catalog the symptoms of mercury poisoning, the methods of exposure to mercury, and the kinds of plants that emitted it. Tom had been unable to connect any of his patients with exposure to the metal. I had to try.

First, though, I had to drop by the dress shop to see Phoebe. I had promised I would, since I was driving her van, and she might need it. I had also promised to bring lunch.

Armed with salads from Burgers & Beans, I went back down Cedar, crossed Oak, and drove on to Willow. This time, rather than making a right toward our house, I made a left and passed more Victorian homes. Quickly, though, residences ended and stores began.

If Oak Street offered necessities such as food, health products, and town services, Willow filled needs that were one step removed. Here were shops selling books, computers, and antiques. There were two beauty salons, a day spa, and the nail shop. There were stores that sold used furniture, office supplies, and candles and lamps. There was a workout place. And a picture-framing store. And an autobody shop. And there was Miss Lissy's Closet.

Miss Lissy was my great-grandmother, Elizabeth, who had first opened the shop. My grandmother, who ran it after Lissy died, might have changed the name to Connie's Closet, which had a certain cachet, had it not been for her obsession with keeping a low profile. By the time Connie passed on and my mother took charge, Miss Lissy's had become too much of a fixture in town to risk a change of name. Besides, with my mother being Alyssa, Lissy's Closet fit.

So, surprisingly, did her stewardship of the shop. She had wanted to be a writer, not a shopkeeper. Her move to the latter came after we girls started school, when it was clear that she could earn more money working for Connie than selling stories to regional magazines. And we did need the money. As a sales rep for the mill — yes, the very same Northwood Mill — Daddy earned a reasonable income, but not enough to save for our education. Mom's income was earmarked for that. Then Daddy died, and Mom's income was all we had.

Miss Lissy's occupied both floors of a small frame house in a row of other small frame houses, each with a tiny front yard and a porch, and just enough room between houses to allow for parking, loading, and fire prevention. The Meade family, which owned this entire end of the street and leased it to shopkeepers, took pride in this foresight. Having lost part of the mill to fire in the fifties before brick replaced wood, they knew what could happen when August turned hot and dry and the town grew parched. This summer was moist enough, but Middle River never forgot the acrid smell of smoke that lingered in the air for days after the inferno.

The shop was on the river side of Willow. The rents were higher on this side of the street, but the ambience was worth the cost. Each house had a back deck perfect for lunches, featured displays, and, in the instance of Miss Lissy's Closet, trunk sales. Moreover, these back decks were connected to the river walk, the scene of the fabled October stroll, when fall foliage was at its height and Christmas shoppers first set out to buy gifts. Those on the landlocked side of Willow, in true sour-grapes fashion, reasoned that they were spared having to look across the water at "th'other side," as Middle River's poorest neighborhood was called. The Meades owned that land as well, and dressed up the riverbank with flowers and trees. Once leaves fell, though, nothing could hide the shabbiness of the homes there.

This August, the earth was moist, the willows grand, and the river world green.

As for Miss Lissy's, it was green every month of the year, inside and out, every shade of green imaginable, all of it blending surprisingly well. Prior to the painting done four years ago, it had been green, but monochromatically so. Now it was variegated in the way of a woodland glen. The shingles on the outer walls were painted celadon, with shutters and doors forest green. The inside walls were painted by room — one room sunshine green, one celery, one sea green, one olive. Wrapping tissue was sage, shopping bags were teal, dress and suit bags a distinctive apple green, and no purchase at all left the shop without a cascade of assorted green ribbons attached. Over and around it all was the store's logo, also redone during my mother's watch when marketing and modernizing came to the fore. It was a closet door done in brushstrokes, with a zippy font presenting the store's name in grass green.

I parked the van in the driveway and

walked around to the front. The look was handsome, I had to say. As fearful as I had been that so many shades of green would be overkill, here on the outside, the celadon, grass, and forest greens worked well. Likewise the hydrangeas that grew in profusion against the front of the shop. They were the palest green imaginable.

Climbing two steps, I crossed the porch. The front door was already open. With the tinkle of a bell, I pushed the screen and went inside. For a minute, I just stood and looked around. I couldn't remember when I had been here last, surely not at the time of the funeral, since the store had been closed out of respect for my mother. I was in the front room; doors straight ahead and to my right led to other rooms. A staircase, farther back on the right, led to the second floor, where there were yet other rooms. Each was a department, so to speak — underwear, outerwear, partywear, even makeup, to name a few.

Marketing and modernization? Oh yes. This front room was a perfect example of that. When I was a child, this room had held racks of the kinds of day dresses that the women of Middle River wore at the time. Now the room held blue jeans and slacks, T-shirts, polo shirts, and sweaters, all popular brands. It was definitely my kind of room.

"Annie, hi," said Phoebe, coming in from the room on the right. She seemed less groggy than she had earlier and sounded less stuffed. Dressed all in ivory — camisole, slacks, and slides — with her hair brushed and her makeup fresh, she looked elegant and in control. She also looked so much like Mom that I felt a catch in my throat.

As she headed for the checkout desk, she was trailed by a pair of customers who had to be mother and daughter. Though the mother was shorter and slimmer than her daughter, their features were nearly identical. Likewise their focus on me — even the daughter, who couldn't have been more than fifteen and therefore wouldn't remember me from before. But she knew who I was now. No doubt about that. Despite the long fall of hair that half covered her eyes, I saw recognition there.

I winked at the girl — why not give her a thrill? my perverse self thought — and nodded at her mother. "How's it goin'?" I said in passing as I slipped into the room from which they had come. This room held shoes. Again, though, the difference between these shoes and the ones that had been for sale the last time I was here was pronounced. There wasn't a leather pump in sight. Here were sneakers and casual sandals, flats and sling-backs and strappy things for evening wear, though surely those evenings were spent in places other than Middle River. I couldn't imagine anything dressy being worn here. Church events, weddings and anniversary parties, birthday bashes — they weren't terribly dressy unless they were held out of town, which they were now more often than not. From what I read, even the school proms were held elsewhere.

"May I help you?" asked a gentle voice.

I turned to face a woman in her late twenties. Dark-haired, she was tall and slim, wore a silk camisole, slim black pants, and black sandals. Classy and composed, she showed no sign of recognizing me.

Nor did I recognize her, for which reason I was able to smile easily. "I'm Phoebe's sister, Annie."

Her eyes did widen then. "Phoebe said you were in town, but she didn't say you'd be coming to the store." She put out a hand. "I'm Joanne. I work here."

"Full-time?" I asked as we shook hands.

"Yes. I started working weekends and summers when I was in high school, but

I've been full-time since I graduated from college. Phoebe made me manager last year."

"Then I owe you thanks," I said. "The past month has probably been difficult here."

Joanne nodded. "I loved your mom. She was always good to me, and she had a great sense of style. Watching her go downhill was heartbreaking. She kept wanting to be here, but it got harder for her."

"Because of the stairs?" I was thinking of the balance problem.

"And illness. If it wasn't a cold, it was the flu. She was in bed half the time, and she hated that. She also hated forgetting people's names. She hated losing her train of thought in the middle of a sentence. The computer was a whole other issue. We had to make sure we were with her when she was entering sales. Poor Phoebe. The strain has taken a toll."

I might have asked about that toll — to wit, my sister's behavior and health. But Joanne was a stranger to me, which made prying seem like a betrayal of Phoebe. So I simply nodded and said, "The store looks wonderful. Very upmarket. How much of it is your doing?"

"Not much," she confessed. "Phoebe

does the buying." She looked past me as Phoebe joined us, and said softly, "You wanted me to remind you about New York."

"All done," Phoebe said with flair. "I made the reservations."

"Reservations for a buying trip?" I asked.

"Yes. Do you want to go somewhere for lunch?"

By way of reminder, I held up the bag with the salads — to which, making light of forgetfulness, she tapped her head, rolled her eyes, and led the way out back.

The deck was warm, but the sun had already shifted enough to bring shade to the wide, weathered planks. A slight breeze came off the river, carrying the scent of wildflowers — yellow wood sorrel and musk flower, blue vervain, purple loose-strife. I spotted a patch of forget-me-nots; it had been growing there forever.

Sitting at a small table, we opened our salads and bottled teas. "How do you feel?" I asked.

"I'm fine. Why do you ask?"

"Your cold seems better."

"It was only a cold." She lifted her fork. It hovered over the salad for a minute — hovered or shook, I wasn't sure which —

before she set it back down, put her hand in her lap, and asked, "Where did you go after you dropped me here?"

That hand had shaken, I decided. She was covering it up.

Nonchalantly, between bites, I listed my stops in town, concluding with the one at the house to put groceries in the fridge.

"Then where?" Phoebe asked with neither an acknowledgment nor a thank-you.

"The clinic. I wanted to talk with Tom Martin."

"Why?"

"To thank him for taking care of Mom. Aren't you going to eat?"

"I will." She glanced at the discarded bag. "Any napkins in there?"

I checked. "No. Are there some inside?"

"In the office." She started to rise, but seemed to struggle holding the arms of the chair at the same time that she was moving it back.

"I'll go," I put in quickly to curtail that struggle. "I have to use the bathroom anyway." I left before she could argue.

"They're on top of the fridge," she called after me.

The office was on the second floor. I used the adjoining bathroom, which had been renovated since I had been here last, and quickly glanced around the office on my way out. It had been renovated too, and was neatly organized, with two desks facing opposite walls, built-in cabinets and shelves, appropriate spaces for computer, fax, and phone. One of the desks was clean, either Joanne's or a spare. The other, marked by a framed picture of our parents, was Phoebe's. It held a mess of papers and wasn't organized at all. A corkboard covered the wall behind it, and was covered with Post-its. There seemed to be duplicates. I saw variations of MAKE RESERVATIONS FOR NEW YORK written on four separate sheets. Apparently, New York was something Phoebe didn't want to forget.

From the looks of those Post-its, New York was also something she didn't trust herself to remember. I wondered how many other of these notes served the same purpose, and whether this was compensation for a faltering memory.

Phoebe used Post-its; Mom had used notebooks. Long before she was ill, she had jotted down thoughts, notes, and reminders in a spiral bound journal, one journal per year. And there they were, in order, occupying a place of their own on the bookshelves to the right of Phoebe's desk.

Another time I would read through them. After all, Mom was a writer. I was willing to bet that there was something of her to be gleaned from all those entries.

For now, though, knowing Phoebe was waiting, I took a pair of napkins from the top of the waist-high refrigerator and returned to the deck. The warmth hit me first, and pleasurably, then the smell of newly cut grass wafting from the mower that droned several houses up. Birds were at a feeder by the riverwalk now — goldfinches, the male a bright yellow and the female a bland yellowish green. They came and went, vanishing into the willows at times before flitting back, at other times flying all the way across the river. On this sunny day, th'other side was at its innocuous best. I couldn't make out homes through the trees, though the riverbank was littered with fishermen. Both sexes, all ages. I counted a dozen, and those, in the small patch of bank I could see through our own willows. As I watched, a thin young man caught something, unhooked it, and dropped it in a pail. This fishing wasn't just for sport. It was for dinner.

The setting was a throwback, yet not — old-fashioned, but very real. Warmth, smells, birds, fish, and leisure — it was idyllic, I had to say.

A Trojan horse, came a whisper. I quickly turned my head, thinking that someone was being very funny. But the buzz had come from a fly.

Swatting at it, I turned back to Phoebe. She had eaten some of her salad while I was gone, but the fork was now idle against the rim of the plastic tray. She was slouched lower in the chair, her head resting against its back and her eyes closed. I let her rest while I ate. When I dragged my chair deeper into the shade, though, the small sound made her bolt upright. Her eyes flew to mine. She looked blank one minute, irritated the next.

"You must be tired," I said, and passed a napkin across.

Relaxing in her seat again, she took the napkin, studied it, then set it down. With her hands on the arms of the chair, she eyed me with caution. "Tell me where you went this morning."

I shot her a curious look. "Didn't I already do that?"

She didn't speak for a minute, seeming to process my question and regroup. "Well, tell me how it felt. Was it embarrassing?"

"Embarrassing?"

"Seeing Middle River. Knowing you

come from here. It must be a pretty ridiculous place compared to Washington."

"I don't compare the two. Middle River is what it is. It doesn't embarrass me."

"But you pretend it doesn't exist."

"I don't. It's my hometown. I've discussed it in interviews. It isn't a secret."

Phoebe furrowed her brow. "Did you say you went to the clinic?" I nodded. "To see Tom?" I nodded again. "What did he say?"

"We have Washington in common, so we talked about that. He's an impressive man. I think it's remarkable the Meades were able to lure him here."

"He came because of his sister," Phoebe said. She picked up her fork, then put it down and picked up her iced tea instead. The bottle went to her mouth with passable steadiness.

"He didn't mention a sister. Does she live here?" I asked.

Phoebe's eyes lit. She was obviously pleased to be the informant. "She moved here with Tom. She's retarded and was institutionalized for a while, until Tom took her out. He can take care of her here."

I was touched. "That is the *kindest* thing."

"So don't expect anything," Phoebe warned.

I didn't follow. "Expect?"

"By way of a date. The two of you might have lots in common, but he doesn't date. He spends all his free time with his sister. She's his mission in life. Some people wonder about that."

"Wonder what?"

Phoebe gave a sly smile. "Whether they have something going, y'know?"

It was a minute before I realized what she meant, the idea was so contrary to my impression of Tom. "That's disgusting, Phoebe."

"I'm not saying *I* think it," she argued, "just that some do. You know how they are. They go looking for anything remotely perverse. I like Tom. He's very attractive, don't you think?"

"I do, and we'll be friends. But anything more?" I shook my head no. There was no chemistry at all.

"How's Greg?" Phoebe asked.

"Fine. He'll be leaving for his trip in another day or two."

"Why aren't you going with him?"

"Because I'm here." But that wasn't really what Phoebe was asking. I sighed. "I've told you before. We're not an item."

"Why not? What're you waiting for?"

"Nothing," I said calmly. "I'm not in a rush."

"You should be. Look what happened to me. Miscarriage after miscarriage, because I waited too long."

This was the first I had heard about Phoebe's age being a factor in those miscarriages — but then, it was something we didn't often discuss. Painful subjects were generally off-limits during those weekends we spent together. But I was curious now that she had raised the issue. "I wouldn't call early thirties old," I said. "It's very much par for the course in Washington."

Phoebe was suddenly irritated. "Well, Washington is *not* Middle River. Maybe those women are different."

"Did your doctor really blame it on age?"

"He didn't have to. It was obvious."

I didn't think it was obvious at all. Very few of my friends had children yet; they were busy building careers. But I knew plenty of women in their late thirties, even in their forties, who had successfully carried babies to term. Conversely, I had heard of plenty of younger ones with a history of miscarriage.

I wondered if exposure to mercury could cause miscarriage. Nearly every article on the subject mentioned the vulnerability of young children. Pregnant women were advised not to eat fish that contained high concentrations of mercury, because even a small amount could affect a fetus.

It struck me that as a Washingtonian I knew far more about the politics of mercury regulation than I did about what mercury actually did to the body.

I had to learn more.

Back at the house, I turned on my laptop and used Phoebe's dial-up to access the Web — and how not to check e-mail first? I told myself I had to do it for work; that was the premise. But of course there was more to it than that. So here was **TRUTH #2: Ego is involved; we want to be wanted.** In my case, given my childhood isolation, I view e-mail as a party. Granted, it's one I throw for myself. But how nice to enter my little cyberhome from wherever I happen to be, and find all sorts of greetings from friends.

I wasn't disappointed now, though the notes in my in box weren't only from friends. I quickly deleted the spam and filed a handful of work-related messages that needed no reply — one from my editor acknowledging receipt of my revisions, one from my agent wishing me a good trip. My publicist wanted to know if I was interested in speaking at a fund-raiser in Idaho the following spring, but since that was my serious writing time, I respectfully declined.

Having saved the best for last, I read notes from my three closest friends — Amanda the graphic artist, Jocelyn the college professor, Berri the professional volunteer — each asking her version of how the drive had gone and how my reception in Middle River had been.

Greg had sent a quickie. His were always quickies, often just a note in the subject line. This one said, *Did you arrive?* I clicked on "reply," typed in, *Yup. Are you packed?* and sent it back.

Done playing, I pulled up Google, but I had barely typed in *mercury poisoning* when I heard something on the stone drive. Recognizing the sound, I smiled and rose from the kitchen table. I was on the side stairs when my niece and nephew, Lisa and Timmy, dropped their bicycles and ran toward me.

I hugged both of them at the same time. This was my homecoming. If there was one single reason for me to spend time in Middle River, these two were it.

I held them back and looked from one tanned, beaming face to the other. "I hope you noticed," I said, "that I'm not even leaning over. You two are getting so tall. What is *happening* here?"

"I'm turning thirteen in three months," Lisa pointed out.

"And I'm gonna be tall like my dad," said her brother, not to be outdone.

"You are both gorgeous," I decided, "and so sweet. You're just what I need my first day back."

"Mom says you're staying the month?" Lisa asked.

When I nodded, Timmy complained, "But that's not fair. We have to go back to school in three weeks."

"We can do plenty in three weeks," I told them. "First, though, I'm making limeade," which I knew they loved but their mother hated, "and then I want the details of Girl Scout camp," this to Lisa, "and I want to know what you've been doing that kept you from e-mailing those details sooner."

"Robert Volker," Timmy said with displeasure.

"Oh, you're so smart," Lisa sang in insult, but she was blushing.

"Robert Volker." I was testing the name,

gently teasing, when Timmy broke away. "And you have to tell me about baseball," I called after him. "Did you win the series?" He was jogging deeper into the driveway. "Come back here, I'm not *done* with you." Suddenly, though, I understood.

"This car is *cool*," came the boy's awe-filled cry as he circled the BMW. "Oh *wow*."

Keeping an arm around Lisa's shoulder — I wasn't ready to let her go — I drew her with me toward the convertible.

From the opposite side, Timmy looked over at me, eyes wide. "Take us for a ride, Auntie Anne?"

Lisa had started the Auntie Anne stuff. She had been two, suddenly talking, but consistently putting an *ee* sound on the wrong word. No one ever corrected her, least of all me. I like being called Auntie Anne. To this day, it makes me feel warm and special and loved — all of which I wanted to wallow in for a while. I figured that if I could distract them long enough, maybe with a batch of sugar cookies to go with the limeade, they might forget. I wasn't yet up for driving topless through town.

"Later," I told him. "Let's visit first."

But Lisa freed herself and ran to the car.

"I *love* this, Auntie Anne. It must be *awesome* to drive. Three years from October, I can do that. Will you bring it back then?" With barely a breath, she said to her brother, "Wouldn't it be *awesome* if we had a car like this?"

"Can we go for a ride — *please,* Auntie Anne?" Timmy begged.

With his close-cropped sandy hair, his broad shoulders, and the promise of height, he was very much his father's son. Conversely, Lisa was a Barnes, with her long black hair — worn in a ponytail now — and her slender build. Both children had their dad's personality. I had always liked Ron Mattain. He was a decent, good-natured sort, far easier to take than my sister.

But I'm being unfair. People always like Sabina. She can be kind and funny and sweet, simply not to me. The same is true of Phoebe, if on a lesser scale, and part of me knows I deserve their hostility. I was awful to them growing up. Totally aside from my gawking at them around the house, they were the butt of more than one of the scathing little editorial pieces I wrote when I was the high school correspondent for the *Middle River Times.*

I had tried to make amends with the vacations I planned, but if Sabina's remarks this morning meant anything, I missed the mark. She was right. This definitely was **TRUTH #1: I should have been here while Mom was sick.** They had shouldered the full responsibility — and it was all fine and good to say that they hadn't let on how bad things were, or that we sisters weren't close, or that I hadn't felt welcome. Alyssa was my mother. I should have helped out.

Our family was shrinking, the older generation now gone. This was no doubt why having sisters suddenly seemed important to me, and I don't just mean *having* sisters. I mean being close to them. The ill will between us had never bothered me before. Now it did.

Of the truths I acknowledged while I was in Middle River, that would be another, but not just then.

"Please," Timmy pleaded, standing on the far side of the car.

Lisa joined his entreaty. "We could go for a ride and *then* talk."

"And where will you sit?" I asked pedantically. "This car only holds two."

"We'll share the passenger's seat," Timmy said.

"We're very small," added Lisa.

"Take us for a ride now, and I'll wash your car."

"I'll make you dinner. I am *the* best cook."

"Is that so?" I asked Lisa, thinking that at not-quite-thirteen, she had remarkable confidence. "What do you make?"

"Chili."

"Ah. That's tempting."

"Wait'll the guys see *this*," Timmy said as he ran a worshipful hand along the rim of the open car. He raised expectant eyes and waited.

Had anyone else asked, I might have said no. But I adored these two children and loved spoiling them. If Middle River saw me driving through town in my vintage BMW with the ragtop down, surely it would know I was doing it for the kids. I certainly wasn't doing it to impress the natives. I didn't care what Middle River thought of me.

Besides, I was suddenly in the mood for a ride. "Okay," I said in surrender. "You twisted my arm."

In short order, with both children belted into the passenger's seat, we set off. It was a perfect afternoon for a drive, just warm enough so that the breeze coming at us felt good. Warmth and breeze were nothing new for me; I experienced them all the time in D.C. What was different here was the lack of urgency. Time was ours for the taking. We were tooling around, with nowhere special to go. I could hear my engine (beautifully smooth, I might add), the occasional lawn mower, the hiss and click of a sprinkler, the kids shrieking at friends. It was fun. Novel. Restful.

I cruised down Willow all the way to the end and turned this way and that under a dappled canopy of leaves, along back roads on the outskirts of town, the kids waving at everyone they saw. We drove along the river for a while, then turned inland and headed back toward the center of town, which was about when I realized I needed gas. So I swung into the filling station at the very bottom of Oak.

It was a tactical error. For starters, nothing in Middle River was self-serve; after all, gossip couldn't spread unless people had the opportunity to talk. I had no sooner pulled up to the gas pump when Normie Zwibble emerged from the mechanics' bay. Normie had barely graduated high school and, ever since, had run the station with his father. The Normie I remembered had more hair, but he had always been pudgy. He had also always been friendly and sweet, neither of which had changed, which was why it took twenty minutes to fill the car with gas. Before the nozzle was even in place, Normie had to properly *oooh* and *ahhh* over the car. Then, while he filled the tank, he kept up a running commentary about all of the people I might remember from Middle River High. He continued talking long after the nozzle had quit on its own. I paid in cash, simply to speed up our escape.

By then, though, Timmy and Lisa were asking about the time, exchanging worried looks, saying that they were supposed to pick up a prescription for their mother at The Apothecary, but that the pharmacy closed at four and it was nearly that time now.

I had no choice. Driving straight down Oak, I pulled into a diagonal space outside the drugstore, and sat in the car while the kids went inside. They hadn't been gone more than a minute when a monster of a black Cadillac SUV with darkened windows whipped around the corner. It passed me and abruptly stopped, then backed right up until it was blocking my tail. The driver rolled down his window. There was no mistaking that square jaw, that beak of a nose, or that full head of auburn hair.

I had known I would run into Aidan
Meade if I was in town for a month. I had
just prayed it would be later, rather than
sooner.

Chapter 4

Kaitlin DuPuis was dying. She hated shopping with her mother in the first place, hated the clothes her mother made her buy (clothes she wouldn't be caught *dead* in when she was with friends) and the noise that went with it — *this one's more slimming, that one's more flattering, the other makes you look smaller, for God's sake get that hair out of your eyes.* Her mom never told her outright that she was ugly and fat — she was too PC for that — but those little digs did the same thing. Being with Nicole was demoralizing for Kaitlin, but there was no way around it. She might hate the docility she had to show, but one thing was tied to the next — docility to trust, trust to privileges, privileges to independence, and independence to Kevin Stark, though of course her mother didn't know about Kevin. Kaitlin had to keep it that way, but she couldn't think straight with her mother in her face, and after Miss Lissy's Closet, there had been lunch and then a mother-daughter tennis match at the club (wearing the *totally* dorky fat-farm whites the club required), and driving back and forth, all with her mother *there*, even in the ladies' room, because this was Wednesday, and during the summer Nicole DuPuis had Wednesdays off.

Nicole was Aidan Meade's executive assistant, meaning that she was his liaison to the outside world. She handled his phone calls and opened his letters, but the crux of her day was spent on e-mail. Aidan liked e-mail. He felt that it effectively countered the image of backwoods New Hampshire, and though little of the e-mail he received was crucial, since his father ran the show, he was forever being cc'd on matters, so there was volume indeed. Nicole's job was to give Aidan the *perception* of importance by replying to each and every e-mail in a manner that suggested he was at his desk, hard at work, and on top of every part of the business.

Basically, as Nicole had told her friends often enough for Kaitlin to know, it was a sell job, and that was right down Nicole's alley. She was good at selling, marketing, packaging. She had built a life doing it for herself, transforming the poor girl she had once been into a woman with just enough savvy and skill to snag a wealthy husband.

The fact that Anton DuPuis didn't have anywhere near the money Nicole had thought he did was only a temporary setback. So she wouldn't have a cushy nest egg for her old age or millions to pass on when she died. Nicole only cared about the here and now anyway. She had enough money to create the *perception* of wealth, and that was all that mattered. The DuPuises lived on Birch Street. They drove late-model cars, belonged to the country club, and shopped to their hearts' content.

So then how to explain the fact that Nicole worked? Power. She didn't have to work, she told friends. She *chose* to work, because, after all, she had only one child, who was in school and didn't need her, and charity luncheons weren't really her thing. She needed an intellectual outlet (Kaitlin nearly gagged each time she heard *that* one, because *she* knew that her mother had lunch at her desk not to get more work done or to read Jane Austen but to watch *All My Children* on the portable TV she kept hidden in the drawer), and Aidan Meade had come to depend on her, so wasn't that nice? What would she *do* with her time and her mind if she didn't have this? If the job paid well — which this one did — so much the better. And she did love those Wednesdays off.

"This gives me quality time with my daughter," she said — another PC sound bite — and planned the entire day to make up for all the time she was at work — which was why only now, *hours* after the fact, Kaitlin was finally alone in her bedroom and able to make the call.

Kevin answered after barely a ring. "Hey, cutie."

"She knows," Kaitlin said in quiet panic. She had her head bowed, hair hiding her face in a way that was usually a comfort, but there was no comfort now. "We're in trouble."

"Your *mother?*"

"Annie Barnes. She saw us last night."

There was a silent heartbeat, then an incredulous, "No way," from Kevin. "It was dark. It was like five seconds in the headlights. She doesn't even know who we are."

"I keep telling myself that, but she walked into Miss Lissy's Closet while I was there with my mom, and she winked at me. I mean, it was deliberate. If you'd seen the look on her face, you'd know it was true."

"How? How could she tell?"

"I don't know," Kaitlin said. "Maybe my hair?" Or my fat butt, she was thinking, though she didn't say it. Kevin claimed that he didn't think her butt was fat, but that was because he knew it would upset her if he told her the truth.

"Like, none of your other friends has long blonde hair?" he asked. "She *can't* know who you are. She doesn't *live* here."

"Kevin, she *winked*. I'm telling you, I don't know how, but she knows."

Kevin was quiet for a minute. "Did she say anything?"

"Of course, she didn't! There was no time for that — I mean, like she went off into the other room, and we didn't see her again — but I'm sure she told her sister, and by now Phoebe's probably told Joanne, and Joanne will tell her mother, and her mother works for James Meade and sees *my* mother at the office all the time. What are we going to do, Kevin? If she finds out, we're sunk! She'll be *furious*. She'll dock me for months, she'll interrogate me every time I go out, she'll send me *away* if she has to. She'll threaten your parents with God-only-knows-what. She'll accuse you of *rape*."

"I never raped you."

"It's a *legal* thing, Kevin. I'm underage!"

"And your mother wasn't doing what we are when she was seventeen?"

"Of *course* she was, which is why she's so distrustful of *me*. She's terrified I'll do what she did."

"She didn't do so bad."

"She hates my father. They barely talk. They don't even make love anymore."

"How do you know?"

"I heard her tell a friend on the phone."

"Well, that's not the situation with you and me. We love each other. Besides, we were just having fun."

Kaitlin might have strangled him for missing the point. "Kevin. Think. Having fun is even worse, because having fun leads to babies, and that's how I came to be. She'll go ballistic if she knows I'm on the pill, and she won't *hear* the part about love. She'll just think about your daddy working at the mill." Kaitlin rubbed her temple. She might have known she would be caught. She was *always* caught. "What were we thinking?"

"That it was nice."

Oh, it had been nice. It always was with Kevin, right from the start. He had been her first. And gentle? Omigod. So sweet touching her breasts, so excited taking off her clothes that his hands shook, and then so careful and apologetic and *upset* when she bled. She had expected to feel grateful

113

that he wanted to make love with her. What she hadn't expected was to feel the fire. But it was there every time. This wasn't the first backabehind they had pulled. Lacking the privacy of a bedroom, they had made love in the woods, behind the school, even out at Cooper's Point. They had made love on Oak Street, Willow Street, and now Cedar.

Kaitlin wouldn't find another guy like Kevin. If it ended, she would be back to being the only one without a date. If it ended, she would feel more ugly than ever. If it ended, she would absolutely, totally cease to exist.

"Annie Barnes will tell," she cried fearfully. "She'll even do it out of spite, because *she* never pulled a backabehind. Like, who'd have slept with her? She had no friends. I mean, ze-ro. She was ugly, and she was odd."

"Yeah, that's what they always said, but I saw her today, and she wasn't ugly. She came into Harriman's while I was stocking the shelves."

"Omigod. *That's* how she knew. You must have looked totally guilty."

"She didn't see me."

"Not once?"

"Not once."

Kaitlin flipped her hair back from her face. "I can't believe Annie Barnes chose *that* instant to drive down the street."

"Maybe she won't tell."

Kaitlin felt despair. "Yeah. Right. Like she won't write it into something? Kevin, do you know who she *is?* She writes books, and she's come here to write about Middle River, because that's what she used to do, only now she's rich and famous, so the whole world reads what she writes. We're in *big* trouble," she cried. "What are we going to do?"

Chapter 5

Heart pounding, I watched through my rear-view mirror as Aidan Meade studied first my car and then me, but that pounding heart had nothing to do with physical attraction. I'm not even sure I had felt that for Aidan back when I was eighteen, when we were meeting in the woods at Cooper's Point. What I felt then was awe; Aidan was the most sought-after twenty-one-year-old in Middle River, and he was interested in me — or so I thought at the time.

I knew differently now, which was why the pounding of my heart came from anger. I tried to get a grip on it during the time he spent studying my car, but it was unabated, even stoked when he opened his door, climbed out, and approached.

Fifteen years was a long time for anger to simmer. *Be cool, Annie,* I cautioned. *Be the deliberate woman you are in D.C. — the one who doesn't act on impulse and has more power for it.*

"That's some car, Annie Barnes," he said

116

in a smooth voice, but the closer he came, the less sure he seemed. "Annie?"

"Uh-huh."

"You look like her, but not. Wow, you've changed."

Had he made it a compliment, I might have calmed, but as stated it annoyed me all the more. "Not you, Aidan," I observed. "You look the same. Older, but the same."

He smirked. "I was hoping you'd say 'older but wiser.' "

"Wiser?" I couldn't help it. "You're on what marriage now? Fourth?"

"Third. Four would be pitiful, don't you think?" I thought three at his age was pitiful, but before I could tell him, he said, "Been following my life, have you?"

"Not yours, per se. I read the *Middle River Times* cover to cover each week. It's better than *People* — more juicy. I'm always amazed. It reports each of your weddings like it was the first."

"Dad-dy!" came a shriek from the car.

Aidan held up a hand to still the voice.

I couldn't see in the windows, though there was truly no need. "And now you're a daddy, too," I observed politely. "How many kids do you have?"

"Five."

"In all?"

117

"Three with Judy and now two with Bev. Lindsey and I didn't have any kids."

I frowned, puzzled. "Lindsey was the first. Didn't you marry *because* she was pregnant?" Of course, he had. The town had been abuzz with the news. There had been a miscarriage and a speedy divorce. The marriage had lasted a mere six months.

"No," Aidan lied, then glanced at his car in response to a cry.

"*Daddy,* he's *kicking* me! *Stop* it, Micah!"

"Micah, keep your feet to yourself!" Aidan yelled. He faced me again. "You have an edge, Annie. But then, you always did. As I recall, we had something going, until you turned sour."

The barb wasn't worth answering. "As *I* recall," I said with a smile, "we never *got* something going, because you were never there. You'd tell me to meet you at eight, and I'd sit alone in the woods until you showed up at ten or eleven. You'd give me some story about work holding you up and how exhausted you were and that you'd call me in a couple of days, and sure enough, you did. Then Michael Corey accused you of having an affair with his wife, and you said it couldn't possibly be so, because on the dates in question, you were with me. You said all that in a sworn affidavit. And I didn't deny it."

"Nope," he said smugly.

"Because to deny it," I went on, welcoming the catharsis, "would have meant admitting to the town that we hadn't been together, and you knew I wouldn't do that. You knew I had never dated anyone else and that I thought it was awesome to be picked by a Meade. You *knew* I would jump at the chance to be yours."

He grinned. "You did."

"And that I would lie, rather than say you had basically stood me up all those times."

"You did that, too."

"Lied, yes — but not under oath like you had, never under oath." I stopped smiling. "I was your alibi right up to the night of my senior prom. You offered to take me."

"In gratitude," he said.

"And then stood me up."

He smirked. "Couldn't be helped. I was tied up."

"So I sat home alone that night, all dressed up in the prettiest dress from my mom's shop. I had told everyone at school that you were my date. When I never showed up, they decided I had made it up."

119

"So then you backtracked and said you lied about the other," Aidan picked up the story, "only no one believed you. After all, I was the one who had sworn to tell the truth. You were such a pitiful thing. People understood why I did what I did."

"Even though you lied."

"My lie was for the greater good. Wouldn't have done Mike Corey any good to know the truth about Kiki and me. They got back together again after she and I broke up."

I gave him my most serene smile. "For the greater good? Huh. What would you do if I told you I was wearing a wire right now?"

I saw a second's surprise in his eyes, but he was distracted when a blood-curdling screech came from the car. This one was higher pitched, if smaller.

"Leave the baby alone, the *both* of you," Aidan roared, "or you'll get it when we get home!"

Beat your kids, too? I wanted to ask, but it would have changed the subject. We weren't done with this one yet.

Aidan was less cocky now. "You're not wearing a wire. You had no idea I'd be coming round that corner."

"No, but, y'know, I'm glad you did," I

said and meant it. I had been dreading this meeting. Now it had happened, and I hadn't crumbled. This was proof that I wasn't the lonely girl I had once been, the one Aidan Meade had left waiting in the woods, the one who had been stood up on the night of her only senior prom, the one who had been disappointed and humiliated and compromised. The woman I was now said in a voice that was forceful for its self-possession, "I've always wanted to tell you what a snake I think you are. You used me, Aidan. I won't ever forget that."

I glanced past him when another big SUV rounded the corner. This one was identical to Aidan's, dark windows and all, except that it had the Northwood Mill logo on the side of the door. It came to a stop as suddenly as Aidan had, idling in the street while the driver opened his door and walked over. Fortyish and intelligent-looking, he wore jeans and a jersey with the same mill logo on the breast pocket.

"Your father's on the warpath," he told Aidan. "The ad folks just showed up, and you haven't answered your cell."

Aidan glared at his own car and shouted, "Did that phone ring, Micah?"

I half turned in my seat to get a glimpse of the shadow of a child, but another

121

shadow caught my eye first. This one was in the passenger seat of the Northwood Mill SUV. Judging from the size of it, it was a man and from the profile, a Meade. That would be James. He was the older brother, the heir apparent, the brains behind the mill's recent growth, and the father's right-hand man.

I don't know whether the child answered Aidan or not, but Aidan was arguing with the man from the mill. "They weren't supposed to be here until four." When he saw his man looking at me, he said with a snide edge, "This is Annie Barnes. She's come back to town to make trouble."

I wasn't bothered by the remark. I looked good, and I knew it. Offering the man a hand, I smiled pleasantly. "And you are?"

"Tony O'Roarke," he said.

"He's our VP for operations," Aidan put in, "which means he's the hands-on guy at the mill *and* the one the old man calls when he has a gripe with one of us." To Tony, who had shaken my hand quite nicely, he said, "Those people said they'd be there at four, so that's when I'll be there."

"He wants you now."

Aidan's look was as cold as his tone. "I'm busy now."

Clearly feeling the chill, Tony raised a low hand and took a step back, then retreated fully. Aidan watched them drive off. Mouth and nostrils were tight when he faced me again, but he picked right up where we'd left off.

"So now you've come back to town to get revenge. Sorry, sweetheart, but there's nothing to avenge."

"Then you have nothing to worry about, do you?" I said offhandedly, and that *did* make him nervous. Everything about him seemed suddenly tighter.

Warily, he asked, "Are you here to write?"

I glanced at The Apothecary just as Lisa and Timmy emerged. "Well, writing *is* what I do."

"How much do you make per book?"

"*East of Lonely* has just gone back to press again. I think the in-print total is approaching two million."

"How much do you make?"

I was amused. "I'm sorry. I don't discuss money."

"I could find out."

"I don't think so. Meades control Middle River, but they don't control New York — or Washington, for that matter." I smiled. "You don't scare me, Aidan." I turned the smile on my niece and nephew. "Get what you needed?"

By way of an answer, Lisa held up the prescription bag. "Hi, Mr. Meade," she said with a deference that was echoed by her brother as they cinched themselves into the single seat belt again.

Politely, I said to Aidan, "I'm afraid I'm going to have to ask you to move your vehicle."

He probably would have argued — Meades prided themselves on getting the last word — had one of his children not yelled, *"Dad-dy, I need to go potty bad!"*

With a grunt of displeasure, he gave my BMW a pat, and walked off.

I watched in my rearview mirror as he climbed into the big black SUV, slammed the door, and drove away. There was no pounding heart now. I might have prayed that my confrontation with Aidan would have taken place at a later time, but Someone upstairs had known better. It wasn't that my prayer hadn't been answered, simply that I had prayed for the wrong thing. I should have prayed to get it over and done. Now that it was, I was composed and content.

I couldn't have asked for a more satisfying meeting.

★ ★ ★

Back at the house, while Timmy washed my car with a ten-year-old's love and Lisa the almost-woman made chili from a mix, I logged onto the Web for a refresher on mercury poisoning.

There were two kinds — acute and chronic.

Acute mercury poisoning results from intense exposure over a short period of time, most notably either from eating the stuff or inhaling undiluted vapors. Symptoms start with a cough or tightness in the chest, and progress to breathing and stomach troubles. Fatalities occur in cases where pneumonia develops. In cases where mercury is actually swallowed, there can be intense nausea, vomiting, and diarrhea, not to mention permanent kidney damage.

I didn't see my mother or sister falling into this category. *Chronic* mercury poisoning, though, was less easily dismissed. It consists of repeated low-level exposure to contaminated materials, and since the symptoms are slow to appear, exposure can occur much earlier. Moreover, the symptoms of chronic mercury poisoning vary widely from victim to victim. One might suffer bleeding gums, another numbness in the hands and feet. Others suffer slurred speech and difficulty walking, or mood changes that include irritability, apathy, and hypersensitivity. In the later stages of chronic mercury poisoning, the central nervous system can be affected, as can kidney and liver functions. Birth defects are a serious risk, hence the warning that pregnant women not eat those kinds of fish that retain higher concentrations of the metal. The relationship between mercury poisoning and autism in young children is a whole other story.

I pulled up more sites in search of other symptoms. By the time I was done, I had found descriptions of all of the ones I had seen in my mother and was starting to see in my sister — the fine tremor of the hand, the trouble with balance, the memory loss and frequent inability to hold a train of thought for long.

Unfortunately, these malfunctions could also be attributed to Alzheimer's or Parkinson's, or to any number of other conditions. Worse, identifying chronic mercury poisoning with certainty is next to impossible. Acute mercury poisoning can be proven, since blood tests done within several days of exposure to high doses of mercury show elevated levels of the metal. After those few days, though, it moves into the nervous system and no longer shows up in the blood, at which point a blood test is useless. Urine tests are even worse; since mercury doesn't *ever* leave the body through urine, it never shows up in a test.

The bottom line? Chronic mercury poisoning can never be diagnosed for sure.

On the other hand, if it could be shown that a person with specific symptoms has been exposed to mercury, a circumstantial case can be made. This was where Northwood Mill came in. Yes, I was biased. I was looking to pin this on the mill. But what else could be responsible? If people in Middle River were getting sick in the numbers I thought they were, the source of mercury had to be big. The mill was big.

"What are you doing, Auntie Anne?" Lisa asked.

"Oh, some research," I said, knowing she would assume the research was for a book. Highlighting the latest batch of information, I copied it into a folder with the rest. "It's kind of a fishing expedition at this point." I clicked the folder shut and turned away from the laptop. "That chili smells really good, sweetie. Did your mom teach you how to make it?"

"Nope. My dad. He's the cook. Mom only gets home in time to eat." Her eyes flew to the door and widened in excitement. "Here she is now. She left work early to see *you*." She ran to the door and opened the screen. "Hi, Mom. Come on in here. I'm making dinner for Aunt Phoebe and Auntie Anne."

Sabina came through the door looking tired and tense. "You are the best girl in the world," she said and kissed her daughter on the forehead. "Want to help Timmy finish the car, so I can have a minute alone with Auntie Anne?"

"I have to stir the chili first," the girl said and returned to the stove. With deliberate motions — carefully taught, I decided — she put on a mitt, lifted the lid of the big pot, stirred the chili in a way that avoided splatter, then returned the lid to the pot, removed the mitt, and smiled at us.

"Well done," I said, smiling back.

Looking proud, she went outside.

The screen door had barely slapped shut when Sabina slipped into the chair kitty-corner to mine at the table and said, simmering, "I just got a call from Aidan Meade. He wants to know why you're here. What did you say to him?"

"Nothing," I replied. I was annoyed by her annoyance. "He didn't ask why I was here." At least, not in as many words.

"Why's he asking you?"

"Because *you* must have said something that set him off. I asked if you were writing a book, and you said you weren't. He thinks you are. He thinks you're still fixated on doing what Grace did."

"This has nothing to do with Grace."

"With you it *always* has to do with Grace. She had a grudge against small towns. So do you."

"She didn't have a grudge against small towns. She just never fit in."

"She *hated* them. Look at *Peyton Place*."

"She painted a realistic picture. There's as much to love about that town as there is to hate."

"See? You defend her."

"I understand her. I know what it's like not to fit in. I have good reason to hold a grudge against Middle River. But why would I want to write a book about it? I have ideas aplenty for future books that have nothing to do with this town. Aidan Meade must have one guilty conscience if all he can think is that I'm writing a book about him."

"Or about us. Why else would you be here?"

"This is my home."

"Correction," Sabina said. "Your home

is in Washington. This is where you grew up, but you left. You rejected us."

"Correction," I shot back, "you rejected me. Middle River made my life so miserable that I had to leave. And I'm not moving back here. Trust me on that. I like my life. But my roots are here. I feel a need to connect."

"Why? Mom's gone."

"But you're here. Phoebe's here. You're the closest blood relatives I have." There it was, **TRUTH #3: My need for family,** bubbling to the surface before I could hold it down — and believe me, I would have liked to. Sharing emotions wasn't something we usually did. Tipping my hand to Sabina made me vulnerable.

But the words seemed to quiet her. She drew in a tired breath and sat back in the chair. "Then try to see it from my point of view, Annie. I'm in a difficult position. He's my employer."

Sabina was Northwood Mill's main computer person, very much the jack-of-all-trades where information technology was concerned. When a computer malfunctioned, she was there. When an employee needed instruction, she was there. She was there when computers were added to the network, there when the system had to be

130

wiped clean of viruses and worms, and she had a major say when it was time to upgrade. The last, of course, meant that she had to train every last employee when upgrades were made.

Being only functionally computer-literate myself — i.e., I could do what I needed to do, namely e-mail, write, and search, but little else — I had the utmost respect for her. I had a feeling she worked longer hours than any of the Meades.

"They need you more than you need them," I said on that hunch.

"Not true," Sabina argued. "They pay me well, and the benefits are twice what I'd get elsewhere. We have two kids to take care of. But you wouldn't know about that."

No. I wouldn't. Steering clear of that discussion, I said, "Sabina? Do you know anything about mercury poisoning?"

"Should I?"

"The symptoms Mom had are very similar."

"Mom had Parkinson's." She scowled. "Why can't you accept what she had? Are you so afraid you'll get it too?"

"It's not that. It's just that these symptoms bother me. Same with Phoebe's symptoms. And from what I've read in the

Middle River Times, it seems like lots of people are suffering from one or another of the same symptoms."

"Are they?" she asked doubtfully.

"If what I've read is correct. You know the column —"

"I do, but the ailments go across the board. Face it, Annie. Middle River is getting older. Older people have more ailments."

"More frequent miscarriages in twenty-somethings? More autism in children?"

"What's your point?" my sister asked blandly.

"The mill. Do you think it could be a polluter?"

"No."

"Have you ever heard the word *mercury* spoken there?"

"No."

"Are you aware that mercury is a political hot button?"

"*No.* Where are you heading with this?"

I backed off. "I don't know. I'm just wondering about these things."

Sabina rose, tired and sad now. "I know you, Annie. Wondering leads to no good. Please. I'm begging you. *Please,* don't do anything to make life difficult for us here. My husband works for the mill. *I* work for the mill. This is our livelihood, our future, our *children's* future. We can't afford to have you meddling."

I wasn't meddling. All I was doing, I decided, going online again that evening after Phoebe went upstairs, was learning more about a problem that maybe, just maybe, was causing harm.

Basically, there are two sources of mercury emissions — natural and man-made. Natural mercury emissions come from volcanic eruptions, the eroding of soil and rocks, and oceanic vapors. These have been around forever, and can't be contained.

Man-made sources of mercury pollution are another story. There are two major villains on this end. The first are trash incinerators that dispose of mercury-laden goods such as thermometers, fluorescent lightbulbs, and dental fillings. The second are oil- and coal-powered plants. These plants are the nation's single largest mercury polluter; once emitted, their toxins remain in the air for centuries. Moreover, once airborne mercury drifts to earth and mixes with bacteria in the soil, it becomes methyl-mercury, and methyl-mercury is extraordinarily toxic. It is also bioaccumulative, meaning that it grows more potent as it climbs the food chain. Mercury in a minnow isn't as bad as it is in trout, which isn't as bad as it is in swordfish or tuna, which are larger. Man, being at the top of the food chain, suffers the harshest effects.

Although some airborne mercury comes from industrial plants in the Midwest, nearly 50 percent is generated in New England. New Hampshire has yet to prohibit mercury pollution and, hence, is one of the worst offenders.

That was something. But I was still in need of a crucial piece of information. I had to dig for it; clearly the industry didn't want the past rearing its ugly head. Beneath layers of links, though, I finally found what I sought: paper mills were indeed known mercury pollutants.

If Northwood Mill released mercury, its most probable victim of contamination was the river. My mother's shop was on the river, not far downstream of the mill. She had spent much of her working life there. Now my sister was taking over. And all those other people worked in all those other shops on the shores of the Middle River. And all those customers sat for hours on those back decks drinking in sunshine and potentially harmful vapors. And all those people on the other side fished for dinner and *ate* what they caught.

The possibilities were endless.

I didn't know whether to be excited or horrified. In need of grounding, not to mention direction, I turned off my laptop and phoned Greg. I half expected that he would be out somewhere celebrating his last night in Washington, but my luck held. He was home.

"Hey," I said with a relieved smile.

"Hey, yourself," he said back and answered my e-mail query. "All packed, thanks."

"Then why aren't you partying?"

"I am."

Ah. He wasn't alone. "Oh dear. Can we talk another time?"

But he was easygoing as ever. "We're waiting for take-out delivery, so this is a great time. What's up?"

It was all the encouragement I needed. "I might be onto something here," I said eagerly. "My mother's symptoms are identical to those of chronic mercury poisoning."

"Mercury? Huh. Any idea how she might have been exposed?"

"Our paper mill."

"Does it produce mercury waste?"

"Not now. But it did. Paper mills are known polluters. Their waste goes right into the river. My mom worked along the river for years. Now my sister's been there awhile, and she isn't well."

"Same symptoms?"

"Some. And she has a cold. One of the effects of chronic mercury poisoning is a weakened immune system. Lots of colds, the flu, pneumonia."

"I'm not sure you can get mercury poisoning just from working alongside a river. I think there has to be direct contact, like something eaten or touched."

"That's possible," I conceded. "But refresh my memory. What's the latest on mercury regulations?"

Greg didn't hesitate; recapping the news in layman's terms was his forte. "Everyone is in agreement that emissions need to be reduced. The disagreement comes in how much and when. The Clean Air Act suggested guidelines and deadlines, but the EPA has scaled back the guidelines and extended the deadlines."

"Under pressure from lobbyists?"

"You bet. And then there's the credit-trading business. All plants pollute. How much they're allowed to pollute is spelled out in pollution credits. A plant that cleans itself up so that it doesn't have to use its credits can sell them to a plant that doesn't want to clean up. The clean plant makes money to compensate for getting clean, and the dirty plant pays to stay dirty. Opponents say this will create hot spots where the pollution is worse than ever. Do we want to live in one of those spots?"

"No. But my mother and sister — much of Middle River — may be doing just that."

"Direct contact, Annie. Keep that in mind. Besides, I wouldn't accuse anyone until you know more. The issue is disposal. If it followed the rules, your mill may be on the up-and-up."

"How would I find out?"

"Ask."

"I can't ask at the mill. They'd go berserk."

"Then call the state environmental agency."

"Like they'd know if the mill has broken rules? Wouldn't Northwood cover it up?"

"They'd try. If they were caught, they'd pay a fine and cover *that* up. But it'd still be in the state records."

It was a good thought, precisely why I had called Greg. His suggestions were always intelligent, purposeful, and diplomatic. Prone to impulsiveness, I'd had, especially, to learn the last.

State environmental agency, I wrote down, then said, "I'm going to go back through the archives of the local paper to find out who is sick and with what. The health column is thorough."

"It would be better to talk with local doctors."

"But then the cat would be out of the bag."

"Would that be so bad?"

"Yes. The Meades own the mill, and they're evil. If they get wind of the fact that I'm looking into this, they'll take it out on my sisters. I did talk with my mother's doctor. He heads the clinic. He put the bug in my ear about mercury, but he's in a precarious position. The mill controls much of the town, including the clinic." I paused. "When you talk Middle River, you talk the mill. It always comes down to that."

"And you'd love to get back at the Meades," Greg said.

"Mom had something. Phoebe may, too."

"And you'd love to get back at the Meades," he repeated.

I was silent. He knew me too well. "You

bet I would," I finally admitted.

"Thinking of doing the Grace thing?"

"Definitely not. Grace wrote a book. I'm not doing that."

"Even if you find a connection? Even if you follow this all the way and manage to bring about change?"

"If things change, there's no need for a book."

"What if you find a cover-up? It would make a terrific story."

"That's *your* field, Greg. You're the journalist. I write fiction."

"So did Grace."

"I'm not Grace."

"So you've said," he teased but with a gentle whiff of truth. "You've said it over and over again in the twelve years I've known you. But she is your model. You cut your teeth on her legacy."

"My career has been totally different from hers."

"And you've made it big now, which means you can write what you want and be guaranteed a large audience."

"My audience would hate it."

"But you'd have quite a platform." On a genuinely curious note, he asked, "Did Grace do it on purpose — write *Peyton Place* with the explicit intention of upsetting the apple cart? Did she do it to create a scandal?"

"With malice aforethought?" I asked with a smile. It was a phrase Greg's lawyer friend Neil — our friend — used all the time. "I don't think so. She loved writing, and she knew small towns. She was simply writing about what she knew."

"But she did have gripes."

"Yes. She was never one to conform to the traditional expectations of women — just couldn't be the pretty, smiling, docile wife and mother that people wanted her to be. She wore jeans and men's shirts. She never cleaned house, except for the very corner where she kept her typewriter, which is such a telling thing," I mused. "She disdained the fifties image — couldn't function as the schoolteacher's wife and do committees and chaperoning and bake sales. She was a brilliant writer who antagonized her landlord with the constant banging of her typewriter keys. Writing was what she did. She just didn't care about the rest. So she was ostracized."

"And she lashed back."

"She told the truth."

"And got revenge."

"That's arguable, given how fast and far she fell after the book came out."

"But she did make a point."

"She did," I had to concede. "What's yours, Greg?"

"I love you. I don't want to see you hurt. I admire you for being there and wanting to know what's wrong with Phoebe, and if you can show a pattern of illness that suggests large-scale mercury poisoning *and* that the mill is the culprit, I'll *help* you write the book. I just don't want you to suffer in the process."

"How will I suffer? People in Middle River already hate me. What do I have to lose?"

He was a long minute in answering. Then he spoke with the kind of caring I was desperate to find. "You've come a long way, Annie. When I first met you, you were still working to distance yourself from Middle River, and you've succeeded. But you revert when you talk of the place. You're prickly, and you're defensive. I'm not sure that town is good for your health."

"Neither am I," I said with new meaning and deepened resolve. "I love you too, Greg. Travel safe."

Chapter 6

Tom Martin was late leaving the clinic again. Today, he'd had to referee a clash between two radiologists fighting over assignments, but more often, his lateness was patient-related. Medical emergencies were forever cropping up at the end of the day, and Tom was a softie. He didn't have the heart to make a patient worry through the night about what ailed him, when an extra thirty minutes of his own time would do the trick. Fortunately, the woman he employed to look after his sister understood.

That said, he hated to push his luck. Making a beeline for home, he whisked out the side door of the clinic and was striding toward the parking lot when he heard his name called. He didn't slow, simply looked around. Eliot Rollins had left the building and was trotting toward him.

Eliot was an orthopedist, a large teddy bear type with a close-cropped beard and a wide white smile. He was a nice guy, a genial sort with more social skill than intellectual curiosity. Thanks to partying in college, much of it with Aidan Meade, he'd had to take several shots at medical school before finally getting in. He had come to Middle River straight from his residency and had been at the clinic for three years before Tom was hired.

Tom might have blamed the distance between them on that; Eliot wouldn't have been the first to resent the new guy on top. But there was more. They had different manners, different tastes, different friends. As a matter of rule, each went his own way.

That was one of the reasons Tom was surprised to see Eliot now. Another was that Eliot was usually among the first to leave work, not the last. He had a rambling old home on the south end of town, where he kept a wife, two children, and a cooler of beer by the pool. Summers, he was usually gone from the clinic by four.

"Hold up," Eliot said in his usual genial way. "I have a question."

Tom slowed only marginally. "Sorry. I'm running late. Have to get home."

Eliot drew abreast and matched his pace. "How's Ruth?" he asked.

"She's doing well, thank you."

"It's working out with Marie Jenkins, then?"

143

Marie was the woman who looked after Tom's sister. She had been an ER nurse on the verge of burnout when Tom hired her, and the job suited her well. Ruth required custodial care, but there was no trauma in her day. To the contrary. Everything about Ruth was slow. She had to be helped with washing and dressing, and had to be driven to and from programs three times a week in Plymouth. She needed help with the DVD player; though, if allowed, would watch *Finding Nemo*, *Beauty and the Beast*, and *The Lion King* for hours on end. She loved being read to, even when she didn't understand the content, and often fell asleep before the first chapter was done.

Marie was so grateful for the respite from the tension of the ER that she didn't mind the tedium. During quiet times, she read or cooked. Tom had no problem with that.

"It's working really well," he told Eliot. Having reached his pickup, he opened the door, tossed in his briefcase, rolled down the window. "What's up?" he asked as he climbed in.

"Julie and I are having a cookout Friday night. Want to drop by?"

Tom smiled. "Thanks, but I can't. Marie is taking off for the weekend, and Ruth has been nervous with strangers lately, so it could be more trouble than not." He pulled the door shut.

"Oh," said Eliot and curved a hand over the open window. "Well, maybe another time." He caught a quick breath. "Say, was that Alyssa Barnes's daughter who dropped by today?"

And *that*, thought Tom, was the question Eliot had really wanted to ask — and with some urgency, if the price of asking it was having to invite Tom to his cookout. Amused by that, and curious enough to set aside his own rush to get home, Tom said, "It was. She wanted to thank me for taking care of her mother."

"Well, that was nice. She didn't catch you at the funeral?"

"Not for that."

"Huh. So she caught you now. She's here for a month, y'know. Did she say what she'll be doing?"

"I don't think she knows for sure."

"Then she didn't mention doing some writing?"

"Not to me," Tom said with more innocence than was perhaps justified, but he sensed where Eliot was headed. "Are you worried she'll write about us?"

"That depends," Eliot mused casually.

145

"People are saying she might. I don't know about you, man, but I wasn't in town ten minutes before someone was telling me about *Peyton Place*. I mean, Aidan used to talk about the connection, and, sure enough, there it was. It's an obsession."

"*Peyton Place* is history. That all happened nearly fifty years ago."

"Middle River says it could happen again. They're saying Annie Barnes could to it. I'm not sure we want her doing that."

"Why not?" Tom goaded. "We're good folk."

"Sure we are, but we help each other out in ways we don't always want strangers to know. You want her writing about Nathan Yancy?"

No. Tom didn't. Nathan had been a staff hematologist when Tom had first arrived at the clinic. It was a full year before Tom had a credentialist in place who discovered that Nathan had bogus degrees. He was quietly asked to leave, and he went without benefit of recommendation. It would be all well and good to say Tom wasn't responsible for a doctor who had been hired on someone else's watch. The fact remained, though, that if word got out about Nathan, confidence in the clinic would weaken and its reputation would suffer.

The same thing might happen if word got out about Eliot Rollins. Unfortunately, Eliot Rollins was in the Meade inner circle and hence felt a certain immunity. That said, Tom had no intention of taking the fall for the powers-that-be, if and when the issue erupted.

"What can I say, Eliot. I've warned you. If you're overmedicating certain patients —"

"I am not overmedicating anyone," Eliot cut in, suddenly less genial. "I've said it before, and I say it again. Pain management is a vital part of practicing medicine. It's the cutting edge."

"Sure it is, for geriatric patients. Our police chief doesn't fall into that category."

"You want to tell him he has to suffer?"

"He doesn't have to suffer," Tom argued. "He could lose forty pounds and start exercising. Add a little physical therapy, and his back would be fine."

"You're an expert on orthopedics now?"

"Nope. Don't have to be. It's common sense. You gave him a crutch, Eliot. He's addicted now, so the problem is compounded."

"You have no proof that he's addicted."

"Anyone who takes the painkillers he

does with the frequency he does is addicted."

Eliot put his hands in his pockets. He was chewing on a corner of his mouth. "Was she asking you about that?"

"Who?" Tom couldn't resist asking.

"Annie Barnes. When she talked with you today."

"No. She was thanking me for taking care of her mother." He had already said that, but it bore repeating.

"That wouldn't take more than a minute or two. You were out there longer than that."

"Were you watching us?" Tom asked, but didn't wait for an answer. Eliot hadn't had to watch them to know they were there. Middle River was a town filled with spies. He had known that his having coffee with Annie would make the rounds. So, casually, he said, "We were talking about Washington. We both graduated from Georgetown."

Eliot didn't look convinced. "All that time you were talking about Washington?"

"Most of it. We talked some about her mom. That's foremost in Annie's mind." Tom fished out his key and started the engine. "Sorry, but I really do have to get home. Hey, tell you what. If I think of someone to stay with Ruth, I'll try to drop

148

by Friday night. Fair enough?"

Eliot didn't answer. But then, Tom didn't give him the chance. Backing out of the space, he turned the wheel, stepped on the gas, and, with satisfaction, left the teddy bear of an orthopedist behind. Glancing in his rearview mirror, he saw that Eliot had put his hands on his hips. And Tom knew two things for sure — first, that he would opt to be with his sister over Eliot any Friday evening, and second, that Eliot wasn't done with the matter of Annie Barnes.

Chapter 7

I started running when I was eighteen. Having just moved to Washington, I was erasing the past and reinventing myself — new attitude, new friends, new interests. Middle River did baseball, basketball, and football, but running? Not in *our* town. That alone would have been reason enough for me to take it up. There were, of course, other reasons, the prime one being Jay Riley, a junior who had helped freshmen move into my dorm and, yes, was a runner. I had a crush on him from day one.

As fate had it, my roommate, Tanya Frye, whom I adore to this day, had been running competitively since she was twelve, and though I had nowhere near the natural aptitude she did, I took to the sport with remarkable ease. Granted, she started me slowly. By the end of freshman year, though, I could do a 10K in forty-six minutes — which, FYI, is nothing to sneeze at.

I never did catch Jay's eye, but my new

150

persona flourished. I dated other guys. Some were runners, some were not. All admired my legs in shorts. It was a whole new experience for me.

Over the years, I have come to race less and run more for the simple enjoyment of it. I always feel better after I run. I'm told it's a chemical thing having to do with endorphins, though I've never delved into the science of it. I do know that after a run my head feels more clear, my limbs more limber, my insides more in sync with the rest of me. After a run, I feel well oiled. Conversely, when several days pass without a run, I'm logy.

That's how I felt waking up Thursday. So I put on a singlet, shorts, and running shoes, stretched right there in the kitchen, and slipped out the door while Phoebe slowly emerged from her own lethargy over coffee and eggs.

Normally I run at six in the morning to beat the heat and then return for my prime hours of work, but Middle River was cooler than D.C. and I wasn't working. Running at eight here, though, raised a different problem. Middle River would be up and about.

So, as I had done in my convertible the day before, I stuck to the back roads, and it was really nice. There were no cars on the road; the area was strictly residential, houses spaced farther apart, and though I spotted the occasional native watering the lawn or weeding the beds, there was enough land between us so that I was barely seen.

Running north up Willow to the end, I turned east and cut across town on pavement that was buckled and cracked but forgiving in the way of a withering hag. These roads weren't named after trees; when the town's founding fathers had run out of those, what recourse did they have but to name streets after themselves? So there were Harriman, Farnum, and Rye streets. There were Coolidge, Clapper, and Haynes streets — and, of course, Meade Street. None of these namesake families lived in this neighborhood; they were closer to the center of town in homes that were larger and more imposing. The houses here were even more modest than ours on Willow. These were small Capes that, if enlarged, had been done so in the form of caboose-type additions tacked on. All were well-tended, though, with pretty walks and flower beds, and matching shutters and doors.

I had a favorite here. It was a bungalow

at the very end of Hyde Street, tucked under a clan of hemlocks and looking like a gingerbread house, with its chocolate siding and pale pink trim.

Omie lived here. But more on Omie later.

Feeling good, I ran on at a steady pace. I turned right at the end of the road and was in the process of returning to the center of town when I spotted another runner.

Another *runner?* I mused wryly. What was Middle River *coming* to?

I might have asked him — yes, the runner was a guy — had he been closer, but he was on the cross street several blocks ahead. He glanced at me as he passed, then disappeared.

Oh boy, sweetie, he's a good-looking one, said a salacious little voice in my head.

Unable to see much this far away, I promptly dismissed the remark, but my commentator didn't leave. Neither a fly nor the purr of a cat this time, the words were crystal clear.

He's tall. I like them tall, she reminded me. *Who do you think he is?*

Haven't a clue, I thought.

There's nothing like a bare-chested man to stir the juices.

He's a runner, I argued. It's a different kind of bare-chested. He's probably all matted and sweaty.

Sweat is sexy as hell. Follow him, sweetie.

I will not.

No? For God's sake, what good are you?

"Hey! Aren't you Annie Barnes?" asked a man who had emerged from his front walk during my brief distraction. He was short and beyond middle age, very much the opposite of the runner (okay, I did get a *general* impression), and he seemed to expect me to stop and talk.

Stopping and talking was something Middle Riverites did. Not me. Especially not while I was running.

I raised a hand as I ran past, but didn't slow down. I had hit my stride. I felt good.

Was I being rude? Probably. When in Rome, as the saying goes.

But my feelings of guilt only went so far. The town already thought the worst of me. What was a little rudeness but a validation of that?

By now, you may be thinking I was disliked by *everyone* in Middle River during the years I lived here. This is not so. I had a few friends. Granted, they weren't exactly my peers. But they were supportive.

One of those was Marsha Klausson. For as long as anyone could remember, she had owned The Bookshop. It was located on Willow, three doors down from Miss Lissy's Closet, and it had been something of a second home for me. As a child I spent hours cross-legged on the scuffed wood floor in front of the bookshelves, browsing through everything appropriate for my age before picking one to buy. That was the deal my father made — we could each buy one a month. Though at that time we had little money to spare, he wanted us to build our own little libraries. One book a month would give us a good start, he announced.

Then he died. I was ten at the time, and my mother carried on the practice, but she never beamed over my purchases the way Daddy had. She also directed me toward what she felt to be the "proper" book, at which point I began spending more time at the town library. My tastes were mature. I had moved on to J. D. Salinger, Jack London, and Ursula K. Le Guin when most girls my age were still on Louisa May Alcott. I'm not sure my mother would have approved of my reading *Lord of the Flies* or

The Great Gatsby, but these books intrigued me. They were my escape.

Mrs. Klausson seemed to understand that. I was her "staff reviewer" long before the practice became commonplace. By mutual agreement, we kept my reviews unsigned. We were co-conspirators in this. I got to read books without buying them; Mrs. Klausson got to talk books without reading them. I continued to send her reviews even after I left Middle River. Once in a while, I still did. We corresponded by traditional mail. As computerized as the store had become, she wasn't an e-mail person. Nor could I ever call her Marsha. Nearing eighty now, she would always be Mrs. Klausson, and not only in deference to her age. She had been natty before nattiness reached Middle River. I suspect I was drawn as much to this difference in her as I was to her books.

I was also drawn to her scent. Everything about her was honeysuckle, from the oil she dabbed behind her ears, to the sachets that scented her clothes, to the soap with which she washed her hands. She generated an aromatic little cloud that followed her around the store. Honeysuckle might not have been my favorite scent, any more than roses were. But just as the smell of roses conjured up Road's End Inn and told me I was on my way home, honeysuckle conjured up the haven of The Bookshop. Like one of Pavlov's dogs, I no longer needed the scent to capture the feeling; one step in the door of this shop and the welcome came to me all on its own.

Fifteen years had made little difference in Mrs. Klausson's appearance; she still wore a pressed blouse and neat linen slacks. I could see that she was shorter than she had been when I left town, and more wrinkled — neither of which I'd had the presence of mind to see when she had come to the house to pay her condolences in June. But her eyes lit up when she saw me enter, and, abandoning a pair of clients at none other than Grace's table, she was by my side in a flash.

"Well, well, well," she said with a twinkly smile and a fond once-over, "look at you. Our most famous writer."

"Second only to you-know-who," I reminded her. It was our long-standing joke.

"She's dead, but you're alive," the woman declared. Favoring her arthritic neck, she turned her whole body and, clutching my hand, pulled me toward the clients she had left. "This is Annie Barnes. Annie, you remember my old friend

157

Carolee Haynes. And this fabulous woman with her is the daughter of an old friend of hers. Her name is Tyra Ann Moore, and she's in visiting us from Tucson with her husband and two girls."

Carolee smiled dutifully. She might have been a friend of Mrs. Klausson's, but she had never been a friend of mine. Nor, come to think of it, had she ever been a friend of my mother's. The Hayneses lived in a Georgian mansion on Birch; Carolee had always considered those of us in Victorians on Willow to be beneath her. She was tall, lean, and starched. Even the wrinkles around her mouth looked ironed in, no doubt from pursing those thin lips in disdain.

Tyra Ann Moore was another story. Blonde-haired and standing barely five-four, she exuded warmth and generosity. Her voice held both. "You're Annie Barnes? I don't believe it! You're one of my favorite writers."

"Then we're even," I said with a crooked grin. "Tucson is one of my favorite places."

"Annie grew up here," said Mrs. Klausson with pride, "which was what I was about to tell you right before she arrived. She was a fixture in this shop for more years than I can recall. That's why I keep her books on the shelf nearest to this table."

"In the shadow of Grace," Carolee intoned dramatically.

"*East of Lonely* was the best," Tyra said with a hand on her chest. "I can't believe it's really you! You look so normal. I mean, down to earth. Do you spend your summers here? Do you come back to write? Are you working on something new?"

"I'd like to know that too," Carolee remarked.

"I've already finished my next book," I told Tyra. "It's being published in the spring."

"Which didn't answer the question," Carolee said.

"Oh, Carolee," scolded Mrs. Klausson, "let her be. She's just lost her mother. She's back to be with her sisters, aren't you, dear?"

I barely had a chance to nod when a third customer joined us. She was close to my age, and had dark brown hair and deep olive skin. Her voice was vibrant. "This has to be the best place for a writer. There's a secret around every corner."

"Juanita," Carolee scolded.

Mrs. Klausson made the introductions. "Annie, this is Juanita Haynes. She's married to Carolee's youngest boy, Seth."

I had never had cause to care for Seth, who had never had cause to care for me. But my feelings changed in the instant. Knowing that he had fallen in love with a Latino woman and had dared bring her to Middle River endeared him to me. Likewise, knowing what this poor woman would face with a mother-in-law like Carolee in a town like Middle River endeared *her* to me.

"I'm glad to meet you, Juanita. Do you and Seth live in town, or are you visiting?"

"Just visiting," Carolee answered for her daughter-in-law. "They're both in hedge funds in New York. We rarely get to see them. A few days here, a few days there. Surely not enough to hear secrets."

Juanita grinned mischievously. "But I did hear about Father William."

Carolee shushed her, but Tyra was clearly interested. "What about him?"

"He has a sweetheart."

"Mary Barrett is his housekeeper," Carolee corrected primly. "She lives in, because there happens to be an extra room in the parish house, and Father William welcomes the rent."

"He doesn't charge her rent," said Mrs. Klausson.

"I know that, Marsha, but we're quibbling with words. He lets her use the room in exchange for cleaning the house and the church. It's a business arrangement, very much the *equivalent* of rent. There is nothing going on between them."

"That's not what Seth's friend Peter said," Juanita teased. "Peter does carpentry work for Father William. He saw them in bed together."

Carolee's mouth was as pinched as could be. "Peter Doohutton is a drunk, like his father was before him, and he's no friend of Seth's. They happened to have been in the same class in school. Truly, Juanita, I wouldn't trust what Peter says. Father William is a man of the cloth, and he's been here a *lot* longer than you."

I would have spoken up on Juanita's behalf, if Juanita hadn't been so clearly enjoying herself. A beautiful woman, she exuded confidence and smarts. I figured that Carolee had met her match with this one.

"Hey," Juanita said now, "I'm fine with Father William *whatever* he does. He's a great guy."

"Then let's not spread gossip."

"Spread?" Juanita echoed, barely containing a smile. "There's no spreading

161

when it's already done — at least, that's the impression I got when we went to church."

"*We* are Congregationalists," Carolee remarked. "Father William is a Catholic. We got *no* impression of him, because we were not in his church."

"But plenty of people were," Juanita said. "Seth's friend John was telling us about it at brunch — and neither he nor his father are drunks. They're selectmen, both of them, here in Middle River. John says attendance at Our Lady is as high as ever. He says that most people don't really care what Father William does at night, as long as it's with a woman."

Carolee glared at Mrs. Klausson. "Do you see what's happening here? They're condoning it."

Mrs. Klausson humored her friend. "No, no, Carolee. They're just leaving well enough alone."

"But the talk —"

"The talk does no harm. It dies at the town line."

"Unless," said Carolee, "someone chooses to write a book about it." Lips pursed, she looked at me.

I was annoyed enough by the woman to want to lash out, and probably would have disgraced myself by saying something like, *Write a book? That might be a good idea after all, because Father William isn't the only one having an affair with his housekeeper, and in fact, maybe he got the idea from your husband, who for years and years and years was slipping home every Friday while you were having your nails done, to settle up the bill with your longtime housekeeper, what was her name?* if Tyra Ann Moore, still starstruck, hadn't jumped in and saved us all.

"Will you tell us about your next book, Annie? What's the title? Will you carry any of the characters over from *East of Lonely*? When is it coming out — I mean, what month?" Before I could begin to answer, she said, "I just can't believe you're here. I'm buying a copy of each of your books for you to sign. Would you do that? No, I'll buy two copies, one for me and one for a friend back home who loves your work as much as I do. . . ."

Sam Winchell was another of the few I had called a friend during my Middle River years. Sam was younger than Mrs. Klausson, probably sixty-five now, which meant he had been in his forties when we had worked together and fifty when I left town. Like Seth Buswell in *Peyton Place*,

163

Sam was the son of an influential man, in this instance a United States senator. Like Grace's Seth, Sam had inherited enough money to own and operate the local weekly and, at the same time, afford a house on Birch. Like the fictitious Seth, Sam was disdainful of bigots and impatient with those who threw their power around, meaning that he had limited patience not only for people like Carolee Haynes, but for Sandy Meade, as well.

That said, Sam was an avid golfer, part of a foursome that played eighteen holes at a club forty minutes away on all but the most rainy of Thursdays. He had been doing this when I had worked for him those high school summers, and judging from the reverence with which he still talked of golf in the paper, he hadn't changed.

Sam's foursome included Sandy Meade. Stories of their bickering on the greens were legendary, as were those few occasions when a game was played minus one of the men when a particularly strong disagreement cropped its ugly, if short-lived, head.

By the way, I had every bit the respect for Sam that I had for Mrs. Klausson. But Sam was always called Sam. The only people who called him Mr. Winchell were from away, and it lasted only until he could wave a hand and say a brusque, "Call me Sam."

I timed my visit so that I would arrive at the *Middle River Times* office on Thursday at eleven. Yes, I wanted to say hello to Sam, but even more, I wanted to pore through the archives to make a tally of the town's sick. Granted, it wouldn't be exact. Greg was right; doctors could give me better figures, but only if they chose to, and it was a big *if*. They could easily stonewall, and then turn around and tell the Meades I was asking. Was it worth the risk? Not yet. I figured I could visit with Sam until he left to play golf, then peruse the paper to my heart's content. Sam's staff wouldn't be around. The paper came out Thursday mornings, and this was Thursday. Within an hour, the newspaper office would be deserted.

The place was front and center on Oak Street, its brick newly painted, mullioned windows washed, trim freshly painted. Sam had always been fastidious about things like these, and clearly that hadn't changed.

No sooner had I let myself in the door, though, when I was hit by the smell of

165

cigar. Sam's fastidiousness had never included his lungs. The cigar in his mouth was as much a fixture of the man as his gray pants and bow tie. No one working for Sam ever complained about the smell; to do so would have meant instant dismissal. I figured that come the day Sam was gone, this place would have to be fumigated *big*-time to remove the last of that smell.

The front desk was deserted, the nearby leather chairs empty. Two offices branched off the main room. I went to the one on the right, led there as much by the strength of the scent as by habit.

Sam, who was tipped back in his chair reading the hot-off-the-press edition of the *Middle River Times*, spotted me over the paper and broke into a grin. His chair creaked as it straightened; the paper landed on the desk with a careless rustle. Rising, he came forward, put an arm around my shoulder, and gave me a fatherly squeeze.

"It's about time you got here," he complained gruffly. "You've been most everywhere else in town first."

"I have not been most everywhere else," I returned. "In case you've forgotten, there are not too many places where I'm welcome."

166

Sam made a sputtering sound. "That was history. You're a noted writer now. You can go anywhere you want. I'm real proud of you, Annie."

I smiled. "Thank you. That means a lot. The rest, well, you know, people jumping on the bandwagon, it's pretty empty."

"And that, right there, is why you'll continue to be a success. Nothing goes to your head, and that's just one *other* way you're different from our Grace," he added, picking up the thread of a conversation we had often had before. Sam, like Mrs. Klausson, shared my fascination with Grace.

I defended her as always. "I don't know that success went to her head. She was just unprepared for it and had no idea what to do. I'm not sure I would have known either, back then. *Peyton Place* was the first of a new breed. No one knew what to expect."

"Well, we do now," Sam concluded, arching a brow. "So I want you to make me a promise. Whatever you write while you're here, I want to serialize it in the *Times*."

I laughed. "I am not here to write."

"Sandy says you are. He called me earlier and ordered me to wheedle what I can from you." He shot a look at the wall clock. "I'm meeting him in forty minutes, and you can be sure he'll know you've been here and want to know what we said."

"Is he nervous?" I asked, enjoying myself. After growing up powerless in this town, I was feeling a definite satisfaction at their reaction to me now. I had felt it with Aidan in a very personal way. With Sandy it was broader, more general, and, given the extent of his power, even sweeter.

"Oh, you know," Sam said dismissively, but I wasn't letting go.

"No, I don't. What have the Meades done?"

Sam gave a grunt. "What haven't they done? But don't get me started on this. Sandy and I walk softly around each other. I could cite you half a dozen things he does that drive me crazy."

"Cite one," I invited.

Separating himself from me, Sam went to the desk and neatly folded the paper. "One? If I told you one and you proceeded to write about it, I might find my computers not working next Tuesday, and if that were to happen, there'd be no paper next Thursday. Not that my livelihood depends on one week of the paper, but it would be a royal pain, not to mention cause a big mess with advertisers who pay by the week."

"Sandy wouldn't sabotage your computers. My sister is his computer person, and she would never do something like that."

"Not if her job was on the line? Not if her husband's was, too? They both work for Meade, and he would use that for all it's worth. If they lost their jobs, you can be sure they wouldn't find others in this town, so how're they going to support their kids?"

"They could bring charges against Sandy."

"And who's gonna testify?" Sam smiled sadly. "So there's your one thing he does that drives me crazy. This is nothing new, Annie. Nothing's changed."

I was thinking that it *ought* to change, that the Meades were truly evil, that if I could prove the mill was contaminating the town with mercury waste and was breaking laws to do it, the family might finally get what it deserved, when Sam said, "I gotta run or I'll miss my tee time. Come on. I'll walk you to your car. Let word get back to old Sandy about *that*."

"Actually, I'd love to sit here awhile and read the paper. Catch up a little."

"Why? I send you the damn thing every week."

I slid him an apologetic look.

He sighed. "And you don't read them."

"I skim," I said, not quite a lie. I often did skim one article or another. Usually, though, my reading was thorough. Not so my memory, which was why I needed this time.

Sam, in his innocence, was flattered enough to leave me to my work.

I started with the current issue, the one he had been reading. It told me, in grand detail, that the library had been given another Meade grant to buy new books, that a full-time ophthalmologist was now affiliated with the Middle River Clinic, that a fire on th'other side had gutted two houses, leaving eleven people homeless, that the state was cutting the money for our schools again, necessitating an emergency town meeting in September to discuss what to do, that a local plumber had been detained for driving under the influence, that for the third weekend in a row vandals had taken baseball bats to mailboxes on Birch and Pine, that the Hepplewaites, who owned Road's End Inn and sponsored the Peyton Place tours of the town, were celebrating their fiftieth wedding anniversary on Saturday, and that Omie was recovering from pneumonia.

The news about Omie concerned me. I liked Omie. She had been old since I could remember, everyone's grandmother and a great-grandmother in her own family many times over. Never a big talker, she was kind to the nth degree. When I used to sit by myself in a booth at the diner, she would bring over her tea and keep me company. There were times when that made things worse — like going to the movies with your mother on a Saturday night and seeing all your friends with dates. Other times, it was a godsend.

Omie's heart was kind. I made a vow to stop by and see her.

Setting aside the current issue of the *Times*, I relocated to the front room, where the most recent months' issues hung on tidy wood racks, and began to peruse the archives. The "Health Beat" column was always on the fourth page, top left. Sam was fastidious in this, too. He believed that people should know exactly where their favorite columns were, and didn't want phone calls coming to him when readers couldn't find what they wanted.

Working backward chronologically, I read column after column. It didn't take long to exhaust the hard copy, at which time I moved to the left inner office to access those on microfiche — and all the while, I kept notes on a pad beside me, marking dates, names, and illnesses.

Most newspapers probably wouldn't list enough sick people to make this search worth my while, but Sam was a clever marketer. He knew that people loved seeing their names in print. Middle River was small enough and the *Middle River Times* hungry enough for copy, to make details not only feasible but advisable. What another town might consider irrelevant was included — a chicken pox outbreak in the local Cub Scout den with the names of children stricken, or random cases of Lyme disease or asthma. Broken limbs were reported case by case, with names, cause of the break (e.g., auto accident, fall from bicycle, soccer game), and often even the color of the cast applied and by whom. The column also listed what doctors in town attended which conferences out of town. Our Tom Martin took the lead in those, both attending and conducting seminars. His specialty was general practice, or the revival thereof, which didn't tell me much about the possibility of mercury poisoning.

Other things did, though. I noted each mention of Alzheimer's and Parkinson's disease. I noted references to autism (e.g., Alice Le Claire's three-year-old son had started at a special school for autistic children), references to breathing difficulties and digestive problems, and I put asterisks beside those instances in which a history was mentioned (e.g., Susannah Alban was recovering from another miscarriage). I noted when babies were born either very early or with illnesses that kept them hospitalized.

In skimming the microfiche reel, I found an announcement of the wedding of Seth and Juanita Haynes. It was on the front page of the paper two years ago last June. The event was in New York City and sounded elegant, from the elaborate description. Interestingly, there was no picture, though I had no doubt pictures did exist. Carolee Haynes was not only a bigot, but a coward.

I went back through five years of the *Middle River Times* — not because I planned to go that far or spend so long at it, but because I kept munching on my chocolate pennies thinking that I would read just one more issue, and those "just one more"s added up. By the time I was done, I had many pages of scribbles.

I flipped slowly through, hoping a pattern would jump out. Oh, the potential was there. Lots of people were sick, many with symptoms like my mother's. But was it mercury poisoning? I had no idea.

I told myself that I needed more information, that I had to sit down with a map of the town and put dots in the spots where each of the afflicted lived to see if there were pockets of illness, that I had to learn whether Northwood did indeed produce mercury waste and, if so, I had to go to the next step, whatever that was. I told myself that I shouldn't worry about the lack of instant answers, that this was just the start.

But I was discouraged. Having exhausted my supply of chocolate pennies, I was also hungry. It was midafternoon, and I was craving protein. I could have gone home to Phoebe's, but by now everyone in town knew I was here, so keeping a low profile was needless. Besides, I kept thinking of Omie. She was the third and last of the friends I'd had in town. I had seen her briefly at the funeral but hadn't had the state of mind to talk with her, any more than with Mrs. Klausson or with Sam. Today's paper said she'd been sick. I really wanted to say hello.

So I returned the microfiche reels to their drawers — neatly and in order, so that no one would know I had been here — and left the newspaper office. Though Middle River was no humming metropolis on a hot Thursday afternoon in August, the center of town was far from deserted. My car was one of a dozen or so parked in those diagonal spaces that ran up the street. Granted, mine was the only convertible. Convertibles weren't practical in towns like Middle River, where winters required four-wheel-drive vehicles, chores involved carrying large loads, and family space was a necessity.

I tossed my purse into the car and slid in. Fortunately, I was wearing jeans. Even through the thick fabric, I could feel the heat of the sun-baked seat. Feeling the heat all over, actually, I slipped on sunglasses, started the engine, and looked behind to back out of my space. I saw no cars in the road. But I was being watched. Directly across the street, several people looked on from the sidewalk in front of Farnum Hardware, and down a bit, several more from just outside Harriman's Grocery. A pickup was idling nose-in at the curb in front of News 'n Chews, driver waiting — watching me too — until a trio of children ran out with small brown bags of candy and climbed up into the cab.

I didn't acknowledge anyone. My Middle River persona wasn't attuned to social niceties. Shifting, I drove on down Oak, crossing Pine, then Cedar, where the roses at Road's End Inn positively burst with sweetness in the midafternoon sun. At School Street, I made a left and passed several frame houses with daylilies growing orange and yellow and wild, before turning left again into Omie's lot. There were only a handful of other vehicles, which was good. Much as I wanted to see Omie, I wasn't in the mood to wait for a seat, and it wasn't only a reluctance to be stared at. My stomach was growling, and the food smells even out here were strong.

The diner was the real thing. Originally built for Omie's father in the early 1900s as a lunch wagon with (new at the time and quite the thing) wooden counters that folded out to make a walk-up window, it had been modified, enlarged, and reno-vated many times over. Through it all, though, it retained the look and feel of a diner.

Omie was similar, in a way. A small woman with white hair in a bun, a face filled with creases, and eyes that were eternally blue, she was either ancient or not, depending on what one wanted to think. Her actual age was irrelevant. Same with her last name. The few of us who knew it could neither spell it nor pronounce it, and it didn't matter. Her daughters had Americanized the original Armenian, and then had all married local men of French-Canadian descent, so the original name was basically gone. Though Omie had great-grandchildren, perhaps even great-greats by now, she remained a grandmother to everyone who opened the diner door and went inside.

Indeed, though she still had the look of a traditional Armenian grandmother, inside she was anything but. For one thing, she had an exquisite business sense. For another, she thrived on work. Long after other great-grandmothers in town had retired to their back porches to alternately rock and crochet, she was at the diner overseeing hiring, firing, redecoration, and menu changes. She had officially passed ownership to her eldest daughter years before, but the transfer was only on paper. The diner was Omie's.

Where wheels had been in the structure's infancy, now stood a base of solid brick. The body of the diner had sides of stainless steel with burnished circles, and panels of decorative tiles between wide windows. The tiles were blue, green, and white, as was the sign high on the roof. OMIE'S, it read in acknowledgment of the woman's force. It had been a gift from her family several decades before, prior to which there had been no sign at all.

I heard a little whispering, but this wasn't Grace. It was my own inner someone telling me that this place was special, and it was all the urging I needed. Grabbing my purse, I climbed from the car and went inside.

Chapter 8

Something was cooking — chicken fajitas, I guessed, from the smell and the sizzle — but with Omie I could never be sure. As Americanized as she was, as wise to the needs of Middle Riverites, Omie prized her Armenian heritage. That meant she cooked as often with lamb as with beef, baked as often with phyllo dough as with flour, seasoned as often with cinnamon, cardamom, nutmeg, and clove as with salt, pepper, parsley, and thyme. New items like fajitas, pastas, and Caesar salads popped onto the menu to keep the diner current, but there were always old standbys — chicken pot pie, macaroni and cheese, and Omie's hash — all of it cooked with an Armenian flair. For that reason, any food smell that wafted from the diner carried the uniqueness of Omie.

Moreover, the scents lingered, because Omie hated air-conditioning. She liked having the windows open, and kept her customers comfortable with old-fashioned fans. Since these never quite eliminated the humidity, smells clung.

Those fans whirred now, stirring the air. Simon and Garfunkel sang softly through ceiling speakers, while the cold drink case hummed an even softer refrain. These things I heard clearly, because whatever conversation had been ongoing when I walked in the door had come to a dead stop.

Feeling awkward, I retreated to my Washington mantra. I was successful in Washington. I had friends in Washington. I could walk into Galileo, Kinkead's, or Cashion and be just like everyone else. That was what I had wanted most when I left Middle River — not the walking into restaurants part, but the being just like everyone else part. Isn't that what most of us want, to be part of something, to belong? Here was **TRUTH #4: We can thumb our noses all we want at people who are different from us, but in the end we ache to belong.**

Standing now with the nearest fan stirring loose wisps of my hair, and all eyes turned my way, I ached for that in this town too. Middle River was where I was born. I had spent the most important eighteen years of my life here, many of those wishing, praying, *yearning* to be part of it all. Of course, I wouldn't have admitted it back then. I hadn't *realized* it back then. It was only now, in this very instant, that I saw how true it was.

I needed Omie.

Drawing myself up, I ignored stares and looked around. Over the years, the diner had grown deeper. To the right of the kitchen, through an archway, were tables that sat sixty, but they were empty now. This time of day, the action was up front, in the diner's heart. Five men sat at the counter — a trio along the front arm, another two at the rear of the L. Of a dozen booths hugging the front of the diner and its adjoining right side, three were taken.

I didn't see Omie. But she would find me. She always did.

My favorite booth was five away from the door, the one in the corner before the line of booths turned and, like the counter, shot toward the back of the diner. I had always felt enveloped in this booth, and hence safer. Unoccupied now, it beckoned.

Heading there, I passed a booth with two women I recognized as neighbors of Sabina's. Their eyes met mine. They didn't smile. Same with the family of four in the next booth.

The third occupied booth was midway

among those running from my corner back along the side wall of the diner. Pamela Farrow and her husband sat there, snuggled side by side, holding hands. Hal was fully engrossed in his wife. Pamela's eyes flicked briefly to mine before returning to his — no smile, no hello, just a glance — quite different from the way she had fawned over me the day before.

So maybe she was just so in love with her husband that she couldn't think of anything else. More likely, someone had gotten to her.

Or, perhaps she was simply acutely aware that one of the two men at the far back end of the counter was James Meade. He couldn't be missed, with his straight back and dark, brooding look — not to mention striking salt-and-pepper hair. I could see the latter now as I hadn't seen it when he had been in the shadow of his car, and might have been surprised by it — James wasn't quite forty — had not the father been silver forever.

James didn't intimidate me. I wasn't in his employ and didn't owe him a thing. Naturally, Pamela would be thinking that if she gushed over me, James would tell his father, who chaired the School Committee, which determined the tenure of her husband as high school principal.

And that was fine. I didn't miss her fawning. I wasn't here to make friends and influence people. Class reunions had never been my thing. I had friends. I had *lots* of friends.

Thinking about them now, I slid into my booth. As James Taylor took over the airwaves, I set my purse by my hip on the wood bench and my elbows on the dark green Formica. In that moment, at least, I was confident.

A menu was wedged between the napkin holder and a jar of ketchup. I pulled it out, opened it, and began to peruse. Little by little, conversations that had been interrupted by my arrival resumed.

"Just when I needed a cup of tea," came a sweet, familiar, and very welcome voice.

I looked up as Omie lowered herself to the opposite bench. Those endless blue eyes had faded some, and her cheeks had the texture of washed crepe. She looked paler than I recalled, but her smile was as sincere as ever. On impulse, I rose and, bracing myself on the table, leaned across and kissed her cheek.

"You look better than last time," she remarked in a grandmotherly voice that held only the faintest trace of an accent. She had been a small child when her parents reached America, and had grown up speaking English with other children. What accent she had she chose to have. It gave her voice a distinctive ring.

"Time has passed," I said. "The shock has worn off. I hear you've been sick."

"It's nothing."

"Pneumonia isn't nothing."

"Well, it is if it's gone," she said with the dismissive wave of a hand. "These things happen when you get to be my age. Two, three times a year it's a cold or such. Too many people in here with their germs. I can't throw things off like I used to. I'm getting old."

I wondered if it was that, or if her immune system was being depleted by something else. It was definitely worth considering, but later. I gestured toward the menu. "From the looks of this, you could be forty. There are lots of new things mixed in with the old."

Omie smiled. "I have to please everyone if I want to stay in business."

I lowered my voice. "If the goal is staying in business, you shouldn't be having your tea with me. I sense that your other customers would rather I not be here." The women who lived near Sabina had already left their booth and were at the cash register.

Omie, too, spoke more quietly. "Ignore them. They're frightened of you."

"Frightened?"

"You speak the truth."

"And they don't?"

Omie didn't answer. We both knew that hypocrisy festered in towns like Middle River. Under the facade of beauty, there was a stratum of dirt. Grace had known this. It was a major theme running through *Peyton Place*, a major theme running through her *life*. She'd had dreams and ideals that were all too often betrayed.

"What are they hiding?" I whispered now.

"What aren't they hiding?" Omie whispered back.

"Tell me the latest."

Omie seemed happy to do that. "Those three at the counter? Doug Hartz is the one in the middle, the one looking uneasy. See how he keeps glancing back at you?"

I did. "What's his problem?"

"He prides himself on not paying taxes. Tells enough people so the whole town knows. Seems to think that if he runs a cash business, he'll slip by under the radar."

"So why do I make him nervous?"

"You're from Washington. The IRS is in Washington. He thinks you'll tell."

"That's pretty funny," I said, because the connection was absurd. "And the two women who just left? What chased them off?"

"Your success. They meet here every afternoon at two to work on a book they're writing. They've been doing this for three years, and there's no sign of any book. And now here you are. For many people in this town, you're everything they can never be."

"Even James?" I asked, because his presence at the counter with his pal was so *there*.

"Even James," Omie said and gave a little snort of dismay. "Staying at that mill under the thumb of his father — can you imagine? It's a waste. James is the smartest of the bunch."

"Not smart enough to leave Middle River," I remarked.

But Omie drew the line there. "Why would he leave?" she asked with a softness that made its point. "Life here is better than it would be most anywhere else. He's tasted what it's like to live away. He was away for college and graduate school.

There was a time when he was on the road four days a week doing work for the mill. He knows what it's like, and he chose to come back."

"Chose? Or was forced?" I could imagine Sandy telling James he was free to leave, but that if he chose to, it would be without a cent of Meade money. "Extortion can take different forms."

Omie didn't reply to that. Instead, she beckoned her grandson over and asked me, "What will you have to eat?"

I ordered the balsamic chicken salad and an iced tea. The latter arrived before either of us could resume the discussion. By that time, the family of four had skedaddled, Van Morrison was singing, and I was studying the man with James. He sat with his shoulders hunched, his eyes on his hands, and his hands on a bottle of beer. He had the look of a man besieged. I might have guessed he didn't even know I was here.

I had a sudden start of recognition. "Is that Alfie Monroe?" I whispered. At Omie's nod, I looked at him, then away, then sipped my tea and studied him over the rim of the glass. Alfie Monroe had been at the mill all his life. Hardworking and decent, he had worked his way up until he was one step below the Meade sons, and well respected for it. The man I remember was good looking and proud. He would be in his early fifties now. This man looked older than that, and I wouldn't have noted either good looks or pride.

Had I read anything in the paper about him? I didn't think so.

"Is he not well?" I asked but my imagination had already taken off. If toxic waste had been released by the mill, someone who worked in its bowels stood an even greater risk of affliction. The Meades worked in offices far from the nitty-gritty. Not so the plant manager.

"He's well in body, but not in mind," Omie said. "He was passed over when Sandy hired Tony O'Roarke to manage the plant."

No. I hadn't read this. There had been nothing in the paper, and I knew why. Sam Winchell would have disapproved of an outsider displacing Alfie, but Sam was a pragmatist. He knew that nothing he said in his paper could either change what Sandy had done or help Alfie. His protest was to say nothing at all.

I pictured Tony O'Roarke driving James Meade around town in that big black SUV, and felt a stab of annoyance. "Why didn't Alfie get the job?"

"The Meades wanted someone more experienced."

"Who could be more experienced than Alfie? He's been with the company all his life."

Omie thought about that as she sipped her tea. Eyes sad, she set down the cup. "Sandy felt they needed a new approach."

"Approach to what?"

"Keeping things streamlined."

I interpreted that to mean cheap. "Sandy wants more productivity for less money."

Omie didn't argue. As she took another sip of tea, Pamela and Hal left their booth and passed by without a glance. My salad arrived. I began to eat. Doug Hartz and his friends slid off stools, dug into pockets, and dropped cash by plates, then followed Pamela and Hal out the door. In their wake, a group of teenagers entered, girls identical with their low-cut jeans, skinny tops, and ironed hair. Two of the five had cell phones to their ears. Several glanced my way as they passed. One did a double-take.

She looked familiar. It was a minute before I placed her as having been with her mother at Miss Lissy's Closet the day before. At the time, I would have guessed she was no more than fifteen. Now with friends, all of them long-haired and mascaraed, she looked eighteen.

I raised several fingers in a covert wave, a simple acknowledgment that we had seen each other before. After all, she was Phoebe's customer. I didn't want to be rude.

The poor thing seemed horrified. I could only begin to imagine what nonsense someone had fed her. Quickening her step, she followed her friends to the very last of the booths, where they all crowded in. Shania Twain began to sing.

"So," Omie said with a gentle smile, "they say you've come to write. Are you still Grace's girl?"

"No. I've made my own way."

"Do you two still talk?"

Had anyone else asked me that, I would have been mortified. Hearing voices — having conversations with people who no longer existed — wasn't something sane people normally did.

But Omie knew about these conversations. I had confided in her once, when I thought I was losing my mind. I was fifteen at the time. My body had finally — just barely and very late — begun to change and, while my family of women was relieved that I was "normal" in this sense at least, they were themselves too blasé about things like periods, breasts, and emotions to want to hear my qualms, even if I *had* been able to express them, which I hadn't. Me, I was feeling like a stranger in my own skin. Well aside from those physical changes, I was terrified of my relationship with Grace.

"You need a friend," Omie had offered by way of explanation back then. "Grace understands you."

"Grace is *dead*," I had replied with a touch of panic.

"Well, yes. But that doesn't mean she isn't here with us."

"Like a ghost?" I asked skeptically.

"That depends. Have you seen her?"

"No. I just hear her. But how can that be? I never heard her voice in real life. How do I know what it sounds like?"

"You know enough about her to imagine how it sounds."

"Grace is dead," I repeated.

"This is her spirit."

"Oh, Omie. I don't think so."

"Well, I do. You came to me to ask, and this is what I say. Grace Metalious was not a happy woman. She died alone and unfulfilled. You may be her vehicle for fulfillment." Before I could argue, Omie asked, "When she talks to you, what does she say?"

What had Grace said? She had given me encouragement, even goaded me on at times. We could argue — I said some awful things — but she always came back for more. She told me I had the makings of a good writer, and, back then, it was what my battered fifteen-year-old ego needed to hear.

We continued to talk, Grace and I, until I left Middle River. Once in Washington, I became a different person. I no longer needed Grace, so our conversations stopped.

Did Grace and I still talk? Omie asked.

There were those few whisperings I had heard, but I couldn't be sure they weren't just the purr of a cat or the buzz of a fly. And the woman goading me on when a well-formed man in running shorts and sneakers had crossed my path this morning? That was Grace all right, but just for fun — my alter ego, more than anything else.

"No," I told Omie in a version of the truth. "Grace doesn't do Washington. She was there once to promote the sequel to *Peyton Place*. The press wasn't kind."

"She was a small-town girl at heart, I think."

"Yes and no. She hated the scrutiny of small-town life, hated the expectations of small-minded people. Cities fascinated her — Paris, Los Angeles, Las Vegas, New York. But she couldn't hold her own in those places. She didn't know what to wear or what to say. She never became savvy and was forever putting her foot in her mouth and then, after the fact being hit in the butt by her own words."

Omie beamed. "Not you. See how far you've come?" She leaned in. "So, about the writing. Is it true?"

My initial hunger sated, I put down my fork. "I'm already involved with a book. It's due to be published next year." I paused. "Omie?"

"What, sweetheart?"

"Do you think people here are unusually sick?"

She considered that. "I don't know what it's like anywhere else."

"The doctor says my mother had Parkinson's disease. She isn't the only one in this town who has it."

Omie studied me more closely now. "No."

"Do you think there's a reason why so many do?"

193

"What kind of reason?"

"I don't know. Has there been any talk — you know, maybe about something in the air making people sick?"

"There's always talk. Someone gets a cold, they blame it on airborne germs."

"That's not what I mean."

"I know."

"Alice LeClaire's three-year-old son is autistic," I said. "Would she talk with me?"

"I doubt it. In addition to that child, she has four other children to care for, and no man to help."

"No man? I thought there were at least two." My mother had maintained — with proper scorn — that pairing up fathers with Alice's children was a popular game in Middle River. Apparently, Alice never quite broke it off with her exes.

"The latest count has it at three," Omie confirmed, "but since the little one was diagnosed, they're all staying clear. They don't want to be blamed for it. They're convinced it has to do with genes."

A muffled phone rang. Instinctively, I went for my purse, but this ring came from somewhere back in the kitchen. Seconds later, a closer phone rang. James Meade flipped open a cell.

"Autism can also result from exposure to

toxicity," I told Omie. "Wouldn't Alice want to know that?"

Omie smiled sadly. "And think she had let her baby be exposed to something bad?" The more distant phone rang again. "Besides, the Meades pay for medical insurance for their workers."

Ah. And Alice had a job at the mill. Considering the special needs of an autistic child, she would be lost without insurance, not to mention that job.

James Meade pocketed his phone. Alfie Monroe pushed himself off the stool and strode past.

"What about the Dahills?" I asked Omie when he was out of earshot. "How many in that house have kidney problems?" My reading told me they were on the third generation of it. All three generations worked at the mill, though I didn't recall in what capacity.

"Kidney problems are hereditary," Omie said.

"Possibly. Okay — probably. But what if they're job-related?"

Omie seemed about to caution me when her grandson called from the kitchen cut-through, "Omie, it's cousin Ara on the phone."

Her eyes lit. "I have to take this," she

said. Rising, she leaned close, kissed my cheek, and whispered, "Try the Mc-Creedys. They've suffered a long string of problems. They're looking for a reason."

I had barely taken that in when Omie was gone, and a separate movement caught my eye. James Meade had risen. He put money on the counter and approached me. There was nothing casual about his course. He knew I was here and meant to stop.

James was impressive. Not only was he the tallest of the Meades, but he was the best looking, and I don't say that to get back at Aidan. It was simply true. Like Sabina and me, James and Aidan had similar features — thick hair, deep brown eyes, pointed nose, square jaw. But with James, like Sabina, the whole was more than the sum of its parts. You might notice Aidan's hair, or his eyes, or his mouth. What you noticed with James was his authority. He was quiet. But when he spoke, you listened.

Now, eyes somber, he stood before me. He wore jeans and a pressed blue shirt, neck open, sleeves rolled to the forearm. Those threads of silver in his hair lent him greater bearing.

"My brother just called in a stew," he said in that quiet, authoritative voice. "He

196

saw your car here. He thinks you're up to no good."

Something about James unsettled me. I wished he wasn't so tall, wished those eyes weren't so penetrating. Feeling a need for distance, I sat back. "I was hungry," I said. "I came here for food."

"You make him nervous."

"Why?"

James seemed to consider the question, but his eyes never lost their intensity. Imaginative on my part, yes, but I felt they were searching me for motive and thought. Finally, quiet still, he said, "I'd say Aidan was feeling guilty for what happened all those years ago, but I doubt that's it. More likely, he's afraid of your pen. He doesn't know what you're going to write."

I smiled. "If he's afraid of my pen, then he has something to hide. I wonder what it is."

James almost smiled back. "I wouldn't do that if I were you."

"Do what?"

"Wonder. It could create problems. Aidan doesn't want that."

"Should I care what Aidan wants?"

"Yes," James said in a factual way. "We employ Sabina and her husband, and we hold Phoebe's lease. There's a lot at stake here."

I felt an inkling of anger. "Is this a threat?"

"Not from me. I'm just passing on what my brother said. He also wanted to remind you that we were good to your father when he was sick. Northwood paid him long after he stopped being a productive employee. We did it out of loyalty."

The implication, of course, was that we owed loyalty in return — or rather, that I did, since I was the one threatening the status quo — and that angered me all the more. I didn't owe the Meades a thing.

"Was it loyalty?" I threw back at him, perhaps rashly, but I didn't like James Meade. "Or was it fear? My father worked at your plant all his life. Maybe he knew things you'd rather he hadn't known. You treat all your employees a little too well. Is that to instill loyalty, so that they won't blow the whistle if they see something wrong?"

I shouldn't have said it. I knew that the instant the words were out of my mouth — and if I hadn't realized it on my own, James's expression would have tipped me off. He seemed suddenly alert, suddenly personally invested in the discussion.

Eyes barely leaving mine, he slid onto the bench where Omie had been. He put his forearms on the table, large hands maddeningly relaxed. "Is something wrong at the mill?" he asked with a calm that could grate.

I nearly backed down. Then I caught myself. Call me impulsive to have blurted out what I had in the first place. But backing down was idiotic when something higher was at stake.

So I said, "I ask you. Is something wrong at the mill?"

He sat back. He didn't answer, just looked at me. At one point I saw his jaw move, but otherwise he was still. He seemed very intelligent. That bothered me the most.

He stared. I stared back. Elton John was singing. I liked Elton John, but took no pleasure in him now.

"What," I finally demanded.

"Are you writing about the mill?" he asked.

"Should I?"

"Are you?"

"It's amazing," I mused. "No one seems to want to talk with me here except to ask if I'm writing a book. The more they ask, the more intrigued I get. If one more person asks, I may do it."

He didn't speak, just continued to look at me.

"*What,*" I said again, more irritably this time.

It was a minute before he responded, and then he seemed genuinely curious. He frowned. His voice dropped even lower. "Do you hate me?"

The question took me aback. "Not you. Who you are."

"My family."

"What it represents."

"Power."

"No single family should have that much. People shouldn't have to fear for their lives if they speak up."

"Their lives?"

"Their livelihood," I corrected. "You just threatened my two sisters and my brother-in-law."

"I didn't. Aidan did. I'm just the messenger."

"Same difference."

"No," he said with calm assurance. "It isn't. I'm not my brother. And I'm not my father."

I eyed him dead-on. "Then you wouldn't commit perjury like Aidan did, and then bribe enough public officials like your father did so that nothing would come of it?"

James didn't blink. "I have never committed perjury."

"What about bribing public officials? Ah, but you don't need to do that. Daddy does it for you."

I was hitting a nerve. I could see that in his dark eyes and tight jaw.

"You don't know me," he said. "I wouldn't burn bridges if I were you."

"Does that mean if I were to write a book about the mill, you'd cooperate?"

"It depends what you want to say in your book. If it's simply the diatribe of a woman who hates this town —"

"I don't hate Middle River. If I went to the effort of writing a book, it would be because I *care* about the town."

"Do you?"

"I grew up here. My family still lives here."

"Answer the question."

"I would *never* write a book out of spite. I don't think I'm capable of doing that."

Still his question hung in the air. He eyed me steadily, daring me to confess. And suddenly, what he asked wasn't so bad. I was a big girl. Spite didn't have to play a part in my response. I could rise above the past.

"Yes, I care," I admitted. "There's lots that's positive here."

"Like?"

"Four seasons. Trees and flowers. Good schools. Marsha Klausson and Sam Winchell. This diner. Omie." When he said nothing, I added, "The barbershop. The nail shop. Miss Lissy's. Brunch at Road's End Inn. Chocolate pennies." He remained silent. "The October Stroll," I tacked on, because it was a lovely tradition, and there were others. "Christmas Eve at the intersection of Oak and Pine. Fireworks in the stadium on the Fourth of July. Even the Backabehind Club." I smiled. "Can't believe the kids are still doing that, but I caught a pair of them at it on my way in the other night."

"Did you ever do it?"

My hackles shot back up. He was ridiculing me. He knew I hadn't dated. The whole town knew I hadn't dated.

But his expression wasn't so much smug as curious.

"No," I said flatly. "I spent most of my senior year at Cooper's Point waiting for your brother to show up."

"For what it's worth," James said, "he was wrong when he did that."

"Which part — carrying on with someone's wife, or using me to get away with it?"

"Both."

As apologies went, it was indirect. But it did seem genuine. And that struck me as odd. Reminding myself that James was a Meade, I put my elbows on the table and leaned in just a bit. "If you're trying to soften me up, don't bother. I'm here to keep an eye on my sister. She doesn't seem well."

"What's wrong with her?"

"I don't know."

"Did Tom have any thoughts?"

"Tom?" I asked in surprise, but quickly regrouped. "Tom isn't treating Phoebe. I was just thanking him for taking care of my mom."

"What about Sam? He have any thoughts?"

There was clearly a point here. James was giving me a message. It was a continuation of the one he had set out to deliver in the first place, namely that I was being watched.

"Sam's a friend," I said. "I dropped by to say hello."

"And stayed for three hours after he left," James reported.

"And that," I declared, "is one of the things I *detest* about Middle River. Whose business is it but mine where I go and what I do? Do you Meades have a spy in every corner?"

James snorted. "No need for spies, and we're not talking corners here. That car of yours can't be missed. Leave it home next time."

"Next time, I will," I said with resentment, then added dryly, "Any more warnings? Words of advice? Messages?"

James slid out of the booth and rose to his full height. "Just a question. Aidan wants to know why you aren't in D.C. with loverboy."

Mention of Greg made me feel stronger. "Loverboy? Cute."

"The correspondent."

"I know who you mean. I'm not there with him, because I'm here," I said quite logically and tipped up my chin. "Does Aidan have any more questions?"

Chapter 9

Kaitlin DuPuis didn't have much of a choice as to where she would sit in the booth. Totally distracted by the sight of Annie Barnes, she had just been carried along by the others. When the dust cleared and they were seated, she found herself on the bench that faced the front of the diner, and a lucky thing it was. If she had been sitting on the opposite side of the booth, she wouldn't have seen Annie talking with James Meade, and this was important. Annie talking with James was bad.

Kaitlin didn't care what Kevin thought; Annie *did* recognize her. First a wink at Miss Lissy's Closet, now a wave. Annie wasn't waving at any of the other girls. She knew about Kaitlin and Kevin. Oh, she knew. And what if she was telling James at this very moment, just as part of the conversation, like, *You'll never guess what I saw the DuPuis girl doing the other night?* James would tell his brother, who would tell Kaitlin's mother, who would then have heard it from *two* sources, if Phoebe's manager's mom, who was James's secretary, was counted, and no *way* would Kaitlin be able to talk her way out of it then. Not that she would have had much of a chance of doing that even with one source. Nicole was *obsessed* with her daughter's virginity, even more than she was with her weight.

What to do? In Kaitlin's dreams, Kevin would have already taken the lead, sought Annie out, and sworn her to secrecy. But Kevin still thought she was imagining things. Besides, Kevin would be totally intimidated approaching someone like Annie. And why would he bother? His parents didn't care if he was with Kaitlin. His dad would cheer him on and reach for another beer. And his mom? His mom *loved* Kaitlin. It would be her *dream* to have her son marry up.

Kaitlin wasn't marrying Kevin until she was older. But she sure didn't want him in jail now.

"*Kaitlin.* Where *are* you?"

She blinked and looked around to find her friends staring at her. Embarrassed, she shot back at no one in particular, "Can't I think about something myself?"

"What was it?"

"Had to be Kevin. She's *always* thinking about Kevin."

"Not always," Kaitlin replied, even in that, though, feeling pride. She was the last of her friends to be with a guy. For the longest time, she thought it would never happen. Fearful that something would screw it up now, she had an idea. "I was actually thinking of Annie Barnes. Do you know that's her back there?"

"I saw," said Bethany.

Kristal nodded. "Me, too."

"Annie Barnes *here?*" Shawna asked, twisting around to look, and in the next instant, Jen was twisting around, too.

"No, no," Kaitlin cried in hushed alarm. "Don't turn around. She'll know we're looking."

"Why's she here?"

"That's what *I* want to know," Kaitlin declared. "Any ideas?"

"Look. She's with James Meade. Oh wow."

"Like, they're *dating,* Kristal? No way. He's too old."

"He isn't so old. My mom says the gray in his hair is from grief from his dad."

"I think it makes him look like Richard Gere."

"Talk about *old.*"

"Annie Barnes isn't so young herself. They could be dating."

"He's not interested. He has a little kid."

"What difference does *that* make?"

"Are we really *not* supposed to know about that baby?"

"Pu-leeze. Everyone knows. Sam Winchell didn't say anything in the paper, 'cause Sandy Meade told him not to. Sandy's annoyed that James went and adopted a baby. He doesn't understand why his son couldn't make one the usual way."

"Maybe he can't."

"Can't?"

"Like, is sterile?"

"Yeah. Right."

"Has anyone seen the baby?"

"I don't know, but it's a girl. My mother saw James at Harriman's buying Snow White Huggies. The baby was home with the nanny."

"The nanny's from East Windham. Can you believe? He couldn't hire someone from Middle River?"

"Sandy probably told him not to. He doesn't want people seeing or talking. The baby's from China."

"Vietnam."

"Whatever."

"Talk about raising a kid with zero of its heritage. Does James know what he's doing?"

"James Meade always knows what he's doing," declared Bethany.

Kaitlin agreed with that, all right. James did always know. So maybe what Kaitlin had to do was to talk with *him*. Maybe she could convince him not to tell. Now that he was a father himself, he might appreciate her dilemma.

Right, Kaitlin. And pigs could fly. She returned to her original idea. Annie was the one to corner. "Is Annie Barnes staying with her sister?"

"Yes."

"She isn't very friendly," Bethany complained. "She was running this morning and just ran right past Buzz Madigan after he said hello."

"Would *you* have stopped to talk with Buzz?" Shawna asked. "Like, I mean, he can go on and on and on. If I was running to get a workout, and I stopped to talk with him, the workout would be shot."

"Do you think she'll spend much time at the store?" Kaitlin asked casually.

"At Miss Lissy's Closet? No. She's going to write."

"Where'll she do that?" Kaitlin asked. "At the house?"

"Who knows?"

"Why does it matter?"

209

Kaitlin shrugged. "I was just thinking that if everyone is saying she's come here to write, maybe she's rented a place of her own."

"No. She's staying at Phoebe's."

Bethany leaned forward, eyes wide. "What if Greg Steele comes to visit?"

"That'd be *great*."

"Omigod. He's so hot."

"Could be trouble if she's hooking up with James."

"Does she have any friends in town?" Kaitlin tried.

"No."

"None."

"Absolutely not."

"What about the gym?" Kaitlin asked. "Your mom's a member, Jen. Think Annie Barnes might work out there?"

"Mom didn't mention it," Jen said and shot her a suspicious look. "Why are you asking these questions?"

"I'm *curious*."

"Don't tell me you've read her book."

"No. I'm just curious. Is there a law against that?"

Eliot Rollins left the clinic early, but not to go home. While his car sat back in the lot, he walked down a block, crossed the

210

street, and entered the low brick building that housed the police station.

The police station. He still choked a little calling it that. Yes, the place had a holding cell — two, actually, but it was questionable as to whether either one could actually hold a person who wanted to escape. Eliot had grown up in New York, where police stations were the real thing. This one was mostly for show. Likewise the chief of police. Marshall Greenwood did what he could to give the illusion that Middle River abided by laws. The truth was that little crime occurred here that wasn't committed by someone directly or indirectly related to the mill, and the mill took care of its own.

Marshall was out and about three times a day, patrolling the streets in his cruiser. He stopped to talk with whomever he saw, so that what would otherwise take only half an hour sometimes stretched to two. The rest of the time he was at his desk.

He was there when Eliot entered, and yes, indeed, he was overweight. Tom Martin had that one right, but then, it wasn't something the man could hide. Winters, he wore a jacket to cover the gut hanging over his belt. Summers, the gut strained against the buttons of his shirt.

That shirt was blue to match his jeans. He called this his uniform, which meant that he didn't have to waste time picking out clothes in the morning. Blue shirt, blue jeans, Demerol, OxyContin, Xanax.

He sat straight in his wide-armed, high-backed chair. It was an ergonomic one bought for him by his friend and benefactor Sandy Meade, and it probably cost more than the rest of the office furniture combined. He was doing a crossword puzzle in a fat book of crossword puzzles. A stack of others leaned against the file cabinet behind the desk. Marshall was addicted to these, too.

He spotted Eliot. "Good timing, Dr. Rollins," he said in his gravelly voice. "I need a word for a skin disease. Six letters, third one's a *z*."

Eliot felt a stab of annoyance. He didn't want to be here at all. The problem wasn't his. He was just the man in the middle, and he didn't do zits. "I'm an orthopedist, not a dermatologist."

"Come on," Marshall coaxed. "You studied everything in med school. It can't be real difficult if it's in my puzzle."

"Put the puzzle down, Marshall. We have to talk." He put his hands in the pockets of his slacks. "Annie Barnes is snooping around. She was at the clinic yesterday talking with Tom, and he says she didn't raise this issue, but it's only a matter of time. You and I could both be in trouble if she gets wind of certain prescriptions."

Marshall frowned. "Why in the world would she get wind of that?"

"Because she's here looking for dirt and this particular dirt is hot stuff. Think about it. 'Middle River police chief addicted to painkillers.' Makes a good headline, y'know?"

Marshall set his pencil down. "I take painkillers for a back problem. I'm not addicted."

"Want to prove that by going cold turkey?"

The look on Marshall's face said that he did not. Then he frowned. "You're acting like this is my fault. I didn't ask for Jebby McGinnis to drive drunk right into my car. I was injured in the line of duty, and you were the orthopedist who headed my case. I'm just following doctor's orders. You're the one writing the prescriptions."

"You're the one demanding them," Eliot shot back, because he wasn't taking the fall here. "You're the one who suggested I write prescriptions in the name of your wife so that insurance will pay for the stuff you take above the normal allowance. That's health care fraud. There's another hot topic. Want to try for that one?"

"I don't want to try for any one," Marshall said in a gruff, law-and-order voice that told Eliot he had his attention. "Is there a point to this discussion?"

"It's already been made," Eliot said with satisfaction and headed for the door. "Sounds like you appreciate the problem. I'm assuming you'll do what you can to make sure nothing comes of it."

"What in the hell'm I supposed to do?" Marshall called, but Eliot was already on the threshold.

"You'll figure something out," he said. "And it's eczema. *E-c-z-e-m-a.* Don't you wish *that* was your only problem?"

Chapter 10

I had my list of people who were sick in Middle River. And I knew that paper mills produced mercury waste. Now I had to connect the two. Specifically, I needed to know whether Northwood was one of the paper mills that had cleaned itself up, or whether it continued to pollute.

How to find out? That was the dilemma I grappled with as I stood at the kitchen window with my coffee early Friday morning. The window was a bay with a three-sided view of the yard. I saw a soft stretch of lawn, bordered by my mother's flowers — the purple, orange, and white of asters, daylilies, and hostas, respectively. Deeper into the yard, gangly black-eyed Susans swayed in the breeze along with the low-hanging willow limbs farther behind them. And farther yet, the river flowed, a rippling swath of gray-blue.

The day was overcast, seeming torn between rain and shine, and the indecision mirrored my mood. Yes, the state environmental agency would have information about the status of the cleanup at North-wood Mill, but going there wasn't my first choice. All it would take was one tattletale phone call by a person there with Meade ties, and the you-know-what could hit the fan.

An alternative was to talk quietly with a mill insider, but my choices were limited. Whoever it was had to be high enough up the mill ladder both to have legitimacy and to know the truth about what the mill did. I wouldn't put it past Sandy to tell rank-and-file workers that the mill was clean, when it might be anything but.

As candidates for mole went, I could think of four. One was Alfie Monroe. If he had an ax to grind against the Meades after being passed over for the position for which he had worked all his life, he might help me out. Another was Tony O'Roarke. He would have an insider's knowledge of the workings of the mill, without a history of Middle River ties to make him beholden to the Meades. Suppose, just suppose, he had found something amiss at the mill, had complained to Sandy Meade and been re-buffed. He might become my ally simply to save his own skin down the road.

Aidan Meade was another possibility.

That's right. Aidan Meade. Aidan had a huge ego, always had, always would, and it was common knowledge that he was concerned about his rightful place at the mill. If he was fed up with playing second fiddle to James, I might goad him into staging a coup around the issue of mercury. Would he listen to me? Oddly, I think he would. I had the distinct impression that he was intrigued, perhaps even excited, by where I lived and what I had become. Perhaps I was deluding myself — or buying into my own hype — or simply thinking too Washington — but I half suspected that I could seduce him if I chose to.

I wouldn't, of course. Even aside from the ethical issue of his being married, I despised him too much to want his skin touching mine. But I could lead him on, right up to the brink. I could get what I wanted from him, then drop him when I had enough dirt on the mill. I could use him the way he had used me. That would be poetic, don't you think?

And then there was James. He had hinted that he stood for what was right. But if that was so, and mercury waste was a problem, he should have acted on it already. He was first in line for the throne. Did I really think he would risk that position by bucking his father? No, I did not.

A loud thud came from the hall, then two more fast thuds. Terrified, I set my mug on the table and ran. I found Phoebe halfway up the stairs, sitting upright, rubbing her elbow. Relieved that she hadn't fallen far, I quickly climbed the steps. I pushed up her pajama sleeve to see the elbow. There was nothing protruding.

"I don't think it's broken," I said. "Does anything else hurt?"

Phoebe looked awful, more washed-out and disheveled than ever. She stared at me fuzzy-eyed and asked in a feeble voice, "Why do I keep forgetting you're here?"

"Can you bend your elbow?"

She did it, albeit gingerly. "I banged it on the banister. I don't know what happened. My foot just slipped."

Had she been wearing slippers with a smooth sole, I might have bought her explanation. But her feet were bare, like mine, and the carpeted stair was textured. "You lost your balance. Were you feeling dizzy?"

"No. I'm just slow waking up."

"You never were when we were kids."

"It's my cold."

"The cold sounds better," I argued. Her voice was far less nasal than it had been.

"How did you sleep?"

"Like a log," she replied.

It was not the truth. I had woken up to the sound of floorboards creaking not once, but twice in the night. I didn't think she was lying. She simply didn't remember.

"Here," I said, taking her other arm. "Let me help you down."

We started slowly; she was shaky. By the time we reached the kitchen, though, it was clear she was unhurt. I poured her a cup of coffee and sat with her.

Gently, I asked, "Does it worry you that you have some of the same symptoms Mom had?"

"*Mom's* symptoms? Oh, I don't have those. I have a *cold.*"

"With symptoms just like Mom's. Phoebe, what if Mom didn't have Parkinson's disease at all? What if something else was making her sick — something environmental like, say, mercury?"

Phoebe eyed me as if I were crazy. "Where on earth would she have found that?"

"The mill."

"*Our* mill?"

I nodded.

"There's nothing wrong with our mill.

Besides, Mom and I don't go *near* the mill."

"You don't have to go near it," I said, speaking hypothetically. "If the mill is polluting the river and you eat fish —"

"Not from the river. We buy our fish at Harriman's. Besides, Sabina works right *there* at the mill, and she's fine. They're *all* fine. I was at her office a few weeks ago, picking her up from work. We were going to plant flowers at Mom's grave."

Mom's grave. My heart lurched at the words. It was one thing to think about Mom being sick or Mom falling down the stairs or Mom visiting the mill. It was another to think of her buried in the graveyard on the hill behind the church. I felt a great yawing inside.

It grew worse when Phoebe's eyes drifted to the window. "We need rain, it's been a *horribly* dry summer," she said in a voice so uncannily like Mom's that even she looked quickly back at the stove, where Mom should have been. When there was no Mom, she started to cry. She bowed her head and covered her eyes, and for the life of me I didn't know what to do. We weren't a touchy-feely family, and I was grieving, too. But Phoebe needed something.

Tissue, I decided and made a dash for the bathroom. I returned with several, which she instantly took. While she pressed them to her eyes, I pulled a chair close, sat down, and rubbed her arm. It seemed paltry comfort to offer. When her crying slowed, I said, "I'm sorry, Phoebe. The past few weeks have been hardest on you."

"It's just that I don't know what's wrong," she cried in a broken voice, holding the tissue to her eyes. "I keep tripping and losing my train of thought and doing all the things Mom did, but I'm too *young* to have what she had, aren't I?"

"Yes," I said. Suddenly I was thinking that it might not be mercury poisoning or anything else at all. My sister could well be clinically depressed. "I think you should see Dr. Martin."

Phoebe shook her head at that. Uncovering her face, she drew herself up and seemed to calm. "No. I'm really all right," she said as she wiped her eyes. "It's only natural that I worry sometimes. Summer colds hang on forever."

"Maybe you need to take time off from work."

She looked alarmed. "And do what?"

"Rest."

"No. I'd only sit here and worry more.

Besides, the store needs me." She blew her nose and managed a wobbly smile. "There. I'm better now."

I was feeling helpless again. "Can I get you anything? Eggs? Cereal? . . . Pizza?"

Phoebe smiled more naturally then. "Mom hated it when we ate pizza for breakfast, didn't she?"

I smiled back. "She did."

"You were never into it as much as Sabina and me. We would deliberately leave slices from dinner so we could have it for breakfast the next day."

"I haven't seen any in the fridge."

"No. No pizza. But that's okay. Food tastes lousy to me lately." Her eyes met mine. "Even coffee doesn't do it the way it used to. What does that mean?"

"I don't know. Dr. Martin might."

"I'm not seeing Dr. Martin."

"If you're afraid of what he might find, that's self-defeating."

"Fine for you to say. You're not the one feeling lousy."

No. Not lousy. But in need of fresh air. I glanced at the clock. It was nearly eight. "Are you going to sit here a bit?" I asked.

Phoebe nodded.

"Mind if I go for a run?"

"Why ever would I mind?" she snapped.

I didn't answer, just drained the last of my coffee and went up and changed. When I returned to the kitchen, Phoebe hadn't moved. She was staring at her coffee mug, just as I had left her.

"Can I get you anything before I leave?" I asked.

She looked up and frowned. "Where are you going?"

"Running," I said, though I had already told her that. "I'll be gone forty minutes. Don't have breakfast. I'll make it when I get back." I went out the door before I could worry, stretched quickly, and set off.

The sky had grown darker, and the air was heavy. Slogging through it, I began slowly, then picked up the pace once my legs warmed. I followed the same route I had taken yesterday — at the same time, yes, I did notice that — and I was on the lookout. I don't know why. I certainly wasn't in the market for a love interest here. Maybe someone with whom to talk about running?

And hell is spiked with ice. Face it, sweetie. You liked the way he looked.

I didn't *see* the way he looked, I argued. He was too far away.

You saw enough. Why else would you be chasing him now? Hey, is that him?

No. It's a man mowing the grass at the edge of the street.

Oh. Too bad. I want to see our guy, too. Who is he?

How would I know? I replied, breathing harder as I increased my pace again. I haven't lived here in fifteen years. I don't know half the people in town.

But they know you. Now you know how it feels to be stared at. I kept telling you it was bad, but you didn't believe me.

It's not so bad if you know to expect it.

Not so bad? People eyeing you like you have horns, then asking why you can't be more like Harriet Nelson?

You're dating yourself, Grace. Besides, it was worse for you because you drank and swore and wore men's clothes.

By Jesus, that was my right.

True, but there are consequences to some behavior. You went out of your way to shock people.

And you didn't?

I did. But I was young. You were in your twenties and thirties. Why were you so contrary?

How else could I know who was friend and who was foe? People are two-faced, sweetie. They're all peachy-

keen when they want something from you, then once they have it, they'll stab you in the back. I thought you learned that with Aidan Meade.

I was thinking that not all people were two-faced — certainly not Greg and others of my Washington friends — when I was suddenly distracted, and not by the light rain that had started to fall.

There! Oh boy. That's him.

Indeed it was. I had just turned a corner, and there he was, running a block ahead. My breathing seemed suddenly louder. I was amazed that he didn't hear, but I suppose the patter of rain hitting leaves overhead covered it up. He didn't slow, didn't turn. I had a fabulous view of his tapering back. He was shirtless again; his shorts were close-fitting and hit at the thigh.

That's an impressive backside.

Uh-huh.

Run faster.

I can't. I'll mess up my workout. Besides, I like watching him — even if he isn't the best runner I've ever seen. He's not terribly graceful. I think he's flat-footed.

But he's tall and broad-shouldered. And dark. I like them dark. My George had dark, curly hair. He was Greek. Did I ever tell you that?

Uh-huh. Many times.

Boy, did my mother hate that. She wanted me to marry a purebred American. We were French-Canadian ourselves, like so many of the others who came to Manchester to work in the mills. My mother wanted to be better than them. Nothing my father did was ever good enough for her. She drove him away. Shit, he's turning the corner! Don't let him get away!

What do you want me to do? I thought with a crazy half laugh. I was running faster than I normally did and had gained on him, but I was breathing perilously hard. Flat-footed or not, he was fast.

Call him! Grace ordered. *Make him stop. He may be the one.*

What one? I asked.

The perfect one. The Adam.

I'm not looking for any Adam.

Sure you are, honey. We all are.

The perfect man doesn't exist. Isn't that the point you made in your books? Your men were all scum.

Not all of them. I liked Armand Bergeron and Etienne deMontigny. They fell hard for their women in **No Adam in Eden.**

Etienne was an abuser.

226

His wife drove him to it. She turned into a real bitch. But what about Gino Donati? He's as good as they get. I would have loved a man like Gino. He had the potential for being perfect. So does that guy up ahead. Christ, sweetie. Move it. He's around the corner. Run faster.

I had no intention of doing that. Soothed by the coolness of rain on my skin, I settled back into a saner pace and ran straight ahead. I might never have known who the other runner was if that little voice inside hadn't prodded me into glancing to my right as I ran.

Well, well. I'll be damned.

The runner had stopped halfway down the block and was standing there in the rain, looking back at me with his hands low on his hips. I could see that he was breathing hard and that because he was dripping wet, his hair looked darker than it really was. In the seconds before a huge oak tree came between us, I saw the gray there. Then the next block began, and he was gone.

I ended up going to work with Phoebe — I mean, actually working at the store. It wasn't something I would have normally chosen; when I was a child, Miss Lissy's Closet had been my least favorite place. It represented everything I was not. Understanding this at some level, my mother put me to work in the back room. Naturally, I felt I was being hidden so that I didn't hurt sales.

It struck me that I still might hurt sales, albeit for entirely different reasons. But I was concerned enough about Phoebe to ignore my misgivings. She had warned me that mornings were bad, and this morning saw that out. She couldn't find her pocketbook, though it was in plain sight at the foot of the credenza in the hall, and once she found the pocketbook, she couldn't find the keys to the van, though they were right there inside. She searched for these things while she was still in her bra, because she couldn't find the blouse she wanted to wear, and when she finally located the blouse, it was on the laundry room floor, fallen from its hanger.

She lost it then — just fell apart. "Look at *this*," she cried, holding up the blouse. "I pressed it so carefully the other day, and now look. *I* can't wear *this*."

"It looks okay."

"It's *wrinkled*. I can't wear a wrinkled blouse."

"Then pick another," I suggested.

"But *this* blouse goes with this skirt, and now look at it. I hung it *so* carefully — I don't know why it fell down — but I can't show up at work this way, so *now* what should I do?"

I set up the ironing board, heated the iron, and ironed the blouse. Phoebe took it back upstairs and returned holding the banister and looking lovely, but she was clearly unhappy. She said it was the rain, then murmured something about buying the wrong things.

"Wrong things?" I asked.

She waved a hand in dismissal.

"What wrong things?" I asked, to which she replied a testy, "What are you talking about?"

Sensing a losing battle, I sat her at the table with a glass of juice, eggs and toast, and a cup of coffee, and while she picked at the food with a shaky hand, I showered and dressed. When she appeared to have finished, I took the keys, held an umbrella over us going out to the van, then drove her to the lower end of Willow.

It had been years since I had been at the store this early, and though computerization had streamlined things, certain chores remained the same. Tallies from the previous day had to be re-checked; messages left by West Coast suppliers after closing time the day before had to be accessed; bank deposits had to be prepared. Newly received shipments had to be checked, ticketed, and shelved; customers waiting for those clothes had to be called. Yesterday's coffee grinds had to be disposed of and a fresh pot put on to brew.

Like Mom, Phoebe had a crew that cleaned weekly, but vacuuming was done daily. Shelves had to be neatened and racks straightened; clothes that had been disturbed the day before were refolded and rearranged by size. Dressing rooms had to be checked, errant clothes put away, and the soft green privacy curtains hooked open.

Since Miss Lissy's had built a reputation for carrying lines of clothing that few other stores in central and northern New Hampshire carried, telephone orders were a constant; most such orders were filled during slow spots in the day, but others were done prior to opening to assure that they shipped with the morning mail. This day, there was only one order to box.

Phoebe assigned it to me. She made it clear that she and Joanne (who, to my relief, was already at the computer when we arrived) were the only ones who knew enough to handle the *complicated* stuff (Phoebe's italics), and I wasn't offended in the least, not then, nor when she directed me to refold T-shirts and jeans and put wayward shoe boxes in order of size. It was a lovely exercise in helping — not greatly taxing, but practical — and it enabled me to watch the give-and-take between Joanne and her.

This held no surprises. Having already sensed Joanne's competence, I figured that she would be doing most of the work. Yes, it discouraged me. It was further proof of Phoebe's impairment. That said, Joanne was wonderfully gentle and understanding and kind. She worked with Phoebe in a way that made my sister feel she had done her part.

Joanne was an enabler. So, for that matter, had I been that morning, helping Phoebe get ready for work. We were making it easy for her to blame the problem on a lingering cold or, worse, to ignore it entirely. But we did that for those we loved, didn't we? And we did it for ourselves. *We* wanted Phoebe to be well too.

And she did seem to be, once the store opened, but I suspected it was a triumph of will. I could see the mask of sweet competence take over her face when a customer appeared, then fall away as soon as the *ting-a-ling* announced that the customer had left. And there were plenty of *ting-a-lings*. While the store would never be a high traffic zone, à la Neiman Marcus the day before Christmas, the clientele came in a steady stream. Granted, it was Friday. If ever there was a time for the impulse buy of shorts, a T-shirt, or sandals for a weekend that promised sun despite the continuing rain, this was it. The mailman came and went, with *ting-a-lings* and wet footprints on the floor. Same with the UPS driver, who delivered three large boxes.

"August is busy," Joanne explained as I helped her check out what proved to be jeans, long-sleeve T-shirts, and sweat suits. "Hot as it is, people are starting to think about fall. School clothes have to be out on display. Same with fall sweaters and slacks. These were ordered back in March."

"Were you at the show with Phoebe?" I asked. I knew that Mom had been too sick to go.

"No. She did it alone."

That made me feel better. I could see from the boxes' contents that whatever she had done was done right. Colors, styles, and fabrics were all appropriate and smart.

But that was March. This was August. "Is she up for New York?" I asked.

Joanne met my gaze and said a quiet, "I've offered to go with her, but she insists she needs me here. What do you think?"

I thought no, she was not up for New York, and I became even more convinced of it during lunch. I had run out for salads, but since it continued to rain, we ate in the office — and was the place a mess? *Big-time*. Apparently Phoebe, in a frenzy while I was out, had decided that since she couldn't *find* anything, reorganization was needed. In the space of those minutes, she had unloaded bookshelves and drawers. Aghast at the mess, I offered to help put things back, but she insisted she had to do it herself. I suggested we eat somewhere else. She nixed that idea too.

So we sat there, but Phoebe did little eating. Seeming lost, she picked up her fork, put it down, ferreted through the clutter on her desk to pull out a note. Barely reading it, she put it down, picked up her fork and seemed about to eat, when she put the fork down and unearthed another note. Back and forth it went, with nothing accomplished on either end, and it struck me how closely she guarded herself when customers were in the store, how deliberately she spoke, how casually she touched whatever she passed — wall, doorjamb, counter — for balance, how desperate she was to create the perception of well-being, when she wasn't well at all.

When the phone rang, it was even worse — clearly a supplier, I gathered from the one-sided conversation, but Phoebe was bewildered, couldn't remember the supplier or putting in an order. Muddling through, she was close to tears when she finally hung up the phone.

Seeming to forget I was there, she put a hand on her head and murmured, "I'm *so* losing it — oh God — what is the *matter?* I can't be sick — I'm too young — I have the store and without me the store isn't — isn't — won't run — and I don't have anyone to take over for me if I get worse — and it's bad enough here but now there's New York."

Aching for her, I asked, "What does New York entail?"

"Next week — will I be better? I just don't know — and if I'm not I won't be able to handle it — I mean, it's one thing waiting on customers here — I've done it so long I could do it in my sleep — but the other is hard — you have to be able to think straight and sometimes now I am *so* far away from that, that it *terrifies* me."

"Phoebe," I shouted to get her attention. When her eyes flew to mine, I asked again, "What does New York entail?"

She blinked, swallowed, looked away and then back. "It's a day or two of shows. There are aisles of booths. My vendors will all be there showing the holiday line."

"Do you have to order things on the spot?"

"No. I can wait until later in the month. But there's a load of paperwork and it's hard keeping things straight — who's selling what — and seeing the trends and deciding what'll work here." She pushed a hand through her hair and said plaintively, "I just *need* to be better."

If she had Parkinson's disease, medication could help. Of course, if she had Parkinson's, the long-term prognosis wasn't good, in which case the buying trip might be a practice in futility, since the store would eventually have to close.

But I didn't believe she had Parkinson's, and if the symptoms were psychosomatic and related to depression, missing the trip would make them worse. Besides, if I could get her to New York, we could see a specialist. I wouldn't even tell her ahead of time. She might be furious with me, but the deed would be done, and with no one the wiser in Middle River.

"I could go with you," I said.

Phoebe was startled. "You? *You* don't know anything about buying clothes."

"I do it all the time," I said with a laugh.

"It's not the same."

"I know." I grew serious, because she was, very much so. "But I could handle the details and the paperwork. I'd be your assistant. I'd take care of peripheral things, like flights and hotels and what vendor is where. You'd just have to look at the clothes and decide which you like. It would be fun, Phoebe. We've never done anything like this, just the two of us."

She seemed interested, but cautious. "No. We haven't."

"I know some great restaurants. We could make it a mini-vacation, a real breather for you. You haven't had that since Mom died."

Her eyes lit. "I might finally kick this . . . whatever it is I have."

"Definitely," I said.

"Well, then . . ." Her voice trailed off. Her brow knit. In the silence, I first feared she had lost her train of thought. But she hadn't. To the contrary. We were in a lucid stretch, as was evidenced by the clarity in her eyes. With that clarity came concern, though, and it suddenly hit me that she might not want to be stuck in New York alone with me. As it happened, her concern was different. "What about Sabina?" she finally asked.

Sabina and Ron lived on Randolph Road, another of those quiet streets named after early Middle Riverites. Their house was a sweet Cape, older than some but kept in mint condition, thanks to Ron's skill with a hammer and nails, and painted a perfect pale blue with white trim. There was no lawn to speak of, no elaborate shrubbery, no cultivated flowers. Landscaping here was entirely natural, consisting of pine trees overhead, their needles underfoot, and clusters of wild ferns.

After a stop at Harriman's, I arrived midafternoon with the makings of a fabulous dinner. Sabina and Ron were at work, and Timmy was nowhere in sight. Lisa, who had been reading a book in the hammock out back, was delighted to see me. Excitedly, she peered into the grocery bag I put into her arms. "What do you *have*, Auntie Anne?"

"I have a tenderloin of beef," I said,

taking the second bag and heading for the house. "And fresh green beans and little red potatoes and makings for a spinach salad. I have Brie and crackers. I have blueberries and raspberries and a recipe for shortbread. Want to help me surprise your parents?"

We had a ball. I set her to work washing things, then showed her how to trim the ends off the beans and halve the potatoes. We mixed the former with slivers of almonds and the latter with chopped fresh oregano. We mixed the shortbread batter, clumped it on a baking tin, and put it in the oven. We fixed a rub for the tenderloin, applied it, and put the meat aside. We washed the fruit. We washed the spinach. We set the table.

I didn't often cook, but when I did, no recipe was too complex — at least, not with a friend like mine. Berri Barry was into cooking. All I had to do was tell her what I wanted — as I had in an e-mail from the store, to which she had promptly replied — and I was given a menu plan with recipes, plus schemes for substitutions in the event that the ingredients she called for weren't at hand.

I went simple here, mainly because Ron was a meat-and-potatoes man. Nonetheless, by the time Timmy rode his bike up the drive, the kitchen smelled divine.

Phoebe joined us a short time later, and then Sabina. I handed both glasses of wine. Tired, Phoebe was content to retreat to a chair on the porch. Sabina was more watchful, clearly unsure of why I was there.

And why *was* I there? Officially, I wanted to make a dent in her distrust, so that she wouldn't object to my taking Phoebe to New York. But here too, there was a deeper truth, one that was tied to the last. I was reaching out to Sabina. I was acknowledging that I knew how hard she worked, and trying to make things easier for one night at least. I was thanking her for taking care of Mom when I hadn't. I was celebrating her two incredible children and her home.

One look at Ron rushing in late, though, and I forgot all those things. I don't know why it didn't occur to me sooner. My source was right under my nose. Ron worked in the maintenance department at the mill. If anyone would know about mercury at the plant, he would. Right?

Wrong. And wrong on *two* counts. But I had to wait until dinner was nearly done to learn that, because I couldn't ask him point-blank when he walked in the door, any more than I could ask in front of everyone at dinner. Sabina would have hit the roof. So I bided my time as we ate, and I made a point of being open and agreeable. I answered the kids' questions about Washington, Ron's questions about Greg, Sabina's questions about the herbs I had rubbed on the tenderloin. My opening came when we moved on to dessert. I had forgotten whipped cream for the shortcakes. Sabina offered to run out for some.

She took my convertible and the kids. Phoebe returned to the porch, while Ron and I set to washing pots and pans, and I didn't mince words. As soon as we were alone, I told him what I suspected and, outright, asked what he knew.

"Not much," he said, long arms up to the elbows in a sink filled with suds. "I work mostly in packing and shipping, over at the garage and the shipping docks. That's way on the other side of the mill."

"Have you heard talk?"

"We talk about cars and boats and sports."

"No one mentions the words *mercury* or *pollution* or *regulations?*"

He didn't answer, simply rinsed a serving dish and passed it to me.

"Is there a pattern of ill health at the mill?" I tried.

When he took a steel wool pad to the roasting pan, seeming content to let the matter ride, I asked if he would tell me if there was.

He looked at me then, eyes filled with affection, though serious indeed. "I like you, toots. I always have. I've fought for you sometimes when I thought Sabina was being too hard. But this is different. This is our lives. Even if I did know, which I don't, there's too much at stake."

"Something more than life and death?" I asked in amazement. I would have thought *nothing* was more important than life and death. But that was just another premise of mine, in rebuttal to which Ron calmly offered **TRUTH #5: More than life and death? You bet. My work and my wife. Without those, I'm dead anyway.** "You don't understand the power the Meades have. They can ruin us."

"I *do* understand. I felt it once."

"When you were eighteen. It's different for me, Annie."

"But what about *mercury?*" I asked, because that seemed the bottom line. "Yes, you have a family, but what of their *health?*"

"Look at them. They're fine. I'm a lucky man," he said, and returned to the pan.

Back at the house later that night, I was no more decided about where to turn next than I had been that morning. Discouraged and in need of a lift, I went online to commiserate with friends, but there was the usual spam to wade through first. I highlighted the immediate suspects — then paused. One stood out. The username was TrueBlue, and the domain was a common one. I didn't know any TrueBlue, but the subject line caught me cold.

I know about the mill.

Could be advertising a coffee mill, I thought. Or a pepper mill. Or, sickly, a people mill. Could be carrying a virus, I warned myself.

But if someone had information on *our* mill, I wanted it.

As determined as I've ever been in my life, I clicked on.

Chapter 11

To: Annie Barnes
From: TrueBlue
Subject: I know about the mill.

You're snooping. I have info. Ask.

There was no electronic signature, no information anywhere to suggest the identity of TrueBlue. I clicked on every possible spot, but found nothing beyond what I saw on my screen. On the plus side, my computer didn't self-destruct, which meant that TrueBlue wasn't lethal, at least not instantly so.

I hit "reply," but even when I right-clicked on TrueBlue in the address line, I learned nothing. So. What did I know? I knew that TrueBlue had my name and e-mail address, that he (or she — it could easily be a woman) knew I was interested in the mill, and that the e-mail had been sent at nine-thirty that night, roughly an hour ago.

To: TrueBlue
From: Annie Barnes
Subject: Re: I know about the mill.

Who are you?

My finger hovered over "send." I knew that in answering, I would confirm my own existence, which was a major no-no in fighting spam. But this wasn't spam, as in a mass e-mailing that advertised something I didn't want. TrueBlue knew I was curious; he (or she) had mentioned the mill. But *our* mill? Not necessarily. This sender could be an ecology buff responding to my research on mercury. I had visited enough sites; any one of them might be able to track its guests — and reply, if so inspired. Did that imply evil intent? I didn't see how. Besides, it wasn't like there were other volunteers lining up at my door.

I sent the e-mail, then sat for ten minutes, clicking on "send/receive" every thirty seconds, until I realized the absurdity of assuming that TrueBlue was sitting in front of a computer just waiting for a reply on the odd chance I was at *my* computer at this particular hour.

That said, the longer the minutes dragged on, the more I wanted to know who he (or she) was. On impulse, I picked up the phone and called my sister the computer expert.

It did dawn on me while her phone was ringing to wonder if, given the subject matter, calling Sabina was such a great idea. But it was already too late; she had caller ID and would know it was me, or Phoebe, and in either event, she would call back. Then she answered, and the point was moot.

"Hi," I said. "You weren't sleeping, were you?"

"No," she replied, audibly cautious.

"I have a question. I just got an e-mail from someone with a username I don't know. How can I track it down?"

"Is it spam?" she asked, seeming to relax some.

"No. It's about work." I clicked "send/receive" again. Nothing.

"A fan?"

"No."

"Is it threatening?"

"No. I think it's about some research I'm doing. I want to check the legitimacy of the source."

"You don't recognize the domain name?"

"Well, I do." I told her what it was.

"That's not good," she advised. "It's a Web-based e-mail service, which makes it next to impossible to trace. Have you tried a reverse search?"

"No. I just got the note."

"Well, try that. You could also Google the address. That might turn something up."

"On *Google?* A person who wants *anonymity?*"

Sabina ignored my challenge. She was calm, clearly knowing of what she spoke. "Whoever it is may have used the address in a chat room or on a bulletin board. If it's been picked up by a search engine, it could show up — not that you'd necessarily get a real name through that, but you'd have somewhere else to look. Try those things. If nothing works, I could snoop behind the scenes. I might be able to find code that would tell you something."

The offer would have pleased me had the circumstances been different. But I was suddenly feeling guilty for using Sabina to get information that might lead to my getting the kind of scoop she had warned me against. She would be furious if she knew.

"Let me try these," I said. "Thanks, Sabina. This is a help."

"Thanks for dinner," she replied. "Now we're even."

I hung up the phone thinking that tit-for-tat between sisters was sad, but I was instantly distracted when I clicked on "send/receive" again.

To: Annie Barnes
From: TrueBlue
Subject: Re: I know about the mill.

It doesn't matter who I am. I know about Northwood Mill.

I answered immediately.

It totally matters who you are. How can I trust anything you tell me, if you won't give me your name? For all I know, you're an ex-employee who holds a grudge and will say anything to cause trouble. Only cowards hide behind anonymity.

Besides, who says I'm snooping?

And how did you get my e-mail address?

And if you're looking for money, forget it.

As soon as I sent the note, I imagined

Greg's dismay. *You have a potential source, and you're calling him names? That's a no-no, Annie. TrueBlue has something you want. Until you have it, treat him with kid gloves. Lose your source, and you're up a creek without a paddle.*

Click as I might on "send/receive," no reply came through. I was starting to think I *was* up that proverbial creek, when TrueBlue replied.

Sorry, toots, but goading me won't work. I already know I'm a coward. And I'm no ex-employee. I've been at Northwood awhile and plan to stay, so I don't need your money. I know you're snooping, because the whole town knows it. And e-mail addresses are a lot easier to find than to trace.

His answer was telling — and, yes, I say *his.* A woman wouldn't address me as toots. Not even Grace used that word, and she could be tough.

My brother-in-law Ron had used it, barely two hours ago, but if you're thinking Ron was TrueBlue, think again. Ron had meant what he said when we were doing the dishes. He wouldn't risk his job or his wife by telling me mill secrets. Besides,

Ron didn't have a computer of his own, which meant that if he were TrueBlue, he would be using Sabina's, and he was way too smart for that. He was also way too devoted to my sister to be out of the house using someone else's computer at this hour of night.

No, TrueBlue wasn't Ron. He could be any of the four men I had already pegged as possible moles. Or he could be one of hundreds of others. The mill employed that many in various capacities.

Taking Sabina's suggestion, I Googled the e-mail address. There was no match. Same thing when I ran it in a reverse directory. *E-mail addresses are a lot easier to find than to trace.* TrueBlue was right about that. So how had he gotten mine? Possibly, if he was hooked into the Northwood network and was computer savvy, from Sabina's machine. Possibly, totally apart from Northwood but certainly vulnerable to a hacker, from Phoebe's. Or from Sam's. Unfortunately, to ask any one of them would mean tipping my hand.

Actually, tipping my hand was also a problem with TrueBlue. For all I knew, he had no intention of giving me answers but was simply trying to find out what I was after. Aidan Meade, for one, wouldn't *hesi-*

tate to approach me under false pretenses; Lord knew he had done it before. Once he found out I was after mercury, he could make sure I got nothing.

I typed my response this time with more care.

Snooping sounds awfully negative for what I'm doing. I'm just trying to find the truth about my mother's death. I'm not accusing anyone of anything. I'm just spending my summer vacation trying to explain her death.

I don't want to think she had Parkinson's disease. There's no villain there. I'd rather think she was exposed to something toxic. She didn't work at the mill, so that's a long shot.

You say you have info. What's it on?

It was nearly eleven-thirty. Granted, it was Friday night, so TrueBlue wouldn't necessarily have to be up the next morning for work. Still, I wondered why he was alone at his computer. So I added a question to that effect.

And why are you awake and e-mailing so late? Too much caffeine?

Scary movie? Guilty conscience?

As I sent off the note, I realized that I had likely forgotten the most probable reason: confidentiality. TrueBlue wouldn't want anyone else knowing what he was doing. That would include a wife, significant other, whomever.

A reply came within minutes.

Call it dedication to the cause. I ought to be sleeping. I have to be up in a couple of hours. What about you? Are you always a night owl?

I typed quickly, the first of several rapid exchanges.

Only when I get notes from strange people who say they have information for me. Why do you call yourself TrueBlue?

Now, if I told you that, I'd be giving something away. Why do you type in script?

I'm an artist. It's my prerogative. Do you share your computer with anyone?

251

No. What about you? Are you at your sister's computer?

Definitely not. For what it's worth, she does not condone this search. Nor does my sister Sabina, so if you're thinking of ratting on her, save your breath. She would be furious if she knew I was corresponding with you. Do you people have to sign a loyalty oath or something?

No loyalty oath. Not yet, at least. What have you come up with for possible toxins that might have killed your mother?

If I told you that, I'd be giving something away — to quote you. But you've offered your services. No one else has approached me with that kind of offer. Why you? Why now? What's your role here? What's in it for you?

A length of time passed without a reply, but I wasn't sorry for the questions. For one thing, I felt they were important. For another, the pause gave me time to e-mail

Greg. He would have flown from San Francisco to Anchorage earlier that day. He was carrying his Blackberry.

I explained what was happening and asked his advice. To trust or not to trust — that was the question.

It was nearly thirty minutes before TrueBlue e-mailed again. He didn't answer any of my questions, simply asked one of his own.

Are you writing a book?

I'm always writing a book. But it isn't about Middle River. It takes place in Arizona and has to do with a family of packrats.

Packrats? Is this a children's book?

No. Human packrats. They don't say much of substance to each other, but they stash away all the little clues to their lives. My main character is the oldest daughter, who is struggling to figure out who she is and what she wants. When her parents suddenly die, she uses all those little things her parents stashed away to figure out her past.

As my publicist puts it, the things that were hidden away become clues in a personal journey of self-discovery.

Skeletons in the closet? There's a novel idea.

For your information, the only truly novel ideas that exist are those that have to do with new developments in technology or medicine. I write about human relationships. It's all about painting an emotional picture that gives readers pause.

Touchy, are we? But now you've told me your plot. Aren't you afraid I might steal it?

Are you kidding? Give the same plot premise to six different writers, and you'll get six entirely different books. Are you thinking of trying to write?

No. But if I was, I don't know if I'd be as cavalier as you. Wouldn't it bother you if someone was to up and write your plot?

Only if he did it better than me.

Ha ha. What are you doing while you wait for my replies?

It appears that I'm plotting. It helps to talk a plot aloud, or in this case to type it to a friend, not that you're a friend, but you know what I mean. I do a lot of my best thinking at night. Speaking of thinking, I have an idea. Want to call me on the phone? I could give you my cell number, so no one would be the wiser that you called. Or you could give me your number. This waiting for a few sentences to go back and forth is pretty silly. Do you IM?

No. I don't IM. I don't have time for that. And no. No phone calls. This is safer.

But you're anonymous and I am not. What fun is that?

I think it's great fun. It's nice to be free of who I am and what I do. Are you working at a desktop or a laptop?

I tried to decide which of my suspects might want to escape himself. Surely not Aidan Meade. He was too much of a narcissist to want distance. Any of the other three could want it, I supposed. Didn't most of us want to escape our identities from time to time?

Laptop. You?

Same. In bed?

No. In the kitchen. I need a phone jack. What about you?

In bed. I'm wireless.

Wireless? In Middle River? I'm impressed.

I had no sooner said that when I realized two things. First, if he was using his computer in bed, he was sleeping alone. And second, we were actually flirting.

Here too, that ruled out Aidan Meade. Aidan didn't flirt, he took. And I ruled out his brother James; no sense of humor there. TrueBlue could type — not a mistake yet — and was more articulate than I imagined, which made me think he wasn't

Alfie Monroe. Alfie was a large-motor, big-machine kind of guy.

Tony O'Roarke was a possibility. I knew nothing about Tony, least of all whether he slept alone.

And I would have included Tom Martin, except that he worked at the clinic, not the mill.

Flirting. Interesting. I had never cyber-flirted before. Greg might not approve at all. But would it hurt to milk the thing? It was in that spirit that I added a quick line to my e-mail before sending it off.

Are you male?

Last time I looked.

Ha ha. What do you do at the mill?

Enough to know what I'm talking about. What are you looking for?

Something to convince me that you're legit.

Try this. Paper mills like Northwood take wood and turn it into paper. Part of the process entails using bleach to make the paper white. Bleach, or chlorine, as it is more commonly called, is produced in a chlor-alkali plant. Northwood has a small one that fills its needs.

Did you know that?

I did not. Go on.

Chlor-alkali plants use salt and electricity to produce chlorine. Traditionally, mercury was used to stabilize the product when electricity was passed through the salt. I say "traditionally," because we now know that mercury is extremely toxic. When it is released from chlor-alkali plants as waste, it fouls air, ground, and water near the plant. Add flow patterns and wind currents to that, and you have serious pollution.

Do we have serious pollution here?

Northwood has complied with every state mandate. We no longer use mercury.

So what's the problem?

Your turn. You tell me.

He might be strong enough to resist goading, but I was all too human. I was also impatient. Flirting was all fine and dandy — *caution* was all fine and dandy — but he was the one who had mentioned mercury. If he had information, I wanted it.

Mercury. Either you still use it in some illicit capacity, or there is pollution from the past that was never cleaned up. How'm I doing?

Not bad. Forget the first; we don't use mercury now. But the past continues to be a problem.

In what sense?

If I tell you, what'll you do with the information?

That depends on whether I decide I can trust what you say. You still haven't told me why you're doing this. What's in it for you? What do you expect me to do? And why don't you do it yourself?

Why don't I do it myself? Oh, I've

tried. I've talked to people, but they refuse to listen. And I'm in a difficult position. If I go too far, I stand to lose my ties with Northwood. Those ties mean a lot to me.

What do I expect you to do? There's some information I don't have. I need you to be my legs for that. For the rest, I need you to be my voice.

I thought of Tom. Hadn't he too talked with people? Wasn't he too in a difficult position? No, I didn't think Tom was TrueBlue. TrueBlue said he had been with Northwood awhile. Not only was Tom relatively new to town, but he wasn't with the mill at all.

Still, he was using me. These two men shared that. So now I replied to TrueBlue.

You need me to be your sacrificial lamb, you mean.

I hit "send" with more force than was needed, but I was amazed at the man's gall. He wanted me to do his dirty work. So much for flirting. He was *using* me.

I was tempted to turn off my computer — to hang up on the guy, so to speak — just turn around and walk away. That's what my passionately defensive Middle River persona would have me do.

But I was grown-up enough to pause, to think, to realize that if this man had information that would benefit me, the using was two-sided. If he had information that would explain my mother's illness, and if his information implicated Northwood Mill, wouldn't I be successful on two counts?

How would you be a sacrificial lamb? You'd be righting a wrong. You'd be finding out why your mother died. You'd be doing something good for all the people who live in Middle River. If nothing else, think of the children. Mercury is devastating in children. How can you turn your back on that?

You're doing it.

No. If you don't agree to help, I'll find someone else. I've been at this awhile. I have other coals in the fire. I may not be willing to be out there and in your face. I may not be willing to sacrifice my name and my place. But I'm committed. Think about it —

you may not get a better offer. I'm logging off now.

I did think about it for a good long time and then, naturally, I overslept the next morning, which meant that since I had promised to help Phoebe out at the store, I didn't have time to go for a run. That put me in a bad mood, which probably explained my paranoia. I was convinced that Phoebe didn't want me around, because no sooner did we reach the store, she gave me a long list of menial errands to run — I was sure it was deliberate on her part — bringing trash to the dump, buying cleaning supplies, hand-delivering a new pair of panty hose to a local customer.

Wherever I went, people stared; I was convinced of that too. It was like they knew I was in touch with TrueBlue, like they knew we were conspiring to rock the boat.

In fact, I hadn't heard from TrueBlue again. I did hear from Greg, though, a truncated note Blackberried shortly before his helicopter touched down at a base camp on the Kahiltna Glacier. He said that he was cold but energized, that this would be his last e-mail until they cleared the 12,000-foot mark four days from now, weather permitting, and that I should corroborate whatever any informant said — and even *that* hit me the wrong way. Well, of course, I would check it all out. Did Greg think I was totally naive?

There were more errands to run as the day passed. I mailed bills, fetched lunch, gassed up the van — the last after waiting ten minutes behind the minibus from Road's End Inn carrying its load of weekenders taking the Peyton Place tour.

Phoebe had her good moments; she did clean up the mess she had made in the office the day before. But in addition to assigning me menial errands, she gave me a few that were absurd. For instance, at one point she sent me with a list of places to go in search of the carpenter who had promised to spend Sunday at the store rebuilding one room's worth of display shelves. She wanted to confirm that he was coming. Me, I wanted to know why the guy didn't have a cell phone she could call. Lord knew, most everyone in town seemed to have one.

I never did track him down, which made me think Phoebe had known I wouldn't — and yes, I was being bitchy. She hadn't asked for my help; I was the one who had offered it. Did I really expect she would put me in charge of the store? Maybe that was what she was afraid of — that I *would* try to take over — which was as ridiculous as it got. I was a writer, not a shopkeeper. And I say that with the utmost respect for what Phoebe did. I would have gone out of my *mind* with the indecision of some of her customers — *the black skirt is best — no, the navy one will work better with my shoes — but the black one makes me look slimmer — of course, the beige one will be perfect for September.*

Writing was a solitary profession, meaning that I did what I wanted when I wanted to do it. Yes, I had to conform to a publisher's schedule, but my book was my book. I was in total control of its contents. My modus operandi didn't involve waiting for someone to decide whether to buy loafers or slides, V-neck or crew neck, wool or cashmere. I had no patience for that. No *way* would I want the store.

Maybe *Sabina* had put that bug in her ear.

More paranoia.

And that was *Phoebe's* fault. Had she given me chores that involved thinking, I wouldn't have had time to stew. But what she gave me was busywork, nothing more. Running mindless errands around Middle River? My worst nightmare. Talk about awkward. Not only did people look at me wherever I went, but when we had cause to exchange words, they were guarded.

And then there was my shadow. Someone was following me. I was convinced of it. I can't tell you how many times I felt a prickly sensation at the back of my neck and looked fast over my shoulder.

There was never anyone there, of course.

But someone had been. I didn't find out who it was until I visited my mom's grave the next day. Until then, I was just in a lousy mood, which might be juvenile, but was fact. By the time Saturday night came, I was annoyed enough at Middle River to agree to help TrueBlue with anything his little heart desired.

To: TrueBlue
From: Annie Barnes
Subject: Your offer

You have a point. Where do we go from here?

Chapter 12

Marshall Greenwood was on edge. He knew that if Annie Barnes was on his case, there could be trouble. One solution was to retire. He was sixty-six and would be doing it soon anyway. As chiefs of police went, he was old. But Middle River wasn't demanding of him, and he needed the money. Besides, his wife didn't want him around the house. She hadn't said it in as many words, but that was the general drift.

Barring retirement, the other obvious solution was to ditch all the pills. If he wasn't taking anything, he wasn't an addict. He could simply deny the allegations. Over and done.

He lasted three hours, at which point the pain in his back was so bad and he was so ready to crawl out of his skin, he gave up on that idea. Besides, even if he were able to kick the habit now, the past would be hard to deny. Among his doctor, his HMO, and the drugstore was a paper trail a mile long. No, there had to be another answer.

He spent most of Friday trying to find it. But he had never been good at finding answers. He did things that were obvious. When someone was drunk, Marshall either drove him home or hauled him in to sleep it off. When a car hit a tree, he called the ambulance first and then the tow truck. When a man beat his wife, he drove the woman to her mother's house, and if the guy did it again, he called the county sheriff.

The only clues Marshall dealt with were in his crossword puzzles. Friday night, he agonized over one that read "major backup." The word had six letters, the second an *a*, the last an *n*. He went through every possible version of *traffic tie-up* before squeezing his eyes shut, shaking his head hard, and taking a whole different approach. Bingo. The answer was *patron*.

Taking that as a message, Marshall picked up the phone early Saturday morning and called Sandy Meade. Sandy was his most respected friend in Middle River. They had gone to school together, and though Marshall was two years behind, they had been teammates in every sport. Sandy was inevitably the star, but Marshall was the better athlete. He made Sandy look good on enough occasions that, by way of reward, he had Sandy's un-dying loyalty. Sandy was responsible for his being hired for the security force at the mill years before, and when he won a spot in the Middle River Police Department, Sandy was responsible for that, too.

"Got a minute?" he asked now. He was sitting in the driveway, calling from his car so that Edna wouldn't hear, but he timed the call well. At this hour on a Saturday morning, Sandy would be out back on the stone patio of that big Birch Street home, reading the newspaper over a third or fourth cup of the strong black coffee his housekeeper kept hot in the carafe.

"Perfect timing," Sandy said. In the background was the muted rustle of paper, and in the foreground, that Meade voice filled with steel. "You're the person I want to talk with. Annie Barnes is back. You know that?"

"I do," Marshall said, delighted that Sandy had raised the subject first.

"Well, Aidan's in a stew. He thinks she's here to dredge up old business. You think so?"

The perjury business hadn't occurred to Marshall. But he was implicated in that, too. "Geez, I hope not. There has to be a statute of limitations on that. What does

Lowell say?" Lowell Bunker was Sandy's attorney.

"He says what you do, that the statute has expired, so there can't be any prosecution. Personal assassination is something else. She could write that whole thing into a story, just barely disguised."

"But why would she have to come back here to do that? She knows all the facts."

"She wants more. She can't make a book out of that one incident, so she's back here fishing for dirt."

"On what?" Marshall asked. He wasn't stupid; he wasn't volunteering the business about the pills unless he had to.

"My guess is the mill. She'll accuse us of all sorts of things, and she won't be able to prove any of it, but she'll go on television shooting her mouth off about art mirroring life, and the talk alone can bring the EPA. She's a dangerous woman. There's a good reason they've always compared her to Grace."

Marshall fed off Sandy's strength. "What can I do?" he asked with crusty sternness, just like the stalwart police chief he most often imagined he was. *Stalwart* — as in "tough as nails" — had been in a puzzle of his not long before. He liked that word a lot.

"Hassle her," Sandy said. "The way I see it, the sooner we let her know she's not welcome here, the sooner she'll leave. If she keeps at it, I have an option or two on my end, but before that, let's see what you can do."

Marshall was not a mean person. He saw his job as being reactive rather than proactive — two more good words. But now he had a mandate from Sandy Meade, and Sandy was a man to please.

Finding Annie was easy. The pale green van with Miss Lissy's logo on the door was nearly as hard to miss as if she had been in the convertible, and with Annie popping in and out of stores, driving from one end of town to the other — Sandy was right, she was definitely fishing — Marshall had her pegged in no time flat.

For a time, he followed her, staying the proper distance behind, but watching every move she made. Given the slightest provocation, he would have pulled her over and given her a ticket. But she stayed within the speed limit, used her blinker at every turn, even stopped for two kids in the crosswalk in the center of town. He thought for sure he would be able to get her when she made a right at the corner of School and Oak; half the town slipped around that corner without coming to a complete stop, as the stop sign dictated. But she did.

Unable to hassle her this way, he tried another tack. It was a more backhanded one (*furtive* was a more subtle word), but again, given Sandy's mandate, Marshall felt justified. He became an investigator, visiting those places where she had made stops and fishing for what *she* was fishing for.

"So," he said to Jim Howard, the bottle sorter at the town dump, "I saw Annie Barnes here earlier. What'd she have to say?"

"Not much," said Jim. He was a sad-eyed and silent man, not personable at all, which was why he was a bottle sorter, not a cop, Marshall mused.

"She didn't ask questions?"

"Nope."

"Didn't say anything?"

"She said 'hi.' " He returned to his work.

"Did she talk with anyone else?"

He shook his head. Then he spotted a brown bottle in the midst of the green ones in the large bin, and pulled it out.

"Well, let me know if she does, okay? She's clever, that one. Thinks if she asks people like you, you'll tell all for the sake of the glory. She's writing a book, you know — or trying to."

Marshall repeated the same line a bit later at the gas station, where he found Normie Zwibble to be just as naive as Jim Howard.

"She's writing a book?" the mechanic asked in disbelief. "That's cool."

Marshall knew admiration when he saw it. Needing to nip it in the bud, he was deliberately cruel. "Not if she writes about an overweight grease monkey who spends half his pay on lottery tickets. Who do you think people will point at?" They would point at Normie, and that would mean trouble. Everyone knew Normie played the lottery — everyone except his parents, who believed gambling was evil and who, moreover, believed that what money Normie didn't have in his pocket at week's end had gone into the collection box at church. No matter that Normie was over thirty. He still lived at home, still worked for his daddy, still went to every town dance with his hair slicked back and his face filled with hope.

That face had gone pale. "She wouldn't do that," he protested.

"Oh, she would," Marshall said. "If I were you, I'd steer clear of Annie Barnes. And I'd tell my buddies to do it too," he tacked on and was immediately pleased with himself. Getting other people to do his dirty work was a brainstorm.

So he tried it on Marylou Walker at News 'n Chews, but only after he bought some almond turtles while waiting for a pair of *Peyton Place* tourists to leave the shop. Marylou was in her late forties, the second generation of three running the store. "I saw Annie Barnes in here before," he remarked when he finished the last of his third turtle. "What'd she buy?"

"Chocolate pennies," Marylou answered with pride. "She's been in here nearly every day. She says she's missed our pennies. Washington doesn't have anything like them."

"She walked out with more than a bag of pennies."

"Uh-huh. She bought the newspaper, several postcards, and a map of the town."

"Postcards? And a map? Why a map?"

"I guess to see what streets are new."

"I'd say she was doing research," Marshall advised. "You do know that she's writing a book. How would you feel about being in it?"

"Why would I be in a book?"

"Because you're part of a family that has, let's say, an interesting history."

Marylou was a minute in following. Then she frowned. "If you're talking about my cousins, that's *ancient* history."

"It was incest," Marshall reminded her. "Do you want it revived in a book?"

"No."

"Then I'd make sure you don't get too friendly with Annie Barnes. That's what writers do, y'know. They sweet-talk you into telling things you wouldn't normally tell. I'd warn your family, too. Be careful, Marylou. Your parents were around when *Peyton Place* came out. Ask them. They remember what went on in this town. Grace Metalious did it then. This is Annie Barnes's chance for revenge." Seeing that Marylou was listening, he knew he had made his point.

Taking another turtle from his little bag, he left the store, but he was thinking about other people who needed to get the message. Even past the *Peyton Placers*, there had been kids in the shop. They were all eyes over Annie Barnes. Hadn't he seen the DuPuis girl several times that day, covering much of the same ground as Annie?

Naturally, when he thought of talking with Kaitlin, she was nowhere in sight. So he headed to Omie's for a late lunch, and there, just coming out with his wife, was

Hal Healy. It was a stroke of luck. Hal was even better. He could reach more people in an hour than Kaitlin DuPuis could in two weeks.

"Got a minute?" Marshall asked. It was his standard opening.

Hal smiled at Pamela. "Wait for me in the car, hon?" He kissed her forehead and watched her walk off.

Marshall watched, too. Pamela was a good-looking woman. He never would have paired her up with a formal guy like Hal. Sour grapes? Maybe. But not because he wanted Pamela himself. The thing was, he remembered when he and Edna had been the way Pamela and Hal were. It was really quite sweet.

"How can I help you?" Hal asked in his quiet, no-nonsense voice.

Marshall refocused. "Annie Barnes. Do you know the name?"

"Of course. She and my Pam were friends back in school."

"Do you know the whole business about Annie and Grace?"

"Yes. Marsha Klausson told me. I've read *Peyton Place* several times."

"Then you know what's inside. Hot stuff, huh?"

Hal grew red. He gave half a shrug,

clearly uncomfortable talking about it.

"Yup," Marshall said, letting him off the hook. "Hot stuff. From what I hear, Annie Barnes is of the same mold, and quite frankly, I'm worried. She's been all over town. I see the kids looking at her like she's their newest idol. She could be a bad influence. School isn't in session for another couple weeks, but you're already holding faculty meetings. Think you ought to alert the teachers to what's going on?"

Hal thought about that for a minute. He actually seemed torn. "I'd hate to stir something up that would otherwise rest in peace."

"Rest in peace?" Marshall asked and cleared his throat to keep the frogginess at bay. "The whole town's concerned. Annie Barnes has a national following, and the media are vultures. She says the right thing in the right place, and we're smeared all over the news. Is that what you want?"

"How will my talking with teachers prevent that?"

"It'll keep them from talking to Annie Barnes. You see, that's the key. If we stand together and stonewall, she can't get a thing." Stonewall. He *liked* that word.

Hal must have, too, because he nodded. "That makes sense. Good idea. Thanks,

Marshall." Arching a mischievous brow, he cocked his head toward his car, tossed a thumb that way, and took off.

Kaitlin DuPuis followed Annie around town most of Saturday, but she didn't get her opening until Sunday morning, and that was purely a fluke. She rarely went to church — hated sitting between her parents listening to all that talk of love, when there was none to the right or the left. As far as she was concerned, this was the most hypocritical of the hypocrisies in her home.

But it was important to her parents that people see them together in church, and because Kaitlin didn't know what would come of the Annie Barnes thing, she figured that this week she'd better go too.

Then she saw Annie in the parking lot, climbing out of her convertible and running around to the passenger side to help her sister Phoebe. Once they connected with Sabina Mattain and her family, Phoebe went up the stone steps and inside with them. Annie separated and headed around behind the church.

Kaitlin followed her parents up the steps and inside, then stopped and said the one thing that was guaranteed to buy her time. "I want to go see Gramma. I'll be right back." She went down the side stairs and out the lower door, which put her one walkway, a small span of neatly mown grass, and a white picket fence away from the graveyard.

Hurrying through the gate in the fence, she proceeded down the stone path that led to her grandmother's stone, but she didn't stop there. She continued up over the rise, then down to a hollow ringed by woods. Though this was technically the back end of the cemetery, Kaitlin had always thought it the prettiest part.

Annie was at her parents' grave, and suddenly that gave Kaitlin pause. The stone with BARNES on it wasn't new, but the sod on Alyssa's side was. This death was fresh. If Kaitlin was intruding on Annie's privacy, it wouldn't help her cause.

Then again, for all Kaitlin knew, Annie had been here before. Kaitlin came often to sit with her grandmother, just as she had done at the nursing home in the months prior to her death. Her grandmother had loved her — *really* loved her. When the rest of the world seemed unbearable to Kaitlin, visiting here helped.

So maybe Alyssa Barnes was helping Annie, in which case Annie would be softer, more relaxed, and receptive to

Kaitlin's plea. Or so Kaitlin hoped. Not that she had other options. Catching Annie alone in a place where all of Middle River wouldn't see was proving to be next to impossible.

She slowed when she neared. Annie sat on the grass with her legs curled to the side. She was wearing sunglasses. Still, it was clear she was looking at that stone with its newly etched addition.

Kaitlin waited quietly, hoping Annie would look up and smile. When that didn't happen, she took one step forward. She waited, then took another. She was about to clear her throat when Annie finally did look. After a moment of nothing, Kaitlin thought she saw her eyebrows go up. Surprise? Recognition?

"Hello," she said. Her voice gave nothing away.

"Hi," Kaitlin replied in a voice that gave *everything* away. It was shaky. She was totally nervous. Given the slightest provocation, she would have turned and run. Lest she do that, she rushed out the words. "I have to ask you a big favor. It's about the other night. I know you know it was us, but like, I want you to know that it'll be really, *really* bad if you tell anyone about it, and it'll be even *worse* if you put it in your book. See, my parents don't know about Kevin. They would go *ballistic* if they did because he isn't the kind of guy they want me with, and it doesn't do any good for me to say we're in love, because love doesn't mean a *thing* to my parents." She pressed her heart, which was where she was feeling the ache. "Kevin is *so* special to me. He's the first guy who has ever, *ev*-er been interested in me, and he didn't just do it for the sex, because if he had, he'd be gone, because I don't think I'm very good at that, either. He doesn't care that I'm not pretty. I mean like, he loves me — is that awesome? — *loves* me — like nobody else ever has except my grandmother, and she's dead too."

"The other night?" Annie asked. Her brows were knit now.

Kaitlin felt herself blush. "You know. The other *night*." When Annie didn't say anything, just sat there looking confused, Kaitlin felt her first inkling of doubt. "You saw us, I know you did. You knew it was me the minute I walked into the front room at your sister's store." The inkling grew. "Didn't you?" Still Annie seemed baffled. That came through, sunglasses and all. "Like, if you didn't, why did you wink?"

"I winked because you were staring at me."

"But then it happened again at Omie's — I mean, you waved at me then."

"I recognized you from the shop."

Annie Barnes was perfectly serious. And Kaitlin DuPuis felt like a *total jerk*.

"Omigod," she whispered, then did it again, because she didn't know what else to do. Should she stay? Run? Dig a big hole and crawl in beside Gramma?

She was looking back, then ahead, then back again when she heard a vague "hey" from somewhere. When it came a second time and louder, her eyes flew to the source. Annie had taken off her sunglasses and was gesturing her closer.

Kaitlin didn't budge. "I don't believe I did this," she said in dismay and put a hand on the top of her head. "You didn't know."

"How could I see? It was dark."

"That's what Kevin said, but we were there in the headlights, and I was sure you had. So now *I've* told you." She wrapped her arms around her middle, but that didn't stop her eyes from tearing. "This is so bad. Like, I am such a *loser*."

"You're not a loser."

"What do *you* know about it?" she asked.

She didn't care if she was being rude. Annie Barnes would do what she wanted, regardless of how Kaitlin behaved.

"I've been there," Annie said. "Want to come sit?"

"What I *want* is for you to forget what I said, but that won't happen, will it." No question there. Kaitlin brushed at the tears and looked back in the direction of Gramma. Gramma would know what to do next. Standing here, though, Kaitlin didn't feel any vibes.

"I won't tell anyone," Annie repeated.

Kaitlin should have listened to Kevin. He had been right. Now, she had messed up *everything.* "I'm cooked. I'm *done* for. My parents will accuse him of rape. Do you know how *awful* that'll be?"

"I said, I won't tell."

Kaitlin was embarrassed just thinking about it. She put a hand back on her head, like that would somehow keep her grounded. It was only then that she heard Annie's words. She looked back. Annie seemed serious.

Actually, she looked like she might have been crying. Her eyes weren't exactly red. But the area around them was shiny. Like, wet. And still she said, "Why would I tell? What's the point?"

Kaitlin could think of several, but mentioned only the most obvious. "Uh, your book." Her voice rose at the end. It was a no-brainer.

"I'm not writing a book."

"Everyone says you are."

"They're wrong."

"You could still tell my parents."

"Why would I do that? I don't owe your parents anything. What you do is not my affair. How old are you?"

"Seventeen."

"And you don't think that's a little young for sex in the street?"

Kaitlin stiffened. "See? You agree with them."

"No." She gave an odd kind of smile. "But I'm an adult. I'm supposed to say that."

Kaitlin tried to interpret that smile. "Yeah, are you supposed to tell, too?"

"Why would I bother? No one would believe me anyway. They'd say I'm envious, because I never pulled a backabehind. And they're right. I didn't have many friends, much less of the male variety. Like I said, I've been there." She patted the ground. "Are you sure you don't want to sit?"

Kaitlin *did* want to — not because she needed to sit, but because something about Annie pulled at her. It had to do with that smile, or whatever it was. It suggested Annie wasn't one of them. But Kaitlin already knew that. She wasn't supposed to be talking with Annie. Word around town said she was dangerous.

She didn't seem dangerous to Kaitlin, at least not sitting here at her mother's grave. She looked . . . sad.

Of course, it could be an act. It could be that she would leave here and tell the first person she met that it had been Kaitlin DuPuis and Kevin Stark making love in the middle of Cedar the night she had blown into town. But she wasn't getting up to leave and do that. And now that Kaitlin was here, she didn't see the harm of staying. It was better than sitting with her parents. It could even help. If she and Annie became friends, she might be able to convince Annie not to talk. Wasn't that one of Kaitlin's mother's pet thoughts — win 'em over, then call the shots?

She started forward, but stopped. "Are you sure you want me here? Aren't you, like, talking with your mom?"

"No. I'm just sitting. It's lonely. I'm not exactly Miss Popularity around town."

Kaitlin knew how *that* was. It had only been the last two or three years that she'd had friends — at least, friends that mattered. Coming the rest of the way, she lowered herself to the grass.

Annie gave her the smallest smile, before looking back at the gravestone.

"Are you sure I'm not intruding?" Kaitlin asked.

Annie nodded, seeming content with the silence. And so, for a short time, was Kaitlin. Birds were making noise in the woods, but not so loud as to drown out the distant strains of the church hymns. Kaitlin enjoyed the hymns from here. They helped clear her mind, helped her focus.

"And you really won't tell?" she asked Annie.

"I won't tell."

"You didn't already tell your sister Phoebe? Or James Meade? I saw you talking with him at Omie's."

"How could I tell either of them? I didn't know it was you."

"Will you tell them, now that you do?" Kaitlin asked, cursing herself *again* for her own stupidity.

Annie looked at her. "There are more important things. I don't even know your name."

Unfortunately, everyone else in Middle River did, which meant that even if Kaitlin refused to give it, it was easily found out. "Kaitlin DuPuis."

"Kaitlin. That's pretty."

"Uh-huh. It's pretty and light and perky — all the things my mother hoped I'd be that I'm not."

"Why are you so down on yourself?"

"Because it's the truth. I'm my mother's biggest disappointment. Well, next to my dad."

"I'm not touching *that* one. About the mother thing, though, maybe we're all destined to disappoint them. We just can't be what they want."

"You weren't?" Kaitlin asked in surprise. "Why not? I mean, like, look at you. You're wicked successful."

"My books sell. That's not everything."

Kaitlin thought about it. No, selling books wasn't everything. Still. "You don't seem so bad."

Annie made a throaty noise. "Not as bad as they say?"

"I'm sure they meant when you were little," Kaitlin put in. "You know, before you left here. I also thought you were ugly."

"I thought so, too."

"But you're not at all. I mean, you're really beautiful. I'd give anything to look like you. I got all of my dad's bad features — bad nose, bad hairline, bad skin." She pointed at her eyes. "These are contact lenses, and this nose is fixed. Same with my teeth and my jaw. I had *the* worst receding jaw, but they fixed that with a retainer too. We've done everything we can to make me look a little attractive."

"I think you're *very* attractive."

"I will *ne*-ver be very attractive. I mean, all we can do is patch things up and then watch for the bad stuff popping up again in my own kids."

"Who says that?"

"My mom. She tells me I'd better marry someone rich to pay for plastic surgery for my kids."

"Are you serious?"

"Oh yeah. My mom's into beauty. She's done everything she can for me. She's harping on low-carb now, but she's just about given up on the weight thing, because packing it on is just like my dad, too. I don't know if South Beach will work. Nothing else seems to. I mean, if we're at Omie's and everyone's ordering stuff with fries, am I supposed *not* to order that? It's like I'd be wearing this, this scarlet letter on my forehead — *F* for fat."

"You aren't fat."

"I am. Ask anyone."

"I wouldn't have singled you out from your friends as being fat. Don't put yourself down. You don't want to be as scrawny as some of those others."

"See?" Kaitlin caught her there. "You did notice. I am bigger."

"Not bigger. *Normal.* Much prettier and softer for it."

Kaitlin didn't believe that for a minute. But she did like hearing Annie say it. Prettier and softer? She certainly *wanted* to be that.

Annie was after something. She had to be. Why else would she be passing out compliments? It struck Kaitlin that they could make a deal. Kaitlin could give her something else for her book, in exchange for Annie keeping quiet about Kevin and her.

"I know things about this town that you'd probably like to hear," she said quietly. "I'd be willing to trade."

But the words weren't even fully out when Annie was shaking her head. "Your secret is safe with me. You don't have to pay to make it so."

"Are you sure? I mean, I really don't want them knowing about Kevin. And I will help you. I know a lot of stuff."

Another head shake. "Thanks. But I'm fine." She looked back at the grave.

"I'm sorry about your mom." When Annie simply nodded, she pushed herself up. "I should be getting back. I don't want my parents to come looking for me. They'll die if they know I've been talking with you."

A rustling came from the woods. Kaitlin looked there just as a man emerged. It was Mr. Healy, the high school principal. He seemed as startled to see them as they were to see him. Actually, Kaitlin was more than surprised. She was *appalled.*

"Omigod," she murmured. "Omigod, I'm outta here." Backing away from Annie, she raised her voice. "Hi, Mr. Healy. Just leaving. I was over there visiting with my gramma and I heard a noise down here, so I ran over. Just leaving. Gotta get back. Bye-bye."

Hal Healy watched her go. When she disappeared over the rise, he slicked back his hair with a hand. His tie was neat; he had checked that before. Running his thumb and forefinger along either side of his mouth, he turned to Annie. She was sitting on the grass, looking, frankly, provocative. He didn't doubt for a minute that she was a scandal waiting to happen.

"Why was Kaitlin here?" he asked.

"She was visiting her grandmother's grave."

"Yes, she did say that, but I'm not sure I believe her." He sighed. "I wasn't going to approach you about this, but finding you here says I'm meant to do it. I'm worried, Miss Barnes."

"Annie."

"You know what my job is. So much of what the kids in this town do is my responsibility. Now, here you come, back to town after fifteen years, and you're just about the age Grace Metalious was when she was shocking the living daylights out of folks living here."

"You don't need to tell me about Grace. I felt the effects of her book more than most."

"Then you'll understand what I'm saying. The kids here are impressionable. They're also apt to be a little in awe of your fame. If they see you snooping around, looking for titillating stories, they'll be fired up to give them to you. We have enough trouble trying to control them without that kind of instigation."

He had to hand it to her; she was tough. She stared at him with cold, hard eyes —

and those, here at her mother's new grave. Her voice, too, was cold. "I'm not in the market for sex and titillation."

"Well, that's good," he said. "I'm pleased to hear you say it. These kids are our future. We have to make sure they're up to it. I wouldn't want our jobs to be made more difficult than they are."

She continued to stare, silent now. He figured he had made his point.

"That's all I wanted to say. Thank you for listening. I'm sure you'll keep this in mind. We only want the best for our children, agreed?"

"Totally," she said.

He nodded. Raising one hand in a half wave, he stepped around the Barnes burial plot and made his way up the hill, back toward the church. Once inside, he slipped into a free seat in the back row. He could see Pamela's head up near the front, her black hair distinct. He could also see Nicole DuPuis across the aisle, with Kaitlin dutifully returned to her side.

He was prepared to let it go at that. As the service went on, though, he began to worry that Kaitlin would tell her mother she had seen him coming out of the woods. He would rather Nicole hear his story than hers.

So he waited until the service was over and the congregants were milling around out front. Kaitlin went off with her friends, while her father went off with his friends. Hal positioned himself not far from Nicole's car. Unfortunately, though, before she could reach him, Pamela appeared, and the moment was lost.

Chapter 13

Something happened to me that Sunday in the cemetery, and it had nothing to do with what I learned about Kaitlin DuPuis or would later learn about Hal Healy. For starters, it had to do with having a good cry and accepting that my mother was gone and that nothing I did could bring her back. I could fight. I could rant and rave about what might have poisoned her. I could breathe hellfire and vengeance. But Mom had lost her balance, fallen down the stairs, and died of a broken neck. What good was vengeance? Would it put her back in the kitchen, waiting for me to come home?

Then Kaitlin came by with her fears, and I got to thinking about the ways in which we disappoint our parents. And Hal Healy had suggested I was a bad influence on Middle River's youth, so I got to thinking about that.

I was still at it when the service finished, and Phoebe found her way to where I sat. I watched her come toward me steadily, then not so, seeking preventive purchase on each gravestone she passed. I felt something then — an awakening — but it wasn't until she and I had spent another few minutes of quiet at our parents' grave, before the awakening took shape. It crystallized when Sabina arrived.

"I was worried," she complained, looking straight at me. "I thought maybe something had happened. You never made it inside at all."

Inside? Did I need to see the Hayneses, the Clappers, the Harrimans, or the Ryes? Did I need to see the *Meades?*

"No," I replied calmly. "I needed to be here more."

"I'd argue with that. The pastor's sermon was on respect within families."

"Sabina —" Phoebe warned.

"It was about understanding the needs of others," Sabina went on, clearly not done with me, "even when those needs aren't your own. We saved you a seat. It was glaringly empty through the entire service. Okay, I know you're not into organized religion. Anything requiring conformity goes against your grain. But even *aside* from the pastor's message, which was really good, family is key. You sitting in church with your family would have gone a long way toward showing certain people in this town that you can fit in once in a while. Show them that, and *we* might not be on the hot seat quite so much. My friends are asking questions. My neighbors are asking questions. My boss is still asking questions. But you don't care. It just doesn't concern you." Face filled with disgust, she turned to Phoebe. "My family is waiting. Can I drop you home?"

Phoebe smiled. She might not have had the wherewithal to tell Sabina off. But she didn't cave in. "I'll stay a little."

Sabina strode off. And we didn't discuss it, Phoebe and I. She had made a small statement, and I was grateful.

I was not smug, however. Smugness was a luxury I couldn't afford where my sisters were concerned.

I had moved on — or back, however you choose to see it — and as we sat, my thoughts gelled. Seeking revenge might be noble if a Meade cover-up was involved. But it was also exhausting. It required the sustaining of anger, something I might have done at eighteen. At thirty-three? I couldn't.

Nor, though, could I let it all go. I couldn't bring my mother back, but, **TRUTH #6: She wasn't the only one**

involved. I could fight this fight for Phoebe, who was clearly ill. I could fight it for Sabina, who talked of respect but didn't have a clue about other threats. I could fight it for Hal Healy, whose concern for the morals of the town's kids was almost laughable, when you thought about the possibility of poison in the air they breathed, the water they drank, and the fish they ate.

I'm not sure I can say that I heard my mother speak. I'm not even sure I can say that she would have wanted me to do this. Like Sabina, she was afraid of talk.

I did hear Grace, but only from afar. Grace didn't do graveyards. That said, she did like unearthing things that were buried. Oh yes, Grace was all for it.

Bottom line? Mom was gone. Phoebe was sick. And totally aside from Grace's need to shock people, I knew this was the right thing to do.

To: Annie Barnes
From: TrueBlue
Subject: Where do we go next?

That depends. What are your plans?

To: TrueBlue
From: Annie Barnes
Subject: Re: Where do we go next?

I haven't thought past finding out whether something in Middle River made my mother sick. No, I'm not planning a book. Isn't that what you're asking, again? And if not you, then everyone else, but the question is getting old. Are you willing to help me, or not?

That depends. There are ways besides a book to publicize a wrong. You could turn the information I give you over to *The Washington Post*, which would be no different from your writing a book. Same thing if you give it to your pal Greg Steele.

I take it you don't like those options. Are you getting cold feet?

Cold feet? Not by a long shot. Remember, I live here. I have even more reason than you to want things fixed. But here's my problem. If you do the wrong thing with whatever you find, this town will be transformed in ways

297

your Grace couldn't fathom. Book, newspaper, nightly news — it doesn't matter how the story breaks, but if you go for something splashy, Middle River will be overrun not only by the media, but by lawyers. Know what happens then?

They swarm.

That's putting it mildly. Personal injury lawyers come in droves, making wild promises to every possible victim. They organize their class-action suits and film their front-page stories on the lawn of the town hall, and they get their headlines and their big trial and their hefty settlement. Unfortunately, they're the only ones who make anything on the deal. Northwood loses a bundle paying damages and expenses, and worst-case scenario, goes bankrupt, in which case the economy of the town goes to hell right along with the jobs of the people who live here. And the victims who are supposedly receiving money for pain and suffering? Once the lawyers take their share and the court fees have been paid and the rest has been divvied up between all the people involved, any single victim gets a pittance.

I take it you don't like lawyers.

Wrong. My college roommate is a lawyer. I'd walk through fire for him. But he's the first one to tell me to avoid litigation. So that's what I'm doing. I want things fixed, if not for me then for the kids around here. I don't want the town destroyed, and that's what will happen if you go for headlines.

I don't need headlines. I need answers. If the answers warrant it, I want change.

If that's all, then we're on the same page. The thing is, once I give you information, you can basically do what you want. Can I trust you're telling me the truth now?

I ask you — can I trust you'll tell me the truth? How do I know you aren't an instrument of the Meades and won't send me on a wild goose chase just to keep me busy while I'm here?

Try this. Government regulations allow for a certain amount of pollution. When a mill like Northwood exceeds that amount, it is required to load it into 55-gallon drums and have it carted away to an authorized toxic waste disposal area. This is costly. It cuts into profits. On occasion, Northwood used other methods.

What methods?

Your turn. Give me something. We're trying to establish a mutual trust here. Put up or shut up.

I have just finished marking a map of the town with dots. Each dot represents someone who has been seriously ill during the last five years. In some instances, there's no pattern. In other instances, there are definite clusters. Like along the river. Hyperactivity, muscular dystrophy, autism — lots of trouble with kids on th'other side.
Could be genes. Could be coinci-

dence. Could be toxicity.
What do you think?

I didn't hear back from TrueBlue, but that didn't alarm me. By the time of our last exchange, it was very late. I went to bed and again slept longer than I would have. But I was on vacation, wasn't I? What were vacations for if not to sleep late?

That set me up to go running at eight. Grace couldn't have been happier.

Good girl, playing with fire. You're very boring where men are concerned.

Excuse me, I demurred. You don't see me in Washington. I've dated some unusual men.

Unusual?

Impressive.

James Meade is something else. There's drama here. He's Archenemy Number One.

Actually, he's Archenemy Number Two. Aidan is Number One, based on past behavior, still unforgiven. But don't get excited — there's no drama. So I bump into him running. So what?

You know what. You like the way he looks.

Correction. I like the way he *runs*.

Same difference. Where is he?

We're not there yet. He has a certain route.

Why does he take that route? Is it near where he lives?

I don't know where he lives.

Haven't you asked?

No, I haven't asked. That would suggest I want to know, and I don't.

Is he married?

Not that I know of. There's never been a notice in the paper. There has never been mention of a wife, period — no picture of the two of them at a social event. Had there been one, Sam would have run it. He loves the visual.

What's James waiting for? What's wrong with him?

I don't know, and I don't care. I told you. I like the way he runs. That's it.

I had barely decided that, when I saw him emerge from the cross street ahead. I fully expected him to continue on as he had in the past. Instead, he looked directly at me and slowed. He ran in an oval until I reached him, then, without a word, started up again.

I fell into pace behind him. He must have wanted this, or he wouldn't have slowed, and I couldn't look a gift horse in the mouth. Flat-footed? He was. But he was good. When you run with someone better than you, you run better. It's that way with most sports, don't you think?

I wasn't let down. He ran at a speed that may or may not have been his usual but that was a challenge for me, and I kept up. I wasn't close enough to get the benefit of drafting, but he paced me in ways no one had since I had belonged to a running club years before. Okay, okay. There was an element of pride involved for me. He had issued a challenge; I was determined to meet it. But there was something poetic here. I was using him. I liked that idea.

Staying ten feet behind, I followed him through the back roads of town, and though there were few houses here, we were passed by several cars. Was I worried to be seen running with James? Not at all. My image in town was at rock bottom; I had nothing to lose. James's image was another story. It could be tarnished if he was seen running with me.

But this was his idea, wasn't it? At any time, he could have poured it on and left me in the dust.

I half expected he would, if only to put me in my place. It would have been a very Meade thing to do. Then again, he was a runner. I had come to think of runners as a notch above.

Indeed, he stayed with me — or let me stay with him — until we reached the intersection of Coolidge and Rye, where we had first connected. Then he pointed me off toward Willow, raised his hand in a wave, and continued on straight without looking back.

Tuesday we ran side by side. We didn't talk. He gestured when he wanted to turn, taking a slightly different route from the one the day before, and I was fine letting him choose. More so than me, he knew the roads that were best for running. That freed me to focus on striking the ground with the outside of my heel, on keeping my knees properly flexed, on modulating my breathing, and on keeping up with James. But I did it. Breaking off again at Coolidge and Rye, I felt proud.

He called the house that night. I don't know what he would have done if Phoebe had answered the phone. I didn't ask him that. Our conversation was brief.

"Are you running tomorrow?" he asked.

"Yes."

"Want to try off-road?"

I was game. My knee was bothering me a little. A dirt path would be more forgiving than pavement. "Sure."

"The varsity course at eight?"

"I'll be there."

We were the only two who were there, I realized as I drove through the parking lot to the very back and turned a corner to the strip at the edge of the woods, but that was no surprise. Varsity runners didn't do the cross-country course at eight in the morning, not during the school year, not during preseason, which this was. They would be here later. For now, the place was as empty as the path through the woods promised to be.

Not that I would have missed James, even if the lot had been full. He was driving the large black SUV I had seen him in once before. Tony O'Roarke had been at the wheel then, but there was no driver now. The windows were open — it was hot already at eight — and James was stretching on the grass not far from the start of the path.

I parked and joined him there, and I have to say, I felt a qualm then. Shy? I don't know. He had been bare-chested each of the previous days; today he wore a tank top. Somehow, that seemed more personal — as if, since he had known for sure today that we would be running together, he had given the matter of bareness some thought.

Okay. I know. He didn't want anyone getting the wrong idea — namely, me.

But covering up just that little bit didn't do a thing in terms of propriety, at least, not in *my* mind. His arms and legs remained bare — long and firm, with lean ankles and wrists — and the tank top didn't hide wisps of chest hair or the darker shadow under his arms. Or the shadow of his beard. Or his Adam's apple. James Meade was very male.

Then again, maybe he seemed more imposing simply because he was standing in place rather than running. Granted, he looked something like a heron, holding one foot back by his butt and balanced on the other. But he was impressive even on one foot.

Whatever, I felt vaguely intimidated. Greg and I had been at a media dinner once and I had been introduced to George Clooney. Okay, maybe George Clooney isn't *your* cup of tea, but he stirs something in me. James had the same effect now, possibly for a similar reason. He was a celebrity of sorts, certainly the star attraction of Middle River. Given the synergy between the town and the mill, he was the direction both would take once Sandy retired. In that sense, he was a powerful man.

Power was alluring. That was the intellectual me speaking.

The visceral me suddenly saw raw chemistry. I hadn't felt anything physical for Tom Martin, and with Aidan Meade, I had probably been too young and green to get past who he was. Not so with James. He was hot.

Shy? Intimidated? Baloney. I was *attracted* to him — which was the *stupidest* thing in the world. Was I a *masochist?* James was a Meade, of the same ilk as Aidan. Being attracted to James was just plain dumb.

I was that. I was also tongue-tied.

So I stretched. Make that — *we* stretched. I went through my usual routine, all habit, which was good, because my mind wasn't on it. I didn't have to look at James to be aware of what his body was doing. Long legs stretching — torso bent over spread thighs — chest lifted by hands clasped higher than I could ever reach — head angling slowly from one side all the way to the other.

Foreplay? Oh boy. By the time we started

to run, I was loaded with so much energy that I would have beat my own time even without James's pacing.

The path was narrow, so he went ahead, and I focused my thoughts on the run. Off-road was different from road running. It took more concentration simply because the terrain was less even.

By the way, the varsity course was on Cooper's Hill. *Cooper's* Hill. Ring a bell? If so, you are astute. Cooper's Hill is indeed home to Cooper's *Point,* the site of my humiliation at the hands of Aidan Meade. The point, as opposed to the hill, is a lookout over the town, reached by a path that ascends through the woods. It's an easy climb, even by flashlight at night — ten minutes, max. As for the hill itself, its only other attraction is a slope for sledders in winter.

The running course, on the other hand, is a favorite of cross-country skiers. It undulates gently around the lower part of the hill for a total of two miles. And if you're thinking that two miles isn't much of a run, keep in mind that two miles running off-road is the equivalent of three on a level surface in terms of time and physical drain.

That said, I was game for another go-round when we finished the first, and gestured this to James when he looked questioningly back. Yes, my knee was tired, but the rest of me was eager. Having gotten past the attraction thing — one cross over the path to Cooper's Point and I was cured — the varsity course was the perfect place to run on a hot, sunny day like this. Other than the length of grass that spanned the sledding slope, the path was generously shaded. Here we ran on a bed of leaves, pine needles, and dirt. Yes, there were exposed tree roots to navigate. I tripped over one early on, and barely managed to catch myself before James looked back. I didn't trip again.

The second round was more draining. I kept up, but was nonetheless grateful when we reached our starting point. James was covered with sweat — rivulets dripping down his face until he brushed them away with an arm, that arm and the other glistening, body hair plastered to skin — but I was no better myself. The hair that had escaped from my ponytail was glued to my slick neck, my face was gleaming, my singlet and shorts clung to sweat dripping beneath. We were both breathing hard, but I wasn't thinking about his body then. I was thinking that the run had been fun.

He must have been thinking it, too, because the look on his wet face was surprisingly pleasant. We stood panting for a minute, just looking at each other. And I grinned. Why in the devil not? If returning to the vicinity of Cooper's Point was a test, I had passed. I had kept up with James. He was staring at me, and I refused to look away.

After a minute, he gave a quick little head shake and went to his car. Pulling two bottles of water from a cooler in the backseat, he handed me one. I finished it off in no time, and gratefully took one of a second pair that he fetched. This one I held to my face; it felt delightful against my flushed and sweaty skin. In time, I closed my eyes, tipped my head back, and put the cool bottle against my neck.

When I finally righted my head and opened my eyes, he was watching me.

Actually, he was watching my breasts.

I cleared my throat. His eyes met mine. Was he embarrassed? No. But that was the power thing. The Meades oozed entitlement. They were shameless when it came to using people — and that was what this was. There was no way that James Meade really wanted Annie Barnes, unless it was tied to thwarting my mission here. But I wasn't falling for it. Like the saying goes — fool me once, shame on you; fool me twice, shame on me.

I wasn't being fooled. If anyone was a user, this time it would be me. That decided, I continued to look at him as I stretched. Oh yes, he was male. If I was drawn, what harm would it be to play awhile? If James could do it, so could I. Running was my Washington thing; as long as my contact with him related to that, I was strong.

Did I feel duplicitous? Not on your life. If anything, I took satisfaction in the knowledge that while I was running with James Meade, I was plotting to screw him.

Uh-oh. That was a poor choice of words. Clearly just a figure of speech.

But you get my point. I might have no longer been out for revenge. But if, as TrueBlue implied, it proved to be the case that toxic waste had been recklessly disposed of, James Meade and his family had some answering to do.

We never did say much of anything that morning, James and I. He didn't look at my breasts again. He looked at my mouth, my eyes, my legs — and he seemed puzzled, like he hadn't expected that I *had* any of those things or that they would function like the same body parts on other women functioned. He looked confused, like he had never dreamed I could run, much less keep up with him.

Of course, with a Meade you never knew what a look meant.

But I wasn't virginal and naive, I wasn't employed by the mill, and I wasn't afraid of James. I thanked him for the water. That was all I said before I headed for my car.

Grace was the one who felt the need to talk. I was barely out of the parking lot when she lit into me.

What are you doing? she asked. She was clearly annoyed. *You don't just . . . toy . . . with a man like that. You go after him with all you have. You could have charmed him. You could have said something sweet. You could have told him he's a great runner. You could have batted your eyelashes, for God's sake.*

Batted my eyelashes? People don't do that nowadays.

If you want to play, play. Milk it, sweetie. This could be a central part of your book.

Book? What book? I'm not writing a book.

I think you should. But you need sex

in it. Sex sells. Real sex. Down-home-and-dirty sex.

I'm selling just fine without that.

You'd sell better with it. Remember what happened when I finally sold **Peyton Place**? *My publisher made me add a sex scene between Constance and Tomas. I wrote it in her office in an hour, and I was not happy. But my readers loved it.* **Peyton Place** *sold twelve million copies. Have any of your books done that?*

No, I reasoned, accelerating as I turned left from School onto Oak, because times have changed. Virtually no book today sells twelve million copies. There's too much competition, too many other books, too many other diversions, like movies, DVDs, and cable TV. Besides, in its day, *Peyton Place* was unique with its sex. Sex in books today is commonplace.

So what's your problem? Seduce James Meade, and you have a great plot.

I stopped where Cedar crossed Oak, let a car pass, then accelerated again. Grace was starting to annoy me. I am not seducing James Meade, I insisted. I'd only be burned. And I'm not writing a book.

You're a disappointment.

You're a pain in the butt.

I'm leaving.

Good. Go. I'm stopping in a second anyway. I want *The New York Times*. And chocolate pennies.

Okay, she tried. *Forget the book. Seduce James Meade, and you'll be able to get the dirt you need on the mill.*

That's disgusting, I mused

It's the best way to get information. Done all the time in my day. You all are even more promiscuous, so what's the problem?

Leave.

I will. But when your search goes nowhere, remember what I've said.

Go!

I heard a siren and at first thought it was a warning — to me, to Grace, to us both. Then I realized it came from the car behind me. Car? Make that police cruiser, from the looks of the top bar with its lights popping and flashing.

Sirens and lights were rare in our town. Thinking something big must have happened, I pulled over by the barbershop to let him pass. To my dismay, he pulled over right behind me and killed the siren. The lights remained on.

I was trying to decide why that was so,

when Marshall Greenwood approached. Leading by his middle with his back ramrod straight, he took his sweet time.

I looked up at him. "Hi."

"License and registration, please," he said in a voice that had grown more gravelly in the years I'd been gone.

I blinked. "Did I do something wrong?"

"You were speeding. License and registration, please." He hooked his hands on his belt, waiting.

"Speeding?" I echoed. "Here? I just stopped. How could I be speeding?"

"The limit's twenty. Sign's right up the block. You were going more than twenty."

I looked around. There had been a car ahead of me, and there were others coming along now that were going at the same rate I had been going.

No. That's not right. They weren't going at the same rate. They had all slowed down to stare at me.

I cleared my throat. "*May*-be I was going twenty-five, but even that's pushing it."

"Twenty-five is above the limit."

"Are you using radar?"

"Don't need to. I know when someone's speeding. License and registration, please."

I had never gotten a speeding ticket in my life. Nor had I ever seen — ever *known*

315

of anyone else to get one on this particular strip. "Is this a new crackdown or something?" I glanced around. There were men on the barbershop bench, men on the rockers outside Harriman's Grocery, men and women in the chairs on the lawn of the town hall. All were watching the goings-on — garish blinking lights were definite attention-getters — but not a one of them was crossing the street. "Was I endangering anyone?"

Marshall sighed. "That's not the point, Miss Barnes. The folks who live here, well, they know the ropes. It's you folks from away, come here and try to do things the way you want with no regard for the greater good. When you're in this town, you have to abide by our laws." He put out a hand, waiting.

Short of causing a scene, I took my license and registration from the glove box.

He was ten minutes in writing up my ticket. I'm sure most of the town knew I was getting it before I actually had the paper in my hand. Cars and trucks rolled past, drivers' heads turned my way. People went in and out of buildings, craning their necks to see. And those blinking lights remained on.

I sat, and I sweated — I was parked in

direct sun. I weathered the heat of dozens of pairs of eyes.

Oh yes, he was doing this on purpose. Marshall Greenwood was Sandy Meade's puppet. But if Sandy thought to intimidate me, his scare tactics were laughable. Sitting there waiting for my speeding ticket under the eyes of every Middle Riverite who passed, I was suddenly inspired.

I did stop for the *Times* and some chocolate pennies, but if Marylou Walker was more chilly than she had been on previous days ringing me up, I didn't care. I was out of there in a flash, tossed the goodies in the car, and drove on home.

Fortuitously, Phoebe had already gone to the store. That meant I didn't have to talk low when I picked up the kitchen phone to call the New Hampshire Department of Environmental Services.

Yes, I know. I argued earlier that I didn't dare call the agency lest someone with Meade connections get wind of it. But that had been Friday; this was Wednesday. That was before TrueBlue appeared as an ally, before my epiphany at the graveyard gave me renewed incentive, before I had held my own side-by-side with none other than the powerful James Meade. It had been before Marshall Greenwood gave me a

317

speeding ticket with *Get out of town* written all over it in invisible ink.

And it had been before my devious little brainstorm.

Chapter 14

I didn't call direct. Rather, I called Greg's assistant in Washington, who knew all the little ins and outs of these things and who just happened to be a friend of mine, too. She patched me through on one of the lines that the network used when discretion was in order.

Didn't think that happened? Think again. Media people have all sorts of tricks up their sleeves. Making untraceable calls is the least of them.

I would far rather have taken the high road, of course, but the circumstances called for caution. How would you feel if you had been stopped in the middle of town for doing what everyone else *always* did, and then were made to sit there while everyone watched? Was Marshall Greenwood really checking my registration that whole time? Was he really checking to see if there were any outstanding warrants against me? No, he was not. He was making me wait for the humiliation of it.

For the record, I was not speeding. This was intimidation, pure and simple. Was *that* taking the high road? Marshall was the law, yet he made me feel helpless and harassed. Moreover, of all the people watching, not one came forward in my defense. They were turning against me, and no, this wasn't more paranoia on my part. Heretofore, their stares had been largely benign. Now they were censorious. Marylou Walker's coldness was a case in point.

What had I ever done to them? The injustice of it infuriated me.

If you've ever felt that, then you'll understand my resorting to subterfuge in making this call — and, as it happened, I didn't even have to lie about who I was. I introduced myself as a novelist who was exploring the issue of mercury pollution for a possible book, and in theory it was true. Though I wasn't planning a book on Middle River, who knew whether the book after the one I was now plotting wouldn't include a twist of this type?

The woman at NHDES never even asked me my name. Trusting and pure, she simply asked what I wanted to know.

"I'm interested in plants in this state that produce mercury waste," I began in a most general way.

"We do have those," she replied.

"Mostly paper plants?"

"That produce mercury? Not exclusively. But mostly."

"Do you monitor them?"

"Yes. Any plant that discharges waste of *any* sort into our waters is required to take out a permit. Then there's testing, monthly or quarterly. Water samples are taken from the point of disposal and are sent to the lab for analysis. We test the air, too, by taking samples of emissions from stacks."

"Who does the testing?"

"Water tests are done by the plant itself. When it comes to air tests, there's usually an observer from our department."

"You don't observe the water sampling?"

"Not usually."

This struck me as a case of the fox guarding the chicken coop. "What's to prevent someone from taking bottled water and claiming it's from the river?"

"The lab would see the difference. We know the chemical makeup of the river."

"What's to prevent someone from taking river water and simply filtering out the bad stuff?"

"If someone went to that extreme, it would suggest there was major pollution, and if that's the case, the air sample would show it. We also do annual inspections to see that plants are properly disposing of their hazardous waste. Disposal is key. Not only does on-site disposal need to be done to code, but everything exceeding the legal limit must be loaded into drums and sent to an authorized site. The mills pay for the disposal of this extra waste. They keeps records of how much goes where. They also pay the state up front for every pound of waste produced."

"What kinds of numbers are we talking about?"

"That depends on the plant."

"Say, Baxter Mills. Or Wentworth Paper. Or Northwood."

"Any of those could produce upward of six or seven hundred pounds in a given period. At three cents per pound to the state, there would be an assessed fee of two thousand dollars."

Two thousand dollars didn't strike me as being prohibitive. Northwood could certainly handle that without folding. "Do you check the accuracy of what they report?"

"Only when there's a discrepancy from the norm."

"How do you know the norm?"

"We have records. There's a Web site, if

you'd like to look." She gave me the URL and explained how it worked.

"And test results?" I asked. "Does the Web site show those, too?"

"No. Mills keep the results. So do we, for a while. Then they're archived."

Northwood wasn't about to show me its files. "Can someone like me access your archives?"

"Yes. But there's a process."

I knew how that went. Processes required applications. They also required time. Between the information I would have to give on the former, and the ability that the latter gave for someone from NHDES to notify Northwood, I would be cooked.

"Okay," I said, "in a slightly different vein, exposure to mercury is known to create health problems. Does your department deal with those?"

"We know what the health problems are. Do we monitor them in specific cases? That would be difficult. Mercury poisoning is hard to diagnose. We hear about the occasional acute case, but that's it. A local health commissioner might know more. You could try contacting one of those."

"That's a thought," I said appreciatively.

And it was a thought, albeit a moot one. Middle River didn't *have* a health commissioner. "You're very kind to be helping me this way."

"It's part of my job," she replied pleasantly.

"Then you don't mind another question or two?"

"Of course not."

I spoke hypothetically now. "If, say, a paper plant wanted to cover up the extent of its production of mercury waste, what would it do?"

"It might bury waste improperly. Or falsify records."

"Could it cover up an actual spill?"

"Technically, yes. If the spill was a major one, though, there would be obvious repercussions, people suddenly very ill. In that case, a plant might try to cover up the extent of the spill, but they wouldn't be able to hide the fact of its occurrence."

"What about bribery?" I suggested.

She chuckled. "That would be hard, given the numbers of people who work at these plants."

Clearly, she didn't know the power of the Meades. "How could a person — my protagonist, for instance — uncover an attempted cover-up of a spill?"

"That's a little outside my jurisdiction."

"Take a guess. Pure speculation."

She was a minute thinking about it. "There would likely be memos, but they would be internal. He would need someone on the inside to provide him with those. Same thing if you want to show that records had been falsified."

TrueBlue. He was my man. He could give me this.

Knowing what I had to do next, I gave in to genuine curiosity. "How does one clean up a mercury spill?"

"Not easily," the woman replied. "A cleanup involves decontaminating everything that came into contact with the mercury — clothes, skin, flooring, machinery. Since mercury is heavy, it sinks into the ground, so in the case of a ground spill, a cleanup could entail digging up dirt and extracting whatever of the metal that seeped in. It's very costly, and it's time-consuming."

"Do you believe that there have been spills in New Hampshire?"

"I know there have been."

"Any plants I know?" I teased and added a quick, "I could interview people there for a touch of authenticity."

"Fortunately for us — unfortunately for

you — they've closed. That's the thing. A mercury spill can devastate a company. You understand why they'd try to keep it under wraps."

I checked out the URL she had given me. Much of the information provided was technical, such as identification numbers and codes, but when it came to waste description, total quantity, and weight in pounds, the data were clear. Up until eight years ago, Northwood had produced mercury waste. When I compared the amount with that of other paper mills, it was similar. Not that I cared about other mills. My sister wasn't sick in those towns. Only in Middle River.

To: TrueBlue
From: Annie Barnes
Subject: Possibilities

It appears that Northwood is not on a DES watch list, which is consistent with the claim that it no longer produces mercury waste. So I'm guessing that one or more of the following is true:

(1) Northwood falsified past reports

*to hide the amount of waste pro-
duced.*

*(2) Northwood falsified past tests to
hide the strength of toxicity in that
waste.*

*(3) Northwood improperly disposed
of waste.*

*(4) Northwood covered up the inci-
dence of spills.*

*Do you have – or can you get – in-
formation on any of this? Ideally, I'd
like copies of internal memos.*

I sent it off with a sense of satisfaction.
Moving ahead on the mercury front was
key.

Right behind it was Phoebe. She wasn't
getting any better. I had made reservations
to fly to New York with her, but she was
still worried about Sabina.

I wanted Sabina in my corner. I really
did. I figured she would continue to fight
me on the mercury thing, but I was hoping
to reach some kind of agreement on
Phoebe.

And then there was Tom. I owed him an
update on what I was doing. I also wanted
him to give me the name of a doctor I
might take Phoebe to see in New York.

Killing two birds with one stone, I phoned my friend Berri, the one in Washington who had helped me plan the dinner I made at Sabina's last Friday.

"Hey," I said, delighted to hear her voice at the other end of the line. "I'm so glad you're home." I meant that, and it had less to do with menu plans than with warmth. I had been in Middle River for a full week now. My reception was getting cooler by the minute.

"Annie, how *are* you, sweetie?"

"Better for having you pick up the phone. It's lonely up here."

"Lonely?" she teased. "With your sisters and Sam and Omie and all the other people you've warned me would be watching what you're doing?"

Berri had been an outlet for me during moments of doubt prior to my leaving Washington. I had prepared her well — prophetically, actually, given the earlier scene on Oak. People were certainly watching me. *Loads* of them.

"It's not the same as meeting you and Amanda for coffee. I feel like I've been gone a month."

"Me, too," she said. "By the way, we're all reading *Peyton Place*."

"You are? Amanda and Jocelyn, too?"

"All three of us."

"That's fabulous," I said in excitement. I was also touched. My friends were busy women with limited time to read. One book a month was pretty much their limit, and it was usually a current best seller. The only reason they would have chosen *Peyton Place* was me. That expression of devotion couldn't have come at a better time. I was definitely suffering from a need to feel loved. "So, what do you think?"

"I *like* it. I mean, I'm only into the first fifty pages, but she's a good writer. I didn't think she would be."

"Thought it was just a trashy novel?"

"*Yes.* We're meeting next week to discuss it."

"Oh no," I cried. "Wait'll I get back!" I wanted to be in on that discussion.

"Preliminaries are next week. Trust me, we won't have finished it. Amanda's work schedule is light, but Jocelyn has to have syllabuses ready in two weeks. Me, I have a diversion, too." Her voice lowered in excitement. "I met a guy."

This wasn't news. Berri was *always* meeting guys. When I laughed and said that, she said, "I mean, *met* a guy. His name is John. He is very smart, very handsome, and very cool. He was at the function I ran last night. I'm seeing him Friday night."

Berri was a professional volunteer. Last night was the Kidney Foundation, if memory stood me well. "What does he do?"

She snorted. "This is Washington, so he's a lawyer. But he's not like any other lawyer I've met. He has long hair, for one thing. And an earring. And a tattoo." She tacked on the last with something I can only describe as pride.

"Where's the tattoo?"

"I don't know. Obviously, I saw the earring and the hair, but when I went looking for the tattoo, he got all smug. He said he didn't *do* that on the first date. I mean, he's just adorable. And a good person. He does legal work for the foundation pro bono. And he wants kids."

"How do you know that?" I asked.

"He said it right off the bat, because there was this *impossible* child that someone brought to the event, and John was the only one who could get the kid to keep his hands off the hors d'oeuvres. I mean, the child touched every single one on the tray. When I said John was a natural, he said he adores his nieces and nephews and can't wait to have some of his own. He's twenty-nine."

I caught my breath. "A younger man." Berri was thirty-three, like me. "Oh, Berri, I hope it works for you. I'll keep my fingers crossed." And I would. Berri wanted to be married. She wanted the house, the kids, the cars. She wanted *love*.

But then, didn't we all?

"How was the tenderloin?" she asked.

"Incredible. The whole meal was incredible. They loved it. That's one of the reasons I'm calling. I need another meal plan."

"Who's this one for?"

"Some of the same people, some different. I want to make something here that I can bring to different houses ready to eat."

"A one-dish meal?"

"If possible."

"Give me five. I'll call you back."

The phone rang in three. "That was fast," I said without a hello. "You are such a sweetie. Do you know what it means to me to have someone like you?"

There was a split second's silence, then a low and amused, "Actually not. Tell me."

It was James, of course. I would have recognized his voice even if there were dozens of other men calling me here, which there weren't. Even kept down in

331

volume, his voice was deeper and more resonant than that of most men I knew, and it did the same thing to me as the sight of him did. Chemistry? Big-time.

I would have been lying if I said I wasn't pleased that he'd called. I was glad, though, that he couldn't see the flush on my cheeks or hear the thud-thud-thudding in my chest.

What could I do?

I laughed. "Sorry about that. I was just talking with a friend in D.C. and she promised to call me back. Did you *hear* what happened to me on the way home this morning?"

"I did. Marshall takes his job too seriously sometimes. I assume it's just a fine."

"It's more than that. It's the principle of the thing. He's had his eye on me. He's been waiting. So what's next?"

"Next is you go down to town hall and pay the fine so that no one can find fault. Then you drive very, very carefully."

I had been thinking of what *Marshall* would do next. As for the other, of course, James was right.

He went on, still in that low voice, and it struck me that he was trying to be discreet about the call. "I have a meeting about to start and another one early tomorrow, so running before work is out. Can you make it after work? Say, seven?"

"Sure," I said with remarkable calm. "Same place as today?"

"If that works for you."

"It does."

James's call had made my day. It gave me something to look forward to, something to *plot* about as I waited for TrueBlue's reply. I logged on soon after Berri called back, but there was nothing then, nor when I checked at midday. I checked again when I returned from Harriman's, and again, later, when the chicken pot pie went into the oven.

Yes, chicken pot pie. Make that *pies*, plural; there were actually three biggies. But these were no ordinary chicken pot pies. Berri had merged several recipes to come up with what she called a *Tuscan* chicken pot pie, which contained, among other things, artichoke hearts, black olives, sun-dried tomatoes, and garlic. Had I ever doubted her skill, those doubts would have vanished when the kitchen filled with unbelievably good smells.

The crusts had puffed and turned a warm amber when the timer rang. I took the pies from the oven and put them on the top of the stove, and the smell was even better then.

I checked the time. It was nearly four. Yes, I could drop Sabina's at the house. But I really wanted to go to the mill. I hadn't seen it in fifteen years. I was curious.

I opened the lower cabinet, where Mom had always kept the insulated bags she used for toting hot food to church suppers. When they weren't there, I checked each of the other lower cabinets. I checked the higher cabinets. I checked the pantry.

I could have called Phoebe, but I was trying to leave her alone for the day. I had been in and out of the store Monday and Tuesday. I was tired of running menial errands. I was also tired of seeing Phoebe struggle to hide whatever it was that ailed her, which also raised the issue of whether, given her current state of mind, she would remember whether the insulated bags had been tossed out in the kitchen renovation, or if not, where they were.

I drove back into town. Harriman's had what I wanted. I bought two. Ignoring the pointed stares of the clerks, I paid for them, returned to my car, and drove home.

Five minutes later, with two of those chicken pot pies duly packed and riding shotgun with me, I approached the mill.

So here we are, at the mouth of the ogre's cave, I mused. It didn't look evil, that's for sure. The entrance was actually lovely. Indeed, the whole place was quite attractive, but I'm getting ahead of myself. Let me paint the picture of what I saw; it's what I do well.

The mill complex was located north of town, which, given what we now know about toxicity flowing downstream, was not the wisest choice. At the time of its founding, though, the roots of the town were already in place, and the land south of those roots lay on solid granite. Hence, by default, the mill was built to the north.

We thought of Benjamin Meade as the founder. That was the story taught in our schools and reinforced during the civics course, when third graders were given a tour of the mill, but it was actually Benjamin's father, Matthias, who got the thing going. In the early 1900s, it was strictly a lumbering operation. Forestry done farther north floated logs to Matthias's mill, where they were skinned and cut into wood planks for housing in the cities farther south. By the 1930s, Benjamin had taken over, and in a short time had broadened the scope of operations enough to genuinely merit being credited as the founder of the modern mill.

Even then, though, it began small, a single structure on the river at the end of a road cut through woods, and this same road was what I saw now, albeit with a new, large, and — I have to say — tasteful sign. As it had a century before, the woods that rose around it were filled with hemlock and pine, balsam and spruce — all evergreen, thick and picturesque throughout the year and deeply fragrant in ways the mill itself was not. A stone entry had been added, waist-high and crafted of rocks displaced when the more recent of the buildings was built. The stonemason was always an Arsenault; Arsenaults had been doing stonework around the mill since Benjamin's earliest days. They were actually kept on the payroll. This was one of the little gems we learned in third grade. Did we appreciate it then? Of course not. Now I understood that this fact was yet another nail in the coffin of dissension that might mar the face of the mill. No Arsenault would report suspicious activity. Those you pay, repay you with loyalty.

Arsenaults were artists; their stonework, done without mortar, was a sight to behold. Here at the entry to the mill, the mosaic of rock ranged in color from amber to slate and in size from small, narrow slabs to pieces the size of a desktop monitor. I have watched stone walls being built and know the artistry involved. Here, those rocks were arranged not only in a way to make the wall sturdy, but to make it an interesting tableau of local stone. The finished product curved gently on either side of the road in a pastoral invitation to enter.

Enter I did, and without pause. There was no guard's station here. The Meades didn't need a guard, but ensured their safety in more subtle ways. I guessed that there were cameras mounted on the trees, with a security guard monitoring the comings and goings. I wondered what he would make of my car.

The road was wider than I remembered it, a change made perhaps in recent years to accommodate the Meades' SUVs. The service road would be at the other end of the complex and wider yet to accommodate the gargantuan semis that carried the mill's goods from the shipping bays to the world.

From these beautiful stone walls, the road stole through scented woods for a quarter of a mile before the first of the buildings appeared. They were attractive redbrick Capes with a Colonial feel — mainly single-floor structures, they had tall doorways with pediments atop, dormer windows in the roof, and white shutters and columns out front. No single building was large, but there were many of them, added as the need arose. This was the Administrative Campus, the sign said — don't you *love* the word *campus?* — and beneath the heading were a flurry of arrows. One pointed to the building that housed the sales department, another the marketing department. Individual arrows pointed toward the executive offices, product development, and the Data Center.

Sabina would be in the last, but I didn't immediately drive there. Taking the scenic route, I followed the road around and between these buildings — and yes, I did give a special look to the one housing the executive offices. James's SUV sat out front. Make that Aidan's SUV, since there was a child seat in the back. There was also a large, dark sedan with tinted windows that had Sandy Meade's name written all over it.

The building that held the Meades' offices was similar to the others in its redbrick and Cape style, but the roof was higher and the dormer windows not only for show. This building had a spacious second floor that was largely glass from the back. Sandy Meade had his office here, beside the conference room where he ruled. He claimed that the second floor gave him a view of the river that he wouldn't have if he were downstairs. We all suspected he simply liked being raised above the rest.

With the exception of that second floor, the executive offices matched the other buildings in appearance. Trees and shrubs were well tended, a testament to Northwood's full-time grounds crew. Lawns, newly mown and still bearing the mark of the mower and a sweet, summer-warm smell, were dotted with white lawn chairs. Lilac and rhododendron, their blooms long gone, softened the expanse of brick between windows. There wasn't a weed in sight.

The guts of the mill lay ahead, but they were hidden behind trees. First came a trio of buildings that were as charming in purpose as they were in style, starting with the Clubhouse. Wholly subsidized by the mill, the Clubhouse was a meeting place for town events. I remembered my mother spending time there in the formative days of a group called the Middle River WIBs — Women in Business. Meetings were held over dinner, the latter provided by the mill in the form of a bribe. No one particularly wanted to drive all the way out there to meet, but the promise of a free meal — and a gourmet one at that — brought the WIBs. Other groups followed suit, but only after the place was rebuilt after one of those gourmet meals caused a fire in the kitchen that quickly spread to the rest. No one was injured in the fire, and the rebuilt Clubhouse had every safety feature imaginable. According to the *Middle River Times*, most every major civic group held its meetings here now. Northwood catered them all.

Stifling dissent? Oh yes.

Opposite the Clubhouse was the Gazebo. Embedded in trees, it overlooked the river and was totally charming. Many a Middle River mill couple had married there. The Meades donated flowers and champagne. Wasn't that nice?

And finally, ahead just a bit more, was the Children's Center. Northwood was in the forefront here, opening an on-site day care center before it was the thing to do. Parents paid a small fee, with the rest of the costs picked up by the mill. Can you imagine the gratitude those parents felt for the Meades?

The working plant was so close it was frightening. On certain days there was a faint sulfur smell, but I didn't catch that today. Perhaps I was too focused on the sudden fall-off of the woods and the emergence of those redbrick buildings, risen like a phoenix from the ashes of the big fire. That red brick notwithstanding, there was no charm here. These buildings were functional — large square and rectangular things that housed the machines that produced paper from logs. As a third grader viewing them, I had thought they were cavernous. Looking at them from the outside now, parked at a guard station, I still found them huge. There were also more now than back then, a tribute to Northwood's growth. Looking down the main drag, I saw one redbrick building after another. I also saw people on foot and in cars. The day shift was finishing its work, leaving the plant on the service road.

"May I help you?" asked the guard.

I took in a deep breath. "Actually, I think not. I'm going to the Data Center." Shooting him my most brilliant smile, I shifted into reverse, backed around, and cruised toward the forest again. Was I afraid of getting close to the plant? Probably, and it had nothing to do with exposure to mercury. The Meades didn't like trespassers — and, yes, there was that little sign.

The Administrative Campus was far more welcoming. Pulling in beside Sabina's ageless Chevy in the small parking strip at the Data Center, I climbed from the car, lifted one of the insulated bags from the seat, and approached the door.

The Data Center was unique. For one thing, the air here was cool to accommodate the needs of the machines. For another, rather than four lavish offices, each with a smiling face near its door, there was a large open room on one side with three desks and, on the other side behind a glass wall, the server.

Two of the three desks were taken, the one farthest from the door by Sabina. She wasn't surprised to see me; someone had warned her I was here. I smiled at the other worker, a man, and went over to Sabina.

"This should probably go in your car, so that it stays warm."

Sabina rose quickly and led the way back outside. If I didn't know better, I'd have thought she wanted me gone. Either that, or not seen. Or not *heard*. Who knew how trustworthy her coworker was?

Funny, though, she didn't stalk ahead. Once I cleared the door, she walked by my side. "What's with all the cooking? Is it the old 'way to the heart through the stomach' theory?"

"Actually," I said, "yes. I don't know how else to do it."

"Does it really matter?" she asked without looking at me. Her car wasn't locked. She opened the passenger door and reached for the bag.

"Yes, it matters."

"What is this?"

"Chicken and veggies in a pie. Oh. Wait a second." I ran back to my car, reached into the narrow space behind the seat, and pulled out a loaf of Italian bread. I put it on top of the insulated bag that Sabina had placed on her seat.

"It smells good," she said and closed the door. She leaned back against it and looked at me, more puzzled now than annoyed. "Do you *want* something?"

I might have gone into the thing about wanting family. But I had already done that.

"Today, yes," and rushed out the words. "I want your approval. I've decided to go to New York with Phoebe, because I don't think she can handle the buying trip herself."

"Shouldn't Joanne be the one to go with her?"

"She needs Joanne here. It's either me with her in New York, or no one. She's already told me I know nothing about buying, and she's right, but I do know New York, and at least I can make sure she doesn't fall or get lost or make some kind of gross error."

"She isn't that bad," Sabina said with a tentativeness I hadn't heard before.

"I've been here a full week, and she's no better. It's starting to frighten her, but she refuses to see Tom Martin. So while we're in New York, I'm taking her to a doctor."

"Who?"

"I don't know yet. Tom's my next dinner delivery." I grinned. "I'm hoping he'll be pleased enough with the gesture to help us get an appointment with someone who knows about things like this."

"Things like this?" she asked with a grain of distrust. "You aren't still on the mercury thing, are you?"

"First, I'm on the Parkinson's and Alzheimer's thing."

Chewing on a corner of her mouth, she looked off toward the woods and nodded.

"I'm not telling her beforehand about the doctor," I went on. "She'll fight me on it, I know she will. When I do, I want to be able to tell her you agree with me on this."

Sabina took a breath and looked me in the eye. "I'm worried about her, too."

"Then we're in agreement about the doctor?"

"I still think it's psychological."

"If a doctor rules out the others, she may be willing to see your friend the therapist."

Sabina nodded and looked away again. This time, though, she grew alert. I followed her gaze. Aidan Meade was striding down the drive. He came right up to us, bold as brass, put his hands on his hips, looked from Sabina to me and back, and smiled. "Don't let me interrupt."

Don't let him interrupt? I mused. Planting himself right here?

I was thinking of a pithy response, when Sabina said, "You're not interrupting. Annie can't stay. She was just dropping off dinner for my family. She's a pretty good cook."

He gave me a smug look. "We're Betty Crocker now, are we?"

I might have said any *number* of things then, but none of them would have done Sabina any good, and she was my concern.

We actually had a meeting of minds here. I cared more about cultivating that than cutting Aidan down to size.

Besides, I had a date with James — well, not a date in the traditional sense, but we were forging a bond. Runners were good at that. But I doubted Aidan knew. So we also had a secret, James and I. That gave me a sense of strength.

I touched Sabina's arm. "It's fully cooked, so reheating at three-fifty for ten minutes should do it." Without another glance at Aidan, I went to my car and drove off.

Chapter 15

Aidan Meade didn't like Annie Barnes. He didn't *trust* Annie Barnes. She was up to no good. He had known it from the start. In Middle River for a whole month? That spelled trouble. If he hadn't sensed it from her holier-than-thou attitude when he had seen her in town that first day, he would have known it from the odd things she did. And it wasn't just him. Marshall was concerned, which meant Sandy was concerned, and when Sandy was concerned, he took it out on Aidan. And now Nicole, putting him on the hot seat no more than an hour before. He hadn't been prepared for *that* one, not when everything was going so well.

"Got a minute?" she had intercommed from her desk as she often did when she had material to run through with him, but he knew something was up the minute she entered his office. For one thing, though she usually teased him about it, she didn't even seem to notice that he had his golf club in hand and was chipping balls into a

Chip-Mate on the far side of the room. Nor, ominously, did she have a stack of papers in her hand.

Closing the door, she came right up to him and said in an intimate voice, "We may have a problem. I got a call from Hal Healy this morning. He's seen Kaitlin talking with Annie Barnes. He knew I'd want to know. We've both been concerned about Kaitlin, because she's had a real attitude lately. He's worried that Annie is not a good role model for the girls in town." Her eyes held his. "Me, I'm worried about something else."

"What's that?" Aidan asked. Kaitlin's attitude wasn't his problem.

"I'm worried Kaitlin knows."

"About *us*?" he asked in surprise. "How could she know? We don't do anything outside this office."

"What about Concord? Or Worcester? Or New York?"

"We were working."

She folded her arms over her chest. "Uh-huh, working up a sweat without a stitch of clothes on."

"Come on, Nicki, how could she possibly know about those times?" he asked as he set the club aside.

"Who knows — suspicion, rumor, guesswork, spies? — but if she's angry at me, giving Annie Barnes the scoop would be one way to hit back. She hates that I hate her father. No matter that she caught him cheating on *me*, somehow I'm at fault. The problem is, if word of what we do gets out, Anton will use it. He's been waiting for something like this — just waiting for me to slip up so that he has an excuse to get out of the marriage without being called a cad by everyone in town."

Aidan gripped her arms and gave them an affectionate shake. "You haven't slipped up. You don't tell friends, do you?"

"*God*, no. I don't tell *anyone*."

Of course, she didn't. She knew when she had a good thing going. She was the best-paid assistant in the company, and she was worth every cent. "And you don't know for sure that Kaitlin knows," he reminded her.

"No, and I can't exactly ask. But why else would she be talking to Annie Barnes? What would my daughter have to say to that woman? Kaitlin's been distant lately. I could feel it rolling off her when she was sitting between Anton and me last Sunday in church. According to Hal, that was right after she talked with Annie."

"Get her to a therapist."

"And have her tell what she knows to someone else? Not wise, Aidan. You know how things are in this town. Confidentiality is a pipe dream."

Aidan was starting to tire of the issue. *He* hadn't made the mess of the DuPuises' marriage. "Talk to Kaitlin. Get on her good side. Buy her something. What about a little car?"

"Anton refuses."

"What do you want *me* to do?"

"Shut down Annie Barnes."

Aidan laughed. "Talk about pipe dreams."

Nicole pulled away from him. "This isn't funny." He reached out and pulled her back, but her eyes were flashing. "Aidan, this isn't funny. If Anton divorces me, I'm sunk. Sunk means without money, and that's the whole point of my marriage. I like where I am. I like what I do. I like what *we* do. If Anton finds out, this is done. You think your wife will put up with your playing around? You blew two other marriages because you couldn't keep your pants zipped. Didn't she make you sign a prenup giving her more money if you cheat? Or was that a story you told me, so I'd know to keep my mouth shut? Well, I have. So maybe the leak is on *your* end."

"You really are beautiful when you're angry."

"*Ai*-dan! *Lis*-ten to me!"

But he was feeling aroused. "There's no leak on my end, not yet, but soon. You are so sexy." He kissed her.

"Aidan," she protested against his mouth, but she didn't resist the kiss. So he deepened it. At the same time, he backed her against the door, locked it, and slipped both hands into her blouse.

She always wore a blouse, usually silk, and a bra, usually lacy, and there were times when he played with the feel of those fabrics against her, but he was impatient today. Freeing her breasts in a symmetrical sweep of his hands, he put a thumb to one nipple and his mouth to the other.

"I don't know what to do, Aidan," she said, but it was little more than a breathy murmur. She had her hands in his hair, holding his head close.

"Do *this*, baby," he whispered against her hard flesh. Reaching under her skirt, he lowered her panties, then his fly. In seconds, he was inside her, and she was ready for him that fast. She always was, which was one of the reasons their relationship worked. He wasn't interested in foreplay when the need hit him hard. The way she moved and the sounds she made told him she felt the same.

It was over quickly and here, too, this was good. She was satisfied, he was satisfied. Usually, that was that.

This day, though, she didn't let it go. After righting her clothes, she straightened and said, "The business about your prenup? The only reason I mention it is to remind you that you have a stake in this, too. It's in your best interest to make sure that Annie Barnes doesn't go public with even the slightest hint of what we do. If I go down, I'm not going down alone."

Aidan had been checking to make sure his pants looked all right. Slowly he raised his eyes. "What does that mean?"

"It means that I refuse to be poor. If my husband divorces me because of what we do here, I'm assuming you'll help me out."

That actually sounded like a threat. "What are you talking about, Nicole? Nothing is going to happen."

"Good," she said, then smiled. "I just needed to say that." And she left.

Aidan stared at the door without moving. The longer he stared, the more annoyed he grew. He didn't like being threatened, especially not by a woman. He was irascible when his phone rang, and grew worse when the voice at the other end informed him that Annie Barnes was cruising around Northwood's grounds. When he set off to confront her sister, he was positively gunning for bear — all the more so when he found Annie right there, and then, as calmly as you please, she talked about delivering dinner, then got in her car and took off.

Annie was a loose cannon. He had no idea what she was planning to do. Sabina was another story. She was on *his* payroll. He couldn't control what she did on her own time, but he'd be damned if she would aid and abet the enemy on Northwood's dime.

"What did she want?" he asked.

"She brought dinner," Sabina replied, so much like her sister — he had never seen it before — right down to the calmness, that it ticked him off more.

"That was an excuse," he said. "She drove all the way up to the plant. Why do you think she did that?"

"I didn't know she had. Maybe she just wanted to see what's changed since she was here last."

"Maybe she's scoping out the place."

"Scoping it out? For what?" Sabina asked, sounding amused.

"Well, you'd have to tell me that," he shot back. "Don't tell me she's just curious about changes. This company means nothing to her. She's looking to cause trouble, Sabina — and I'm not the only one who thinks it. Even Hal Healy is worried."

"Hal? What does Hal have to do with Northwood?"

"Nothing. But he's seen her talking with some of the young girls in town. He's worried she's a bad influence."

"She's a best-selling author," Sabina reasoned. "She's a successful woman. That makes her a *good* influence."

"Not if she fires these girls up. Think of Annie Barnes, and you think of *Peyton Place*. Think of *Peyton Place*, and you think of sex. Let's face it. Your sister lives life in the fast lane. You have an impressionable daughter. Don't you worry about things like this?"

Sabina had the gall to laugh. "Of course, I do, but not because of Annie. I worry about the boys in this town. Look at you. We were in school together, Aidan. I remember the things you did."

Aidan had done nothing more than any other healthy, red-blooded male would do. Yeah, yeah. She would say he did do more because he was a Meade and could get away with it, and she would dredge up the case of Annie and Cooper's Point. But that was NA — not applicable — to the discussion at hand. "I didn't touch your sister."

"I know. You were too busy touching Kiki Corey. And there were plenty of others before and after. Come on, Aidan. Don't play the prude."

First Nicki, now Sabina. He didn't like it when women bested him with words. "Am I your boss?" he asked.

"What does that have to do with this?"

"I deserve respect. I'm telling you that your sister is looking for trouble. I don't want you laughing in my face."

She didn't reply. Rather, her face grew blank. And that was worse. That was *insolent.*

"Control your sister, Sabina, or there will be repercussions."

Still she didn't reply, just stared at him with that blank look.

"If I feel," he said, "that your relationship with your sister raises a security problem for this company, I'll replace you."

"Replace me?"

"Fire you. Control her, Sabina. I want her the hell out of town."

★ ★ ★

Sabina watched him walk off. She had known Annie would be a problem. Hadn't she begged her to keep her nose out of Middle River business — hadn't she *pleaded* with her that first morning in Phoebe's house? She had told her what was at stake, and now it wasn't just theory. Thanks to her sister, Sabina might well lose her job. Annie was *the* most stubborn, *the* most bullheaded, ornery, impossible person she knew!

Simmering quietly, Sabina glanced back at the office. She couldn't work now. She was too annoyed.

And why should she work? It was five. Wasn't that her own assistant packing it in?

"See you tomorrow," he called over the roofs of their cars. She raised a hand in acknowledgment.

He left at five every day. She stayed later. Was it pride in her work? A sense of professional responsibility? The desire to please her bosses?

But now Aidan had threatened her job. That galled her. And he wanted her to make Annie leave town. That galled her even more. Annie had as much right to be here as Aidan did. She was nosy, but nosiness wasn't a crime. Sabina would absolutely not tell her to leave.

She might get a little closer to her. Talk with her more. Get a feel for how she spent her days. That would be productive.

Her eyes fell to the dinner that lay on the seat of her car. Aidan was right; Annie had come about more than dinner. She had come about Phoebe, which was actually a good thing. It was actually a *kind* thing. Phoebe needed help. It was time to admit that. If Annie was willing to get the ball rolling, how could Sabina complain?

Chapter 16

I was exiting past those beautiful stone walls, leaving Northwood behind and heading for the Clinic, when I had a thought. It was after five. If Tom Martin had left for the day, my showing up there would create gossip with nothing at all to show for it on my end.

So I pulled over to the side of the road, took my cell phone from my purse, and called just to check. Sure enough, the answering service came on. *"No,"* I replied casually, *"no message, I'll just catch him tomorrow,"* and clicked off. I called Directory Assistance, asked for Tom's home number, and was automatically connected.

I recognized his voice immediately. It had an intrinsic warmth. "Tom? It's Annie Barnes. I cooked you dinner. Can I drop it off?"

His words smiled. "Cooked me dinner? That's *so* nice. When can you get here? We're starved — you know I have a sister, don't you?"

"I do. There's enough for four."

"Then maybe you'll eat with us?"

"I'll sit for a bit, but I promised to be home so that Phoebe isn't alone. Want to tell me where you live?"

He did that with total trust. There was definitely a rapport here.

Smiling, I was returning the cell phone to my purse when the police cruiser came up alongside. There were no lights now, no audience, just Marshall and me. My smile faded. It wasn't that I felt physically threatened being alone with him on a quiet road. Uneasy was more apt. I had passed a few cars, though saw none now. After our last run-in, I was wondering if the man would be better or worse without witnesses.

He didn't get out of his car, just called across the passenger's seat and out the open window, "Got a problem?"

That should be your line, Grace said in a huff.

I agreed, but knew better than to say it aloud. I simply smiled. "No problem, thanks." I started the car.

"We don't like people using cell phones while they're driving," he called.

"I agree. It's dangerous. That's why I pulled over to talk."

"We ticket people for talking while they drive."

359

Is he kidding? Grace cried, indignant. *These people talk on cells all the time. We didn't have them in my day. Far better, if you ask me.*

I wasn't asking her. She sounded like my grandmother would have sounded had she been alive. They were roughly the same age.

But cell phones were a fact of life — as was the power that went with Marshall Greenwood's badge. I might sass him all I wanted, but he'd only get me again. It was infuriating. *And* if I dwelt on how infuriating it was (as I had done after he stopped me in town), his power only increased.

So, still smiling, I said a pleasant, "I'll remember that."

"I'd advise it."

"Thank you."

He seemed to want to carry on the argument, but didn't know where to go with it. I had deprived him of opposition. It was the wisest thing I could have done.

He frowned, still thinking. Apparently realizing there was nothing more to say, he simply faced forward and drove off. It struck me then that Marshall Greenwood didn't have much experience being a tough guy — and that made me wonder why he was doing it to me.

Actually, I *knew* why he was doing it to me. I had struck a Meade nerve. That alone was reason for me to persevere.

I know. I know. There was the matter of James. But my running with James had nothing to do with the other. Then again, if he and I developed enough of a relationship so that I could milk him for information that would help me with the other, so much the better.

With Marshall Greenwood now out of sight, I started the car and headed for Tom's. He lived in a yellow Victorian not unlike our Victorians on Willow but on a far larger piece of land. I guessed he owned acres, much of them meadowed. At the front of the property was the house, surrounded by grass, the occasional shrub, and two enormous trees. A wooden swing hung from the arm of an oak; a large tire hung from the arm of a maple. A wraparound porch hugged the house, broken only by wide wood steps leading to the front door and to a side door. Not far from the foot of the latter was a picnic table with benches on either side. Potted petunias, a striking violet hue and evenly spaced, hung from the edge of the porch roof all the way around the wrap.

I parked at the edge of the road, lifted

my insulated bag, and went up the front walk. I had barely reached the porch when the front door flew open and a young girl appeared. All smiles, she was dark-haired and pretty in an unpolished way. She had Tom's blue eyes and was equally lean, a fact that wasn't hidden by the overall shorts she wore. It was only when I got close that I realized she wasn't as young as I had first thought.

Still, her smile was infectious. "Hey," I said. "I'm Annie."

Though she continued to smile, she seemed to grow shy, hanging now on the post at the top of the stairs. I was wondering whether she talked much at all, when Tom came out the door. He wore shorts, a T-shirt, and sandals, and was handsomely tanned.

"You are a lifesaver," he said, trotting down the stairs to relieve me of the bag. "Mrs. Jenkins took Ruth down to the outlet stores in Conway today, so she didn't have time to cook dinner. I was about to open a can of tuna."

"Then I've *really* saved your life," I remarked. "You never know what's in tuna."

"Oh, I do." He unzipped my insulated bag. "Tuna steaks are iffy. Canned light tuna, eaten in moderation, is fine. Besides,

I'm not pregnant, and neither is Ruth." He put his nose down and inhaled. "Chicken pot pie?"

"You're good."

"It smells incredible."

"It may need reheating."

He touched it. "Nope. Ready to eat. Are you sure you won't join us?" When I shook my head, he looked back. "Ruth. Come meet Annie. And see what she's brought."

Ruth came as far as the bottom step, where she sat. If she was hungry, she didn't show it. She didn't spare a glance at the bag, but continued to look at me.

"I'm pleased to meet you, Ruth," I said.

Tom gestured her over. When she gave a quick head shake, he led me to the steps. "If the mountain won't come to Mohammed . . ." He settled close to Ruth, clearly not forcing the issue of a formal introduction. Gesturing me to sit, he put the bag on his lap. "You said you have to be back for Phoebe. How's she doing?"

I settled on the other end of the step with my back to the post. "Lousy. That's one of the reasons I'm here. I've tried to get her to see you, but she won't. I'm thinking that's because Middle River is . . . well, Middle River, and people will see her going to your office and begin to talk. So

Plan B is to see someone in New York. I'm going down with her Saturday to help out with a buying trip. She's depending on me to organize things and make sure she is where she's supposed to be when she's supposed to be there, so I'll be able to get her to a doctor before she knows what I'm up to. Only I don't know who to see, and time is short."

"I know just the person," Tom said, as I had figured he would. "When do you want to see her?"

Her was even better. "Tuesday morning."

"This *coming* Tuesday?" He gave a sputtering laugh. "You only ask for the world."

"I know. I'm sorry. I've been putting it off, hoping she'd get better. But now even Sabina agrees that something's wrong. And this trip is the perfect opportunity. If you can't —"

"I can," he said. "She's a friend. She'll do this for me. For what it's worth, she's in on the cause."

"*Our* cause?" I asked, though unnecessarily. I hadn't talked with Tom since that first day at the clinic, but I sensed instinctively that we were on the same page, same paragraph, same line.

He nodded. "Judith is an expert in alternative therapies. She's helped me treat some of the people here in town with something called chelation."

"Chelation," I repeated, testing the word.

"It's from the Greek word for *claw*. A synthetic amino acid is used as a chelating agent. It enters the body and gloms onto toxic metals that may be present in body tissue, then pulls them right out. The body doesn't like this synthetic stuff. It can't see the metal under the glomming, but knows that the synthetic substance doesn't belong there. So it directs the whole business to the kidneys and expels it through urine."

The scientific explanation made sense. I still wasn't sure about the politics of it. "Do the people you treat with this know you're trying to rid them of a toxic metal?"

"I've explained it, albeit hypothetically — you know, *if* there's a metal, this will remove it. Obviously, I can't point fingers and make accusations about the origin of the metal. And my patients don't ask."

"Don't ask?" I was amazed.

"Don't ask. They're simply glad to be feeling better."

"Then it does work?"

"I've seen improvement."

"Did you ever suggest it to my mother?"

"Yes, but she wanted to give the traditional medicine time to work. Unfortunately, she fell down the stairs before we could know either way."

That saddened me. But again, my concern now was my sister. "I can make Phoebe agree to do this."

"Assuming Judith recommends it," he cautioned. "She'll do a complete workup to rule out other things."

But my thoughts were racing on. "If the cure for mercury poisoning works, isn't that proof of its existence?"

"No. Is it mercury? Or lead? Or another metal entirely? Lead can be detected in a simple blood test, not so mercury and some of the others."

"But if I can find a connection between the people you've treated successfully and something to do with the mill, isn't that proof?"

"That depends on what kind of connection you find."

"Can I talk with your patients?"

"I can't give you names. That would be a violation of confidentiality. I could call them and have them call you if they were interested in talking. But that raises the problem I cited last time we talked."

"Your position."

"Yes," he said, and his voice said he was

making no apologies for that. I had to respect him for it.

I tried to bargain. "Okay. If I went down a list of people who've been sick, would you give me a yes or a no?"

"As to whether I've treated them? No. As to whether I feel they'd be willing to talk, I could do that. I wouldn't be speaking as a doctor, just as a resident of Middle River. I'd be guessing."

"Guessing is more than anyone else has been willing to do. I'll take it," I said and looked at Ruth. She hadn't moved other than to lean forward a notch when Tom sat down so that she could see me without obstruction. "Your brother is a good man." I looked at Tom. "Naturally, when I need it most, I don't have my list with me. Can we talk later?"

"Sure. You have my number."

I eyed the insulated bag. "You really will have to heat that up now. And I do have to run. Thanks, Tom. It's so nice to know you're a friend." I stood. "It's been nice meeting you, Ruth."

She didn't reply, just continued to look at me with what struck me as doe eyes.

Tom noticed it, too, and said as he walked me to my car, "She's been skittish around strangers lately, so that's a high compliment. I think she's in awe."

"Why?"

"She wants a sister, and you fit the bill. She likes the way you look."

"She seems very sweet. How old is she?"

"Twenty-eight. She was a late-in-life baby for my mom. A *very* late-in-life baby," he added sadly, then brightened. "But she likes living here. The city was too loud, too busy, too big. She doesn't do well with change, and the city is full of that. I couldn't control it. Here, I can. My hours are more regular. I go to work, I come home."

"What happens when you attend conferences?" I asked. Some of those reported in the *Middle River Times* were in places he couldn't possibly do in a day.

"Mrs. Jenkins stays over. She's a godsend. It's working out well."

Phoebe professed to love the chicken pot pie, though I sensed she spoke more from an ingrained politeness than her taste buds. She had withered by the time I cleared the table, and was soon on the sofa in the den with the TV on and her eyes closed. I was loading the dishwasher when Sabina called to thank me for the dinner, of which, she said, they had eaten every last bite. She asked how Phoebe was and said that the more she thought of it, taking Phoebe to a doctor while we were in New York was the right thing to do. She asked what I was doing tomorrow.

Mention of tomorrow made me think of James, which created a perverse excitement that was distracting, so that it wasn't until later that I questioned Sabina's sudden interest. At the time, I simply felt good about the call.

I peeked into the den. Phoebe was dozing. Satisfied that I'd have a measure of privacy, I got out my notes and called Tom. The conversation was simple: I tossed out a name — Martha Brown, Ian Bourque, Alice LeClaire, Caleb Keene, John DeVoux — and Tom said yes or no, depending on whether he felt the person or his or her family would be approachable. There were no guarantees; we both knew that. But given the length of my list, it was a start.

Phoebe continued to sleep. So I set up my laptop in the kitchen, connected to the phone jack, and logged on. I skimmed past the spam and found notes from Jocelyn and Amanda. Saving them as a treat for later, I went straight to two others.

The first was from Greg. I opened it eagerly.

HIT THE 13,000-FOOT MARK IN ONE PIECE, BUT IF WEST BUTTRESS IS THE BEST ROUTE, I SHUDDER TO THINK OF THE WORST. BAD WIND AND SNOW HERE. IS THIS AUGUST? ME, I WOULDN'T BE ANYWHERE ELSE, BUT I'M GLAD YOU'RE NOT HERE. YOU'D HATE THE COLD. HOPE YOU'RE FINDING WHAT GRACE SOUGHT. SEND WORD. LOVE YOU.

Smiling, I shot back a note.

I'm making progress along with a friend or two, and things are actually better with my sisters, which is good. The law here is a problem; I'm beginning to feel harrassed, which is not good. Am I finding what Grace sought? What is that? Small-town caring? Not yet. Acceptance and respect? Not yet. Family? Maybe. I found a running pal. You'd die if I told you who. I'll keep that a secret, one of Middle River's many. Climb safely. I love you, too.

I hit "send," then, with bated breath,

opened a note from TrueBlue.

> You're getting warm. I'm impressed.
> Yes, I have information on this end. Here are a couple of dates — March 21, 1989, and August 27, 1993. Go through your list of people who are sick and see if any of them were at Northwood during the week preceding those dates.

What happened on those dates?

First the names.

And if I give you the names and those "witnesses" suddenly start showing up face-down in the river?

O ye of little faith.

Thursday morning I went at it. I pared down my list to include only Tom's yeses, then pared it down again to include only those people whose ailments most resembled the symptoms of mercury poisoning. I did this before Phoebe came down for breakfast. I waited until she had a cup of coffee, hoping that would wake her up some. When it barely did, I went ahead anyway and asked her about TrueBlue's dates.

She couldn't remember. Had I really expected she would? But I did sense it had less to do with what ailed her than with the passage of time. Would *I* have been able to say what I did on a particular day, week, or even *month* more than a decade ago? A big event, yes. A milestone in my life, yes. An everyday occurrence, I doubt it. Would anyone?

Failure on this first test notwithstanding, I set off at ten o'clock with my map and the highest of hopes. In the ensuing three hours, the map remained, but the hopes faded fast. Of the people I visited, half were either at work (yes, at the mill, apparently well enough to work) or unwilling to talk. The unwillings to talk included two mothers with ill children and a total of six men and women who had been diagnosed with either Parkinson's, dementia, neurological problems, or multiple bouts of pneumonia. Silent. All of them. And I tried hard. Yes, I was tipping my hand. But there was no law against my dropping by to talk with people in town, was there?

That said, Marshall Greenwood was watching. I passed him often enough — and he slowed and stared at me as we passed — to know that he was monitoring my comings and goings. That might well have explained these people's unwillingness to talk, because I certainly made myself innocuous in my introduction.

"I'm Annie Barnes," I would say to each. "My mother was diagnosed with Parkinson's disease last year." Or Alzheimer's. Or pneumonia. I tailored my approach accordingly. "I'm trying to find other people with the same symptoms to see if there may be a mutual cause. I understand that your husband has been sick." Or your wife. Or your son or daughter or mother.

Inevitably, I would get a yes, but that was the extent of the accommodation. "He's fine now," one said and closed the door in my face. Another asked, "How did you get my name? The paper? Well, Sam's a friend, and I'd like to help find your mutual cause, only I don't think there is one, and I'm really busy now." A third, of course, remarked, "I know who you are. I don't think I should be talking to you."

They were more factual than hostile. Several people asked who had sent me or whether I was working for a health organization. But none agreed to talk with me, until I reached the McCreedys. Remember that name? Omie had put them on the slate, and Tom had seconded the nomination. It was one in the afternoon by now, and Marshall was probably on lunch break, which may have explained their inviting me in. Then again, they did indeed have a "string of problems," as Omie claimed, so it was possible that they simply needed to vent.

Tom and Emily McCreedy lived in the same neighborhood as Sabina. Owners of a flower shop and nursery at the far end of Willow, they were in their midforties. Though neither came from families with histories of ill health, Tom had chronic kidney disease that zapped his strength and immune system, while Emily, who was already being treated for bipolar disorder, had just been diagnosed with adult-onset asthma. They had three children ranging in age from fourteen to nineteen. The oldest and the youngest — both girls — were healthy, but the sixteen-year-old — a boy — was autistic. He attended a special school, and though the state paid part of the bill, the McCreedys footed the rest. Given their own medical bills, it was hard.

The fact that I found them at home in the middle of a workday said something about the state of their health. Once I was in their parlor, they described their ailments in depth. They expressed bewilderment that two people who had been in perfect health not fifteen years before could now be so chronically ill. They spoke of their son with genuine anguish. And anger. They were convinced that something in the air had tripped something in their own body chemistries to cause malfunction — and yes, they had run tests on the air and materials in their home and in their shop. All had come out negative, though they didn't particularly believe the results.

When I asked what they thought might have tripped them up, they tossed out a smorgasbord of possibilities. Acid rain, airborne asbestos, bad well water — they were convinced that at some point there had been a problem, and that if the tests didn't show it now, the problem had either been eliminated or was being hidden. In any event, Emily pointed out with visible irritation, the damage was already done.

I asked about the mill.

"What about the mill?" Tom asked blankly.

"It produces toxic waste," I said.

"It's way on the other side of town."

"Do you ever work there?"

"Yes. We do floral arrangements for

meeting rooms and conference areas."

"And landscape design," Emily added.

"Could there be something in the air there?" I asked, trying to carry over the theme they had raised earlier themselves. On one hand, it amazed me they hadn't thought of the mill on their own. On the other hand, they might simply have bought into the hype about Northwood's environmental good health.

"The air there is fine," Tom said. "The Meades aren't sick, and they're there all the time."

"How long have you been doing their floral arrangements?"

"Twenty years. They were one of our first clients, and they've been consistently the best."

That didn't bode well for me. Their first and most consistent client? It was the loyalty issue again. That said, of all the people I had approached today, the McCreedys were my best hope. Every one of their symptoms could feasibly be traced back to mercury poisoning.

So I asked, "Do you have a record of specific dates when you were on the grounds of the mill?"

Tom deferred to his wife, who apparently kept the files but was beginning to look edgy. "We have financial records," she said. "They would show what jobs were done on what days. But I don't see the point of this question."

"What if there had been a toxic spill at Northwood on one of the days you were there?" I asked.

"We'd have known it. The Meades would have cleaned it up and helped everyone who was exposed."

Yeah, right, I thought. "Do you know that the physical problems you've had are consistent with the symptoms of mercury poisoning?"

"I have kidney disease," Tom said, "not mercury poisoning."

"But where did you get it?" I asked. "And why you? Isn't that what you've been asking me?"

"Bad things happen," he replied, at which point I tried Emily.

"You're being treated for bipolar disorder. As I understand it, mood swings are typical of that. Did you know that they're also a symptom of mercury poisoning? Same with asthma. Same with the kind of neurological damage that can result in the birth of an autistic child."

Emily's expression hardened. "If you think we haven't thought about all these things, you're dead wrong. We've thought about everything. But I was pregnant with Ryan sixteen years ago, I was diagnosed as bipolar seven years ago, and the asthma diagnosis came just last year. So when might I have been exposed to mercury? *All* those times? And no one else in town has been? And none of the doctors are worried? And the mill has covered it all up?"

I explained some of what I had learned. "You didn't have to be exposed multiple times. One major exposure would have been enough. You might have felt sick afterward, like you had the flu, and then gotten better — except that the mercury would have remained in your body and settled in your organs, causing you chronic exposure." I looked at my pad of paper, though I knew the dates by heart. "I have evidence of two spills at the mill. One occurred in March of '89, the other in August of '93. Given your son's age, you were probably pregnant with him during the first. If you knew you were at the mill during the week prior to the twenty-first of that month —"

I was interrupted by the doorbell and an almost simultaneous knuckle-rap on the jamb. "You folks all right?" came the gravelly voice of the chief of police. He walked right into the house, entered the parlor with his stiff-backed gait, and eyed me with distaste. "Is she bothering you?"

"No," said Tom. "We're just talking."

"She's been working her way around town all day, bugging people about finding a cause for their illnesses, like we don't know how to take care of our own. Say the word, and I'll get her out."

"She's fine," Tom said.

Marshall looked at me. "Those others this morning weren't happy. They say you were harassing them."

I couldn't let that go. "If they say it, it's because you told them to. I never even *talked* with any of them. They said they didn't want to, so I left."

"Well, I'm sure the McCreedys would appreciate it if you left, too." He gestured with his hand. "Come on. Let's go."

"Am I under arrest?" I asked in disbelief.

"Not yet. Resist, and you will be. We have no use for rabble-rousers around here. I assume you know what that term means?" he asked, seeming pleased with himself.

I might be impulsive at times, but I wasn't a masochist. Quietly, I gathered my things and rose. To Emily and Tom, I said,

"If I've bothered you, I'm sorry. If you'd like to talk more, I'm staying with my sister."

"Hopefully not for long," Marshall tossed back to the McCreedys as he escorted me out of the house.

I was furious. I reminded myself that my anger was what he wanted, but it didn't help. I tried thinking about my real life, tried thinking about my Washington friends and about my book, but still I boiled. What Marshall was doing was grossly unfair. I wanted justice.

I thought of calling Sam and demanding that he print an op-ed piece on police abuse. Only I knew he wouldn't do it. He would remind me that any such piece would be a direct charge against Marshall Greenwood, since he was the only policeman in town. He would remind me that Marshall was backed by the Meades and that I probably didn't want to take them on.

He would be wrong about the last. I certainly did want to take on the Meades — but about mercury, not Marshall. It struck me that I had to keep my focus and pick my fights with care.

The reality of the Marshall business? No

one in town was going to want to take him on, either. He was *their* chief of police. They would be stuck with him long after I left. Much as I adored Mrs. Klausson and Omie, they weren't activists. Middle River didn't have many of those. Except TrueBlue. I might mention Marshall to him. But to what avail? TrueBlue was TrueBlue (i.e., anonymous) because he didn't want to publicly buck the tide. He was using me for that. By Middle River's standards, I was expendable.

Discouraged, I drove to the diner. I parked off to the side, under the shade of a big old oak so that the sun wouldn't beat directly on my seats. Parked there, my car was also less conspicuous, which felt like a good thing just then.

The smell of burgers on the grill and the whisper of the fans hit me just inside the door, along with Elton John singing "Candle in the Wind." Its lyrics had always haunted me. This day was no exception.

And wouldn't you know, just when I could have used it, my favorite booth was taken. A group of high school kids sat there, with others of their friends in the booths fore and aft. Summer vacation was nearing an end. This gathering was something of a last hurrah.

There were two free booths right up in front, but I wasn't in the mood to be quite so visible. Walking to an empty one in the back, I passed other townsfolk. They glanced at me, neither friendly nor not. Feeling distinctly alone, I ordered Omie's hash and an ice cream frappe. It wasn't healthful. But I needed comfort.

I know what that's like, Grace remarked. *They used to make fun of me for being overweight, but when you're desperate for comfort, what else can you do?*

A psychiatrist, I replied, would say you were desperate for love.

Was I?

Of course.

Are you?

I never thought so. My life is full. I'm happy.

My food arrived. I was midway through wolfing it down when Kaitlin slipped in opposite me. I had been too engrossed in eating to see her come in, but there were her friends, settling into one of the booths in the front. Elton John had long since given way to Sting and, again, to Gloria Estefan.

Kaitlin leaned forward and spoke very softly. "I keep thinking about what I said

382

Sunday. I feel like such a fool."

"Don't." I finished chewing what was in my mouth and put my fork down. "There was no harm done. Your secret's safe with me. Truly, it wouldn't even matter if it wasn't. No one would believe a word I said. My credibility in this town is zero. I half suspect that if I dared say something negative about anyone here, I'd be jailed."

"I doubt that. You're so lucky. You get to leave soon. I'd give *anything* to be gone from this town."

"But then you wouldn't have Kevin."

She studied her hands for a long minute, before giving a one-shouldered shrug and raising her eyes. "Maybe I'm not meant to have him. I mean, I don't know what I'd do if I didn't have him now, but I'm not sure love lasts. My parents hate each other. Do I want that? Besides, I want to go to college. I want to work in a hotel someday, maybe in New York or London or Paris. I want to be independent."

"Are you talking about money or parents?"

"Both." She sat straighter, with something akin to defiance. "Like, I *know* someone's going to report back to my mom that I'm talking with you, and she'll get all hot and bothered, but why can't I talk with you? What's so bad about it? You're the most interesting person who's come here in ages."

"That," I remarked, "is the nicest thing anyone's said to me all day. If you're saying it just to make sure I don't tell —"

"No. I mean it. You *are* interesting. Look at who you are and what you've done. Were you really a dork when you were growing up here?"

"Totally."

"And ugly?"

"Very — but part of that was my attitude. An ugly attitude is like a zit." I jabbed a fingertip to the side of my chin. When she smiled, I said, "There. Better. You have a great smile."

She blushed. "You can thank Dr. Franks for that." When I didn't follow, she said, "My orthodontist." She darted a look at her friends. "I gotta get back. Maybe we can talk another time?"

"I'd like that," I said and meant it. Don't ask me why — Kaitlin DuPuis was nothing to me — but I felt better for her coming over. Less alone. Which was pathetic. I was thirty-three. You'd think I could rationalize being alone for a time, wouldn't you?

Wrong.

TRUTH #7: It doesn't matter how

old you are. Lonely is lonely.

Having acknowledged that, I returned to my food. I ate more slowly now, listening to a sweet Sarah McLachlan song, and set down my fork while some food was still left on the plate. Sated, I sat back. Thinking of all those other things — my friends, my book, my *life* — did help then. Marshall Greenwood be damned. I was going to be fine.

"Hello, sweetheart," Omie said, her wrinkled face wreathed in a smile, but the smile fell when she looked at my plate. "You haven't finished the hash. Is it not good?"

She was concerned to the point of pallor. "It's delicious, there's just too much." It struck me that the pallor wasn't from concern. There was none of the color I had seen in her face last time I had been in. "Are you feeling okay?"

"A little tired," she said with a small smile. "I'm not as young as I used to be."

"Will you sit with me?"

"Not today. I'm heading home for a nap. Would you like another frappe?"

"Good Lord, no. Maybe some iced tea. But I'll get it at the counter."

Omie held me in my seat with a fragile hand. "I'll have someone bring it. You stay

385

here and relax. You bring class to this place."

"Your place doesn't need any help," I called to her as she walked slowly back around the counter and into the kitchen. Less than a minute later, her grandson emerged with a tall glass of iced tea. Having exhausted my need for calories, I added artificial sweetener.

I glanced at my watch. It was barely three. Four hours left until I met James.

I wasn't in the mood to stop in at the shop, wasn't in the mood to sit home alone, wasn't in the mood to move from this booth, period. Omie's was friendly turf, and I was marginally invisible here in the back. Did I have anywhere better to be? Absolutely not.

So I pulled the latest *People* from my purse and began to read. Billy Joel sang, then the Beatles, then Bonnie Tyler, then Fleetwood Mac. I accepted a refill of tea, added sweetener, and relaxed. Omie's was unique. There were places in Washington where I went when I wanted to take a break from my writing, but none felt like home the way this did.

No matter that I hated home. Home was still home. Another truth? Sad, but true.

Thinking that I was going to have to look

harder to find something like this in the District, I closed the magazine and just sat for a while. When I hit the three-hours-to-go point until I met James, I studied the tab, left a tip, and slipped out of the booth.

Invisible no more, I felt the stares of the occupants of every booth I passed, and how to deal with that? How to let these people know that I wasn't an ogre, that I meant them no harm, that I was — yes — one of them at heart? I smiled. I nodded. I even winked at a sweet little girl who couldn't have been more than five.

Kaitlin and her friends continued to talk.

I paid up at the register, then went outside and down the steps to the parking lot, and the convertible was where I had left it, parked under the oak where the sun wouldn't burn my seats.

Only I shouldn't have worried about the seats. What I saw — how not to, with your car sitting all alone there like a sinner on display — was that my tires were flat. Not one tire. All four.

Chapter 17

My first thought, given the day it had been, was that I would find Marshall Greenwood on the opposite side of the parking lot, lounging against his cruiser with a stick of grass in his mouth, as casual as you please, claiming not to have seen a thing. And who would contradict him? If he had chosen a moment when everyone was inside, he could have done the dirty deed in private. In the shade of that big old oak, my car couldn't be seen from the street. Nor could it be seen from inside the front half of the diner, which was the only part open for another hour at least.

It was, of course, a writer's imaginative moment. In fact, Marshall was nowhere in sight. And how ironic was that? At the very moment I needed him, he was gone.

Disgusted, I pulled my cell phone from my purse and punched in the number that every schoolchild in Middle River was taught. It hadn't changed. Marshall's voice came right on; there was no dispatcher here. Middle River couldn't afford one, any more than it could afford more than a one-man department. Marshall was it. How frightening was that?

"This is Annie Barnes," I said. "I'm at Omie's. Someone has slashed my tires."

There was a pause, then a bland, "Why are you calling me? I don't change tires."

I sucked in a quick breath. "*Slashed* is the operative word here. Vandalism is a crime."

"Do you see anyone around?"

"No, but —"

"Think I'll find fingerprints? Footprints on raw gravel? Tire marks?"

I was incensed. Forget depriving him of an opponent; I couldn't resist lashing back. "You've thought this out, haven't you? If I didn't know better, I'd think *you* might be the one who did this. Well, that's actually good. You've inspired me. I need a bad guy for my book."

I struck a chord there, judging from Marshall's sharp reply. "Not me. I am no bad guy. Push that line of thinking and you'll regret it. You've already caused trouble here. Want to cause more? Or don't you care about the welfare of your family?"

I was stung. A threat from a Meade was

one thing; a threat from the chief of police was something else. "What does my family have to do with this?"

"They're accepted in this town. Push your current line of thinking, and people here will turn against them, just like they've turned against you. Know what the word *agitator* means? Well, that's you, and it ain't nice. If you ask me, when an agitator shows up here, she needs to be run right out of town."

I had no idea how to address that. Marshall Greenwood hated me. I didn't know why. But there it was.

Shaking with anger, frustration, and — yes — perhaps an element of fear, I returned to the immediate problem. "My car has been vandalized. Will you come here to investigate, or should I call the state police?"

Calm and cool after winning that round, he said, "No need to call the state police. I'm just finishing something up. I'll be there as soon as I'm done."

It took him twenty minutes — twenty minutes to finish up whatever it was and drive all the way around a single block. I used the time to call Normie at the service station, and to seethe.

I was doing the latter, standing with my

arms folded over my chest and my eyes on those pancake-flat tires, when Kaitlin and her friends emerged from Omie's. Three of the five headed for one car. When Kaitlin spotted me and approached, the fourth ran off to join the others.

"What happened?" she asked, eyeing the tires.

"Someone slashed them while I was inside. You didn't by chance see anyone hanging around here when you and your friends arrived, did you?"

"No. And the tires weren't like this when we came. I saw your car right off and pointed it out to my friends. We'd have noticed this."

But they had been inside the diner for more than an hour. That allowed plenty of time for someone to put a knife to good use.

"I called Normie at the station," I said. "He wasn't thrilled at having to come all the way down here." It was an understatement. Friendly Normie hadn't been friendly at all.

"Normie's a total jerk," Kaitlin replied.

Marshall drove up. Kaitlin stayed, and she wasn't alone. By now, other people had left Omie's, seen us, and wandered over. Marshall walked around my car giving due consideration to each of the tires. Then he looked at the people watching.

"Anyone see anything?"

There were head shakes and murmurs, all to the negative.

"I don't suppose you have four spares in your trunk?" Marshall asked me, but looked at his audience and chuckled.

I wasn't answering a stupid question. "Is there a history of this kind of thing in Middle River?"

"You mean, do we have a serial slasher?" he asked with another amused glance at those gathered around. "Nope. You must have annoyed someone. You're good at that. I'd say this is a message."

"A message saying what?" Kaitlin asked. I noticed that she had come a bit closer to me.

Marshall arched a brow. "Saying that Annie Barnes is stepping on toes in this town. Are you a friend of hers?"

She ignored the last. "Whose toes is she stepping on?"

"I can name a dozen people," he said and began shooing away the onlookers. "Okay, folks, nothing much to see here." To Kaitlin, he said, "Aren't your parents expecting you home?"

"No," Kaitlin said, tossing her hair out

of her eyes in a gesture that was nothing if not defiant.

It wasn't so bad now that the other people had left. Still, I feared she would make trouble for herself. "You can go on, Kaitlin. I'm fine."

"Will he do an investigation?" she asked me.

Marshall answered. "I'll do what's needed."

When Kaitlin looked about to ask more, I clasped her arm. "Go on, now. I'll handle this."

The last of my words were drowned out when, with a lumbering noise that didn't say much for the skill of the mechanics at Zwibble's Service Station, the tow truck came down the street and turned into Omie's lot. Pulling up where we stood, Normie climbed down from the cab.

There was no smile this time, no chit-chat as he surveyed the scene. There was no *ooohing* and *ahhhing* over my car, no mention of old friends from school. Rather there was a silent, plodding examination, first one tire, then the other, then a walk around the car to the third tire, then the fourth. When he finally returned to us, he was scratching what remained of the hair on the back of his head. He glanced at

Marshall before acknowledging me at last, and even then he kept his eyes mostly on the car.

"We got a problem here," he said. "I don't have the kind of tires you need."

"I'm not fussy about brand," I replied.

"Not brand. Size. We don't have any cars like this in Middle River."

"These tires aren't unique to convertibles," I pointed out.

"Most everything here is trucks."

"My parents don't drive trucks," Kaitlin said. "My mom's Sebring's not much different in size from this."

"But I don't have the right tires," Normie insisted.

"When can you *get* the right tires?" I asked.

"I'd have to make some calls."

He stood there.

"Okay," I said. "Can you do that?"

"Yeah, but I'd need your car back at my place, only I can't tow it back with the tires this way. I need a flatbed."

I waited. When no explanation was forthcoming for why he hadn't brought a flatbed in the first place, since I had told him on the phone that all four tires were slashed, I said, "Can you get one?"

"It's back at the shop."

"So you need to drive back and switch trucks. What'll that take, twenty minutes?" I glanced at my watch. I still had time. Granted, unless he could get the tires from another station in the immediate area, my car would be out of commission until tomorrow at the least. But once Phoebe got home, I could use her van. The timing would work. I didn't have to be at the varsity course until seven.

Normie made a face. "Y'know, it's not like this is all I have to do. I was in the middle of a job when you called. I gotta have that one done today." He shot Marshall a glance.

Marshall seemed perfectly content. If I didn't know better, I would say the two were in cahoots about messing me up.

"Tell you what," I said, reaching for my wallet. "Since you don't want to help, I'll call Triple A." I pulled out my card. "I gotta say, between you two guys, I have *great* stuff for my book."

Normie's round face paled. "What stuff?" He shot Marshall a different look now. "What stuff does she have?"

"Nothing," the police chief scoffed. "She's making empty threats, because the fact is that no one in town wants to talk with her. She's a pariah — now there's a good word. Tell you what. Be a sport and get the flatbed. The sooner she gets her car fixed, the sooner she'll leave."

I didn't bother to correct him. "What about who did this?" I asked with a glance at my car.

"Look, miss," Marshall muttered, "I'm doing you a favor here. Leave well enough alone, will you?"

He turned and walked away before I could argue. After a word with Normie, he got in his cruiser and drove off.

Normie climbed back in his truck and rumbled out of the lot.

I checked my watch. It was five. Assuming he came right back, I was okay.

"Can I drive you somewhere?" Kaitlin asked. "I have my Mom's old Jeep. It's falling apart, but it works."

"Thanks. I'm okay for now." I rested against the side of my car and hugged my middle. Talk about feeling like I was on hostile turf. And it was only getting worse. "You ought to go. Hanging around me won't help your image."

"I'm not worried."

"Well, I am." I smiled. "Really. I'm fine."

"Are you sure?"

"Yes. I'm sure."

She started off, then turned and came

back. "You told them you were writing a book."

"And I got a reaction, didn't I? Interesting, that reaction."

"But you told me you *weren't* writing one."

"I'm not writing one about Middle River. That's the truth."

Kaitlin relaxed. "In a way it's too bad," she said with a mischievous half smile. "Know what they say about Normie Zwibble?"

I put my hands to my ears. "I don't want to hear this."

She said it anyway, and of course I listened. "He's addicted to playing the lottery, only he can't buy tickets at his father's place or he'd be found out, so he drives over to Weymouth. That's where he'll buy you your tires. It'll give him an excuse to go."

"The lottery, huh?"

"And Chief Greenwood's a junkie."

"I don't believe that."

"It's true. He's hooked on painkillers. My parents talk about it all the time. Like, it's a good thing we don't *need* him for anything, y'know?"

I was wondering about that as she set off again. Four tires slashed. That was violence against my property — violence against *me*. No matter how much I felt the people of Middle River disliked me, I had never been physically threatened before. I felt a trembling in the pit of my stomach as the reality of that sank in.

With each passing minute, I felt more impotent. Needing to *do* something, I called Sam. It was only when the answering machine at the newspaper office came on that I realized it was Thursday. He would be out playing golf or, more aptly given the hour, in the country club bar drinking scotch with his pals, one of whom was the great Sandy Meade.

I shifted from foot to foot. I leaned against one side of my car and studied the diner, then walked around and leaned against the other side and studied the woods. I thought about Sandy Meade and the satisfaction that would come from winning a round with him. It was the only thing that brought me relief as I waited for Normie to come.

When twenty minutes passed and he didn't return, I began wondering whether what Kaitlin had said about him was true. And not only about him. About Marshall. Addicted to painkillers? If he was, and if he truly believed I was writing a book about the town, I could see that he would feel threatened. But to threaten me in turn? If he thought that would shut me up, he had another think coming. I would have no qualms about publicizing his problems if he continued to put me in harm's way.

I wondered if Sam knew about this. I guessed most of the town did.

Ten more minutes passed, and I grew severely antsy. When my watch read five-thirty and there was still no sign of Normie, I turned to Plan B and called Phoebe. She was with a customer, so I waited. I kept thinking Normie would come along, in which case I wouldn't need Phoebe at all. But Normie didn't come. And Phoebe was distracted. "Why are you at Omie's house?" she asked when she finally came on.

"Not her house. The diner. I stopped for something to eat, and my tires were slashed. I'm waiting for Normie Zwibble, but if he doesn't show up, I'll need your help. You close at six. Can you be out of there by six-fifteen?" I knew there were closing chores, but Joanne was there to do them. Six-fifteen would give me enough time.

"Joanne?" Phoebe called away from the phone. "Do we close today at six? Isn't it eight today? Six? Oh, okay." She returned to me. "I don't know if I feel like going out for dinner. I'm exhausted. Should we eat in instead?"

"We agreed on having the chicken pot pie left over from last night," I said, but I was realizing the futility of the reminder. "Listen, Phoebe. I'll call back if I need a ride. Okay?"

I ended the call and tried Zwibble's, but there was no answer. I couldn't believe Normie had forgotten. It didn't make sense. I mean, if what Kaitlin said was true and he thought I was writing a book, wouldn't he be afraid of crossing me, lest I tell his secret to the world?

Of course, if Marshall had told him to make things hard for me, and if he was more afraid of Marshall than of me . . .

I tried Zwibble's again. Still no answer. We were coming up on six o'clock, and I was developing a whale of a headache.

By the way, if you're thinking I was standing in the parking lot alone all this time, you'd be wrong. We were into the dinner hour now. Middle Riverites had been coming and going. They noticed me, noticed my car, and went on inside. When they came out, they noticed me, noticed my car, then got in their own and drove off.

Talk about being stared at. Talk about being the butt of gossip. Talk about being . . . *shunned*. It was as bad as it had ever been.

Now you know, Grace said smugly. **Do you understand why I drank?**

No, I do not, I challenged. When you drank, you made it worse. When you drank, you couldn't write, and that was your tool. You could have hit back that way.

Like you're doing, Miss High and Mighty? Write a book that exposes all the phonies there, and you'll have your revenge.

But then I lose Middle River and my family completely, I thought and felt stymied.

Omie. I wanted Omie, but she was home taking a nap. Had she been there, she would have waited with me. She was that kind of person. And her children and grandchildren were of like heart — *good* elements of Middle River — except that they were surely up to their ears cooking and serving inside.

Six o'clock passed. I tried to phone Phoebe to get her here, but the answering machine came on at the shop. There was a private number, only I didn't have it. Nor did Directory Assistance. Mom's line at the house just rang and rang and rang, and Sabina's line was busy.

By six-fifteen, I was seriously considering walking home. I didn't like the idea of abandoning the BMW — couldn't begin to imagine what little "mishaps" might occur if I left the car here overnight. But I might have no choice. Still no one answered at Zwibble's, which meant that Normie might well have forgotten all about me, and I couldn't wait forever. I had to be at the varsity course by seven.

By the time six-thirty arrived, my head was throbbing. I figured I could run home in less than ten minutes, change clothes, and, assuming Phoebe *was* home with the van, get to the varsity course just in time.

That was when Normie finally showed up, and I was beside myself with impatience. It took him ten minutes to get the BMW on the truck, and another ten to get my credit card information, which he insisted he needed prior to ordering my tires.

I wanted to scream. Instead, I gave him what he needed, then quietly asked if he could drop me at home. He refused, claiming his insurance said I couldn't ride in the cab. I offered to ride in the flatbed of the truck, but he vetoed that, too.

402

By now it was six-fifty. No doubt about it, I was going to be late. I knew James had a cell phone (he had talked on it that day at Omie's), but I didn't have the number. So I got his home number from Directory Assistance and tried him there.

A woman answered.

Stung, I hung up. There was no wife. I was sure of it. A girlfriend? Fine. I was running with James — running — that was all.

That said, I had to *be* there in order to run. He had said seven, and I had agreed. Now I was going back on my word. Meades might do that, but Barneses did not — not even when they had splitting headaches like mine.

"Can I drive you somewhere?" Kaitlin asked through her car window.

I hadn't seen her pull up, though I might have guessed she would come. With my eyes on the road searching for Normie's flatbed truck, I had seen her mother's old Jeep go past several times. Kaitlin was keeping tabs on me.

Grateful that someone was, if only this young woman who might well have a case of misplaced idol worship, I rounded the car and climbed in. "My sister's, as fast as you can drive without getting a ticket," I said, pressing my fingers to my temple to hold my head together.

She got us there in two minutes flat.

"You're a lifesaver." I climbed out. "Thank you." Seeing the van at the side of the house, I ran up the walk, let myself in, and raced upstairs to change clothes. It was seven on the nose when I ran back down and into the kitchen. Phoebe was at the table, eating. She looked up in surprise.

"Annie? What are you doing here?"

To this day, I believe she meant what was I doing in Middle River when she assumed I was in Washington. At the time, I simply said, "Gotta go out for a run. Are you okay with the pie?"

"The pie. Did *you* cook this?"

Call me callous, but I couldn't deal with the mental fuzzies just then. "I'm taking the van." I looked around. "Keys?"

"Uh . . . uh . . ." She rose from the table and, seeming mystified, searched the counter, the drawer by the kitchen phone, then her purse. I was dying, looking everywhere else I could think of, when she said a vague, "In my blazer pocket?"

"Which blazer?" I called as I headed for the closet in the hall.

She didn't answer. I was trying to remember which blazer she had worn to work that morning, when she joined me and said, "I think it was my white linen. It's upstairs."

I ran up the stairs, found the blazer on her bed and, thankfully, the keys in the pocket. Racing back down, I dangled them Phoebe's way and bolted out the door.

I quickly drove down Willow, turned onto School, and flew across town daring, just *daring* Marshall to catch me, though for sure he was at home eating a big meal by way of rewarding himself for hassling me. A handful of cars were in the high school parking lot, close to the school. Dodging them, I cut through to the very rear and turned the corner, but when the parking strip at the edge of the woods appeared, I caught a sharp breath.

No one was there — no person, no car — *nothing.*

Pulling up, I left the van and actually went to the start of the path. Don't ask me why. It was as deserted as the parking strip.

Trembling, I returned to the grass near the van. It was seven-fifteen. I was late. But not *that* late. Wouldn't he have waited? Or just started to run without me? That was what any rational person would do. Wasn't it?

It hit me then, hit me hard. History was repeating itself. I had been stood up.

I should have been furious. But it was one too many turns of the screw on a day filled with them. I was suddenly too tired to process much, and my head was killing me. Sinking down on the grass, I folded my legs, put my elbows on my knees and my face in my hands, and let myself cry. Self-pity? Yes, and I had a right to feel it.

I don't know how long I sat there, only know that the crying felt good. In time, I wiped my eyes with my forearms, raised my head, and took a long, stuttering breath. I released it and continued to sit. My mind wasn't quite revived. I felt numb. That was probably why I didn't hear the approaching vehicle until it rounded that last curve and came into view.

My numbness dissolved. At the sight of that black SUV, I was suddenly rip-roaring mad. I rose to my feet and approached, so that I was no more than three feet from the car when he opened the door and lowered a sneakered foot to the ground.

"You are a major son of a bitch," I cried, rigid with fury. "Do you have any idea what I did to get here — or what my day has been like? I've been threatened and vandalized and stared at and *talked* about, no doubt, because this is Middle River and the average Middle Riverite doesn't have the *balls* to do more than talk, except for whoever slashed my tires, and *that* person is probably on your daddy's payroll like most of the *rest* of the town. I don't know why I thought *you'd* be better, maybe because you're a *runner,* for God's sake, but you're a snake, just like your brother, Aidan — the two of you chips off the old block, because I'm *sure* all this is coming from Sandy, I would put *money* on that. But if you think you can scare me away, you're dead wrong. First Marshall, then Normie, now you — you all are pushing me *this* close," I held up my thumb and forefinger, barely parted, "to writing my damned book and exposing everything possible about this stinking town. Thought you were being cute letting me sit here waiting, like I waited for Aidan back then? Wrong. I have a life. I have connections. I have *power.*" Pressing my palm to my temple, I muttered, "And a massive headache, thanks to you."

"You didn't get my message?" he asked.

I would have screamed if I'd had the strength. "That's the oldest line in the book."

"I called Phoebe and asked her to tell you I'd be late."

"Well, Phoebe *didn't* tell me," I charged. The words were barely out when I realized that Phoebe might well have taken the call and forgotten all about it, but even *that* had a Meade cause. "If she didn't tell me, it's because something's wrong with her mind, no doubt from pollution caused by *your* mill." I waved both hands. "But that's beside the point. I was worried because *I* was late, so I tried to call *you*. A woman answered the phone. Does that give me a hint about why you were late?"

He didn't smile. "I was late because an account I've been trying to land needed another thirty minutes of work. That was the babysitter who answered the phone."

I blew out a puff of air and said to the dimming sky, "Oh . . . Lord. The . . . babysitter." My eyes returned to earth and challenged his. "Do I look like a *total* fool? You don't have a baby."

"I do. Her name's Mia. She's ten months old."

It wasn't his sureness that got to me, as much as the softening of his voice. That gave me pause. "Ten months old, and never a mention in the paper?"

"My father didn't want it publicized. He doesn't buy into single parenthood."

"So you aren't married?" Nothing about that in the paper, either, but I wanted to be sure.

"No."

"And Sandy is *ashamed* of the baby?"

"No. Angry."

"But you wanted to be a parent."

"Yes."

"And you take care of this baby yourself?" I was trying to picture him changing a diaper. He seemed far too . . . big, was the only word that came to mind.

"Other than when I'm at work, I do. She's precious."

He said the last with a half smile, and it did something to me, that smile, moved something inside me that made me forgive him anything that had made him late. It struck me that I had behaved like an imbecile, not the sophisticated woman I wanted to be. And of course he could see that I had been crying. My eyes had to be red.

Bowing my head, I rubbed the back of my neck. "Oh boy." I felt like a fool.

"Did you take something for the headache?"

"No time."

Before I knew it, he had produced pills and a bottle of water. "Here."

I took them without asking a thing. He

wouldn't give me anything harmful; my gut told me that. I don't know why *it* was so sure. After all, James was a Meade. But my gut was also reminding me that he was attractive, and I had no cause to doubt that. He was standing beside me now, so much taller and broader than I, though still lean. And strong. Quietly so.

A large, silent, authoritative man like James rocking a baby to sleep? The image was striking enough to tie up my tongue.

I drank more of the water, then lowered the bottle. My eyes met his for a long moment, and for the life of me, I couldn't think of a thing to say.

Then he said, "Want to run?"

I nodded. Running was *definitely* the thing to do.

So he closed up his car, and we stretched. Then we hit the woods. He offered to have me go first, but I motioned him on, and it was wise. For one thing, though the light was starting to fade, he illuminated the path. I don't know whether it was his tank top, which was white, or the reflective material of his running shoes, or the last of that light on his skin or the gray in his hair. But he was easy to follow — quite a *good* runner, actually, I decided, as it seemed I did every time we ran. And why my surprise? He was athletic; one didn't grow up in Middle River and not know that the Meade boys played baseball, basketball, and football. I guess it was just that running was different. If was solitary, for one thing. I would have thought a Meade would want more of an audience. For another, it was grueling. Typically, Meade boys relied on others to get them the ball when they were in a position to score. Running was not a team sport. Your own two legs carried you, or you went nowhere at all.

We went around once. The cutoff to Cooper's Point came and went.

"Head okay?" he called back.

"Better," I said.

So we went around again. It was darker still this time, but I felt safe — certainly safer than I had standing beside my vandalized car back at Omie's. James ran immediately ahead, his feet rhythmically striking the ground, lean legs in a fluid stride, butt tight, back straight, arms pumping easily. He glanced behind every few minutes to make sure I kept up. Had I fallen, he would have been there. I knew that. It was another gut thing.

Did he alter his pace to help me out? Probably. But he built up a sweat anyway. I could see it on his neck and his arms, in the spikes of his hair and on his face each time he looked back, and when we finally reached our starting point again and stopped, he was breathing as hard and deeply as I was.

Gesturing for me to stay, he got two fresh waters from the car. We drank them leaning against trees at the start of the woods. Dusk had fallen; for all practical purposes, we were hidden away. It was incredibly peaceful — peaceful until his eyes met mine one more time, and one more time I felt the pull.

He pushed off from his tree and came toward mine. "Do you know what in the hell this is?" he asked, sounding truly perplexed.

I shook my head. Oh, it was physical attraction of the most basic kind. But it wasn't supposed to happen. Not between James and me.

Between James *Meade* and me? No way.

But I could see it in his eyes and feel it in my body, and when he put a hand on the back of my neck and pulled my mouth to his, there was something live between us that caught fire and burned. The kiss went on and on, turning this way and that, deepening and withdrawing and deepening again, but it wasn't enough, wasn't nearly enough. By the time he drew back, my arms clutched his shoulders and his clutched my waist, and it *wasn't enough*.

His eyes were dark in the encroaching night, his voice hoarse. "Do we want to do this?"

I shook my head, but my hands betrayed me by curving around his shoulders and sliding over sweaty skin to the nape of his neck — and the sweat was as appealing as everything else. Chemistry? Omigod. Chemistry didn't began to explain the need I felt just then.

He kissed me again. His hands didn't have to guide my face this time, so they found my breasts, and what he did with them was incredible, *but it wasn't enough*.

I could barely breathe, could barely speak, but as I drew back enough to grab the hem of my top, I whispered, "Don't want to do it, but will die if we stop."

I imagined that the strangled sound I heard was a laugh, but it was quickly muffled when he pulled his own top over his head. I wanted my breasts against his chest. He wanted them in his mouth. He got his way. With one nipple drawn in and the other rolled between his fingers, my knees went weak. I clutched him now so that I didn't fall.

A final time, in the heat of it, I thought it — James Meade and *me?* — but in the next instant the thought was gone and never returned. Identity had no chance against raw passion, which was what we shared. To this day, I have no idea how we got out of our shorts, what I leaned against as he thrust into me again and again, whether either of us spoke, or how James knew to withdraw in the instant before he climaxed. But it was good. It was incredible. I couldn't speak for James, though the sounds that came from his throat were something of a testament, but for me, it was the longest and most intense orgasm I had ever had in my life. And as if that weren't amazing enough, we just sat there for a while — James on a log, me astride him, both of us buck naked — sat there until the fire had cooled and evening set in.

We dressed then and went to our cars. We didn't touch. He seemed lost in thought, and I didn't know what to say either. When we stopped, our eyes met, and for a minute longer he seemed confused. Then, quietly and with an odd unsureness, he said, "Want to meet her?"

I followed him to his house. It was a

large brick Colonial, as I had expected it would be, only it wasn't on Birch with the others. It was on the south end of town, not far, actually, from Tom's and with the extra land that James wouldn't have found had he bought a house on Birch. There were no lights on either side of his home or even across the street, just those flanking his own front door and warming the windows inside.

The babysitter greeted us. She looked to be about my age, though her face wasn't familiar. James introduced us, paid her, and she left.

I was assuming that the baby was asleep when he led me through the kitchen to an open family room, and there was a very little girl, sitting in the middle of the floor holding the corner of a fleece blanket, while the rest trailed to the side. Her hair was short, thick, and dark, and her footed pajamas were pink. More vivid colors — shapes, numbers, animated animals — came from the large-screen TV to which she was riveted.

We didn't speak, and for the longest time she didn't know we were there. I looked at James. He didn't take his eyes from the child.

Then something tipped her off. She

looked back, saw James, and her entire face lit. In an instant, she was crawling our way. Not once did she take her eyes off his face. He was on his haunches when she reached him and caught her up into a hug.

I actually took a step back then. It seemed such a private moment, such an *adoring* moment, that I didn't belong. But then James stood and brought the child closer. She had a small arm around his neck and large eyes on me.

"This is Mia," he said in an exquisitely gentle voice.

Seeing her close up, I caught my breath. She was beautiful, and I told him that. Unable to resist, I took her little hand. "Hello, Mia," I said in a voice that was as gentle as his, but then, there was no other way to greet this child. With creamy skin, tiny rosebud lips, and dark eyes with just the slightest slant to suggest Asian descent, she was all innocence. Her hand was warm, but it didn't quite grasp mine. I was a stranger.

She kept her eyes on me through a tour of the kitchen, where James filled her bedtime bottle, and then it was up to her room, done up in yellows and pinks, where he settled into a rocker and let her drink, and still she looked at me. By the time she was done, she was comfortable enough to give me a smile, but it was a sleepy one. She babbled a little while James changed her diaper, but even the babble was sleepy. By the time he put her in her crib, with her favorite bear in the corner, her favorite square of fleece in her hand, and her favorite mobile playing a lullaby, she was asleep.

He turned down the light and turned up the monitor. Then he took my hand, led me into a master bedroom suite that I couldn't see because he didn't bother with a light there at all, and made love to me again.

He was truly incredible. Totally aside from stamina, which he had in spades for a guy with more gray in his hair than black, he was so strong and at the same time so *gentle* that I was beside myself with need when he finally entered me. He wore a condom this time, which meant that he stayed there through not one, but *two* orgasms — and I'm talking simultaneous ones, which is so rare. But it was like his excitement spurred mine, which then spurred his, which spurred mine more . . .

I'm sorry. I'm not being very articulate, certainly not poetic here, but you get the idea. Suffice it to say that when we finally separated, I was totally spent. I thought he was, too, until, with little warning, he scooped me up and carried me into the shower.

We needed it. After four miles of running and two bouts of sex, we were pretty ripe. Soap took care of that — lots of soap and lather and scrubbing. Ah-hah, and I know what you're thinking. You're thinking we were going to make love again, there in the shower.

Nope. There was plenty of feeling and touching — he scrubbed me, I scrubbed him — but we didn't go farther than that. Actually, a kind of shyness set in when those oversize bath sheets of his covered each of us up. For my part, I was trying to understand what had happened and why and what I was going to do with it. He must have been thinking something similar because, with his towel hooked around his hips, he straightened his chest, dusted with wisps of newly washed and dried hair, and said with vague amazement, "Annie Barnes? Who'd a thought it?"

I blushed. How flattering was that?

And being waited on for dinner — how flattering was *that?*

After checking in on Mia, he led me to a sleek kitchen with ash cabinets and state-of-the-art appliances, and plied me with a fabulous Pinot Noir while he grilled us a foursome of burgers. I ate my two as quickly as he ate his. I was starved.

By the time we were done, all sorts of little warning bells were dinging in the back of my mind, but I kept them there — muted, way in the back — until I was in the van and on my way home. Then they rang out, and it struck me. If James Meade could have chosen anything that would keep me in the Meade corner and out of mischief, it was this.

After I'd been floating for the last two hours, that realization grounded me.

Then I walked in and found Phoebe in the kitchen waiting, only not in pajamas. She was fully dressed. With more lucidity than I had heard from her in months, she told me that Omie had suffered a massive heart attack earlier that evening and was dead.

Chapter 18

Phoebe and I weren't the only ones driving over to the diner that night. The kitchen had closed as soon as word came of Omie's death, so it wasn't as though food was being served, but people streamed in to console the family and also each other. Omie was widely loved in Middle River. She had touched most of our lives.

For Phoebe and me, as well as for Sabina, who arrived soon after us, there was a special mourning. Omie had been a close friend of our mother's. So we were there for Alyssa's sake as well.

Those of us who had come — and then some — were back the next morning, now bringing the cakes and cookies, casseroles, finger foods, and soups that we had made late into the night. None of us expected Omie's family to work in the kitchen that day. We streamed in and out, heating this, chilling that, putting the other on platters and carrying it out front — and I say "we" meaning Middle River in the largest sense.

If ever there was a sense of community, it was here. Coming together in times of need was what small towns did. I could appreciate that. I could even admire it.

So yes, here was another truth. **TRUTH #8: Small towns have their strengths. They can offer comfort and support in ways that a city may not.**

But as long as I was onto this business of truths, there was more. What was it I said earlier — that I looked at my sisters and saw intelligent women whose lives were wasted in a town that discouraged free expression and honest thought? I wasn't entirely right. I had seen Phoebe at work; she provided a vital service for the townsfolk. Likewise Sabina; that Data Center of hers, with its server behind glass and Sabina its mastermind, was impressive. And now here they both were, communicating easily with all of these people, joined in their grief, taking comfort and giving it back. Honestly? I envied it.

That said, for this day, at least, I was part of it all. No one doubted my having loved Omie, or my grief now that she was gone. We worked side by side in the kitchen, feeding each other and all those children, nieces and nephews and grands, that Omie had left behind. Her body rested in the local funeral home, but she was waked here, and her spirit was strong.

Under the spell of that spirit, people seemed to forget that they hated me. Omie's death was a distraction that mellowed them.

It had that effect on me, too. I was able to smile at Marylou Walker, though she had been decidedly chilly last time I was at News 'n Chews. I could nod politely at Hal Healy without staring at that arm around his wife, which seemed more inappropriate than usual. I even acknowledged some of those who had slammed the door in my face the day before.

Kaitlin was a sweetheart. She spent a lot of time helping wherever I was, and my acceptance by her triggered acceptance by her friends. They talked with me, and they smiled. Hal Healy wouldn't have been pleased.

There were moments when new people entered the diner and I wondered if a tire-slasher was among them. There were certainly moments when I wondered if TrueBlue was here. Marshall Greenwood was. I saw him numerous times, but he steered clear of me. I wanted to think that in the presence of Omie's goodness, he was wallowing in guilt.

Most important, though, without the distraction of mourning Omie, I would have been agonizing over James. It was a pretty big thing that had happened out there on the varsity course, and I'm not just talking about erasing the humiliation of my wait for Aidan at Cooper's Point. I'm talking about sex in the woods and again at his house.

I take sex seriously. I didn't have it until I was twenty, and in the thirteen years since, I'd been with three guys, each of whom I stayed with for multiple years. I didn't sleep around, and I certainly didn't sleep with guys I barely knew, and I barely knew James.

Did I make a conscious decision to sleep with the enemy? No.

Was I scheming to ruin him while his tongue was in my mouth? Absolutely not.

Grace would have been disappointed in me. She would have said I had squandered a golden opportunity. But in all honesty, who James was and what he did was the farthest thing from my mind when we were making love. In those moments, he was a guy to whom I was powerfully attracted and who — omigod — was powerfully attracted to me! I felt a tingle just thinking about it even hours after the fact.

So I kept busy. I did talk with people, but I felt most comfortable working in the kitchen. Washing platters was perfect. Same with loading and unloading the dishwasher. It kept me out of the spotlight, with my hands busy and my mind on Omie.

Did James show up? Of course. I think that I sensed it the instant he walked into the diner, and I was in the kitchen at the time, which says something about the sexual antennae we humans have. I had a weird feeling; I glanced at the passthrough, and there he was.

I stayed off to the side so that he wouldn't see me. I mean, what could I say? Even in *spite* of that powerful attraction, I was confused. I would have thought that James's last name alone would have been a depressant. But it wasn't.

He found me in a moment when there were few enough people in the kitchen so that he could say a few words without being heard.

And that's all he said — just a few words — the first of them while he kept his eyes on the lavash I was taking from a large plastic bag and arranging in a dish. "Got your tires straightened out?"

"Uh-huh. Normie managed to locate the

right ones over in Weymouth." I looked up in time to see a twitch in the corner of James's mouth that suggested he knew what else was in Weymouth. Then his eyes met mine, and an instant something passed between us.

I could barely breathe, certainly couldn't look away. I was relieved when he finally broke the spell by saying, "I can't run on weekends. No babysitter. Can we do Monday?"

"I'll be in New York Monday with Phoebe. We're due back Tuesday night."

"Wednesday morning, then?"

"Okay."

He nodded, tapped the stainless steel counter, and turned to leave, and I thought that would be it. Then he looked back. "I don't do one-night stands."

Well, what in the devil did *that* mean? That there wouldn't be a repeat of what we had done because it had, in fact, been a one-night stand and he didn't do those? Or that there *would* be a repeat of what we had done because that would make it something *other* than a one-night stand, which was fine?

I couldn't ask, of course, because by the time I wanted to, he was halfway across the room. All I could do was watch him work his way around counters and shelves. His back was straight, salty hair neat, blue shirt neat, gray slacks neat, loafers neat.

To this day, I don't know for sure whether people saw us talk and thus deemed me worthy of trust. But after James left, I did get some questions. People were wondering whether Omie's death was from simple old age, or whether it had been hastened by something external to her. Apparently — I hadn't known this — longevity ran in Omie's family. Her mom had died at ninety-six and her dad (who was much older than his wife, hence his death when Omie was still relatively young) at ninety-eight. Omie had only been eighty-three, which sounded plenty old to me, but not to these others. They wanted to know why she had been sick on and off for the past year, why the bouts of pneumonia, why the massive heart attack at the end.

They were nonchalant about it, asking quietly, almost rhetorically. But they did ask. And they asked *me*. That meant something. It was like they knew I was looking, and that made me their advocate. Like they didn't have anyone else to ask. Like they *trusted* me.

Maybe the last was pushing it a little.

Still, by the time I left Omie's at midafternoon, I was feeling a sense of heightened responsibility.

I turned on my computer. My friend Jocelyn had e-mailed to say that she had reached the part in *Peyton Place* where Tomas Makris was stripping Constance MacKenzie with his eyes, and that she thought he was absolutely fabulous. I wrote back telling her that, yes, Tomas was totally sexy but that the *point* of the relationship was Constance coming to accept her own sexuality. How far we women have come in this sense. I could never have done what I did with James if I didn't like sex — but I didn't write Jocelyn this part. My friends knew nothing of James at this point.

Greg e-mailed to say that they had reached fourteen thousand feet but were being slowed by wind and snow, and I have to say I felt an inkling of unease. People died climbing mountains, and Mount McKinley was a biggie. Was being caught in a blizzard at fourteen thousand feet any less dangerous than walking through the wartorn streets of Afghanistan? I wasn't so sure.

My thoughts were brought back to the dangers here at home when, just as I was about to reply to Greg, an e-mail arrived from TrueBlue. *Any luck?* he wrote, and, knowing he was right there at his computer, I was suddenly annoyed.

No luck yet, but you're setting me up to fail unless you give me more information. I can't ask people questions without backing those questions up with facts. I can't win their trust unless I sound halfway intelligent, for God's sake.

What happened at Northwood on the dates you gave me? Was there or was there not a mercury spill?

There were fires on both of those dates. On March 21, 1989, a fire destroyed the Clubhouse, and on August 27, 1993, a fire destroyed the Gazebo.

On those dates, huh? Okay. But the fires themselves aren't news. We all know they happened. Sam gave them front-page coverage. What's the significance here?

Those fires were made to look accidental. The Clubhouse fire was blamed on faulty wiring in the kitchen. The one at the Gazebo was blamed on a torch that hadn't been properly extinguished. But neither fire was accidental. They were set by representatives of Northwood at the order of Sandy Meade. The purpose was to level the structures so that Northwood could make a big deal about rebuilding from scratch. What never made the paper was the fact that prior to the rebuilding, mercury was removed from the soil underneath.

Mercury at the Clubhouse and at the Gazebo, but not at the plant itself?

Remember I told you that Northwood used other methods of disposing of mercury waste? There were huge drums buried under both of those structures.

Under the Clubhouse and the Gazebo? Why? Why not bury them out in the middle of nowhere?

Sandy Meade thought it would be

clever — and less suspicious if ever there was a probe — to build something for the good of the town on top of those dumps. In fairness to him, the drums were supposed to hold. There wasn't supposed to be any leak.

But there was?

During the week prior to each of the fires, events were held at each of the places. Following those events, there were outbreaks of something alternately called flu and food poisoning. It was enough to make the Meades test the air. They found evidence of a major spill that had likely seeped into the air vents.

The fires were a cover-up then?

Yes. A cleanup was done in every sense of the word. Internal memos were wiped from the files. There are still records of what events were held during those days leading up to the fire, but there's only a scanty record of who attended each. The outbreak of illness wasn't widespread enough to attract the attention of state authorities. The Meades were satisfied that they had caught the spill early and had totally cleaned it up.

And they thought that absolved them of responsibility? Did they do anything for any of those people?

A few things have been done, but quietly enough so that the people involved don't know why those things were done.

Are there more sites like this?

Yes. The day care center sits on top of one. It was built there under the same premise. For what it's worth, there have been no other leaks. Given the years that have passed since the last leak, Sandy Meade is assuming that those two simply had problems, and that these others will hold.

And they're willing to take the risk, knowing that children are in harm's way?

Apparently. They grow more secure

with the passage of time. They see the lack of a leak as proof that there won't ever be one. I see it as a tragedy waiting to happen. That's why I need you.

I was appalled. Even aside from what had happened before, I couldn't imagine what kind of evil mind could do that to children, and that raised a new issue.

If, say, Sandy Meade were to drop dead today, what would happen? Would the sons continue this practice?

That depends which son takes over.

James is in line.

Don't be so sure. By the way, you looked like you were really into it at Omie's.

You were there and didn't present yourself to me? When will we meet?

When we have evidence that's workable. We need names. We need people who were at one of those two sites during the week in question, who have suffered physical problems since, and who are willing to talk.

What's in it for them? Can we offer them help of some sort?

<u>WE</u> can't, but I assume the Meades will as part of a settlement. Isn't that where we're headed?

It was. Of course, before any settlement could be reached, there would have to be a confrontation with the Meades. I didn't look forward to that. Their three to my one would be formidable odds. If TrueBlue came out of the closet, that might make it their three to my two, but I couldn't count on his doing that. By his own declaration, he wanted to continue to work at the mill. That would be impossible if he stuck it to the Meades.

Nor could I count on Tom. Oh, he was being a *huge* help to me. Not only had he gotten us an appointment with his friend in New York, but he had also given us my mother's files, so that we would be able to show the doctor something of the family history with regard to Phoebe's ailments.

But his job, too, would be on the line if he came forward.

The public side of this fight appeared to be mine and mine alone.

Chapter 19

Nicole DuPuis was feeling complacent after her talk with Aidan. She had him over a barrel, and he knew it. If her marriage fell apart, he would have to help her out — and it wasn't blackmail, exactly. But the truth was, he had a good thing going in her, totally *aside* from the sex. She held up his end of the business in ways she was startled by herself sometimes. She was Aidan's voice; she made him articulate. Sandy Meade was certainly fooled. He was relying on Aidan more and more to be the front man for the mill. If things continued as they were, Aidan was a shoo-in for chairman of the board after Sandy, and that was in Nicole's best interest, too. With Aidan as chairman, she would be all the more indispensable. Moreover, if he were chairman, he would have unlimited access to funds. If enough came her way, she could kick Anton out on her own.

She would like that, would like it a *lot*. Anton was a lying cheat. They no longer shared a bed, but there were still meals and

435

social events to endure. Nicole hated the constant tension. It was wearing on her.

Precisely because of that, she had put off talking with Kaitlin, because that would invite *more* tension. Kaitlin was touchy enough as it was. Oh, she put on an act. She smiled and nodded and said, *Yes, Mom, I will.* But Nicole could see the anger beneath. Confronting her about what she might have told Annie Barnes could be unpleasant.

Then Omie died, and everyone was at the diner on Friday, and how to miss Kaitlin's connection with Annie? Every time Nicole looked, it seemed, Kaitlin was either talking with Annie or standing close by. Add Hal, pointing it out and expressing concern about what appeared to be a blossoming relationship, even suggesting that Kaitlin had become the liaison between Annie and the other young girls, and Nicole couldn't put it off any longer.

She waited until the funeral was done Saturday morning and Anton had left to play golf. Kaitlin was out by the pool, wearing a bathing suit that was at least a size too small. Her body was smeared with oil. She was stretched out on a lounger, talking on the phone. When she saw Nicole approach, she ended the call, dropped the cell phone onto a towel on the ground, and closed her eyes.

"Who were you talking to?" Nicole asked in a friendly way, one that was actually sincere. She did want to be friends with her daughter. She truly did. It just hadn't happened yet.

"No one," Kaitlin replied.

Nicole smiled. "Couldn't have been no one all that time."

"No one important."

"Kristal?"

"Jen," Kaitlin said. Without opening her eyes, she put a hand down on the far side of the lounger, took a cherry from a bowl, and put it in her mouth. Removing the stem, she dropped it back in the bowl.

"Ah. Jen." Nicole liked Jen. She and her mother had the kind of relationship Nicole envied. Pulling over a second lounger, she sat on its lower half. "Can we talk?"

Kaitlin was chewing the cherry. "Mm-hm."

"You were with Annie Barnes a lot yesterday. Any special reason?"

She shook her head, spit the pit into her hand, and dropped it into the bowl.

"You've been seeing her a lot."

"No more than anyone else in town."

"They don't talk with her. You do."

Kaitlin slit open an eye and raised her head just enough to look at Nicole. "How do you know? Is someone telling you this?"

"I could see it for myself yesterday at the diner." Kaitlin had looked perfectly comfortable with Annie — not only comfortable, but happy. Nicole hadn't seen her that way in a long time. "What do you two talk about?"

Kaitlin dropped her head back again. "She was telling me how to arrange the chicken fingers on the platter. There's a knack to it."

That was exactly the kind of remark that irked Nicole — innocent on the surface, mocking beneath. "Don't be fresh, Kaitlin."

"I'm serious. That's what we talked about."

"Lots of people in town are concerned about Annie Barnes," Nicole said in self-defense. "It isn't just me."

"Like who else?"

"Mr. Healy, for one thing. He thinks she's a bad influence on girls your age."

"Mr. Healy would think that. He's *so* full of hot air."

Nicole agreed with her on that, but wasn't about to admit it. For the current purpose, Hal was simply the high school principal. "He's concerned about Annie Barnes."

Kaitlin rose on her elbows, both eyes open. "Concerned about *what?*"

"That she'll worm her way into your lives, then turn around and write about it."

Kaitlin made a face. Sitting all the way up, she reached down for the cherry bowl and settled it in her lap. "She is not writing a book about Middle River." She put another cherry in her mouth, pulled off the stem, and dropped it in the bowl.

"How do you know?"

"She *told* me," she said around the fruit.

"And how did that subject arise?"

She spit the pit into her hand. "I *asked* her, Mom. Half the *town's* been asking. Do you have a problem with that?"

"No problem," Nicole said, because she really *didn't* want to fight. But there was still the whole business about what Kaitlin knew and what she might have told Annie. This whole conversation was about damage control, wasn't it?

So she reversed herself and said with greater force, "Actually, yes, I have a problem. Women like Annie Barnes are devious. They act like they're your friend, then they stab you in the back. She may be using you, Kaitlin. I hope you haven't told her anything you could come to regret."

"Like what?"

"Well, *I* don't know." Nicole wasn't about to mention Aidan. There was always a chance Kaitlin was still in the dark about that.

"I trust her."

"Oh God. You have told her things."

"All I mean," Kaitlin said, "is that she isn't using me. She isn't that kind of person." She took another cherry.

"And you know what kind of person she is?" Nicole asked. "You are seventeen, Kaitlin. You are *not* an authority on who to trust. Do you have any idea what happens when someone like that takes your confidences and spreads them around? Do you know the harm that can be caused? Annie Barnes does. She knows it firsthand. You tell her stories about *any* of us, and once they're out, there's no taking them back. Some things are meant to stay private. And stop eating those *cherries*, for God's sake. They're filled with sugar. That bathing suit is tight enough already."

Nicole knew she had made a mistake the instant the words were out of her mouth. Kaitlin's face grew stony.

"And that," the girl announced coldly, "is why I *like* Annie Barnes. She wouldn't say something like that. She doesn't think I'm fat at all. She was ugly, too, when she was my age. I'd like to grow up to be like her."

Nicole was startled. "You're not ugly."

"No? Then why do we work on my nose, my teeth, my jaw, my hair, and my skin?"

"I have never said you were ugly."

"You don't use that word, but you say it in all sorts of other ways. 'My bathing suit is tight enough,' " she mocked. " 'Stop eating those *cherries,* for God's sake.' Mom, I'm not deaf. I hear what you're saying. Well, maybe I'm not *meant* to be as beautiful and thin as you are."

"I *never* said you were ugly."

"Fat is ugly, and you're always telling me what to wear that will make me look thinner. Now you're even saying I'm dumb."

"I am *not.*"

"I am *not* an authority on who to trust," Kaitlin mocked again. Cradling the bowl of cherries, she grabbed her cell phone and stood. "Well, maybe I'm smarter than you think. Maybe I do know who to trust. Annie Barnes understands me more than you do. She *knows* what I'm feeling. She's *been* there. If she says she isn't writing a book, I believe her — and if *you* have a problem with that, it's because you're afraid all *your* secrets will come out. Well, she doesn't *know* your secrets, and it has nothing to do with whether I trust her with them or not. There are people in this town I'd talk about before I talked about my own parents. Do you think I'm proud of what you and Dad do? Why do you think I don't have friends over?"

"You do," Nicole argued, but a hole was opening up inside her.

"Not for dinner. Not for weekends. Not when there's a chance you and Dad will both be here, because it's like anyone can *see* how much you hate each other — and don't try to deny it. I've heard you say things to friends on the phone."

Nicole was appalled. "You had no business listening."

"I was in the *room*. How could I *help* but hear? I'm not three anymore, Mom. You can't just say things and think I don't know what they mean — and besides, I *saw* Dad with that woman. They were in bed, and they were naked in the middle of the day. They were having sex. Do you think I don't know what that is?"

Nicole gave an uneasy laugh. "Well, yes, I was kind of hoping that."

"Because I'm ugly? Because I'm fat? Y'know, there are some guys who don't care."

Her unease increased. "What are you saying?"

The girl looked angry enough to go on. Then she caught herself, let out a breath, and calmed. "I'm saying that it is *the* most obvious thing how bad your marriage is, and if I had my friends over more, they'd see it in a sec, and it'd be embarrassing. So if I feel that way, why would I ever tell Annie Barnes what goes on here? I am not *totally* stupid. Give me credit for that at least, will you?" Grabbing her towel, she walked off.

Sunday morning, Sabina went to church with her family. She was feeling a particular need for comfort. Part of it had to do with losing Omie, who had symbolized all that was stable and safe. The rest was more complex. It had to do with accepting that Phoebe was sick, with appreciating Annie's help, and with feeling that, deep down inside, something in her own life was about to shift.

She didn't understand what the last was until the service ended and she went around back to visit her parents' grave. The grass had filled in over Alyssa's coffin, the rhodies flanking the stone had grown, and the impatiens that she and Phoebe had put in earlier that summer were a bright orange, pink, and white — all attesting to the strength of the growing season in Middle River this year.

The setting was lush, and so, in its way, was her life. Ron and Timmy had stayed out front, but Lisa was with her, holding her hand in a way that Sabina knew was precious, given how grown-up the girl was becoming. Sabina was truly blessed with her children, certainly with her husband, and, yes, with her sisters. Her parents were pleased that she understood it; she could feel that here in the warmth of the sun.

After a few minutes, they headed back. Just beyond the graveyard gate, they bumped into Aidan Meade and Marshall Greenwood. When Aidan spotted her, he broke into a crooked smile. "We were just talking about your sister," he said.

Sabina gave Lisa's hand a squeeze. "Go on out with the others. Tell your dad I'll be right there." When Lisa ran ahead, Sabina turned to Aidan. "Which sister?"

"The troubled one."

Sabina gave a curious smile. "Which one is that?"

"Annie," Marshall said in his sandpapery voice. "I had quite a time with her on

Thursday. She's riling up people all around town."

"Huh," Sabina mused. "No one seemed upset with her Friday at Omie's."

"They were being polite," Aidan advised. "After all, it was a wake. But she annoyed someone enough to get her tires slashed the day before. I'd call that a message."

That was when Sabina felt the shift. It was subtle, but distinct. "Kind of like the one you gave me on Wednesday, the one where you threatened to fire me if I didn't get Annie to leave town?" She looked at Marshall. "If I didn't know better, I'd say you guys were behind those slashed tires."

"Uh-huh," said Aidan. "And have you shared that theory with anyone?"

"Not yet," Sabina replied with a smile. "It just came to me now, seeing you two out here talking, by your own admission, about Annie."

Marshall tugged on his belt. "So she's gone off to New York? How long's she staying?"

"She's with Phoebe, so it's *they*. *They* will be back on Tuesday." Sabina raised her brows. "What's next? Think someone'll take a potshot at the house? String up roadkill on the porch? Burglarize the store?" Looking from one to the other and feeling a distaste for both, she identified that little shift inside. It had to do with loyalty. "Here's a promise. If something else happens, first thing *I'm* doing is calling the state police."

Aidan drew himself up. "That sounds like a warning. I don't like warnings, Sabina."

"Yeah, I know," Sabina commiserated. "They really make you feel small and powerless, don't they?" She smiled again. "You, though, are big and powerful. All it takes is a word from you, Aidan. Let Marshall here know that Annie is to be protected, and she will be protected."

"I want her gone," Aidan stated flatly.

"Well, she will be that, too. She's only here for the month, and nearly half of that's passed. Two more weeks, Aidan. That's all. Can't we make this work?"

Chapter 20

Phoebe and I left for New York immediately after the funeral, and the timing couldn't have been better. For the tiniest while I had actually felt *comfortable* in Middle River. But feeling comfortable was a luxury I couldn't afford. My life was elsewhere. I needed a reminder that there was, indeed, life beyond.

That reminder came as soon as we passed through airport security in Manchester. Had I truly felt unsafe because someone had slashed my tires in Middle River? The thought of bona fide terrorism put that in perspective and, emotionally, it was uphill from there.

New York was my kind of town. When I had decided to join Phoebe, I had upgraded our reservations, not because I didn't want to stay in the more modest hotel she had initially booked, but because I had promised her a good time, and location was everything. Our room overlooked Central Park and couldn't have been more lovely. We had barely unpacked when a bottle of wine and a bowl of fruit arrived, and Phoebe felt pampered. The feeling remained when we shopped. We hit Fifth Avenue and did more window-shopping than anything, though I did buy Phoebe a beautiful scarf at Bergdorf's and, at Takashimaya, bath salts and body lotion.

We also stopped at the Godiva boutique at Rockefeller Plaza. You already know I love chocolate. What you don't know is that I have a thing — a *real* thing — for Godiva truffles. And not just *any* Godiva truffles. I would beg for a roasted almond truffle and steal for a smooth coconut, but for a hazelnut praline, I could be tempted to kill.

I'm kidding, of course. But I was happier once my shoulder bag contained that little box of truffles.

We walked over to Madison and shopped more. I kept an elbow linked with Phoebe's to steady her, but it brought us closer even beyond the physical. We talked as we walked — about Mom and Daddy, about Sabina and rivalry and happy times, too. Then Phoebe flagged. We returned to our hotel for high tea in the lobby, and, reinvigorated, visited the Central Park Zoo. Phoebe needed a nap after that, but she loved the restaurant where we ate dinner. I was gratified. It had always been a favorite of Greg's and mine.

We spent Sunday and Monday at the buyer's show, held at the piers on the Hudson, and I gained a new respect for what Phoebe did. This was hard work. I have never seen so much merchandise of so many different kinds, with so many people so skilled in the sell. How much of what to buy and in what colors? Amazingly, Phoebe was able to sort through it all.

I know what you're thinking. You're thinking that her problem wasn't physical at all but purely mental, that it was depression, and that removing her from Middle River had lifted her spirits. I had been hoping that, too. But it wasn't the case. The physical problems remained — the odd gait, bad balance, fine tremor. She still easily lost her train of thought and had trouble finding words. What she did with regard to work, though, was to compensate. She had brought along notes and reminders, and not only checked them often herself but had prepped me on them, so that I could assist her as smoothly as possible.

Using the past as a guide, she moved methodically down a list of known vendors. And she was remarkable. She might have faltered at first, but she always ended up asking the right questions of each, expressing reservations when the pitched merchandise was inappropriate, approaching new vendors when their goods caught her eye. She drew on every bit of her inner wherewithal to stay focused. But it exhausted her. We had room service deliver our dinner both nights.

Then came Tuesday morning. Phoebe had expected that we would sleep late and leisurely return to the airport. She was not at all happy when I told her what I had done. I do believe that if she had been rested, she would have flat out refused. She protested, but feebly. She said she didn't need a doctor. She said that I had no business making an appointment behind her back, and that I was causing a rift between Sabina and her. She argued that Alyssa had not had mercury poisoning and therefore why in the world should she?

But she didn't have the strength to fight for long. Any last protest died when Sabina called on the phone in support of my plan.

Judith Barlow was a surprise. Anticipating a specialist in alternative medicine, I had expected someone close in age to

Tom, but she was easily approaching sixty. I had expected someone who looked eccentric, but she was elegant in a simple and conservative way. Likewise her office, which, contrary to my expectation, was in a prime (read "high rent") area, and was large, professional, and polished. The woman clearly had a successful practice.

She smiled when I was drawn to the diplomas on the wall. "People come here half expecting that I got my degree from Sears Roebuck."

"Harvard?" I was impressed.

"Undergraduate and medical school, with my training at Mass General. The fact is that I practiced traditional medicine for twenty years before I moved into the other."

"Why the move?"

"Too many people came in with problems that I couldn't touch with traditional treatment. When you reach the point of having tried everything and getting nowhere, you have to look farther."

"We're not quite at that stage," I cautioned with a glance at my sister. She was sitting in a chair, looking frightened. "Phoebe hasn't seen a doctor, but her symptoms are identical to those we saw in our mother. I was hoping we could skip treatment that didn't work on Mom."

Judith sat down at her desk, put on wire-rimmed reading glasses, and studied the file I had brought. When she was done, she opened a clean file on Phoebe and proceeded to ask more questions than I had ever heard a doctor ask at a single sitting. More important, she asked the *right* questions. I'm still not sure whether Phoebe had decided to cooperate or was simply worn down by what ailed her so that she had no defense. But I was stunned by some of her answers. I knew about the obvious symptoms. But joint pain? Itchy skin? Night headaches? These were all news.

There was a physical exam, followed by more tests than I thought a single doctor's office was capable of performing. But Tom had known what he was doing in recommending Judith. She had a remarkable facility, with nearly every diagnostic tool at her fingertips, and those that she didn't have were in nearby office suites. Moreover, she was able to get quick readings on tests, so that she could decide which ones to do next.

We missed our plane. And Phoebe grew increasingly cranky. Taking one test after the other was grueling and, of course, there were waits between tests. But Judith was methodical. At every turn, she explained what she was testing for and why. As Tom had told me she would, she ruled out every conventional ailment before she ever mentioned mercury.

That came in the final sit-down. "If these symptoms were new," she told Phoebe, "say, within the last three or four months, I'd test a hair sample for the presence of mercury. Given how long you've had symptoms, though, mercury from an initial exposure would have long since grown out. Absent our ability to actually isolate it through other tests, I can only make an educated guess. Mercury is the leading suspect. Things like grogginess and itchy skin aren't indicative of Parkinson's or Alzheimer's. Nor is asthma, which is what that lingering cold of yours appears to be. So we have a choice. We can treat the symptoms. Or we can go for a cure."

I looked at Phoebe, but she didn't seem to know what to say. So I asked, "What does a cure entail?"

Judith explained the general premise of chelation therapy to Phoebe, much as Tom had to me. But she went further, patiently explaining the details. "The specific protocol for this treatment is evolving as the results of new studies come in. Normally, I would recommend the oral route, which would entail a varying schedule of pills taken every four hours on alternate weeks, then, depending on your progress, a switch to pills taken three to four days every week or two. We do it slowly over a period of months, and we give you breaks. It's gentler. But it does take a while before you feel better."

"What's a while?" I asked.

"Two to six months. On the other hand, given your proximity to Tom, he could administer a newer protocol that involves an eight-hour intravenous infusion. Some believe that this is the only way to remove mercury from the brain. The infusion hits your body hard. Following it, you have a bad couple of days during which you can't do much of anything. But then suddenly you *do* feel better. We repeat the infusion every few months, until the mercury is gone."

"How can you tell when it's gone?"

"When mercury is pulled from the organs, as happens in chelation therapy, it is expelled in the urine."

"I thought mercury wasn't expelled that way."

"On its own, it isn't. Attached to a

chelation agent, it is. In those few days following the infusion, we closely monitor the urine for its mercury content."

"How long until it's gone?"

"Not knowing exactly how much is there, I can't tell for sure. In general, though, it takes one to four years until you're free of the metal."

"*That* long?" Phoebe cried feebly.

Judith smiled. "It isn't so long when you stop and think about how long you've been experiencing these symptoms." She patted Phoebe's file, which had mushroomed in a day. "According to what you've told me, you've been symptomatic at some level for several years." She shot me a glance. "Now the thing to do is to find out when and where you were exposed."

I called Sabina from the cab on the way to the airport. She had been trying me every few hours and was waiting for word. To her credit, she listened. More than that, she *heard*.

"Not Parkinson's?" she asked.

"The doctor doubts it."

"Does that mean Mom didn't have Parkinson's either?"

"It's hard to tell. Mom was older than Phoebe when she got sick, and in fairness to Tom, the symptoms could have fit Parkinson's. But Phoebe has other symptoms." As I spoke, my poor sister was tucked into a far corner of the tattered leather seat, staring out the window in something of a fog. I'm not even sure she heard what I said. I asked Sabina, "Did you know that she gets intense skin rashes on her stomach?"

"No."

"Or that she has pain in her joints?"

"She thought that was the flu."

"She's had those pains on and off for several years."

"Several years, and she didn't *say* something?"

I had been frustrated, too. But I could see Phoebe's point. "She thought it was age. Early arthritis. Then Mom got really bad and Phoebe was frightened. Mom died. It's scary when you have the same symptoms. But there's hope for Phoebe." I explained what chelation was about.

"Attaches to metal?" Sabina echoed. "Couldn't that metal be lead?"

"The blood workup says no. No lead there. Mercury won't show up in the blood, but that's what the doctor thinks it is."

"The doctor, or you?" Sabina asked with the old distrust.

"I was quiet, Sabina. I didn't say the *m* word once. She came up with mercury all on her own." When Sabina was silent, I said, "I know you don't want to hear this. It complicates things, because if mercury is the problem, there's only one possible source." I waited for her to argue, and still she was silent. "Do you know what I mean? Sabina?" I checked the bars on my cell. There was barely one.

We weren't able to reconnect until Phoebe and I reached the airport, and then I couldn't talk. There was too much to do, what with supporting Phoebe and our luggage. We managed to get seats on the last flight to Manchester, but time was short and the security lines long. I had visions of our missing this plane, too, and sweated it out. We actually made it to the gate with a handful of minutes to spare before boarding began. Moving off to the side, I called Sabina.

"Hey," I said. "Can you talk?"

"Yeah. I'm trying to take in what you said. How's Phoebe handling it?"

"Hard to tell, she's so tired. She says she's relieved. Poor thing must have been terrified of getting worse and worse."

"Mercury? Are you *sure?*"

"Yes. And I have to tell you more,

457

Sabina." It was time. I needed an ally. Sabina's mind seemed open. I spoke quickly, wanting to get it all out before we boarded the plane. "Remember the fires that totaled the Clubhouse and the Gazebo? They were set." Without mentioning TrueBlue, I told her what he had said.

Sabina was fast to respond. "I find that very hard to believe. There was a clandestine clean-up, and *none* of the people involved told *anyone* about it?"

"What if they weren't told what had spilled? Or what if they had been sworn to secrecy? The Meades give bonuses for that kind of thing. *Big* bonuses."

"Wouldn't they have gotten sick themselves?"

"Not if they were wearing protective gear."

"But you're talking arson — and *fraud*. That's big-time criminal behavior. It's a lot to swallow. A lot. Who's your source?"

"I can't say yet, but think about it, Sabina. If this plot was in a book, it would make total sense, wouldn't it?"

"But do you know how many events take place at the Clubhouse?" she continued to argue. "If there was a mercury spill beneath it, wouldn't *all* those people be sick?"

"Not if they weren't there on one of the few days between the spill and the fire. What if we found that Mom was? What if Phoebe was? She can't remember. At the time of the Clubhouse fire, she was already working with Mom. We need to try to reconstruct her schedule. Same with other people who might have been there. I talked with the McCreedys."

"Annie —"

"Don't worry. They deny any connection. But look at the physical problems they've had. They're florists. They do work for the mill. Isn't it feasible that they were at the Clubhouse delivering flowers for an event that Mom attended?"

"I don't think you should be involving other people yet. This is *so* off the wall."

I didn't snap at her, just stayed calm and cool. "Look at it this way. If Phoebe does have chronic mercury poisoning and can be helped with Dr. Barlow's protocol, how many other people in Middle River could use the same?" I had been listening to airport voices with half an ear, but suddenly heard the right words. "They're calling our flight, Sabina. I have to get Phoebe. We won't be arriving in Middle River until late, and I want to go running early tomorrow. I'm feeling emotionally stuffed up, if you know what I mean. Can we talk later in the morning?"

Emotionally stuffed up? Well, that was one way to put it. Another was curious. I wanted to see James.

Wanted to? Was *dying* to. What can I say — he was an incredible lover. I would have thought that being a Meade, he would have made love in an egotistical, *Me, Tarzan!* sort of way. And he was strong. And forceful. And definitely took the lead — but he also took care to make sure he satisfied me.

Granted, it wasn't a hard thing to do. One look at James, and my insides quickened.

About now, you're probably thinking that I am a total hypocrite. After all, since I'd last seen James, I had learned that he and his family had been involved in the dirtiest, most immoral of activities. I mean, knowing that people were exposed to mercury and not telling them what it was that they had? That was as low as it got.

I could rationalize and say that something didn't fit about all this, and it didn't. James didn't seem all bad. Hadn't he tried to separate himself from his father and brother that first day we talked at Omie's?

Besides, could a man who had adopted a baby he clearly adored actually raise her in the shadow of poison? Granted, he didn't bring her to the day care center at the mill. He had a nanny. Still, I had to believe he cared for his child.

So that was one reason I wanted to see him in spite of all that I had learned. But there was his parting shot at Omie's last Friday. *I don't do one-night stands.* I didn't know what he had meant by that, but I also didn't know what I *wanted* him to mean. He was my summer fling. That's all. We had no future, James and I. James was a Meade. End of story.

That said, as summer flings went, he was hot and heavy — and that was *not* my imagination. So maybe I was curious to see if I could make him hot and heavy again. Was my ego involved? Of course, it was! Remember, another Meade had made a fool of me once. Egos don't forget things like that.

Despite getting home after midnight, I was up at six Wednesday morning. By six-thirty, I was sitting in the yard with Mom's flowers, the willow, and my second cup of coffee. I called Tom at seven to tell him to expect a call from Judith. At seven-thirty, I checked on Phoebe, who was sleeping still.

I left her a note, propped it on the kitchen table, and set off for the varsity course.

The high school parking lot had a sprinkling of cars now, more than last week, fewer than next week. By then, if we continued to run at eight, we would be seen. Of course, James had no choice but to run at that hour. I understood that now. He couldn't leave the house until Mia's nanny arrived.

Skirting the cars in the lot, I drove to the back and rounded the corner. James's SUV was there. The man himself was stretching on the grass.

My pulse gave a hitch, then raced on ahead. I parked, climbed from the car. He shot me a small smile, which I returned. Then I joined him stretching.

You are such a coward, Grace declared. *He is the man to talk with. Are you going to stand there and stretch, when he has answers you need? "My pulse gave a hitch, then raced on ahead." Oh please!*

Whoa. Weren't you the first one to tell me how sexy he is?

I never slept with the enemy. For that matter, I never slept with men I didn't love. But all that is beside the point. The point is that the man stretching

*right over there is someone to chal-
lenge. His family is bad. You need to
talk to him about this.*

But we don't talk, James and I. We run.
And we make love. We don't bring in the
rest of the world. Hey, he could be asking
me about my trip right now, but he isn't.
I'm okay with that. It works on my end.

*That's why I say you're a coward.
Life is about confrontation. I lived in a
time when women didn't dare speak
their piece, and I did speak my piece.
That took guts.*

And look where it got you. You drowned
in a bottle and died. What do you want
from me?

*Confrontation. You live in a time
when you can speak out against
wrongs, and you do have the goods on
the guy. So speak. You owe it to me.*

To you? I was startled.

*Yes. I coddled you when you needed
it. I gave you your identity, for God's
sake.*

Hah. It's been a yoke.

*It's been a boon. So now I'm asking
for your help. I need the Meades destroyed.*

Why?

Because I can't do it myself. Because

463

I died too young. Because I had too many other problems, and those problems mucked things up. You don't have those problems. Don't you see, Annie. If you do this — if you go home to your little New England town, turn over those rocks, and expose the dirt — it'll validate what I did myself. I was vilified. That wasn't fair. I was living in the wrong place at the wrong time. I need you to set things straight.

"Ready to run?" James asked.

The sound of his voice silenced Grace. I knew she'd be back. She had raised a valid point. We needed to discuss it, she and I. But not now.

Pushing myself to my feet, I nodded. We headed for the woods and set off on the path — and it was a relief from the start. I did need the airing-out. It was only as I ran that I realized how tense I had been those days with Phoebe. Running now, the tension began to melt from my limbs. I focused on the warm air and the trees, on the pine needles and the sun that pierced them. I focused on being back here doing something I liked — and when we passed the cutoff to Cooper's Point, I focused on how far I'd come. Feeling strong, I lengthened my stride.

That was when I hit James — just ran smack into him — because he stopped short. Turning quickly, he caught my arm and steadied me. We were both breathing hard.

Our eyes met, and it was there again, every bit of what we had shared the Thursday before and then some, because this time we knew where it could go. He dipped his head and caught my mouth, and it was almost comical, trying to kiss that way with the two of us breathless from running, but amazingly it worked. He deepened the kiss — or did I? — because a simple kiss wasn't enough. Nor was not touching. My back found a tree that fit, and he pressed me there. His hands moved from my thighs over my middle to my breasts — both hands, both breasts — while I worked my own against his groin.

I heard a cry. I might have thought it had come from James, if it hadn't been so high. And it wasn't from me. At least, I didn't think it was.

Apparently, neither did James. He stopped what he was doing and lifted his head. "There it is again," he said in a raggedy way. "I thought that was you."

"Again?"

"I heard it before. That's why I stopped."

"You thought I —"

"Wanted me." He looked off into the woods.

I might have been embarrassed — like he had stopped only because he thought *I* needed *him*, like I was a charity case — if I hadn't felt his erection against me. It had been there all along. The need was mutual.

But that cry came again, and I, too, looked toward deeper woods.

"Trouble?" I whispered, quickly forgetting my own need.

"I don't know," he whispered back, apparently past his own need as well. Taking my hand, he led me off the path and into the woods. We worked our way between trees, over pine needles and moss, around rocks.

Still holding my hand, James stopped and waited. The cry came again, definitely human and female. Our eyes met.

"Distress?" I whispered.

"Doesn't sound it," he whispered back, "but can we be sure?"

We couldn't. On the chance that there was indeed trouble, James put me behind him. I clutched the back of his shirt and measured my steps to his and we moved on.

We didn't have to go much farther. Just when another cry came, we rounded a tall patch of ferns to an opening in the woods — and, looking around his arm, I caught my breath. A woman was there, bound to a tree.

No, I realized. Not bound. Her back was to the tree and her arms curved around it behind her, but there were no ropes. Her eyes were closed, head turned to the side, long dark hair draped over her shoulder. No, there were no bonds. Ecstasy held her there, aided by the dark head and pale male body that covered her lower half.

"*Omigod*," I whispered and would have backed up as silently as we had come — we were intruding on *the* most intimate of activities — if James hadn't been so firmly planted where he stood. I gave a tiny tug at his elbow, but he wasn't moving. Even more startling, he put his hands on his hips.

The wait wasn't long. I don't know whether something tipped off the woman (whom I didn't recognize) or whether she had simply reached a break in her ecstasy-driven bliss, but her head rolled to the front and her eyes opened. She didn't cry out then. She screamed. Her arms crossed her torso to cover her breasts. Her lover looked up, then around.

I did recognize him. Instantly. It was Hal Healy — Hal, who was so in love with his voluptuous wife that he couldn't keep his eyes or hands off her; Hal, who had accused *me* of being a negative influence on the impressionable young girls in town; Hal, the illustrious principal of good old Middle River High. We had stumbled across another of Middle River's dirty little secrets.

"You self-righteous prick," James said.

Hal seemed to sink lower toward the ground, trying to hide his buttocks from our view, though he couldn't turn without exposing himself more. He couldn't run, couldn't hide. All he could do was to go red in the face, which he did. It would have been humorous, if it hadn't been so pathetic.

"It's not what you think," he managed in a shaky voice. His eyes were on James, not me. James was clearly the threat.

"No?" James asked. "Then what is it?" To me, James said toward his shoulder, "I assume you know Dr. Healy. The lovely woman with him is Miss Eloise Delay, the guidance counselor he hired last year. She's fresh out of college, which makes her substantially younger than our prinicpal.

468

She gives advice to troubled students."

Miss Eloise Delay was frozen against the tree, covering herself as best she could, her eyes large and filled with horror. She looked like she would have welcomed death, if that were her only means of escape.

"Don't take this out on her," Hal begged.

"Was she unwilling? It didn't look it. I'd heard rumors, Hal. People are wondering why you're all over your wife whenever anyone is looking, at the same time *she's* complaining that you're at school night after night. The rumors hinted that it was someone at school, but could never quite home in on who. So it's you and Eloise, working late evenings? That's bad enough. But here, in broad daylight? What if I'd been one of your students? What if I'd been a whole group of your students?"

Lacking an answer, Hal begged, "Back off so we can get dressed, at least."

"When I'm done," James said with every bit of the authority I had always attributed to him. He didn't have to raise his voice to imbue it with thunder. "What are we going to do with you?"

"It will never happen again," Hal said.

"How many times have students said

that, just prior to being suspended or, worse, expelled? How long's it been going on, Miss Delay? Was the spark there when you interviewed for the job?"

Eloise didn't speak. I suspected she couldn't have found her voice if she'd tried.

"Hal?" James prodded. "How long? I remember when you hired her, there was some talk about her being inexperienced. You were her champion before the school board. What was it you said? Stellar academic record? Brilliant recommendations? Personality plus? I guess the *plus* takes on new meaning now."

I touched James's arm. "Let's go," I whispered.

But James wasn't done. "What about your wife, Hal? She's lived in this town all her life. Do you have any idea what happens when the rumors go to work? Think it's fun for her? Okay, so you resign and take a job somewhere else, but what about her? This is her home. Are you going to uproot her and take her along? Is she your cover? Is that it? Or will you divorce her and scoot off with Miss Delay?"

"James," I repeated. I detested Hal Healy, but I was beginning to squirm.

My plea registered. James made a

scornful sound in his throat, turned and strode off. I followed gladly.

"What are you going to do?" Hal cried.

Calling back over his shoulder now, James thundered, and I have to say it was awesome: "Let you *wonder* what I'm going to do."

Back on the path, he continued to stride, taking the shortest route to the parking lot.

"James?" I called from several paces behind.

He held up a hand and went on, stopping only when we reached the grass on the far side of the trees. Bending over, he put his hands on his knees and hung his head. I came alongside, but just stood there and waited until he had regained control. Then he straightened.

His eyes met mine. "I'm not sorry for one word of that. He deserved it. He's a pompous ass. But what about us? Are we any different?"

I knew exactly what he was thinking. Lord knew I had my faults, but I refused to group myself with the Hal Healys of the world. "Yes, we're different. For one thing, when we did it here, it was dark. For another, neither of us is married. For a third, *we* don't preach abstinence and restraint. He does — all the time, from what I hear.

471

My niece was telling me that he's even cracked down on the showing of bare skin in school, and I agree completely, except that he has some gall to be calling for that, when he's out here without a stitch of clothing on *and* with someone who isn't his wife."

James's eyes were dark. "Are you Greg Steele's lover?"

"No."

"You live together, but you don't do it?"

"No."

"Did you ever?"

"No. We're very good friends. The cost of condos in the District has gone through the roof, but because we pooled our resources, we could afford something good. Neither one of us wanted to live alone. We'd rather live with each other than with anyone else. We see other people; if one of those relationships ever gets serious, we would sell the condo, but for now, this works. We have separate bedrooms on separate floors. We've never been sexually involved."

I'm not sure if my answer pleased him. His eyes remained dark, not so much doubting as haunted. "So what we did hasn't broken any moral code. And yes, we did it before in the dark. But just now, would we have stopped what we were doing if we hadn't heard her cry?"

He had me there. I couldn't answer. The truth was that when I was with James like that, the rest of the world didn't exist.

He grunted. "Yeah. I know. So what are we going to do about it?"

"Do we have to do anything?" I asked with a half smile. "Can't we just enjoy it while it lasts?"

He studied me for another minute, then pushed a hand through his rumpled hair. Leaving that hand on the back of his neck, he regarded me with what seemed like amazement and returned my half smile. "I keep saying, is this really Annie Barnes? The old Annie Barnes, who was such a royal pain in the Meade butt way back when? I don't understand why I'm attracted to you."

"Thanks."

"You know what I mean. Don't you feel the same way?"

Suddenly I was very serious. I wouldn't have picked this time or place. I actually would have let it go awhile, because it was so nice just . . . feeling James Meade against my body . . . and surely this kind of discussion would ruin that. But here was another truth, but I've lost track of the count, so what is it, maybe **TRUTH #18? Time and place have a mind of their own**. We can decide one thing. Then another thing happens, and our decision is moot. We can't go back, only ahead.

"You bet I do," I said, and what came out of my mouth then had nothing to do with Grace. She had been a victim of her own time and place, but this was mine. "You're the bad guy. I should *not* be attracted to you, especially after what I learned in New York. My sister went through a whole barrage of medical tests there, the upshot of which is that she has been diagnosed with mercury poisoning. The only source of mercury here is your mill."

"I was under the impression that mercury poisoning could come from dental amalgam."

"It can. But she doesn't have silver fillings. Besides, there have been spills."

He stared at me. Doubting? Daring?

"Phoebe isn't the only one who is sick," I said.

"I know."

I pounced on that. "You know, and you do nothing about it?"

"That isn't exactly correct."

"Enlighten me, please."

He looked off toward the field house, which was the only part of the high school that was visible from where we stood. "Not here. Not now."

"But you raised it. If not here and not now, *when?*"

"Tonight."

"I have to take care of Phoebe. She is really bad, James, and it'll get worse before it's better. She goes in tomorrow for the first of the treatments. Tom's doing it — and, so help me, if you people cause trouble for him because of that, I *will* write my book."

"No trouble. When will Phoebe be in bed tonight?"

"Nine."

"Come then."

Chapter 21

Sabina made breakfast for Ron and the kids, but she was distracted. As soon as Lisa and Timmy had left the room, Ron sat back in his chair. "Calling Sabina," he teased. "Come in, Sabina."

Her eyes flew to his. She smiled sadly. Ron did know her well.

Helping herself to another cup of coffee, she sat kitty-corner to him. "I think . . . we have a problem." She passed on what Annie had told her the night before.

"The first problem is insomnia," Ron said. "You barely slept. Why didn't you tell me this last night?"

"Because I didn't want to believe it — and then, when it kept on nagging at me, I wasn't sure what to *do* with it. There's so much at risk. On one hand, there's Phoebe and all those others who are sick. On the other, there's the mill. Aidan is watching me. The slightest provocation, and he'll fire me." She frowned. "And then there's Annie."

"Sweet, successful, troublemaker Annie," Ron said.

"Troublemaker Annie is right."

"Our very own Grace, stirring things up."

"Yes, and I keep telling myself that, only this time, what she says makes sense. I've been going over it in my mind all night, looking for every reason to say she's simply out for revenge. Except that she's right — as plots go, this one is plausible. Not only that, but it explains so much." She raised her mug and let the scent of the coffee soothe her. In time, she sipped it.

"Did you decide what to do?"

"Actively decide? No. But it's like I'm being swept along with something that I can't drop. This isn't just Annie telling the world that Daddy did most of my sixth-grade science project, or that Phoebe sucked her thumb until she was ten. It isn't just Annie accusing Aidan Meade of being a liar or Sandy Meade of manipulating Sam Winchell. This is poison. It's innocent people being robbed of their health. It's Mom — and maybe Omie and a slew of others — *dying* because of something that could have been prevented." She paused, struck again by the weight of it all. "I mean, it really is bad. Can I turn my back and walk away without saying a word?"

Ron chewed on his cheek.

"Yes, I may lose my job," she went on. "You, too. Would you hate me if it happened?"

"I'd be worried about how we'd survive."

"But suppose we figured that out, would you hate me for what I'd done?"

"I might wonder what it accomplished. Look, Sabina, even if Annie's right, can she really take on the Meades and win?"

Sabina had spent the wee morning hours considering that question. She kept trying to find alternative answers, to give herself *choices*, but only one emerged. Could the Meades actually be beaten?

"This time, yes," she said, "because if what Annie says is right, this is bigger than Middle River. This isn't about who's sleeping with who. It isn't about who has power and who doesn't. It's about who's sick and dying, and whether it can go on." She spoke pleadingly, desperate that her husband understand, because, of all the other arguments, this one tormented her the most. "Our kids were in that day care center, Ron. They were there, each of them, from the time they were three months old until they went to school. What if something had happened during those years? Or before they were born? You're up there by the shipping docks all day, but I'm going to different buildings all the time. What if I had happened to walk through an area where there was a spill while I was pregnant? Getting mercury out of Phoebe's body is one thing, but when there's fetal damage, it's permanent."

Ron countered, "What if I fell off the shipping dock, like Johnny Kraemon did last week? He broke his back. He'll never walk again. Bad things happen."

"Accidents do. But what if we have a chance to prevent them? Don't you see, there's my sister Annie, who has a life somewhere else, and she's committed to this cause — and here I am, with a life right here, and I'm on the fence? Who stands to lose more? How will I feel if she actually *wins* this?"

Ron was silent for a moment, his expression grim. Then, with a chill she rarely heard, he said, "Is it still a race between you two?"

Sabina was stunned. "Low blow, Ron."

"Answer the question. Is the motivation Annie, or is it the cause?"

Taking cover in indignation, Sabina rose from the table, noisily put her mug in the sink, reached for her briefcase, and, without another word to her husband, set off for work.

Middle River was its bucolic self, but she saw little of the sun, little of the trees, flowers, or homes. What she saw were the Waxman twins, age five, riding bicycles in their driveway — and the Hestafield boys, ages eight and eleven, throwing a ball into a pitch-back on their lawn — and the Webster children, age one and three, being strapped into car seats by their mom. Middle River was full of children, all innocent of worry and dependent on the goodness of the town. She wondered if Ron realized that when he questioned her motives — wondered if Annie realized it when she pricked Sabina's conscience — wondered if Aidan realized it when he issued ultimatums.

She arrived at the Data Center feeling entirely unsettled, and that, before she discovered a major electrical problem. Yes, there was a backup generator, but it was nowhere near as powerful as the regular current, which meant that anything she tried to do would be painfully slow.

She called Maintenance, then put several backup CDs in her briefcase. Electrical problems happened. She could always work in one of the other buildings.

But not now. She was *so* not in the mood. Once the electrician arrived, she went outside, crossed through the parking lot, and sank into an Adirondack chair.

Northwood Mill was waking up. She saw Cindy and Edward DePaw pass in their pickup, saw Melissa Morton, Chuck Young, and Wendy Smith in their vehicles, all on this road as opposed to the plant road, because strapped safely into the backseat was a child — destination, the day care center.

Antsy, Sabina pushed herself up and headed across the grass, over a knoll and through a cluster of trees to the marketing department. Part of the Administrative Campus, it was housed in a redbrick Cape comparable with Sabina's Data Center. Selena Post worked here. She and Sabina had become co-conspirators in school when aging teachers confused their names. They still had coffee together from time to time.

Selena's office was warm after a night without air, and filled to the brim with stacks of promotional materials. "Major mailing this week," she told Sabina by way of explanation for the mess.

Sabina slid into the chair by her desk and said in a very low voice, "Mercury.

Know anything about it?"

"Oh yeah. We're clean. That's always been part of our marketing claim."

"Always?"

"Well, for the last few years. It was a while before people realized the harm mercury could do. Every new piece of equipment we buy for the plant is either toxin-free, or comes with the mechanism to nullify whatever toxicity is produced."

"What about cleaning up after the mercury produced years ago?"

"Done back then. Northwood is cited by the state for its environmental considerations. We rank among the top in all of New England for the cleanliness of our plant. That's one of the reasons we can afford to provide such extensive health care coverage for our workers and their families."

Sabina knew there was a chance Selena was right — which left Alyssa's death, Phoebe's illness, and the ailments of so many in town unexplained. But there was also a chance that Selena had fully bought into the hype, or that she was truly ignorant of the problem. In any case, Sabina knew a hard sell when she heard it. Her gut told her that further discussion would be fruitless.

Closing the conversation with Selena, she proceeded on, this time walking along the side of the road, one building back to human resources. Her friend Janice worked there. Fortuitously, she was just climbing from her car when Sabina approached.

"Hey," Janice said with a smile, but the smile faded when Sabina drew closer. "What's wrong?"

"I have to ask you something, Jan," Sabina said in a voice that wouldn't carry past where they stood. "Do you ever hear anything about mercury here at the mill?"

"Not lately. Years ago, maybe. But it's been cleaned up."

"How do you know?"

"I have it from the horse's mouth."

The horse's mouth meant one of the Meades. Sabina tried a different angle. "You handle requests for disability benefits, right?"

"Yes."

"Permanent disability?"

"Some."

"Have there been any suspicious ones? Any trends?"

"Like . . . ?"

"Parkinson's. Alzheimer's. Chronic fatigue. Depression."

"A few. That's where the Meades shine. They come in and help. Not only is the basic benefit package solid, but they add things when the severity of the problem merits it."

Sabina hadn't heard about this before. "What do you mean, 'add things'?"

"Money. It's done in a quiet way, so that the recipient doesn't feel as though people are looking and saying they're pure charity cases. The way it's done, they maintain their dignity. But they are taken care of."

Sabina just bet that they were. It was called "hush money." "Do they sign papers promising not to tell?"

"No," Janice chided. "I mean, I have no idea what's said face-to-face in the privacy of Sandy Meade's office. He handles it himself. He says it's one of the best parts of his job, putting people's minds at ease." She hesitated. "Why do you ask?"

Because, Sabina wanted to say, *you have a little girl in the day care center as we speak, and she may be in danger.* But she didn't say it, because she didn't have proof, and it would be wrong to create unnecessary fear. Just because Annie had presented a convincing scenario didn't mean it was so. *Troublemaker Annie,* Ron had called her. *Our very own Grace, stirring things up.*

Sabina couldn't count the number of times she had called her sister these things herself and felt perfectly justified doing it. But this time it didn't feel right. She didn't know why — Annie hadn't revealed her source — but Sabina believed her this time.

She couldn't explain all this to Janice, though. So she simply shook her head, said a teasing, "No reason. Just wondering what to expect in *my* doddering old age. Catch you later," as Janice turned back to take her briefcase from the car.

Sabina headed back to the Data Center, but her thoughts had stalled. No, this was *not* a race between Annie and her. For the first time, truly it wasn't. The dynamics between them had changed. This playing field was new.

Is the motivation Annie, or is it the cause? Ron had asked, and it was actually both, though in a surprising way. Sabina believed in the cause, but she also, for the first time, believed in her sister. If Annie had a source, it was a good one. Sabina wanted to be *with* her on this.

Call it a reaction to losing Alyssa. Call it a reaction to Phoebe's symptoms. Call it the culmination of years of disdain for Aidan Meade. But there it was.

Several hundred yards shy of the Data Center, she abruptly shifted course. She headed north toward the picturesque little threesome just shy of the plant itself, and picturesque it was. There had always been something special about this area. It was typically the first to be cleaned, polished, landscaped. Sabina had always attributed that to the fact that these three — Clubhouse, Gazebo, Children's Center — were used by Middle River. Suddenly there was another possibility. It was possible that the Meades kept the surface here utterly pristine quite literally to compensate for bad stuff that lay beneath.

What was it that Grace Metalious had said so many years ago — that to turn over a rock in any small New England town was to find bad stuff beneath? Middle Riverites had heard that quote more times than they could count. Each time, they nodded, chuckled, and went on with their lives.

Sabina couldn't do that this time. There was merit to the quote, and if Annie was the one to turn over that first stone right here, Sabina was proud of her.

The Children's Center was still dressed in the yellows and greens of summer — decorative flags out front, painted sign, protective awnings. She held the door open for a pair of mothers delivering their children, then followed them inside. It was a minute before she located Antoinette DeMille. Toni was the center's director and one of Sabina's most respected friends at the mill. Sabina found her in the infant room, holding a crying child that couldn't have been more than three months old.

"Separation problems?" Sabina asked.

"Nope," Toni said dryly. "Colic. Should be easing up any day, but until then, it's tough. Breaks your heart to feel these little legs scrunch up against belly pain."

Sabina nodded. She waited until one of the other teachers was free and took the child from Toni. Then she followed Toni out of the room.

Toni glanced at her as they walked. "You look like you need to talk."

"Yes. But in private."

Toni gestured her into her office and closed the door once they were inside.

Sabina didn't mince words. "Not so long ago, Northwood used mercury as part of the process of bleaching the wood. That produced toxic waste, which was disposed of, and the newest processes don't use mercury at all. Still, it's in the river. Know how people aren't supposed to eat fish?"

"They do anyway."

"Yes, because the warning is always half-hearted. But I've been told there's another problem, that some of the mercury waste was buried in large drums here on the campus, and that several of the drums have leaked." She tied the fires and subsequent rebuilding of the Clubhouse and the Gazebo to this. "The Children's Center was built on a burial site, too."

Toni's jaw dropped, but she quickly recovered. "Oh, I don't think so. The Meades wouldn't do that. There are children here."

"What better place to hide illegal disposal of toxic waste?"

"And put children in danger?" She shook her head. "I don't think so. The Meades wouldn't do that."

"Do *they* have any children in the center?" Sabina asked, then answered, "No. So maybe they know something we don't?"

"But the center's been here for more than twenty-five years, and there's been no unusual illness."

"Because the drums are holding. But what if there's a leak, like the leaks at the Clubhouse and the Gazebo? There would be a fire and a cleanup, but what harm would be caused in the meantime?"

"Those fires, Sabina. There were logical causes for both. Who told you they were set?"

Sabina hesitated.

Toni guessed. "This is coming from your sister, isn't it? She's been trying to nail Middle River for years."

"Actually, not," Sabina said. "She's been gone a long time. She could have skewered us in a book, but she hasn't, and she doesn't plan to. This is for our mother and all those other people who've been sick."

"Do you know they were here at the time of the leaks?"

"No."

"There you go. I know you love your sister, but this time she's out in left field. If you'd been talking about a mercury spill at the plant that was covered up, that's one thing. People at the plant know the risks. But to say that the Meades would put innocents at risk is something else. I mean, the Clubhouse and the Gazebo are one thing. They're used only occasionally. But there's no way the Meades would build a day care center over a waste dump, not something that's used every day and by *children*. If they realized there was the potential for harm here, they'd have razed the place early on, cleaned up, and rebuilt. We're safe. Truly we are."

Toni DeMille loved children. She had raised six of her own and had earned a degree in early childhood education prior to being named director of the Children's Center at Northwood Mill. She prided herself on being one step ahead of the Children's Center's insurers, and was putting tots in for naps on their back even before it became the norm. She didn't believe in taking chances when it came to the health of her kids.

For that reason, she found herself thinking more and more about what Sabina had said as the morning passed. As the afternoon progressed and the children of part-time moms started to leave, she was taking good, long looks at those children and thinking about it even more. She debated calling her husband, who worked in the plant. Or her neighbor, who worked in sales. Or her cousin, who worked with Sabina's husband in shipping.

But that was how rumors started, and the Children's Center couldn't function in a maelstrom of rumors. So she went to Aidan Meade and told him what she had heard. She didn't mention Sabina's name until Aidan did, and then she couldn't lie. When he made mention of Annie Barnes, they shared a chuckle. Annie did have that element of Grace in her. But Middle River was no Peyton Place. They agreed on that.

On the matter of mercury waste being buried under the Children's Center, Aidan put her worries to rest. He denied there was anything buried anywhere. He said that the Children's Center was the pride and joy of the mill, largely thanks to Toni's vision and care, and that his family would never, ever do anything to jeopardize that.

Aidan Meade wasn't upset. Quite the opposite, he was very pleased. He was a master at trumping up charges, but when real ones presented themselves, it saved him the work. When *real* ones presented themselves, he didn't have to explain himself to anyone.

He stood at his office window until he saw Toni DeMille cross the road and head over the grass toward the Children's Center. Then he picked up the phone and called the mill's security chief. He didn't check with Sandy; Sandy would only ask why he had waited so long to deal with the problem. Nor did he need Nicole punching out the extension for him. He knew what to do and wanted the joy of doing every part of it himself.

Within five minutes, the chief and two of his trusted guards reached Aidan's office. Setting off on foot down the road, Aidan explained what they were going to do. When they reached the Data Center, he led the way inside and went straight to Sabina's desk.

The two others in the office had looked up, but she was so engrossed in something on her computer screen that she didn't appear even to know he was there. That clinched it. He felt no mercy at all.

"Sabina," he said sharply.

She looked up in surprise. Her eyes strayed to his companions, then returned to his. She frowned.

Feeling immense satisfaction, Aidan said, "You're fired. You have five minutes to take whatever personal belongings you have from your desk. Joe and his friends here will watch to make sure that's all you take. Then they'll escort you to your car and follow you out."

Sabina drew back her chin. "Fired?"

"Done. Gone. Outta here."

"*Why?*" she asked with what actually sounded like indignation.

"You're spreading rumors about Northwood that have nothing to do with reality. Mercury? Excuse me. There's no mercury here. Check with the New Hampshire DES. They'll vouch for that."

"I'm not spreading rumors. I'm asking questions."

"Same thing," he said and shot warning looks at her coworkers. If they wanted to keep their jobs, this was a lesson for them. "We expect loyalty. If you have a problem, you take it to the top. You don't go skulking around asking little people here and there. Honestly, Sabina, I thought you were smarter than that. You aren't good for this organization." He shot a thumb toward the door and couldn't resist adding a firm, *Now.*

She stared at him for a minute, and he could see her mind working. She was trying to decide how she could keep her job, whether apologizing would work, whether she ought to actually *grovel*, like a Barnes woman knew how to do that. Aidan didn't envy Ron. He had his hands full with this one. She knew computers. Aidan had to give her that. But she was no match for a Meade.

Averting her eyes, she opened a drawer, removed her briefcase and purse, then stood. She had the gall to look amused.

"Who'll take care of your computers?" she asked.

"We have two others right here who can do what you do."

"Is that so?" she asked with a crooked grin.

"What's in the briefcase?" asked the security chief.

She opened the briefcase wide. Aidan watched while the chief thumbed through a few papers. From where he stood, they looked pretty worthless. He guessed that anything of value was there on her desk. Of course, if he and the guards hadn't been there — say, if he had been stupid enough to fire her in his office and let her return to her office alone — she would have been filling that briefcase with everything she could that would help her double-cross Northwood. The Barneses were vindictive. This all went back to Annie and Cooper's Point.

"She's clean," announced the chief.

Looking at Sabina, Aidan put his hands on his hips and hitched his head toward the door.

She actually smiled. "Thanks, Aidan. You've been a help."

"A help in what?" he asked. Helping her was the *last* thing he wanted to do.

"Sorry. I gotta go." She started off.

"A help in *what?*" he repeated, turning as she went.

She stopped at the door. "Since you are no longer my employer, I don't need to answer that." She raised a hand to the two workers at their desks, who had been watching every minute of the show. Then she winked at the guards, gestured them along, and, leaving Aidan totally up in the air, was gone.

Sabina drove straight to Phoebe's. She found Annie in the kitchen making balsamic chicken salad for dinner.

"Can't stay long," she said at the end of the same breath in which she had told Annie she was fired. "Ron'll hear through the grapevine, and I want to be home when he gets there. But Aidan was a huge help — so arrogant and heavy-handed and condescending and *defensive* that if I still doubted your theory, I can't anymore. He's despicable. And he's hiding something. So I'm with you, Annie. Tell me what to do."

Chapter 22

I was stunned — oh, not that Sabina had been fired. Aidan would do that, if for no other reason than to flex his muscle. What stunned me was that she hadn't blamed me. After the way she had warned me off when I first came to town, this was a turnaround. She wasn't even angry — at least, not at me. At Aidan, yes. She called him a first-class asshole, a word I'm reluctant to repeat, but which gives you a sense of where my sister was at. I don't think she had thought out the long-range implications of being unemployed. Right now, she was actually happy about it. I never would have imagined that.

Nor would I have imagined that she would have taken up my cause. Of course, there was always the possibility that she was doing it to validate having been fired, or that she was simply filling a void. But that she had come to my side after a lifetime of dissension? That made me feel good. Made me feel *really* good. Like she was validating what I was doing. Like I wasn't bucking the tide in this. Like I wasn't *alone*.

I was in a good mood making dinner for Phoebe and myself that evening. My chicken salad was another of Berri's recipes, given to me spiritedly that afternoon. Berri was in love with her philanthropic lawyer, with whom she had spent the entire weekend. I suspected she would have even given me her great-grandmother's top-secret waffle recipe, she was feeling that magnanimous.

The chicken salad was enough. Made with poached chicken, chopped peanuts, and sliced green grapes, drizzled with a uniquely sweet dressing that made all the difference, and served with mini corn muffins, it was delicious. Even Phoebe liked it, and she did eat, hungry after spending the day at the store. Tom was doing her first IV infusion the next morning. Knowing she might miss a few days of work, she had been trying to get things in order.

We talked about that possibility over dinner. I had promised her that I would fill in, and now Sabina planned to join me. Though Phoebe was tired this late in the day, which meant that her mind was more cloudy than clear, she was able to answer most of my questions.

I took notes. After dinner, I cleaned up the kitchen. I checked my e-mail. I looked at the clock.

By nine, Phoebe was upstairs. Sitting on the edge of her bed, I said, "I'm going out for a little while. I'll just drive around, do some thinking. Will you be okay?"

Dryly, in one of those clear moments, she said, "I'd better be. You won't be staying here forever."

I felt a twinge. Guilt? Nostalgia? Regret?

Whatever, she was right. She would be on her own soon enough. "But you're going to be feeling *better*," I said in an urgent whisper. When she simply looked concerned, I asked, "Are you nervous about tomorrow?"

"Yes. She said it would get worse before it got better."

"That's why I'm here. That's why Sabina's here. That's why *Tom's* here. You'll be better in no time, Phoebe. I *promise*." Giving her arm an encouraging squeeze, I left the room.

You may be thinking that I had some gall being so positive about something that was really quite iffy. But I didn't think it was iffy, and Phoebe needed my confidence.

Then again, that's probably not at all what you're thinking. You're no doubt wondering why I didn't tell her I was going to James's house. Why I *lied*.

Well, I didn't really lie. I did plan to drive around and do some thinking. I just chose not to tell her that I was making a stop. And I had good reason for that. James was a Meade, and the Meades were the enemy, not only in terms of abuse of power, but in terms of mercury leaks and, now, Sabina's firing — which James *had* to have known about. He could have stopped it in a second. He was higher on the ladder than Aidan.

At least, that was the perception. For the first time, though, as I crossed town to his house, I wondered about that. What was it TrueBlue had said with regard to which of the Meade sons would take over after Sandy? I had said James was in line, but he had written, *Don't be so sure.* TrueBlue worked at Northwood. Maybe he knew something I didn't. Maybe he knew something most of the *town* didn't know.

Maybe James wasn't the crown prince after all. Hadn't he cautioned me not to clump him with his father and brother? He did seem different — for starters, in temperament. I needed to ask him about that. All in all, we had *lots* to discuss.

Naturally, I forgot about everything else

the instant I went up the walk and was greeted by James holding Mia. The child was absolutely precious in her pajamas, a slim little girl with diaper padding, her small legs straddling James's torso, one arm around his neck. Her face was already familiar to me — creamy skin, dark eyes, rosebud mouth. She had a tiny barrette in her dark hair. I leaned closer to see it.

"Mia," I read, then said to the child, "That is the prettiest barrette I've ever seen." She smiled. "On the prettiest little *girl* I've ever seen." To James, who was smiling, too, I said, "She really is the sweetest thing. Can I hold her?"

When he started to shift her, I held out my arms, but Mia's lower lip went out and began to tremble. Wary eyes stayed on me, but she leaned closer to James.

"Another time," he said. "Come on in."

We went to Mia's room and played with her for a few minutes. By the time he put her on the dressing table and changed her diaper, she was warming to me, playing with the furry puppet I held, even laughing aloud when I made it tickle her neck.

There is nothing like a child's laugh. I had discovered that when Sabina's kids were young, and was reminded of it now. A child's laugh is infectious. It is uplifting. It is innocent and pure and filled with hope and light. It is about prioritizing life, putting the good things first, placing exquisite value on moments of harmony.

I say all this to explain why, after Mia was settled in and the monitor turned on, James and I went right down to the leathery den on the first floor to talk and made love instead, which actually answered one of the questions I had. What he had meant about not doing one-night stands was that this wouldn't *be* a one-night stand. And it wasn't me who started it. He was the first to make a move — a hand on my neck as we left the baby's room, fingers linking with mine as we went down the stairs, an arm circling my back as he guided me to the den. He couldn't keep his hands off me, and after his hands, it was his mouth. That mouth touched *everything*.

Did I object?

Of course not. I loved what he did.

I didn't hear Grace once, but then, she had no need to speak. She approved of this, probably wished *she* could have done what we did with the impunity we had. A free spirit in the buttoned-up fifties, she had taken flack for the role sex had played both in her own life and in the lives of her characters. To this day, I'm convinced that much of the negative reaction to *Peyton Place* had less to do with sex, per se, than with the sexuality of its women. Those women threatened people. Take Betty Anderson. After dating *her* for months, Rodney Harrington had turned around and taken Allison MacKenzie to the school dance. Furious, Betty went to the dance with John Pillsbury. Halfway through the evening, though, she lured Rodney to John's car for some heavy petting, got him thoroughly aroused — then kicked him out of the car onto the ground and stormed off.

Call her the worst kind of tease, but she had the guts to make a statement. It was a statement of strength, and it was threatening both to men, who feared being on the short end of a stick like that, and to those women who didn't dare do it themselves.

I dared. But then, I lived in a different time from Grace. Part of the transformation I experienced in college had to do with discovering my sexuality. With the right partner, I thoroughly enjoyed sex.

There in the den of his house, James was the right partner. End of discussion.

Actually, *beginning* of discussion. Once

we were satisfied (make that, physically exhausted), we had to talk, and I did start that part of it, but he didn't object. We sat in the dark on the Berber rug in the den. Still naked, we faced each other, but we no longer touched. I could make out his general features, but details were lost, and that helped. Between the scents of leather and sex, and the dark, I was emboldened.

"Sabina was fired," I began.

"So Aidan said. I'm sorry he did that."

"You disagree, then?"

"Yes, I disagree."

"But you didn't stop him from doing it."

"I couldn't. I don't control Aidan."

"Who does? Sandy?"

"When he wants to. He's getting older. He likes it when Aidan makes the tough decisions."

"Like that was the *right* decision to make?" I asked in alarm.

"Tough doesn't mean right. I've already said I disagree. But Sandy doesn't. He doesn't like dissension within the company."

"And Aidan's his hatchet man."

"You could say."

"What are you?" I asked.

"What do you mean?"

"What role do you play for Sandy?"

"I do product development, and not for Sandy. It's my own thing."

"Isn't Sandy involved?"

"No."

"Or Aidan?"

"No. I work independently."

"I was starting to get that impression. Don't you three get along?"

"We've had issues."

"Like mercury?" I asked. After all, that was the crucial issue for me.

James was silent for the longest time, during which I would have liked to have seen the details of his face. I could tell that he was frowning. At least, I thought he was.

Finally he said, "Like mercury. I'm sorry about Phoebe. Are you sure that's what's wrong?"

"We won't know conclusively until she has the treatment. James, I meant what I said about Tom. I don't want him being made a scapegoat. He's an innocent party in this. He just happens to be the one who can administer the treatment."

"Tom won't be punished," he said with the quiet authority that made me believe.

"And if he treats other people after Phoebe?"

"I'm all for it."

"What if word spreads that the mill has a mercury problem?"

"The mill doesn't. Not now."

"But it did, and it could again. I know about the toxic waste buried under the clubhouse and the gazebo."

"There's no toxic waste there."

He was playing with words. Annoyed, I reached for my blouse. "Not anymore," I conceded, "but there was. And what about under the Children's Center?"

"There's no problem with the Children's Center."

I put my arms in the sleeves. "Did you say that about the clubhouse and the gazebo, too?"

"No. But I'm saying it about the Children's Center. It's being monitored. If there's a problem, we'll know before anyone is harmed."

"What about all the people who have *already* been harmed?" I asked, buttoning up.

He sighed. "Annie, I'm doing what I can."

"What does that mean?"

"It means I'm doing what I can."

"What does that *mean?*"

"It *means*, I can't *say* any more right now."

I groped around in the dark, found my shorts, and pulled them on.

"You don't have to leave," he said quietly.

Standing, I stepped into my sandals. "I do," I said. I pushed my hands into my hair and held it off my face. "Talking about this tears me apart. If you can't *say* any more, it's because you don't trust me —"

"I trust you."

"— and if you don't trust me, that demeans what we just did. So that leaves me thinking about why I'm here — I mean, not only here, in your house, but here in Middle River. I came to solve a mystery, and I have. It's starting to look like my mother died, James — *died* — because she was exposed to mercury from your mill. Phoebe has been suffering from the same thing. God knows how many others are, too. I don't know how you can let that happen. I don't know how I can *be* with you, knowing you let it happen. How do you live with yourself? How do you *sleep* at night?" I pointed toward the stairs. "And how do you justify letting that child stay with a nanny here in the safety of your home, while the rest of the children in town risk being poisoned every time they go to day care?"

★ ★ ★

A shrink would say that I deliberately provoked James — deliberately painted him as the bad guy — because I needed to put distance between us, and I suppose it was true. I was feeling too drawn to him. I was liking him too much. And how not to? He had never been anything but respectful to me, had never been anything but solicitous and caring, whether we were running or making love. Moreover, he was an exquisitely gentle father. My heart melted when I saw him with Mia.

Fine. I could blame the Northwood problem on Sandy and Aidan. But James was there. He knew what was happening. And no, I *didn't* think he was doing enough.

I told myself that at least a dozen times on the drive from his house to Phoebe's, and then I turned on my computer and found two e-mails that helped me focus again. The first was from TrueBlue.

Do you have people to connect with those dates yet? We can't do anything until you do. Even if they don't agree to talk, if you find enough sick people who were at the sites in question on or around the dates in question, the circumstantial evidence may suffice. Finding those people was your job. Are you going to do it or not?

He sounded impatient. He sounded *annoyed*. But he was right. I was slow.

I'm working on it. I have reinforcements coming in to help tomorrow. And what about your job? I need copies of internal memos showing that the Meades knew about the mercury. And then there's the issue of the showdown. Do you plan to show up when I confront the Meades?

I sent it off with a determined click and opened the second e-mail. It was from Greg.

WE SUMMITED THIS AFTERNOON, AFTER THE MOST UNBELIEVABLE ASCENT. WHAT AN EXPERIENCE! WAIT'LL YOU SEE MY PICTURES. THEY MAY BE THE LAST I TAKE FOR A WHILE, THOUGH, BECAUSE SNOW'S PICKED UP. GOTTA CONCENTRATE ON THE DESCENT. BESIDES, PHOTOS TAKEN UNDER WHITEOUT CONDITIONS DON'T

SHOW A HELL OF A LOT. WOW. THIS IS
AMAZING. CAN'T WAIT TO FILL YOU IN.

Knowing Greg as well as I did, I felt his
triumph. And I couldn't wait for him to fill
me in, either. I missed seeing him, missed
bouncing ideas off him, missed our dinners
together and evenings spent with friends at
local bars. I had a *great* Washington life.
Soon enough I would be back.

In the meantime, he was an inspiration
for me to plod on.

Chapter 23

I ran at six the next morning, in part because I knew that I had to deliver Phoebe to Tom at eight and that this would allow me to spend time with her before we left, and in part because I knew James couldn't run that early. I was annoyed at him. I was annoyed at men, period, because TrueBlue hadn't answered me yet. He wanted results from *me* but wasn't willing to produce any himself. Did he distrust me, too?

The old feeling of being alone returned. It was me against the world.

Good, said Grace. **Maybe now you'll do what needs to be done.**

Forget it, I argued. I am not doing your bidding. I am not writing a book. I am not destroying the Meades just to validate you.

Then you're a fool. James Meade didn't prove to be so perfect, did he? What did I tell you? They're all two-faced rats. They take what they want and then, by Jesus, they're gone.

Well, I'm not gone. I'm still here. The

510

Meades will answer for what they've done. But a book is a wasted effort. Times have changed, Grace. Tell-all books are a dime a dozen. No. I want direct confrontation.

Oh, honey. Come on. Do you truly think that will work? You need the masses behind you. You have an audience. Use it.

I didn't need the masses behind me, I realized. I needed the *law* behind me.

Inspired on that score, the first thing I did when I reached Miss Lissy's Closet was to go up to the office and phone Greg's lawyer friend Neil in Washington.

I know. I had an agreement of sorts with TrueBlue not to take the lawyer route, but there were different lawyer routes to take. TrueBlue decried the splashy, very public class-action one that might destroy the town in the process. What I had in mind was more subtle. If I could gather enough evidence to show the Meades that they stood to lose big if there ever *was* a public legal case, I might get them to deal. Call it blackmail if you will. I call it gentle persuasion.

As it happened, my phone call was unproductive. Neil was on trial, and I knew how those trials went. He could be tied up in court for weeks. The fact that this trial

511

was ongoing in August, when most law-enforcement personnel — not the least of whom being judges and their clerks — wanted to be on vacation, spoke of the demands of the case. Neil would definitely return my call. I just didn't know when.

I might have been discouraged if Sabina hadn't arrived at the store just then looking utterly defiant. "Ron is furious with me," she announced, plunking her shoulder bag on the office desk. "He says I was irresponsible talking to *anyone* at the mill about something that may not be true. He says I put my own needs before those of his and the kids, and that *infuriates* me. In the first place, if Aidan is going to fire *him* because of me, why would Ron want to work there, period? Isn't my speaking up a matter of principle? In the second place, why do *I* have to be the major breadwinner in the house? What about *his* responsibility? If he's worried about money, let him get a second job. Me, I'm worried about the health of my children — because something's up, Annie. You hit pay dirt this time. Aidan wouldn't have fired me if I hadn't touched a nerve."

"We need proof," I warned.

She grinned. With a conspiratorial gleam in her eye, she reached into her bag and pulled out a handful of CDs. "We had an electrical problem at the office yesterday morning. I was thinking I could work in one of the other buildings until it was fixed, so I stuck these in my briefcase. I didn't use them after all, but I never removed them. When Aidan and his goons arrived to escort me out of my office, the security chief searched my briefcase, but apparently he isn't familiar with CDs in skinny little jewel cases. I had them in a side pocket. He never even saw them." She waved the CDs in delight. "These are backups of some of my most important information, including access codes. I can get into any account I want, Annie. Anything that is in the mill's computer system is ours."

"Even e-mail?" I asked with growing delight, because my gut told me that's where valuable information might be.

Her grin widened. "Piece a cake."

The ease of it gave me pause. "That includes personal e-mail?"

"*Everything.* If it's in the company system, it's the company's property."

"If the government went to the company, could they see everything, too?"

Sabina nodded. "It's scary."

"But legal."

"Based on recent legislation, yes."

"What about what we're doing? Is this legal?"

Sabina didn't seem concerned. "Probably not, but I could always say I was looking for material of my own in there. Besides, they won't find out. Aidan is too arrogant to think I'd dare hack into the system, and Sandy isn't savvy enough to realize it's possible. The only one of the Meades who knows anything is James, and he sticks to his own end of the business."

I jumped at that opening. "So James is separate? Who takes over when Sandy dies?"

"Aidan."

"Not James?" I asked, wanting to be sure, because though TrueBlue had implied there was doubt, this went against conventional wisdom. "James is the older."

"James might succeed if there's a power struggle. The mill is what it is today because of him. He's been behind everything new in the last ten years, and without new direction, the mill would have lost ground. So if Aidan takes the helm, will James leave? And if he does, what happens to the mill? They're troublesome questions. And I don't know the answers."

"Do you think Sandy does?"

"I think Sandy tells himself what he wants to hear."

"Even if it's not for the good of the mill?"

Sabina shrugged. "He likes Aidan better than he likes James. They're two peas in a pod."

"Was it always that way?"

"Sandy preferring Aidan? No. It's developed in the last couple of years."

"Why does the town still talk of James as the heir?"

"Wishful thinking. Most everyone hates Aidan."

Joanne arrived to prepare to open the store, seeming to be totally on top of everything Phoebe had told me to do. While she rechecked the closing charge tallies from the day before and packaged several customer sends, I put on a pot of coffee, vacuumed, and refolded sweaters. I finished just as the store opened, at which point UPS delivered four huge boxes of goods. While Joanne waited on customers, I inventoried the boxes and found an immediate problem with a dye-lot discrepancy, tops mismatched with bottoms. So Joanne and I switched; she got on the phone with the supplier while I waited on customers.

It was enlightening. For one thing, I was greeted warmly, as though I belonged there. For another, word of Phoebe's treatment had spread. Indeed, the doorbell *ting-a-linged* often enough to suggest that people were stopping by as much to get news as to shop. Apparently, Phoebe hadn't been as adept at hiding her symptoms as we thought. The townsfolk knew she wasn't well. They were concerned.

The circle of customers around me grew until, at one point, there were six women asking questions about Phoebe, and I tried to be vague. But these women weren't dumb. They could tell an answer from an evasion. When yet one more of them asked what Phoebe was being treated for, I gave in. Quite honestly, I didn't see why I shouldn't. They wanted to know. And I *wanted* them to know.

"We suspect she has mercury poisoning," I said.

There was a collective gasp, then a flurry of questions of the when, where, and how type.

"We won't know anything for sure until the treatment is done," I said. "It's all very tentative."

There were a few more questions, but they generally tapered off to expressions of support. I shouldn't have been surprised when every one of those women left Miss Lissy's Closet and began to spread the word.

After an hour or so, Sabina took over helping Joanne, while I drove to the clinic to sit with Phoebe. She was in a large room with two patients with chemotherapy drips, and there were more people checking on the three of them than I would have imagined, including Tom. He and I talked for a few minutes — talking with him was so easy that yet again I thought of Greg — before I returned to the store.

The first person to greet me there was Kaitlin. She had heard that Phoebe was at the Clinic and that Sabina and I were at the store, and she wanted to help. Joanne put her to work unloading additional boxes of goods that had arrived. I sent Sabina back to the office, and so it went. We took turns helping Joanne work the store and running to the clinic to be with Phoebe. But Sabina was as focused as I was when it came to what had now become our shared mission. Operating on Phoebe's computer with code from her CDs, she infiltrated Northwood's system and went looking for dirt.

Me? I had to find people who would talk. To some extent, my past efforts had been blind. If I hoped to find something soon, I had to narrow the list of those I approached. That meant finding people who had in fact been at either the Clubhouse or the Gazebo in the days immediately prior to the fire.

I began with a visit to Sam, catching him as I had two weeks before, just as he was setting off to play golf. "You're ruffling feathers," he said around his cigar as he gathered his things, "but I love your spunk. Whaddya need?"

"I want to know who held events at either the Clubhouse or the Gazebo immediately preceding the fires at each. That's the kind of thing you print in the *Times*. When you report on town events, you tell where they took place. I want to go into the archives again."

"You have the dates?"

"I do."

Sam went to his office door and bellowed, "Angus!" I had thought the place was deserted, what with the *Times* having come out that morning, but a fair-haired, bespectacled boy showed up at the door. Sam pointed at me with his cigar. "She needs information. Research the archives for her, like a good kid. She'll give you the dates and the place."

Pleased, I not only gave him that information but also my cell phone number. While he went to work, I visited Marsha Klausson at The Bookshop. As always, the scent of honeysuckle welcomed me, but if that hadn't done it, her personal warmth would have. "Did I tell you I had to re-order all three of your books?" she asked the instant she reached my side. "We've had a rush on them since Omie died. Must have been seeing you there at the diner that made people curious."

"Is curious good?" I asked cautiously.

Mrs. Klausson nodded. "They're intrigued. You were a big name before, but they've always associated you with Grace. I think they're starting to see you as different, and it's about time. You're *very* different from Grace."

I was starting to think so myself. When I was a kid, I never disagreed with Grace. Now I did.

But I wanted to hear Mrs. Klausson's take on it. So I asked, "In what ways?"

"Grace had an edge. It showed in her writing. People were either really good or really bad. You've always been more nuanced. You see the middle tones in people. You're more constructive."

"Constructive?"

"Perhaps practical is a better word. Yes, you rebelled. But you were always more into finding solutions to things. Your books do that. Your characters grow."

"So, here's a question," I said, because there was definitely a solution that I needed right now. "You helped organize the Middle River Women in Business, didn't you?"

"I certainly did. There were six of us who got it going — Omie, Elaine Staub from the home goods store, the realtors Jane and Sara Wright, and, of course, your mom."

"Elaine died," I realized the instant she mentioned the name.

"Yes. Several years back. She had a rough time at the end. If it wasn't the flu, it was colds, even pneumonia or *shingles*. That's painful, you know."

So there was another person whose death might be related to a long-ago exposure to mercury. "And the Wrights moved away," I said, pulling that vague thought from my past reading of the *Middle River Times*.

"Yes. They weren't very old, but Jane suffered from rheumatoid arthritis. When it got bad enough so that she had to struggle to work, they moved to Arizona for the warmth and the sun. Jane died a year or two ago — nothing to do with the arthritis, it was her heart. Sara has stayed out there."

"And she's well?"

"Far's I know. We exchange cards each Christmas, but she's made a whole new life for herself. I believe she found a well-to-do widower. She sounds happy."

"So of you six women, four have died and two are healthy."

"Yes." The bookseller frowned. "It is frightening, the fragility of life, isn't it? Jane wasn't old. Your mother wasn't old. Nor, come to think of it, was Elaine."

Omie had been old, I reminded myself, but not as old as her parents had been. I was feeling like I was getting somewhere. "Do you remember when you started meeting at the Clubhouse?"

"It was before the fire."

"*Right* before the fire?"

"Oh yes. I remember thinking how lucky we were that we weren't there at the very *time*. The fire started in the kitchen while the meal for a meeting was being prepared. It wasn't for *our* meeting, but it might have been. We did meet that week." She frowned again. "Twice? Why am I remembering that? Was the fire on a Monday?"

"Tuesday."

Her eyes brightened. "Tuesday. I remember now. We were going to meet for breakfast *that* day — Tuesday — but called it off because a stomach bug was making the rounds. The others — Alyssa, Elaine, Omie, and Jane — all had it. Sara and I had been sick the week before, so we missed the lunch meeting on *Friday. That's* how it was."

"If that's how it was," I said, repeating the story to Sabina at noon, "there's a distinct possibility that one of those buried drums sprang a leak that Friday. Mrs. Klausson and Sara missed the meeting because, coincidentally, they had the flu. When the others got sick, it was assumed they had the flu, too — but remember, acute mercury poisoning produces flulike symptoms. Maybe others had similar reactions — you know, the cook, the waitstaff. When the powers that be at Northwood saw this, they knew they had a problem, and they knew just what it was. So they burned the place down. That gave them an excuse to clean up underground and rebuild with no one the wiser."

"And Mom and the others who were sick?"

"The acute symptoms let up, the mercury drifted to different organs and lay dormant for years, then erupted as chronic mercury poisoning in the form of immune deficiency disease, rheumatoid arthritis, and, in Mom's case, Parkinsonian symptoms. All four of the women who were at the Clubhouse that day are dead. That says something."

"But not about Phoebe. Do we know if she was at that Friday meeting?"

"I asked Mrs. Klausson. She thought and thought, but she wasn't there herself and had no recollection of hearing that Phoebe was. Phoebe wouldn't have worked all that long for Mom. She certainly wasn't a seasoned businesswoman at the time. So why would she have been there?"

"I don't know. So we still don't know where she was exposed."

I glanced at the computer. "Have you had any luck there?"

"I've found lots of chatter, but nothing usable. I was hoping to find e-mail from Aidan either to his father or to James mentioning mercury, but there's nothing yet."

"You said Sandy isn't a computer person. Does he e-mail?"

Sabina smiled dryly. "He e-mails like Aidan does — tells his secretary what he wants sent and she does it."

"Maybe the secretaries would talk with us?"

Sabina was shaking her head even before I finished. "Dire loyalty," she said as my cell phone rang. "They like their jobs."

I fished the phone from my purse. It was Angus calling from the newspaper office. Pulling up a pad of paper, I wrote as he spoke. According to the *Times* archives, four events had been held at the Clubhouse and the Gazebo in the days immediately preceding their fires. Thanking him profusely, I closed my phone and put the list before Sabina. At the same time, I pulled out my original list of ill people and set it alongside the other.

"Can you match any up?" I asked.

Sabina didn't have to look long. She placed a finger at a spot on each list. "Here. Susannah Alban has had one miscarriage after another. And here. The Alban-Duncan wedding was held at the Gazebo two days before the fire." Stricken, her eyes met mine. "I know about Susannah's miscarriages, because the first of them coincided with one of Phoebe's miscarriages."

"Was Phoebe at the wedding?" I asked, hoping, hoping.

But Sabina shook her head. "Susannah's more my friend than hers. Ron and I would have been there, except that the wedding was really small, and afterward we were grateful. The guests all had food poisoning. It was a hot day in August. The food was sitting in the sun. It made perfect sense."

It certainly did, just like the WIBs having the flu, which was going around town at the time. "Any others?" I asked with growing excitement. TrueBlue was going to love this.

Sabina refocused on the lists. A minute later, she pointed again, one finger to each list. "Sammy Dahill. Rotary Club meeting. Sammy was chairman of the club a while back. I only know it because he lives on our street. He's had kidney problems."

I knew about those kidney problems. They had been reported in the "Health Beat" column of the *Times*. "Omie said that runs in his family. According to the paper, three generations of Dahills have had kidney problems."

"That's true," Sabina acknowledged, "but what the newspaper doesn't say is that Sammy was adopted."

"Adopted? Why didn't Omie know that?"

"A senior moment? But it makes kidney problems mighty coincidental, wouldn't you say?"

I struggled to contain myself. "More importantly, what would Sammy say?" I gathered my things. "I'm going to go see him. And Susannah. If one or both are willing to talk, we're in business."

Neither would. Susannah, for one, had her hands full caring for three children under the age of five, all adopted after so many miscarriages. She was convinced that the problem at the wedding had been nothing more than food poisoning. After all, she said, she and her husband both worked at the mill at the time, the Meades had paid for the wedding, and those in attendance really couldn't complain about a few stomach cramps. Moreover, the Meades had been extraordinarily generous when the children arrived, even transferring Susannah's husband to the Sales Department and letting him work out of the house when a sleeping disorder (yet *another* possible by-product of you-know-what) made work at the mill a risk.

As for Sammy Dahill, he owned the

printing company that printed not only stationery but annual reports and marketing material for the mill. He claimed not to remember whether there had been a general illness following a meeting of the Rotary Club in March of '89. Too many years had passed, he said.

Personally, I didn't believe him. Memory was a convenient excuse.

Starving by now, I picked up a bag of chocolate pennies and, eating as I went, headed for the clinic. But I'll bet you're wondering where Marshall Greenwood had gone. I certainly was. He had been harassing me right up until Omie died. It didn't make sense that he would suddenly stop.

So I asked him. No, he wasn't following me. There was no sign of him at or around Susanna Alban's or Sammy Dahill's, but after I left News 'n Chews, I spotted him parked in front of the Sheep Pen. He actually appeared to be minding his own business. Swinging around the corner, I pulled over behind the cruiser and swallowed down a chocolatey mouthful as I parked and walked up.

"Hey," I said, smiling at him through the open window. I could see on the passenger's seat the crumpled Sheep Pen bag that suggested he had just eaten some kind of bar fare — likely chicken fingers or nachos; still, I held out the bag of pennies. "Want one?"

Marshall eyed me with distrust. "What's in 'em?"

"Pure chocolate."

"You didn't add anything?" he asked in his usual rasp.

I couldn't decide if he was serious. But I was remembering what Mrs. Klausson had said that morning about my being more nuanced in my judgments of people. So I smiled again. "I should have, after the trouble you gave me last week. But I really am not an ogre." To show him there was nothing but pennies in the bag, I ate one myself.

This time when I offered, he helped himself to a few. He didn't thank me, but I didn't need thanks. "Are we friends now?" I asked.

"That depends," he said.

I leaned closer, spoke more quietly. "On whether I'm going to tell the world what I know about you or Normie or Hal Healy?"

Trite as it sounds, Marshall did have a deer-in-the-headlights look just then. "What's Hal Healy done?"

"I'm not telling, because that's my point.

I don't *do* that, Marshall. We all have our personal little secrets — our personal little *problems*. I don't care about those. It's not why I'm here. I am not writing a book, and even if I were, I wouldn't write one about you. So if that's why you were after me, please don't be. You are perfectly safe."

He thought about that for a minute, then said a grudging, "You're safe, too, even without that assurance. You have friends in high places."

I straightened. "Who?"

He shot me a crooked smile. "You tell me about Hal, I'll tell you about your friend."

It was a test. Did I betray people, or did I not?

I did not. And it was far more important that Marshall know this, than that I know who had spoken on my behalf. Besides, it wasn't that great a mystery. I knew it wasn't Sandy Meade, and it sure wasn't Aidan. There was only one Meade left who had enough clout to get Marshall off my back.

James. I had been trying not to think about him.

Not wanting to now, I simply said, "Checkmate." I held out the bag. "A few more for the road?"

Marshall took a handful, which left precious few for me, but my hunger had been eased, my craving satisfied for now. Returning to my car, I drove on to the clinic. I hadn't been with Phoebe for more than five minutes when Tom appeared at the door and hitched his head. I joined him in the hall.

"How's she doing?"

"Fine," he said. "Her vital signs are good. She's starting to feel zapped and disoriented, which is the part that gets worse before it gets better. The IV drip is just about done, but I'd like to keep her overnight. I want to monitor everything that comes out, and she's apt to be unable to do it herself. Are you okay with that?"

I was fine with it. I was actually *great* with it. If Phoebe stayed over at the clinic, I could work longer with Sabina, and the longer I worked with Sabina, the more evidence I might amass and the less I would think of James. "Totally. Has any mercury come out yet?"

"It takes a little while for that to start. Late tonight, early tomorrow — those are the critical times."

"What'll you do if the tests are positive?"

He looked me in the eye. "Face a moral crisis. There are lots of people here who are sick. Do I treat them for mercury poisoning, or do I not? I need evidence that they were exposed."

"You didn't have evidence that Phoebe was exposed."

"I know. That's the problem. Can you find it?"

Determined to do just that, I returned to the store, but the place was humming. Sabina was helping Joanne, and they needed me, too. It wasn't until we had locked the door, closed the register, and tallied up cash, checks, and credit slips, that Sabina and I had time to think, and then we were hungry. Sabina had already left a message at home that she would be staying here at the store with me awhile. Needing air, she volunteered to pick up dinner at Omie's.

While she was gone, I went up to the office and logged on to check my e-mail. There was nothing from Greg, though I pictured him sliding down Mount McKinley in the snow. Berri sent a note saying that she and John were still hot and heavy. There was a note from my editor saying that my revisions were fine and she was clearing out of the city until after Labor Day, so I wouldn't hear from her again until then, which suited me fine. I was feeling distanced from work. Not so from my friends. I felt a warmth inside reading a note from my friend Jocelyn, who was nearing the end of *Peyton Place* and wondered how much was autobiographical. She was trying to picture me there, she said. I clicked on "reply."

Grace wouldn't say that Peyton Place *was the most autobiographical of her novels. She would say* No Adam in Eden *was that. But there are similarities between Grace and Allison MacKenzie. Both grew up without fathers in the house. Allison was something of a social outcast, as Grace was. Allison was slow to reach puberty, as Grace was. Grace was actually called "slats" when she was a teenager, because she was flat as a board. By the time she was sixteen, she had made up for it, but being called names may have enlarged the chip on her shoulder.*

As for trying to picture me in the town of Peyton Place, don't. Middle River was like Peyton Place when I was a child, but returning here now, I see how different it is. For one thing, there's fifty years of modernization. Middle River hasn't stood still. Everyone has cell phones, Omie's plays popular music, businesses are computerized, FedEx comes twice a day. Even the Sheep Pen has gone modern with beer from microbreweries.

Funny, but I don't feel isolated here the way I thought I would. Isn't e-mail a fabulous thing?

I clicked "send," then pulled up True-Blue's last note — the impatient one — and reread it. Rather than impatience now, I sensed urgency. So I clicked "reply."

The good news is that I've located two people who were at the Clubhouse and the Gazebo prior to those fires, and who have had chronic problems in the years since. The bad news is that neither of them is willing to talk. I put the bug in their ear and am hoping they'll come around. In the meantime, I'm working on finding others.

You've probably heard that my sister is being treated at the clinic. If it proves that she did have mercury poisoning — and if the treatment works — her mind may clear up so that she'll remember more of the when and how. But that could take a while.

What are you getting on your end?

I sent the note, and quickly got one in return.

Lots of flack. The Meades are feeling threatened. Aidan is using your sister's defection as a sign of looming trouble. A board meeting's been called. You need to work fast.

I was reading his note when Sabina returned, and I might have hidden it from her. I had enough time. But she was my ally now.

"He's my source," I explained. "He has given me information on the mill's use of mercury. He was the one who told me that a toxic cleanup was done after the fires."

She finished reading. "Who is he?"

"He won't say. He works at the mill, has for years and hopes to for a lot longer, but his user identity is all I have. TrueBlue. Any ideas?"

Sabina looked at me. I could have sworn

I saw a flicker of smugness. "Actually, yes. I'd guess it was James."

"James." My heart tripped. "James *Meade?* Why do you say that?"

There was more than a flicker of smugness now. She seemed downright lordly. "I've spent much of today reading e-mail that's come into the system. James is currently going back and forth with a friend who lives in Des Moines, a lawyer, from the gist of the conversation. I gather they're old college buddies. The guy calls him Blue. Sounds like a college nickname."

Hadn't TrueBlue said that his college roommate was a lawyer?

"That's bizarre," I argued. I did *not* want TrueBlue to be James. James and I had been too intimate for him not to have told me something as important as that. Besides, Sabina's tone grated. I didn't want her to be right. It was like we were kids again, and she was one-upping me. "Are you sure James's friend was calling *him* Blue? Maybe he was referring to someone else."

Sabina had an answer for that, too. "He did it multiple times — as in *Hey, Blue, good to hear from you,* and *So, Blue, how's Mia?* and *Good thought, Blue. Don't e-mail.*

I'll call. James had legal questions that he wanted to keep confidential. Is it a coincidence that he's asking a pal legal questions at a time when Aidan and Sandy are getting nervous about mercury?"

No, it wasn't a coincidence. So was James asking legal questions on behalf of Aidan and Sandy? Or was he asking on behalf of TrueBlue?

"And he has information on a board meeting," Sabina said. "The rank and file wouldn't know that."

"Why would his college friends call him Blue?" I asked, resistant still.

Sabina put the bag of food on the desk. "Because, Annie, he wears blue all the time. Blue shirts, blue jerseys, blue sweatshirts and jackets. Ask me, and I say that's boring as hell, but hey," she opened the bag, "each to his own." She removed takeout containers and handed me one. "Omie's hash, in memory of Omie. She always told my kids that her hash was brain food. Maybe it'll help us. If a board meeting is coming up soon, we need something more than we have."

We sure did. Phoebe was our best bet, but she wasn't thinking straight, and now I had to think about James, too. There were oh-so-many reasons why his being

TrueBlue made sense, and the more I thought about it, the more sense it made. But it raised the major question about whose side he was on, and how could I possibly know? James didn't trust me enough to share more than a very general *I'm doing what I can.*

Well, from what I could see, that wasn't enough. Bottom line? I didn't trust him either.

As soon as Sabina and I had eaten, we phoned Susannah Alban, Sammy Dahill, and Emily McCreedy in the hope that maybe if Sabina voiced the appeal, one of them would talk. No luck. We did get the full Rotary Club roster. It was in the town hall files, and since the Meades so generously allowed the town to use Northwood's server, Sabina was able to pull it up. We matched three other names from that list to mine, but two were dead, and the third wouldn't talk.

Moreover, the fourth event held prior to one of the fires was a photo shoot at the Gazebo for a clothing catalog. Since the *Times* hadn't listed names (I asked Angus that on the phone), and since most of the participants were from out of state, Sabina was going to have to dig into the Northwood system for details.

For now, we scrutinized more of the mill's e-mail. It seemed that this very day Aidan had initiated a dialogue with an agent of the state Department of Environmental Services suggesting that Northwood sponsor another of the public information days that the department periodically held. Northwood had done this before. The mill was a best friend of the DES, enough to make one wonder. And then, there was the timing. It was fishy. But the correspondence was clean.

Frustrated, we left the shop at ten. We stopped briefly at the clinic to find Phoebe in a private room now, sound asleep. It was past ten-thirty when I finally got back to the house. I had barely set my things on the kitchen table when the phone rang.

Caller ID told me it was James, and I was suddenly furious, hurt, and confused, all at the same time. I debated not answering. I simply didn't know what to say to him.

But I couldn't just let it ring. So I picked it up. "Yes, James."

There was a pause, then a quiet, "How's Phoebe?"

"She's sleeping at the clinic."

"How's she feeling?"

"Lousy, I'm told."

"I'm sorry."

"That she's sick? That half the *town* is sick? That *you* can't trust me enough to confide in me?" I could *feel* Grace telling me to confront him about being TrueBlue, but I didn't want to. I wasn't ready.

"We need to talk," he said in that same quiet voice.

I rolled my eyes. "Have I heard that before?"

"We need to talk about us."

"Us?" I cried, realizing in that instant that I wouldn't be asking about TrueBlue at all, because this phone call had nothing to *do* with TrueBlue. This was between James Meade and me. "What us? There is no us."

"I think there is. That's why this is so hard."

"What's so hard?" I shot back. "Lying?"

This time he was silent so long that I half expected he had hung up. I was surprised when he said, more quietly than ever, "I want to see you."

Fingers closed around my heart. Eyes tearing, I said, "Well, you have a child, so you can't leave your house, and I have obligations to my family and dozens of other people in this town, so I need to be up early tomorrow to work, and I'm not sure there's any *point* in our seeing each other, because I'm going back to Washington in two weeks, so even if there *was* an us here, it's done. It's been fun, James, y'know?"

As I waited for him to reply, I cursed myself for sounding like a petulant twelve-year-old.

When he remained silent, I rubbed my chest. It *hurt*.

When still there was nothing one minute, two minutes, three minutes later, I realized that this time he truly had hung up.

Chapter 24

Naturally, I didn't sleep well. I ran early to work out the kinks, but James spoiled that, too. I kept looking for him. Yes, I knew he couldn't leave Mia until the nanny arrived, but I kept thinking that if it mattered enough to him to see me, he would have found a way. Hell, he knew Phoebe was at the clinic and that I was alone in the house. James was a resourceful guy. He could have found a way to come at two in the morning, if he chose.

He didn't, which was probably just as good. My mission was never more narrowed than now. With no one else in town willing to talk, Phoebe was our only hope. Assuming the tests proved mercury in her body, I had to link her to an incident of actual exposure.

After showering, I dressed quickly and went to the clinic. Phoebe was groggy, dozing on and off throughout the *Today* show as it came from the monitor high on the wall. She was still catheterized, but she seemed comfortable. Comfortable? I half wondered if she was on morphine, she was that spacey.

"Hey, Phoebe," I said.

She was slow to turn her eyes to mine, then a minute in recognizing me. "Hello," she replied in a distant voice.

"Feeling okay?"

"What's it doing out?"

"It's warm and humid. They're predicting thunderstorms for later."

"Oh dear," she murmured and closed her eyes. "No golf."

"You don't play golf."

"Michael does."

"Oh, sweetie." Michael was her former husband. He lived three towns over, had remarried since their divorce, and now had two kids. "Do you ever see him?"

Phoebe didn't open her eyes. "Who?"

I let it go. But I clutched her hand. "I have to ask you something. I know you're feeling kind of out of it, but remember I asked if you were with Mom at the Clubhouse right before the fire?"

Phoebe opened her eyes wide. "Mom's dead. What are you talking about?"

"The Clubhouse fire. A couple of days before it, Mom was there with the WIBs. Were you there?"

Phoebe closed her eyes again. "Tell them I can't move," she said, back to murmuring. "I'm sorry. If there's a fire here, it'll have to go on without me."

"The *Clubhouse* fire."

"What Clubhouse fire?"

I didn't say anything else. As the minutes passed, I'm not sure Phoebe even realized I was still there. In time, I left and went on to the store.

Tom called shortly after noon to say that the tests were positive, that there definitely was mercury leaving Phoebe's body. I found the news almost anticlimactic; I'd been that convinced even before all this. That said, I was definitely relieved. We would never know for sure whether Mom had mercury poisoning, too, because we weren't about to exhume her body for an autopsy, but in my heart I knew. Though the satisfaction was bittersweet, it was satisfaction nonetheless. Wasn't this why I had returned to Middle River? Granted, my mission had changed. But I did feel a certain vindication on Mom's behalf.

I e-mailed Greg with the news. I knew he was somewhere in his descent and wasn't sure whether he could send or receive, but I wanted the message waiting for him.

I did not e-mail TrueBlue. The idea that he was James still had me reeling. I kept remembering remarks in his earlier e-mails — had even reread a few that morning. The clues were there. He slept alone; he had to be up early; he liked the anonymity of being TrueBlue so that he could be free of who he was and what he did. Even the flirting felt familiar, though with James in the flesh, it had been — well — in the flesh.

Besides, James had hung up on me. And now TrueBlue wasn't e-mailing. Did either of them have to know that the mercury theory was a go? Not from me, they didn't. At least, not right now. After all, the theory would only be good if I could show that Phoebe — or *someone* — had been exposed to mercury at the mill.

We spent the day at it, Sabina and I, but it seemed that no matter how many Rotarians we called, no one was willing to talk. Likewise, no matter how many leads we followed trying to track down Sara Wright (now married and presumably using another name) in Arizona, on the chance that she might know whether Phoebe had been at the WIBs meeting that March day, we had no luck.

And through it all, we had to help in the store. It seemed that we were no sooner into something in the office, when Joanne gave a yell — and this, even with part-timers at work and Kaitlin and Jen in the back room. August was one of the busiest months of the year, Joanne kept saying by way of apology, and I'm sure that between back-to-school wear and general fall mer-chandise, it was true. What became ap-parent as the hours passed, though, was that, once again, many of the customers came by in a show of concern for Phoebe. They wanted to talk as much as to buy, and for that, they wanted Sabina and me.

I was surprised by the last part. Totally aside from Omie's wake, where emotion, compassion, and grief snuffed out other re-alities, I would have thought that Middle Riverites had such a deeply ingrained image of me as a wretch of a writer that they would never have been able to warm to me as a person, much less *trust* me in the retail setting. Enter **TRUTH #9: All people have the capacity to change their minds, even people who live in small, insular, parochial towns.**

In fact, with regard to that issue of trust, I swear they came to me more. It was as if they wanted my advice on what they should buy, whether one size or color or style was better than another, precisely because I was now from the big city.

Perhaps it was my own need to think that. But the end result was that I was every bit as busy on the floor as Sabina.

So she and I talked with the people who came in. We sold lots of clothes. We ran up to the office to catch a minute here or there at the computer, and, through thickening clouds, dashed over to see Phoebe. Tom wanted to keep her at the clinic one more night, more for his own education than anything else. He figured that if he might be treating others this way, the data the nursing staff collected with regard to vitals would be a help. And again, neither Sabina nor I minded.

She headed home at seven for dinner with the kids, but I stayed on. I had a bag of chocolate pennies that (surprise, surprise!) Marylou Walker had brought over herself, and I still had the second half of my lunch sandwich. I wasn't in the mood to go out, because distant thunder was rumbling and the air was as thick as it could possibly be without rain.

The thunder neared, the rain began, and Sabina returned — at least, I thought it was her. Shortly before nine, I heard the downstairs doorknob jiggle, then the front door open.

"Up here!" I called. I was following yet another lead in trying to locate Sara Wright, and didn't think anything of it when Sabina didn't answer. At the sound of footsteps on the stairs, though, I was frightened. This wasn't Sabina. These footsteps were heavier, definitely male.

I stood and looked around frantically for something — letter opener, scissors, *anything* — with which to protect myself, which was, of course, what my Washington self would have done. That this was Middle River, hence the open front door, was a minute in registering. By the time it had, James was on the office threshold, shrugging off a hooded rain parka. Underneath, he wore sneakers, shorts, and — yes — a dark blue T-shirt. His limbs were long, lean, bare, and hair-spattered, but the most notable aspect of his appearance was Mia. Wearing a thin pink sleeper, she was strapped to his chest, facing out, arms and legs dangling free. She was wide awake, looking straight at me, and I must have been starting to look familiar to her — she certainly was looking familiar to me — because she smiled. I saw two teeth on the bottom and two on the top, plus eyes that had narrowed with the smile but were beautiful, indeed. That smile plucked at my heart.

"What a coward you are," I scolded, speaking to James but looking at Mia. "Hiding behind a *child?*"

He might have said, *I told you I was a coward at the start,* which would have acknowledged that *he* knew *I* knew that he was TrueBlue. So maybe he didn't know I knew? Well, I wasn't clueing him in just yet. I wanted to see just how long he would drag out the ruse.

"I had no choice," he said, hooking the hood of his jacket on the coat tree by the door. "The nanny's gone, and I needed to see you."

"Shouldn't the baby be asleep?"

"Yes, but this is urgent. She'll probably doze off right here. We need to talk, Annie."

I sat back down at the desk, swiveled to face him, and folded my arms over my chest. Thunder rolled, though not loudly. When it was gone, I said, "I'm listening."

Not only hadn't Mia been alarmed by the thunder, but she didn't look at all ready to doze off. She was kicking one leg and craning her head back, looking up at James now. He took both of her small hands in his, but his eyes were on me.

"I didn't expect this," he began and stopped. Those dark eyes — dark brown eyes, actually, and quite deep — suggested confusion.

"This what?"

"You. This attraction. I'm not supposed to be attracted to Annie Barnes. She's trouble."

I grinned.

"See?" he said, pointing at me. The spontaneity of the moment made him look younger. "There. That grin. It *does* something to me, and I don't know why. But I keep thinking about things like that and telling myself that there's no way anything between us could work. For one thing, we live in different places, which I *swore* I would never do again. And for another, you'd like nothing more than to bring down my family business."

"That's not true," I argued. "If I wanted to bring down the business, I'd have gone to the press long before now. It's a hot issue, so there'd be no trouble getting coverage. There'd already be producers from *60 Minutes* up here and investigative journalists from the big papers. What I *want*," I said with emphasis, "is for Northwood to finally take responsibility for two very serious mercury spills, compensate the people who've been hurt, and make sure it doesn't happen again."

He didn't deny that there had been two spills. Nor did he ask how I knew. He was distracted, because Mia had started to squirm. Perhaps it was the suddenly heightened slap of rain on the roof, perhaps it was simple restlessness, but she clearly wanted out of the carrier.

Holding the child, he unhooked the straps. "Do you think I haven't done things? Do you think I haven't compensated the people I knew who were hurt?" He set the child on the floor and straightened. "Why do you think those people won't talk with you? They won't talk because I've set up funds to help them with the things they need."

So here was another thing. TrueBlue knew I was having trouble getting people to talk. James and I hadn't discussed it.

But suddenly the distinction didn't matter. "You, personally, set up funds?" I asked. Mia was crawling toward the far end of the room.

"Me, in the name of the mill," he said, watching the child. "We call it a civic disability package, but I know what it is. So do my father and my brother."

"Then you know that those spills have caused illness?"

"We've known since it happened back at the Clubhouse."

"And some of that illness has caused death?"

He nodded slowly, grimly.

"Did you set the fire?" I asked.

"No. If I'd had my way, I'd have been blunt and just torn down the building and cleaned up the spill. But it was a fight. My father wasn't going to do a damn thing at all, until I badgered him enough."

"He'd have *ignored* it?" I asked, appalled.

I had barely finished speaking when a loud clap of thunder came. Seeming more puzzled than frightened, Mia looked back at James. Picking up on his lack of concern over the noise, she resumed crawling.

"He'd have prayed it would go away, which, of course, means it would seep deeper into the ground and move toward the river with each rainfall until the river was more polluted than ever." He sputtered scornfully. "Talk about burying your head in the sand. So I threatened him. I talked about lawsuits and media attention. I told him we had to do something. But I was as surprised by the fire as the rest of the town." Stretching forward, he scooped

Mia up and returned her to his spot. The instant he set her down, she took off again, this time toward the bookshelves beside my desk.

"Why didn't you speak up then?" I asked, because what James was telling me implicated him in deception, and I didn't want that. "Couldn't you have told *someone* the truth?"

"Oh, I tried," he said dryly. In a gesture of frustration, he scrubbed the top of his head, ruffling salt-and-pepper hair that was already ruffled — and in this, too, he seemed younger than his usual, composed, authoritative self. His eyes were on the child. "And every time I did, my father would cover my tracks so that it was like I hadn't said a goddamned word." His voice rose. "At one point he told his golf buddies that I was full of radical ideas I got at business school. How's that for a smear? He knew they would spread the word, but in the kind of subtle way that has more weight for its semblance of confidentiality. Sandy is a genius at creating spin and making it stick. It's a natural marketing skill. And yes, it's the power thing that you hate."

I wanted to believe him. He sounded genuinely upset — guilt-ridden, angry, and dismayed. "What about the Children's Center?" I asked.

He showed no surprise that I knew about that, either. Mia had begun taking books from the shelves, a soft *thu-thunk* of each, audible only because the rain had eased again. He went after her and began putting back the books. "Yeah, well, that's an ongoing argument," he said. "Sandy claims that the other leaks were a fluke, and that since there hasn't been a problem under the Children's Center so far, the drums there are solid and that to do something will only draw attention to the presence of those drums, which are illegal, by the way." He sat back on his heels, looking up at me from there, "And before you lambaste me for that, please remember that those drums were buried before I became part of the company. I was away in college at the time. Sandy had no reason to ask my opinion. I sure as hell wouldn't have built civic buildings over a toxic waste dump. Is that *idiocy?*" he cried.

"The Children's Center is a tragedy waiting to happen."

"Yes," he shot back, "and I have nightmares about that. But you have to understand, my relationship with my father is tenuous. That's why I keep to myself and run my own part of the business. He and I don't see eye to eye on things, and the more I push, the more he marginalizes me. So I have a choice. I can let myself be marginalized so much that I'm no good to the company. Or I can pick and choose my fights — which is what I do. The mill is the lifeblood of Middle River. If it folds, the town is in dire straits."

Hadn't TrueBlue said something similar?

Thunder struck. Mia shot a frightened look at James. His hand on her head soothed her.

"But what about the Children's Center?" I pushed. "Would you want Mia there?"

"Why do you think she *isn't?*" he asked with a tortured look. I had touched a raw nerve. His voice was impassioned as the thunder rolled off. "Do you think I don't want her with other children? She needs to learn how to play. She needs to learn how to *share*. She needs to have friends, and playdates with children with mothers, because, Lord knows, I'm no mother, but I'm doing the best I can, damn it. Okay, she's only ten months old now, so keeping her home with the nanny is okay, but in another few months I'll have to do something. My father would be perfectly happy to keep her hidden away. I refuse to do that."

"Hidden away because she's adopted?"

"Hidden away because she's *not* adopted!" he said so sharply that Mia began to cry. Quieting instantly, he drew her up into a hug. "Shhh, I'm sorry, baby," he murmured against that short, shiny black hair. "I'm not angry at you, never at you."

Mia cried for another few seconds before responding to his calm.

"There," he said by her ear. "Want to take the books out again?" With an economy of movement, he put every last book back on the shelf and sat her down. She went right to it with a resumption of the same soft *thu-thunk, thu-thunk* as each book hit the floor first with the bottom of its spine, then with its side.

Me, I was stunned. Arms no longer crossed, I had my hands on the edge of my seat. "She isn't adopted? Does that mean what I think?"

There was no thunder to punctuate his revelation. It was striking enough on its own.

James bowed his head toward Mia, then raised it and faced me. "Up until last year, I was on the road often. When you develop new products for a company like ours, there's a lot to consider, from the machines that produce it, to the raw materials those machines need, to the markets that will purchase the product when it's complete. I've been doing this kind of thing for ten years. For six of those years, I had a relationship with an advertising executive in New Jersey. It started off as professional — she created an ad campaign for us — but then it became personal. She wasn't supposed to get pregnant, but it happened. She wanted to abort; I wanted the baby. I finally made her an offer she couldn't refuse."

"You bought her off?"

"Don't judge me," he warned.

"I'm not," I said quickly. "I'm just amazed. Was she after money all along?" It was a definite possibility. Anyone dating a Meade of Northwood Mill knew she was dating money.

His eyes held mine. "No. She wasn't after anything. When push came to shove, she didn't *want* anything — not me, not my baby. She had a town house she liked, and a job she liked, and there was no way in hell she was giving up either, much *less* moving to a small town where she would stick out like a sore thumb because she was Asian American. Well, she was right about that part. I argued that it wasn't so, because she was such a dynamo of a woman that she would have made friends here, and the color of her skin wouldn't matter. But Middle River isn't ready for someone like her, not so long as Sandy Meade is at the helm, because he sets the tone for the town. He's not exactly a bigot; it's just that he's threatened by anything different. He went berserk when I told him about April — that's Mia's mom — so I knew how he would react to the baby. I picked her up at the hospital when she was two days old, and my father dictated the spin."

"That she was adopted? How could he do that? And how could you let him? You're her biological father."

The *thu-thunk* of Mia's mischief had kept up, but I'm not sure James even heard. He looked disgusted. "Well, I can be bought, too. He told Middle River the story he could swallow, and told me that if the truth came out, he would disown me."

"Why?"

"Because Mia's different, and Middle River doesn't do different. Adopting her is acceptable because it makes me a remarkable person who is giving a poor orphan a good home. Siring her myself is something else."

"I think you're wrong," I said. "I think Middle River would love that you insisted Mia be born. Doesn't Sandy see that?"

"No. And if you're going to accuse me of going for the money like April did, all I can say is that Mia is my flesh and blood, and I want her to have every advantage money can buy. It's bad enough that her mother wants no part of her. Amazing how history repeats itself, isn't it?"

"Your mother died."

He was looking at me, slowly shaking his head. It was as though Pandora's box had been opened, and he just couldn't close it back up. "That's what Sandy would have Middle River believe. Aidan even believes it, but the truth is that my mother is alive and well and living in Michigan with her second husband and the three daughters she had with him."

My jaw dropped. The dead mother had been part of Middle River lore. With a concerted effort, I closed my mouth. Another round of thunder grumbled past. "Do you ever see her?"

"I go there once in a while."

"And you never told Aidan?"

"Oh, I told him, but he chose to carry on the myth. That means he doesn't have to think of visiting or sending a note. It means less responsibility for him. And hey, I hear what he says. He doesn't owe her anything. She wasn't here when he was little, and he was younger than I when she left. It was lousy growing up without a mom. But Sandy's even more at fault. He was miserable to her while she was here. I want him to pay for that. One way is through my daughter. I want Mia to have a piece of his estate. There'd be poetic justice in that on several scores. So I'll keep my mouth shut until the inheritance is safe." Seeming purged, he turned his attention to the child. She had crawled farther along the floor to the next bookshelf and, with more rhythmic *thu-thunks*, was pulling those books off, too. "Oh, little girl," he said, making a face, "look at this *mess*." He began to pick up the books.

Beak of a nose? Had I really thought that once? Yes, his nose was straight and more pointed than some, but when he made a face for his daughter, there was nothing beaky about it.

"Leave them," I said. "She can play. There's no harm." I was trying to ingest what he had said. "Who else knows she's biologically yours?"

He kept his eyes on the child. "No one."

"And you told me? Annie Barnes? The

town loudmouth?"

His eyes met mine. "I trust you."

The simplicity of it — the honesty I heard and its implication — made me cry out, "Then why *TrueBlue?*"

He didn't blink. "When I talked with you that first day at the diner, I thought maybe you could help. But it was awkward, given who I was. You didn't trust me. And I didn't know if I could trust you. I sensed that TrueBlue's being anonymous would appeal to your novelist's imagination." He gave a crooked grin. "Besides, you're from Washington, aren't you? That's Deep Throat country."

"Uh-huh, and Woodward and Bernstein got a book out of it, but I'm not writing a book. I've said that from the start, and still you hid behind TrueBlue."

"Hid?" He considered that, then lightened up. "I actually thought it was kind of fun. And it was a relief. I said that — or TrueBlue did. Because I wasn't me, I could ask you questions without your asking *me* questions that I wasn't comfortable answering."

I was feeling vaguely used. "So I'm asking them now. Why do you need me to find people who were exposed at the time of those two spills? You know who they are. Isn't that what your 'civic disability package' is about?"

"There are people we don't know about. I want an inclusive list."

"Ask the guard at the gate."

"I would if I could, but sixteen years ago, he was a token presence. He wasn't there all the time, and when he was, he didn't keep a paper trail of who went where. He does now, because security is an issue everywhere, but he didn't do it then. So we don't know for sure who was at those sites at the time of each spill. I can't exactly put an ad in the paper. And I can't go around town asking people, because that would create a rumor that could grow out of control. Beside, we've never had proof. We never wanted it — and I'm using the royal *we*, meaning the voice of the company. When we created those disability packages, we suspected illnesses related to mercury poisoning, but we give generous disability packages to our own employees anyway, so this was simply perceived to be an extension of that. We never made connections to mercury, certainly not publicly. So we never got that proof. Did Tom find it in Phoebe?"

I was saved from answering by Mia, who chose that moment to make a pitiful sound. It wasn't from the storm, because the thunder was more distant now and the rain a bearably light patter on the roof. She was sitting in a sea of books, rubbing one tiny fist back and forth over her nose. Her other hand was pulling her hair. She was tired.

James caught her up and cradled her on his shoulder.

Me, I wasn't quite there yet. I was still looking at that sea of books. Well, yes, they were books, but not like novels or reference books or even sample books. For the first time, I realized that they were my mother's notebooks, apparently displaced during Phoebe's recent reorganization frenzy. Hidden down by the floor, they hadn't made it either to my radar screen or to Sabina's. Now it struck me that they might tell us whether Phoebe had been with the WIBs that fateful day.

I didn't say anything to James.

And don't ask me why, because I don't *know*. Yes, he had said he trusted me, and given what he had confided in me earlier, I believed him.

The problem was me. Maybe I didn't know what to do with that trust?

Mia was quiet, her eyes closed, cheek on James's shoulder. Putting my elbows on my knees, I leaned forward and whispered, "She's very sweet."

James stroked the child's head with a large, strong, masculine hand that reminded me of things we had done in the dark. Not knowing what to do with that thought, either, I simply met his eyes and said in a voice soft enough not to wake the baby, "Why do you need proof now?"

"Proof is the only surefire lever I have."

"For what?"

"A bloodless coup. There's a board meeting Monday at four. Can you come?"

He didn't kiss me. I knew he wanted to. I could see it in his eyes, in the way they looked at my mouth. I could also hear it in his breathing, which was less steady than it had been. Mia was back in her carrier, asleep now and totally limp, hanging over his front so that if he was aroused, I couldn't see.

But he had to leave. I wanted him to leave. Something was happening too fast. I needed time to focus.

I got it, though in an unexpected way. James was no sooner out the door when my cell phone rang. It was Greg's friend Neil, calling not from Washington but from Anchorage, where he had flown after being granted an emergency recess in his trial. It seems Greg had fallen during the descent of Mount McKinley and smashed his leg. He had already had surgery. Now Neil wanted to help him return home, and fast.

My first sense was sheer envy that Greg had someone who cared enough about him to drop everything he was doing to fly to his aid.

My second was that I wanted to be there when Greg got home. I could help make him comfortable in the condo, could stock the fridge, do some cooking, air the place out after it had been closed up for two and a half weeks.

I told Neil I would be at the condo by noon the next day.

Then I called Tom. "Too late?" I asked.

"Nah," he said easily. "I'm reading."

"I was wondering what your thoughts are about Phoebe coming home. There's an emergency in D.C. I'm flying out early tomorrow. If she's coming home, I'll have Sabina take care of her."

"Have Sabina take care of her," Tom said. "She's starting to feel better. Now that we've identified the problem as mercury, there's no need for constant monitoring. The occasional test next week is fine.

Is the emergency something to do with this?"

"No. It's my roommate, Greg. Broken leg. His partner flew out to be with him in Anchorage. I think they're already flying back."

"Huh," Tom said in a tentative way. "When were you thinking of leaving?"

"Here? No later than seven."

"And coming back?"

"Probably Sunday night."

There was a pause, then, "Want company?"

"Sure. I'd love it. But can you do that?"

"I don't know," he said, but the tempo of his voice had picked up. "I have a friend in the EPA who could answer some questions I have. I'm long overdue for a visit anyway. Let me see if Mrs. Jenkins can come. I'll call you right back."

He called five minutes later to say that he would be with me. I called the airline and booked tickets, then called Sabina to let her know.

I didn't tell her about the notebooks, didn't want her getting her hopes up. Honestly? I didn't want her asking to see them. As the last-born child, I had always had to share. These journals were a link to our mother. For now, I wanted them all to myself.

Chapter 25

Kaitlin was up early Saturday morning, showering and putting on clean jeans and a new jersey and clogs from the store. She took care with her hair and applied only as much makeup as her mother liked — but not to please Nicole. She didn't care what her mother thought. She wasn't dressing for *Nicole*. They had barely talked in a week.

Leaning closer to the bathroom mirror, she studied a little raised dot on her chin. It was a zit in the works, no doubt about it. Taking a tube of acne medicine from the medicine chest, she dabbed on just enough to zap the zit without spoiling her makeup. It used to be that her whole *face* was covered with zits. She loved her dermatologist for helping with that. Actually, she loved him anyway. He was always warm and smiling. He looked at *her*, not at Nicole. He acted as though *she* was the important one there, not Nicole. And in follow-up visits, he would tell her how *fabulous* she looked.

She didn't necessarily believe him. He

told that to all the kids he treated. But it was nice to hear it, anyway.

"You're up early."

Kaitlin jumped. The slight movement brought her mother into the mirror's frame. Nicole was at the bathroom door in her silk robe, shoulder to the jamb, arms crossed. Kaitlin leaned in again to block the view. She pushed her tongue against the spot with the zit. Definitely a zit.

"Where are you going?" Nicole asked.

"The store."

"Again? What's with this? You've been there every day this week. Wouldn't you rather be out by the pool than stuck in the back room of Miss Lissy's Closet with cartons of clothes? Everyone knows that's where you are, Kaitlin. They're not putting you out front, are they." It wasn't a question.

"Today they are," Kaitlin said with pride. "Joanne's been showing me how-to stuff all week. Annie can't be there today, because she's going to Washington, and Sabina will be with Phoebe, so I'll be on the floor." That was the expression Joanne had used when she called last night. On the floor. It meant actually selling clothes to customers. Kaitlin still couldn't believe Joanne had asked. Salespeople had to look good in the store's clothes. Wasn't that a major selling tactic?

"Joanne, Annie, Sabina, Phoebe — on a first-name basis with *all* of them?"

"Yes," Kaitlin said. Finished in the bathroom, she headed for her bedroom. That meant slipping past her mother. Fortunately, Nicole stepped aside. Unfortunately, she didn't go away.

Following Kaitlin to her room, she said, "I'd be careful of aligning myself with those people, if I were you."

Kaitlin was in the process of reaching to neaten the bed when she stopped and straightened. "Those people?"

"The Barnes women. They're not in the mainstream in this town. I'm sure you know Sabina was fired."

Kaitlin stared at her mother. "By your boss, because he's *so* afraid of what she knows. I'm sure *you* know Phoebe has mercury poisoning. What does your boss have to say about *that?*"

Nicole frowned. "What are you talking about?"

"Mercury poisoning. She's being treated for it, and it's absolutely pouring out of her body."

"I don't believe you."

"Call Dr. Martin. He's the one who's

treating her. And there's only one place mercury could come from in Middle River, and that's the mill. If I were you, I'd be worried about working there. But your boss hasn't told you that, has he?"

Nicole looked momentarily flummoxed. It was all Kaitlin could do not to smile. And, of course, her mother recovered. Nicole *always* recovered. "See?" she charged. "That's the foolishness you're getting from those Barnes women. Hal Healy is right. They're a bad influence on this town."

Kaitlin did smile this time. She couldn't help it. "Hal Healy is history."

"What are you *talking* about?"

"He submitted his resignation yesterday."

"How do *you* know that?"

"Because I'm at the store, where Middle River comes and goes, while you're at the mill hearing only what the Meades want you to hear. Mrs. Embry came by the store yesterday to ask about Phoebe. She's the vice chairman of the school committee, second only to *your* boss's father, so either Sandy is keeping Aidan in the dark, or Aidan knew about it and chose not to tell you. Mr. Healy resigned."

"Why did he do that?"

"It wasn't only Mr. Healy. It was Miss

Delay, too. Isn't that a coincidence?"

"Kaitlin."

"Oh, come on, Mom. Everyone knows they're fooling around. Like he's in her office *all* the time talking about students, only no one believes there are *that* many students with *that* many problems, and if it's only school business, why do they lock the door?"

Nicole was quiet. She looked confused. It was such a rare thing that Kaitlin almost took pity on her — almost, but not quite. The moment was too good to waste. "So, if I were you, I wouldn't worry about the Barnes women being a bad influence. I'd worry about people like Mr. Healy and Miss Delay, and I'd worry about your boss, because if it's true that the mill is poisoning people, he'll get his. You may get yours, too. Want me to tell you the symptoms of mercury poisoning?" She raised her voice to follow Nicole, who had turned and was walking down the hall. "Because I know about those, too. It isn't Alzheimer's, and it isn't Parkinson's. It's sometimes both, and it isn't *pretty*, Mom!"

Since Anton left early for golf or whatever it truly was that he did, Nicole liked her Saturday mornings. Weather permitting, she spent them out by the pool with coffee, strawberries, and the catalogs that had arrived in the mail that week. Last night's storm had left thick clouds and dense humidity, so the pool would have been a bad idea today, but the sunroom at the back of the house would have been fine. It was air conditioned.

But she didn't go there either, instead just sat at the kitchen table. She had the coffee, but no strawberries and no magazines. She wasn't in the mood to eat or to read. She was bothered by what Kaitlin had said — bothered that Kaitlin knew more than she did, but not simply because as the mother, she should be the one to know things first. She was bothered because Kaitlin was right. *You're at the mill hearing only what the Meades want you to hear.* It was insulting. It was *humiliating.*

Aidan knew things he wasn't telling her, and it had to be deliberate — a concerted effort to hide certain things — a calculated absence of the word *mercury* in any e-mail she might see — a willful withholding of the news about Hal. There had been phone calls yesterday. She knew there was a board meeting on Monday, but was it anything out of the ordinary?

Aidan had said it was not. He had specifically said that, when she asked. Apparently, he had lied. Apparently, he hadn't thought she was important enough to know.

So where did that leave her? Was she or was she not his executive assistant? Was she or was she not his right-hand man? Was she or was she not the one who had to know *everything,* if she had *any* hope of representing his interests in the best possible way?

Picking up the phone, she dialed his cell number. He didn't answer, but she knew how that went. He didn't answer his cell when he wasn't in the mood to talk.

But she was. She had too much invested in their relationship to let this go. He owed her an explanation or two.

So she called on his home line. Beverly answered, which, had Nicole been a lesser woman, might have been reason to hang up. But she was used to talking with Aidan's wife. The woman often called the office.

There was a bedlam of children's voices in the background. Nicole spoke loudly and with authority. "Hi, Bev, it's Nicole. I'm sorry to be bothering you at home, but I've run into a problem with one of the spreadsheets I'm preparing for Monday's board meeting. Is Aidan around?"

"Are you sure this can't wait?" she asked, sounding annoyed.

"Yes," Nicole replied firmly.

"Aidan! It's your secretary!" The phone hit the table with a clunk. The cacophony of background noise went on and on.

Nicole simmered. Secretary? She was a lot more than Aidan's secretary. This woman had no *idea* how much more than Aidan's secretary she was.

She waited for what seemed an eternity through yet more bratty child sounds, and she knew exactly why it was taking Bev Meade so long to get Aidan. He was hiding somewhere in the house where he wouldn't have to hear the kids' noise.

"Yuh," he finally barked into the phone.

"I need to see you."

"What spreadsheet?"

"Mine. Everyone here is gone for the day. Can you come over?"

"And this can't wait the hell until Monday morning?"

"Absolutely not," Nicole said and slammed down the phone. Then she sat back, fuming, thinking every vile word she could about Aidan Meade until he pulled into her driveway and stormed out of his car — and still she sat. Unshaven and uncombed, he let himself in the kitchen door and slammed it shut.

"What spreadsheet?" he asked, looking at the half of her silk robe that showed.

She ignored the look. "Why didn't you tell me about Hal Healy resigning?"

His eyes rose to hers. He seemed taken aback. "Why should I? What's he got to do with the mill?"

"My daughter knew he'd resigned before I did. But more important, what's the business about mercury?"

"*What* business?"

"The *business* about Phoebe Barnes having mercury poisoning."

Aidan scowled. "She doesn't have mercury poisoning."

More lies? Nicole fumed. "Yes, she does. She's being treated for it at the clinic. I thought the mill didn't use mercury anymore."

"It doesn't. Phoebe Barnes is a bizarre person. She hasn't been right for months."

"Exactly, and now they know why. So there I am sitting up in that office at the mill five days a week, forty-nine weeks a year."

"There's no problem with the office."

"Then the plant. I'm up *there* three, four, five times a week doing your bidding. Do I stand to become a . . . a . . . bizarre person, too?"

Aidan made a face. "Geez, Nick. I can't believe you got me over here for this. You know who started the trouble, and you know why. Annie Barnes was waiting for an excuse. Sabina being fired was it."

Nicole might have bought into that excuse before. But to do it now went against common sense — not to mention Tom Martin, Sabina Mattain, and everyone else walking in and out of Miss Lissy's Closet. To do it now said that her daughter, Kaitlin, was as much of a troublemaker as Annie, and somehow, suddenly, Nicole didn't believe that. Suddenly, Kaitlin seemed perfectly reasonable.

"And if you got this from your daughter," Aidan was going on, "it's because she is furious at you because *you* have failed to hide your lousy marriage from her. By the way, did you ever find out if she knows about us?"

By the *way?* Like it was an inconsequential aside? Even *that* annoyed Nicole. "She doesn't know."

"Are you sure?"

She rose, went to the sink, and put her mug down none too gently. She turned, her back to the counter. "For God's sake,

Aidan, I couldn't exactly ask directly, or she would have known something she might have only guessed up until now. *Are you sure?* Pu-leeze."

"She knows."

"She does not. She talked about Hal Healy and Eloise Delay and would have talked about us in the same breath, if she'd known."

"Good," Aidan said. "Wouldn't want the girl ruining a good thing." His eyes fell to her robe. "Where is she now?"

"Out. Define *a good thing.*"

He took a step closer. "And Anton?"

"Out. Define *us,* Aidan."

Smirking, he came up close and gripped the tie of her robe. "What's under this?"

"Absolutely nothing," Nicole said, as much in defiance as anything else. She wasn't turned on. She didn't know whether it was the fact that this was Anton's house, or the fact that Kaitlin had been eating breakfast in this very room not that long before, or the fact that Aidan had just come from his wife and kids, and Nicole had never set out to cheat them. Perhaps it was just the fact that here in her own home, where there was no pretense of work, where Aidan didn't have the aura of the would-be heir to gild him, he wasn't as attractive to her. "I need you to tell me this, Aidan."

"Tell you what?" he said, distracted as he untied the robe.

"What *we* are. You just called us a good thing. What does that mean?"

He opened the robe. "Quick. Easy. Sex." His eyes were on her along with his hands, and she let him do it. She let him fondle her breasts, bury his mouth against her neck, put a hand between her legs. She even moved against that hand, moved against his crotch, until he began to breathe in that half-gone way he had, "Ooooooh, baby. Ooooooh, that's good."

"Is it, Aidan?" she whispered breathlessly, pressing her hips forward.

"Oh yeah, it's good. It's always good."

"Is it good and hard?"

He grabbed her hand and showed her just how hard it was, and that made it easy for her to squeeze, to squeeze tightly and twist, then shove him away.

"Bitch!" he cried hoarsely, doubling over.

She pulled her robe together and straightened. "A good *thing*, Aidan? Is that what I am, a *thing?*"

"Bitch," he repeated, adding several other pithy epithets under his breath. He raised threatening eyes, but before he could say a word, she spoke.

"Don't even think it, Aidan," she warned. She was the brains behind their duo. It was about time he realized that. "You fire me, and I'll say it's in retaliation for my rebuffing your sexual advances. I'll say that what you just did was attempted rape."

"It wasn't any freaking rape," he snapped, still trying to catch his breath, now with both hands on his knees.

"Okay, then," she said calmly. "Let's call it consensual sex that's been going on for three years, and how will your wife take to that, Aidan? How will Daddy take to it?"

"You can't prove a thing."

"But I can. I have hotel receipts, plus the names of clerks everywhere we went. We were a handsome couple. They'll remember us."

"You go public about us, and Anton will divorce you."

"Well, maybe that wouldn't be such a bad thing," Nicole said. She was thinking about Kaitlin, who was no longer fooled. And she was thinking about herself. Aidan was right. What they had was quick, easy sex. Having Aidan gave Nicole a good excuse to stay with Anton. So she was beholden to two men, neither of whom she personally cared for. Didn't she deserve more? Wasn't she *worth* more? There had to be someone who would see that, someone who would worship the ground she walked on.

"This relationship is taking its toll," she said with both men in mind. "Maybe it's time we call it quits."

Chapter 26

I was up late Friday night reading Mom's journals, then up again at dawn to pack, which meant that two nights in a row I hadn't gotten much sleep. That might have explained my heightened emotionalism, though I suspect that between James's declarations and those of my Mom, there was good enough reason for it.

I was ready when Tom came by to pick me up for the drive to the airport in Manchester, but I wasn't in the mood to talk. He seemed to know that without my having to say it, which in turn made me wonder why I couldn't fall in love with *this* man. He was good, decent, and compassionate. He was attractive and intelligent. He was a success at what he did, and he wasn't enamored of *my* success. Admiring, yes. But at no point did I feel that he was playing up to me because I had a big name and a solid stock portfolio.

Does that sound arrogant on my part? Well, believe me, it's happened. In the last year especially, after I hit it big with my books, I suddenly became visible to men who hadn't seen me before. I met them at signings, charity events, even Greg's functions. Most were subtle, but others were frank. *I think,* one said, *that it has to be every man's dream to be hooked up with a woman who can keep him in style.* Can you believe he said that? Naturally, I told him that I wouldn't be caught *dead* with a man who wanted to be "kept," and he quickly slunk off, but I'm sure he wasn't alone. I was worth more money this year than last. There were some men to whom that mattered.

It didn't matter to Tom. He fit into my life as a friend in ways that I knew would outlive my return to Washington in the fall. He was going to be a permanent friend. But nothing more.

Had I not been preoccupied, I might have spent the entire trip wondering why that was so, and I might have come up with a handful of possible reasons. But I was thinking about my mother's journals, feeling close to her in ways I hadn't even felt at the cemetery, close in ways I hadn't felt in years.

I know I'm supposed to be

reading about market trends, she had put down in her neat script, *but the bulletins sitting here on my desk will have to wait. I just finished reading Annie's book for the second time, and it was even better than the first. She's such a talented writer. Maybe if I had been as talented as she is, I would have succeeded as a writer. But no. It takes more than talent. It takes drive. Annie has that.*

I always knew that about Annie, but for the longest time I didn't know where the drive would take her. She could have gone in so many different directions, and a lot of them would have been self-defeating. But she took one of the good roads, which put her in a good place, and she did it no thanks to me. I didn't give her the attention I should have. I suspect she took to writing when she was a teenager in part to get my attention. Well, she has. I'm more proud of her than I can say.

I mean, what do you do when you read passages like that? You sit there in a public place, beside a person who is attuned to your moods, and you bite the inside of your lip to create pain as a diversion, because otherwise you'll break down and cry. But you can't stop reading, can't stop feeling, can't stop wishing your mother were still alive so that you could talk about these things.

So you read on, but you have little nuggets of new knowledge tucked in a corner of your brain, and it suddenly occurs to you that if the plane takes off with you and your journals, and something unspeakable happens, everything will be lost. So you wait until the last minute, until you can see the airline personnel preparing to board passengers with children or those who need extra help. Then you buy privacy by moving off to the side, and you take out an insurance policy by calling Sabina's cell phone.

"How's Phoebe?" I asked.

"Feeling okay. I have her home."

"At your house?"

"No. At Mom's. The nurses agreed that she'd be better in the place that's most familiar. Besides, I'm still annoyed at Ron."

"Still not talking?"

"Nope."

"Oh, Sabina."

"It's okay. I believe in this cause, Annie. I look at Phoebe, and I see just this little bit of improvement, and I know it's only the beginning. I think we're doing the right thing."

"I know we are — know it for fact. I found our proof."

I heard a gasp on the other end, then a breathless, "What?"

"That March Friday when the Middle River Women in Business met at the Clubhouse? Phoebe was there. Mom, the would-be writer, was the unofficial scribe of the group, but she had inadvertently picked up the wrong folder on her way out of the store to the meeting. She called Phoebe, who brought over the WIB folder, and it only made sense that she should have something to eat while she was there, so she ended up staying through the rest of the meeting."

I could hear tempered excitement in Sabina. "How do you know this?"

"Remember Mom's journals? The ones she kept on the shelves at the store?"

"Those were Gram's journals."

"Nope. Mom's."

"Are you sure? I haven't seen them lately."

"I know. Phoebe moved them. I hadn't

seen them either and completely forgot they were there until last night."

"And it says all this inside? In Mom's handwriting?"

"Mom's handwriting, with the entry clearly dated." The general boarding was starting. I could see Tom rise and glance my way. "I have to run, Sabina. Is this good news?"

"It's great news!"

"So if the plane crashes, you'll know what to ask Phoebe when she comes to —"

"The plane won't crash."

"— and if she still can't remember, have her hypnotized."

"The plane won't *crash!*"

"And the best?" I said as I hoisted my backpack to my shoulder.

"There's more?"

"The Northwood board is meeting Monday at four. I've been invited. Is this cool?"

We had climbed through broken clouds, leveled off at thirty-three thousand feet, and left New Hampshire airspace, heading south, when I heard from Grace. I was startled. So much had been going on that she and I hadn't talked in a while. I truly thought I had left her behind.

Why are we here? she asked, sounding disgruntled. *I nearly died once on a flight from Dallas to Atlanta.*

That was in 1961. Aircraft were entirely different then.

Why couldn't we drive? I would have much preferred that. This is not where I want to be.

We couldn't drive because it takes too long. Besides, if not here, where?

New York. I always loved the Plaza. I want to go back there. Pay your money, and they love you. They don't care how frumpy you look. I could be myself there. Or Paris. I love Paris, too. Or Beverly Hills. I could live in any one of those places.

In a hotel, I said to make sure I understood what she was saying.

Why not? Hotels are the best. You don't have to cook or clean or make your bed, and no one faults you for it.

That's all fine and good, I reasoned. But for how long? You can't live permanently in a hotel. Hotels are cold.

And towns like Middle River aren't? Oh boy, do you forget fast. I'll take a cold hotel any day over that. Get tired of one hotel, you move on to the next. It's a gypsy's life, but I like it.

You *hated* it, I argued. You were miserable. You were alone, even when there were people around, so you filled the void with booze. Y'know, Grace, maybe your problem *was* that gypsy's life. Maybe you would have been better off staying in one place and putting down roots.

Weeds have roots. I wanted better.

That's right. The grass was always greener somewhere else. You were like your mother that way, always itching for something more. Well, maybe you didn't know what you had. Maybe if you'd let people get to know you, they'd have accepted you. Maybe you could have made friends. Yes, yes, I know. You had friends, but really only ones who reinforced your separateness. You expected friends to be loyal to a fault, but that doesn't happen right away. It takes time. Maybe if you'd made the effort, you'd have built the trust. You'd have been part of a community. You wouldn't have been such an outsider.

"Annie?" My arm was jiggled "Annie?"

Eyes wide, I looked quickly at Tom. He was seated beside me, regarding me with concern.

"Are you all right?" he asked. I nodded, but he said, "You were looking fierce. And you were moving your lips."

587

"Was I?" I asked, mortified. "Oh dear. I'm sorry. It was an imaginary conversation. Argument, actually. Writers do this kind of thing a lot." I waved a hand. "But done. Over. Forget it happened. Please?"

"Can I help with the argument?"

I smiled and shook my head. "Not this one."

"Then the other," he said, and I knew what he meant.

"Time to put our money where our mouth is?" I asked.

He nodded. "That's why I'm here."

It was why we were both here, though that particular meeting would take place on Sunday morning. Saturday was for our personal agendas. When we landed at Reagan National, we got in the same cab, but after dropping me at the condo, Tom continued on to meet his own friends.

Was I thrilled to be in the condo? Not a hundred percent.

But you guessed that, didn't you? You knew that the place would look different to me, that its familiarity would represent only half of what was fast becoming the rooted part of my life. You knew I wouldn't be able to walk in that door and not think of James or Phoebe or Sabina or the backyard willows that overlooked the river.

That said, it was *so*, so good to see Greg when he finally hobbled into the condo with Neil. But if I had expected that he would be bedridden, I was mistaken. Recent surgery notwithstanding, Greg had adapted to the use of crutches with the same ease with which he did most physical things. Yes, there was discomfort. He had been told to expect some swelling and had been advised to keep the foot elevated, but he tired of that quickly. Truth be told, the downer of breaking his leg couldn't begin to compete with the upper of having summited, and that was what he talked about for much of the afternoon. He had more film cards than I could count, and he showed me every shot he took. He claimed he had deleted dozens of bad shots along the way. Had he not done that, I shuddered to think how long we'd have sat there on the sofa, tucked together — me, Greg with the elevated leg, and Neil — looking into the monitor of Greg's camera while he went from image to image with a corresponding narration of the trip — shuddered to think of not finishing in time for me to tell him all of my news, shuddered to think of not finishing in time to allow for leisure — because I wouldn't have missed Saturday night for the world. All Greg had to say was that he wanted to go out, and I was the concierge planning it all.

We started with wine and cheese on the steps of the Lincoln Memorial, because this had always been a fun adventure of ours. We had the cheese in a baggie and the wine in a thermos — I know, I know, not the way to treat good wine, but (a) this wasn't good wine and (b) the wine wasn't the point. The point was feeling that we were elevated physically and spiritually, just that little bit above the city, and from there we went to our favorite restaurant, a burger place in Georgetown where we were known enough so that the waitstaff catered to Greg's casted leg.

Had it not been for that leg, we might have gone to a succession of bars after dinner. Instead, we settled for an old standby in Dupont Circle, where we could drink beer, watch the Orioles battle the Yankees on the plasma TV on the wall, and reconnect with people we knew. Like Neil, these were originally Greg's friends, but I had long since been accepted as one of the guys, which meant laughter, good talk, and total ease. It was a dark-wooded and discreet place; there might be handholding or a hug here and there, but an outsider would be hard-pressed to know who was with whom. And I wasn't the only woman present, because women in the know who wanted a carefree night understood that even beyond the friendship, the laughter, and the beer, the neat thing about being in a gay bar was that there was no risk of being hit on.

That said, it was not an entirely shock-free night for me — and please don't jump to conclusions here. You know my sexual orientation. You know it quite intimately by now. What you don't know — because I didn't know, didn't guess, should have suspected but was too preoccupied with my own world — is the sexual orientation of Tom.

Yes, Tom. Tom Martin from Middle River. To this day I don't quite know why I looked up at that particular moment. But my eyes penetrated the dim light in the bar and spotted Tom, standing with a group on the other side of the room. He was every bit as discreet as Greg, his arm linked with that of a friend in a way that might have been casual had we been in, say, Paris, where physicality between men was more common. But not here in D.C.

This linked arm had meaning, but it was understated, and I'm sure it was done that way for the very same reason that Greg took such care with his public image, including living with me. To be outed as being gay might negatively impact the career of a man like Greg, who was seen as something of a sex symbol to women in the heart of America. Likewise, to be outed as being gay might negatively impact the career of a man like Tom, whose dedication to his retarded sister and to his patients had endeared him to the heart of Middle River.

Tom looked around. When I asked him about it later, he admitted to feeling a prickle at the back of his neck when his eyes met mine. Even through the dark I saw a moment's panic. That was what compelled me to worm my way through the crowd to where he stood. By the time I got there, he had separated himself from the man he was with and was awaiting my judgment. I imagine that in those brief minutes he saw his career roll to the edge of a precipice and hang by a thread. Middle River could accept a bachelor doctor. A gay one? Not now. Not yet.

If he feared me, then he had underestimated me. But then, he was so stunned to see me that he didn't see me with Greg. Had he done that, he'd have understood.

I wrapped an arm around his neck and held on tightly. "This explains so much — how comfortable I felt with you from the start, how much you reminded me of Greg, why there was a lack of sexual chemistry between you and me."

"Are you disappointed?" he asked.

I drew back. "Yes, but not in you. I'm disappointed that Middle River hasn't the goodness to accept people who are different."

"But they are good people, Annie. If I didn't believe that, I wouldn't be there."

Which was one of the things I was coming to love about Tom. He had a big heart, certainly bigger than mine. I was quick to judge; if I could learn tolerance from him, he would prove a valuable friend.

I was up early the next morning, first running through familiar streets in the familiar heat, then going on from there to all the other familiar things that I loved — to brunch with Jocelyn and Amanda, to iced coffee with Berri and John (whom I liked a lot, by the way), to iced tea with another friend. I interspersed all this with errands for Greg and with stops at favorite places, like the Air and Space Museum at the Smithsonian, the Tidal Basin, the shops at Adams-Morgan.

I didn't stay long at any one place or with any one person. There was too little time. But I felt a need to see and hear and feel all that had come to mean so much to me in the last fifteen years. I was crowding it all in, waging a campaign of remembrance, because I was starting to fear that I had forgotten that these things mattered. When I was in Middle River, the town was all-consuming. Here, now, I needed to remind myself of all that I loved that Middle River couldn't provide.

We met at the condo at two in the afternoon. There were Greg and I, and there was Tom, who, after our unexpected meeting, had spent a while with us at the bar the night before. Neil arrived at two, taking time from preparation for his return to court the next day to give us legal advice on the victims' behalf. Nancy Baker, who was a pharmacologist at the EPA and a lawyer herself, was also there. She and Tom had known each other for years. They had been discussing the mercury issue since Tom first suspected a problem at

Northwood. Her role was to advise us, strictly as a friend, on where the government would stand, should word of this get out.

For two hours, we went back and forth. I learned what I needed to know so that I could be better informed at the board meeting the next day. I won't bore you with the details, but when Tom and I were finally back at Reagan National for our return flight, I turned to a fresh page in my mother's journal and made my list. The prospects were quite bleak.

First, Northwood could not be prosecuted for violating regulations for the abuse of toxic waste, because the statute of limitations had expired.

Second, according to the files Nancy had checked, Northwood was in complete compliance with current regulations, which ruled out new criminal charges.

Third, if illegal dumping could be proven to have occurred, civil charges could be brought in the form of a personal injury suit by either individuals or a group, but this would require proof of mercury poisoning in every one of the plaintiffs.

Fourth, the waters were muddied by fish containing high levels of mercury. For years, the state had posted warnings to residents of Middle River not to eat what they caught. For years, th'other side had ignored the warnings, choosing possibly dangerous food over no food at all.

Fifth and finally, the only chance of criminal charges being brought against Northwood was if it could be proven that illegal dumping had resulted in one or more deaths. That would constitute murder. There was no statute of limitations for murder.

"It'll never happen," Tom advised from my shoulder, where he had been reading my list as I wrote it. "Making the connection between illegal dumping and any one particular death will be impossible to prove. We don't know for sure that your mother had mercury poisoning. We can surmise it, based on Phoebe's case. But even if an autopsy were to prove that there was mercury in Alyssa's body at the time of death, she didn't die of it. She died of asphyxiation after a fall down the stairs."

"That's a technicality," I argued.

Our flight was called.

"She was sixty-five," Tom countered, tucking a magazine in the outside pocket of his leather duffel. "She might have fallen on her own. Omie was eighty-three. Older people often get pneumonia. In time their bodies wear out and their hearts stop. Was this because of mercury? It's circumstantial evidence, Annie."

"But what if we were to gather *all* the circumstantial evidence, and it points to a connection? What then?"

"Then we have headlines and lawyers and media, all the things you just told me you didn't want."

"I know," I said as I reached for my bag. "And I don't want those things. But *they* don't know that, and it's a good threat, don't you think? Threats are what it's about. It's about giving the impression that you have a foolproof case. Northwood has to understand what they stand to lose if they choose to fight."

I was, of course, referring to Northwood as though it included the triumvirate of Sandy, Aidan, and James, when in fact James planned a coup. A *bloodless* coup, he had said. I wondered what he had in mind, whether he could pull it off, and what would happen if he didn't. I guessed he would have to leave town. He would get another job. He could get a *better* job. He might even move to Washington. That would be promising.

Promising for me. Not so for Middle River. The town needed him. For that reason, I was praying that his bloodless coup would succeed. In that spirit, I knew that any evidence I could bring to the board meeting would be a help.

"We have Phoebe," I said, mustering hope as we stood and shouldered our things. "There have to be others like her." When I started forward, Tom held me back with a light hand on my arm.

"I haven't thanked you," he said quietly.

"Thanked me for what?" I asked, though I knew.

"Being exactly the same today as you were yesterday."

I was touched by the way he said it, and felt the need to make a point. "Are you a different person today from who you were yesterday? No."

He smiled sadly. "No. It's the perception that changes. In a town like Middle River, that's the name of the game. Y'know?"

Chapter 27

Our flight was delayed. We sat on the runway for forty minutes while mechanics tried to fix a problem. When they failed, we returned to the jetport, deplaned, changed gates, replaned, and finally took off ninety minutes late. By the time we had landed in Manchester, found Tom's pickup in the parking garage, and made the drive to Middle River, it was nearly as late as it had been when I had first returned to Middle River for my vacation on a day that seemed like an eon ago.

I would be lying if I said I wasn't pleased to be back. Of course I was pleased. Returning tonight was different from that other night. There was excitement this time, anticipation.

It was stagnantly warm; still, we rolled down the windows of the pickup as soon as we crossed the town line. We had barely passed Zwibble's when I smelled something odd.

"What's that?" Tom asked, clearly smelling it, too.

"Not gasoline," I said. "It almost smells like the kind of wood fire you'd burn in the middle of winter — almost, but not quite." I studied the buildings on Oak as we passed, but they were their usual inert nighttime selves, lit only to show their wares.

Something was definitely burning. A fine whisper of smoke had begun to collect in the air. As we drove on, the whisper grew louder and the smell more acrid.

We were nearly at Cedar, where Tom would turn to drop me at Phoebe's, when I saw the glow above the treetops ahead, up on the north end of town.

"The mill?" I asked in dismay.

Without a word, Tom drove straight ahead rather than turning. We were passing homes now, too many of which were lit this time of night. Coming up behind the taillights of another car, we drove around it and on. Its headlights grew smaller behind us, but they didn't disappear. Someone else was headed for the mill.

"It's brick," Tom said. "How can it burn?"

"Maybe the insides?"

"There's a sprinkler system."

"Maybe the woods around it?" I didn't know what else to suggest. The Gazebo was the only structure made purely of wood, but that had already been torched and rebuilt.

Torched. It was a harsh word, though it did describe what had been done both to the Gazebo and the Clubhouse. There was only one suspicious building left to burn.

"Omigod," I said as we turned in at the stone wall that marked the entrance to the mill. The smoke was heavier here, the smell sharper. "The Children's Center," I said. "Go there."

We didn't get half that far. Too soon we found ourselves behind a line of cars, with a mill guard flagging us down. We saw flames ahead — heard their crackling, the pounding of water from hoses, the bark of a bullhorn. Parking behind the other cars, we continued on foot.

The crackling actually came from the trees that surrounded the Children's Center. There was nothing left to burn of the center itself. It was little more than a brick shell.

We passed clusters of people. None seemed hurt. Still Tom ran on.

I caught his arm. "A fire here can mean only one thing. There's a mercury leak. Don't go on. It's not safe."

"I have to," he said. "I need to make sure

no one's hurt. You stay here. I'll be back."
He held up a finger in promise, then disappeared into the glare of spotlights and fire.

I had just lost sight of him when someone came up on my right. It was one of Omie's grandnieces. "The building was completely engulfed when the trucks arrived," she said. "It spread to the wood equipment in the playground, went along the whole row of them and up the kids' tower into the trees. That's what we're seeing now. The trees."

"How did it start?"

"No one knows," she said. Several others had joined us. I recognized more of Omie's relatives, Marylou Walker's son, a Harriman or two.

"Is anyone hurt?" I asked.

"No," said the Harriman. "I was up at the front a couple minutes ago. All's left is to contain the blaze. They've got it, I think. Big flames, short life, but more excitement than we've had here in a while."

I was thinking that they should only know what's coming, when I saw James emerge from the smoke. Remaining separate and off to the side, he put his hands on his hips and turned to watch.

I slipped away from the others. He didn't see me until I was close to his side, and then he was startled, but only briefly. His eyes returned to the fire.

I turned to watch with him, moving close enough so that we were arm to elbow. "Is there a leak?" I asked softly.

His voice was tight. "My monitors said no. They're checked twice a day."

"Your monitors. Ah-ha." I should have guessed. Hadn't he told me he would know if the Children's Center drums sprang a leak? Monitors would tell him that. Still, he sounded angry. "Are kids getting sick?" I asked.

"No."

"Did you set the fire?"

"No."

"Your father?"

"Not personally, but I'm sure he ordered it done."

Angry? James wasn't angry. He was *furious*.

"But isn't this a victory for you?" I reasoned. "Isn't it an admission from him that the drums underneath need to be removed?"

"Oh yeah, only no one will ever know it," he said through clenched jaws. "It's another coverup in too long a string. He'll get those drums outta there so that no one'll ever be able to claim his child got sick from something leaking into the water supply in the playground bubbler. He'll tell the board there are no toxic sites at the mill — and it'll be a lie, because there *are* other ones, only he ran out of pretty little diversionary buildings to put over them, so they're away from where people go, which is good, at least — and the board will go home and sleep well with the reassurance that Sandy Meade is on top of things. He knew they were starting to talk. Word about your sister spread faster than this friggin' fire. He was starting to get phone calls."

"Was he the one who called tomorrow's meeting?"

For a minute James's mouth was a rigid line. Then he took a breath. In the orange sheen of the fire — diminishing now — I saw the brief flare of his nostrils. "Nope. It was me. Only he reframed *that* fact by calling each of the board members and setting forth his agenda. The stakes are rising. This is an anti-me move. But it's typical of my father — trying to one-up anyone who crosses him. Well, fuck it, I'm not going away. I'm tired of coverups. I'm tired of working at a place that is dishonest enough to put its employees at risk. There's so much that's good in this mill, but it all gets diminished by the stain of graft."

"Graft."

James shot me a look. "The guys who do the cleanup? Ever wonder why they don't tell what they've done? The answer'll make your blood boil."

"Money for silence?"

"Big-time."

"Do they know they're handling mercury?"

"No. They're told it's 'production waste' that may have turned toxic over time. They're protected — masks, coveralls, you name it. And the work is done after hours, so if you're wondering why the rest of Middle River doesn't guess what's wrong, don't."

He went silent. I might have said he had run out of steam, if I didn't continue to feel his anger. It came off him in a rigid pulse. That arm cocked on his hip? It was glued there, and it was iron-hard. I knew that, because I touched it. It was my pathetic attempt to give comfort.

Very quietly — timidly, actually, because I didn't know him well enough to know how he reacted in situations like this — I asked, "Are we set for tomorrow?"

"I am," he said tersely. "Are you?"

"Yes."

"Good."

That was all he said before he vanished into the night.

Phoebe was upstairs in bed, but Sabina was in the parlor, asleep on the sofa in weirdly similar fashion to the way I had found Phoebe the very first night I had come. The difference came when Sabina awoke. She sat up, instantly alert.

"There was a fire at the mill," she said. "I'd have gone over, but I couldn't leave Phoebe."

"Tom and I just came from there," I said and told her what we had seen. We moved into the kitchen for tea, and it didn't seem to matter that it was one in the morning. I wanted to know the latest on Phoebe; Sabina wanted to know about my afternoon meeting. I wanted to know if Sabina had talked with Ron; Sabina wanted to know how it had gone with Greg.

We went through several cups of herbal tea, went on talking longer than either of us would have imagined, but Sabina didn't seem to want to go to bed any more than I did. We had never done this before, she and I. I mean, *never*. For the first time, we seemed to be more alike than different. For the first time, we were friends.

That was why, when a telltale ring came from my purse at two in the morning, after I answered, talked, and ended the call, I put the phone on the table and met Sabina's curious eyes.

"You heard. I said I'd go over."

"James *Meade?* Calling you at this hour?"

"We have this . . . this *thing* going on. We kept bumping into each other mornings when we were out running, and I had no idea it would amount to anything, because you remember the mess I got into with Aidan, but then it just kind of . . . became . . . something."

"*Sex?*" she asked.

"I'm not a virgin, Sabina. It was only when I was growing up here that I was a total nonwoman."

She was smiling. "Sex with James Meade? That's amazing. He doesn't do it with anybody. I mean, there's a reason he had to adopt a child."

I might have enlightened her on that score if I felt it were my place to do it, but it wasn't. As much as I liked this new honesty between Sabina and me, I couldn't betray James. So I put the cell phone back in my bag and took my car keys from the basket of keys on the counter. "I don't know as we'll be doing that tonight. He's upset about the fire, and he's nervous about tomorrow. I think he just doesn't want to be alone."

Sabina remained amazed. "James Meade is *always* alone. Either that image is bogus, or you've done something to him."

"The image is bogus," I said on my way to the door. I paused with a hand on the knob and looked at her reflection in the mullioned glass. "I may not be back until morning. I mean, it won't be about sex, but if he wants me to stay, it might be in all of our best interests. I'm going to be lobbying for your job."

There was enough teasing in Sabina's smile to make it even through the glass. "I'll just bet you are."

James saw my headlights and was waiting at the side door. He wore nothing but jeans, and much as I might tell my sister that this visit wasn't about sex, I was ready when he pressed my back to the wall.

So was it only about sex after all? Had he called with that in mind, needing physical release in a time of stress, as so many men did? Was I fooling myself, as so many *women* did?

No. Absolutely not. It was just that we were newcomers at communicating, and in this way we did it very well. And then, just to show you how really new we were at understanding each other, he asked a question that took me by surprise. Actually, it wasn't even the question that took me by surprise, as much as the confrontational tone of his voice.

"How was Greg?"

I was tingling inside. He had just left me, but my legs were still wrapped around his waist, with his hands holding them there. My back was still to the wall — my bare back, now, because our clothes were strewn about — and my arms were around his neck.

Freeing one, I swatted at his head. "You jerk!" I cried. I would have separated from him completely, if his torso hadn't been so fixed. "Is *that* what this is about — you marking your territory?"

Had he smiled, I would have hit him again. But he didn't. His face was as sober as I'd seen it. "It's about my feeling too much for you and wondering when the hurt's gonna come."

My heart melted. "You *are* a jerk," I said, but more gently. Then I told him about Greg. It was not a betrayal of Greg's privacy, because James and I had crossed some kind of line into a relationship that included trust. He trusted me with the truth about Mia; I trusted him with the truth about Greg. I didn't make him promise not to tell anyone about Greg, any more than he had made me promise not to tell anyone about Mia — any more than Tom had made me promise not to tell anyone what I'd learned about him. Trust was implicit in each of these instances. It went with the territory of being a true friend.

Tom was that. And yes, James was that, too.

We talked more. We spent most of the night at it. The light of day had already risen beyond his bedroom window before we finally fell asleep, but Mia woke us shortly thereafter. Since neither of us felt comfortable having her see us in bed, I let James go to her while I showered and slipped back into my clothes.

James caught me at the door just as I was about to leave. Yes, he was holding Mia, but she didn't see anything remotely untoward. All he did was put a hand on my cheek.

"Thank you," he said. "I needed that."

I nodded. "Today is important."

He raised his brows in wry agreement. "See you at four?"

I nodded again. Touching the tip of Mia's tiny nose, I said, "Bye, Mia."

She put a finger in her mouth and smiled.

You love him, Grace said, but it wasn't an accusation. After my blasting her on the plane, she had mellowed.

I don't know, I said.

I think you do. Will you marry him?

Aren't we getting ahead of ourselves here?

Are we? she asked. *Isn't this what girls do? We dream, and then we picture how things will be in those dreams. When I was in high school, I'd doodle "Mrs. George Metalious" in my notebook.*

Well, I'm not in high school. There are weighty decisions to be made, and I don't have the facts. James may or may not take over his company, he may or may not be leaving Middle River, and he may or may not love me. He has never used those words.

Do you want him to?

I don't know.

Do you want him to take over the mill?

611

I don't know.

What about leaving Middle River? Do you want him to do that?

I don't *know*. Why are you asking me all this? I've told you I don't have the facts.

Facts? Facts don't matter. It's the heart that counts.

Thank you, Dear Abby.

Now wait just a minute. Aren't you the one who spent half a plane ride giving me advice? You said I moved around too much and that maybe if I'd stayed in one place and put down roots, I'd have been happier. So was that about facts? It was not. It was about heart. That's what happiness is. It's about heart.

I couldn't argue with that. Nor was I surprised that she said it. Grace had lived life with her heart on her sleeve. It made sense that she would see it. And me, I was prevaricating. That was all.

I may have botched the execution of it, she went on, *but I knew what I wanted. I wanted success. I wanted the freedom to live life on my own terms, and I wanted a man to do it with.*

You wanted a man to dote on you.

Okay. Yes. Fine. And I wanted children, lots of children, only my body

*gave up after three, so my books be-
came my children, and then they failed
me, too, but at least I tried, because
those were the things I wanted. So
maybe you don't want those things.
But do you know what you want? Do
you know?*

I did not. And I couldn't spend time
right now thinking about it. A revived
Phoebe — not perfect, but improved after
a day of therapy, three days of rest, and a
huge dose of optimism — insisted on being
at the store, and if the crowds were big
when she had been at the clinic, they were
even bigger now. Sales were strong. But affection? Through the roof. It was one large
community show of love for our sister, and
Sabina and I were impressed.

That said, we were also distracted.
Mindful of a four o'clock deadline, we
made phone call after phone call trying to
find one more person who would testify to
the tie between exposure to mercury at
Northwood and chronic illness. We had a
significant list by this time, though, of
course, most of the people on it were being
taken care of by the Meades and had no
desire to rock that boat. I ran down the
street, caught Emily and Tom McCreedy

at their store, and made my arguments yet again. I drove across town and did the same thing with Susannah Alban, but none of the three would commit. Sabina even managed to dig deep enough into mill records to identify the chef who had prepared dinner for the Women in Business that night in March so many years ago. He had cooked; his wife had served. They had left Middle River soon after the fire to work at a resort in Vermont, but when we called there, the manager said that the pair hadn't been reliable enough to keep on for more than a year, and he had no idea where they had gone.

Very possibly their "unreliability" had to do with health problems stemming from the leak of those underground drums. But if we couldn't locate the two, the point was moot.

Badly discouraged and needing respite, we took to filling the time between calls by reading Mom's journals. There were a remarkable number of them, going all the way back to the time when she gave up writing for shopkeeping, and it wasn't that they held any major surprises, just that they were so . . . so *Mom*. There's reason why she had wanted to be a writer — she was good. That came through when she wrote about her feelings for Daddy even years after his death, when she wrote about all that she wanted for us that she feared she couldn't provide, when she wrote about Phoebe's divorce (which pained her) and Sabina's absorption in computers (which confounded her) and my leaving Middle River and never returning (which hurt her deeply).

More than once, Sabina and I would sit back with tears in our eyes after one or the other of us read a passage aloud. I'm not sure I would have wanted to do this alone. It had more meaning being with her. There was certainly more comfort.

But four o'clock approached. Setting the notebooks aside, we made a final round of calls, reminding all we spoke with of the meeting at the mill, and then Sabina went out on foot again to lobby for help, while I returned home to shower and dress. I put on a skirt, the only one I had brought with me. It was white and worked well with a red blouse and red sandals. I was definitely going for power. To that end, rather than letting my hair shout *WOMAN*, I swept it back and anchored it with a clasp. I put on makeup with care, then lined my lips with a pencil and applied lipstick with a brush. I straightened before the mirror and checked to make sure I approved.

Feeling reasonably attractive and suitably professional, I set off — and only then did it occur to me that not once since I had been back in Middle River had I seen Sandy Meade in person, which means, of course, that you don't know what he looks like.

Picture a lion with a large head and a full mane of silver hair. Erect, he stands at the same height as Aidan, several inches shorter than James. Picture a barrel chest above slim hips, and legs that are strong and agile enough to allow for stalking, which he had always done, and which, I'm told, hadn't slowed with age. Picture strong hands that like tapping a table with a pen, a mouth that is turned down, and eyes that drill whatever they see.

Intimidating? Definitely. By the time I arrived at the executive offices, I was wondering if I was up to the task. It didn't help that the last time I had faced Sandy Meade in a confrontational situation, I had lost badly.

But I was here. And I wasn't turning back. The lingering scent of the fire stiffened my resolve. Last time, the Meades had succeeded in sweeping truth under the carpet. This time, I had maturity, evidence, and James on my side.

Since there were more cars than usual, I had to park a short distance down the drive. I was walking toward the redbrick Cape with its tall pediment, dormers, and white shutters, when a man emerged from a car immediately ahead. He was very much like James in appearance, though I realized afterward that it was only the height, the neatness, and the air of authority that corresponded.

He put out his hand. "Ben Birmingham. I'm James's friend."

In that instant, I recalled what TrueBlue had said. Adding that to what Sabina had learned hacking into the system e-mail, I said, "His college roommate, the lawyer from Des Moines."

Ben smiled. "That's it. He described you well, too. I couldn't have missed you."

"Cute. I'm the only woman around. This is still an all-male board."

"There's Sandy's secretary."

"She's sixty."

"True." He hitched his head toward the building and said more seriously, "The board members are all inside. They'll be conducting business on their own for a while. While they do that, James wants us to wait outside the conference room. I'd be honored if you'd let me walk you there."

"Are you my lawyer?" I asked, only half in jest.

"If you're on James's side, I believe I am."

Chapter 28

The conference room was large and paneled in dark wood, with thick Persian rugs underfoot and weighty oil portraits on the walls. The oils were of Sandy Meade's parents and grandparents, painted from timeworn photographs but depicting each subject doing the kind of aristocratic activity that, even James knew, was more fiction than fact. His great-great-grandfather hadn't hunted for fox, any more than his great-great-grandmother had been a socialite. James believed that the dishonesty detracted from their memory, that it somehow said that who they really were wasn't good enough. He had always felt that the truest things in this room were the open meadow, the scattered trees, and the river, pictured in all their glory in the wide wall of windows.

He didn't see those today; his back was to the glass. He did see the long mahogany conference table, with a glass of iced water for each attendee and, evenly spaced, a pair of paper cubes. Sandy was at the far end, with Aidan on his immediate right, and the non-Meade members of the board, five in all, randomly seated between those two and James. They included Lowell Bunker, the mill's lawyer; Sandy's longtime friend Cyrus Towle, president of the country club; and Harry Montaine, vice president of a private college in nearby Plymouth and the token intellect. Brad Miller, a state senator and the newest member of the board, was a friend of Aidan's and had been brought on the year before for that reason alone. And finally, at the far end of the table, was Sam Winchell. A sometime friend, sometime adversary of Sandy's, he was on the board to show that Sandy wanted the town to know the truth about the state of the mill. Unfortunately, since meetings were carefully scripted, Sam had nothing to report to the town that Sandy didn't want known.

James wore a navy suit, not his everyday attire, but that didn't keep him from resting easily in his seat with his elbows on the upholstered arms, while Sandy gave his opening. It always followed the same chatty format, more a personal update than business, and it seemed all the more outlandish to James today, given the fire the night before. Not that the lingering smell of it penetrated the conference room. The air here was as carefully controlled as the agenda of the meeting. If the board members hadn't already learned of the fire, they might not have known it had happened at all.

But that was how Sandy worked. A master at manipulating the opinions of others, he was saving the real purpose of the meeting for last, solely to minimize its importance.

Setting a pair of slim reading glasses halfway down his nose, he began reading excerpts of papers pertaining to the financial health of the mill. He went on to discuss the newest paper being produced by the mill for digital-imaging processes, put due emphasis on the customization capability of its coatings and the resultant demand by hospitals, praised it as being the wave of the future — and he did all of this without once mentioning James, whose brainchild it was. He talked of other directions the mill hoped to take and presented more figures and charts, and by the time he was done, more than one pair of eyes had begun to glaze.

But not James's. He knew what his father was doing and had to work harder to swallow his fury as the minutes passed, had to work harder to keep his mind on his father's words. And then, finally, there they were.

". . . really too bad," Sandy was saying about the fire at last, "because the Children's Center is a vital part of this community. But Aidan has already found temporary quarters for the day care center until it can be rebuilt here on our grounds. Aidan, please speak about that."

Aidan came to. He had been sitting in something of a trance with his fingers steepled and his eyes out the window. It was his rendition of the thinking man's look.

Thinking man's look? James knew damn well what he was thinking about, and it wasn't business. It was his Executive Assistant, who was giving him some kind of trouble, to judge from Aidan's ranting that morning.

More galling to James, though, *Aidan* hadn't found a thing with regard to the Children's Center. Sandy was the one who had called the Catholic church and convinced Father William that it was in Our Lady's best interest to shift CCD classes to the evening and offer the space to the Children's Center during the day. Sandy knew about Father William and his house-keeper, and would have had no qualms in using that as leverage.

No, Aidan hadn't *found* a thing. Sandy had laid it all out for him an hour before the start of this meeting. Presenting it as Aidan's idea was the typical spin. Aidan had to be established as being competent, active, and concerned.

James might have laughed at that ruse, if it hadn't been so pathetic. Putting Aidan in charge would be the beginning of the end for the mill. Aidan was a puppet. He nei-ther knew nor cared about the nuts and bolts of the mill. Sandy wanted a tool for promulgating secrecy, bribery, and fraud even long after he was gone. Aidan would be that tool.

James was angry, but not out of envy. He was angry because he cared about the mill, and because he cared about Middle River. Had either not been true, he would have left town and tried to salvage his relation-ship with April for the baby's sake. Like-wise, had either not been true, he would be thinking of leaving town to follow Annie Barnes. But that was a whole *other* can of worms.

"So we're on top of this," Sandy assured the board, taking over again that quickly, because Aidan hadn't had a whole lot to say. "Now," setting one piece of paper aside, he cleared his throat and pulled up another, "there's the matter of mercury. Rumors have been going 'round town that the mill has problems, so if you move on in your folders, you'll see copies of the latest certification we received from the state."

James knew how this would go, too. By way of damage control, Sandy launched into a presentation of scientific facts and figures that were far too complex for the board to understand, but understanding wasn't the point. Sandy didn't understand them himself. He had admitted that to James more than once, back in the days when they talked, when he thought he was grooming James for his job and wanted to teach his son how to lead. The goal, he claimed, was simply to have the board *believe* that he knew what he was talking about, in this case that the state had truly declared that Northwood was mercury free.

"Hold it," James said now. They were the first words he had spoken, and they brought all eyes his way. "That's only half the truth."

Sandy shot him an ingratiating smile. "Well, it's the half we need to hear," he said and turned to the others, prepared to go on.

"No," James insisted, straightening in his seat and thereby drawing attention. "That's wrong. We need the whole truth."

"What's the whole truth?" Sam Winchell asked.

"Christ, Sam, don't encourage him," Sandy snapped.

James held up a hand to appease Sam. The man had a natural curiosity, not to mention a few philosophical differences with Sandy, hence the question. But James knew what had to be said. "The whole truth is that there are potential hot spots scattered around the mill campus, where toxic waste was buried in drums. If those drums start to leak, the potential for causing harm to human health will spawn the kind of legal action against Northwood that will run us out of business and take the town down with us."

"James," Sandy said with an exaggerated sigh. "You're being dramatic. There is no such risk."

"It's already happened twice," James said.

Apologetically, Sandy looked at his board. "I'm sorry. He simply doesn't know the facts."

James was satisfied. Sandy was playing right into his hands. The more he said to discredit James, the more he cooked his own goose.

Meanwhile, Aidan wasn't saying anything. He wasn't good on his feet. To his credit, though, he did look alarmed.

James took his briefcase from where it had rested so innocuously on the floor by his chair. He stood, put the case on the table, undid the strap, pulled out papers of his own, and began passing them around — and still Sandy tried to act as though James were nothing more than a misguided son who didn't know any better.

He gave a long-suffering sigh. "What are you doing, James?" To the others, he said, "I wouldn't bother yourselves with whatever it is that's on those sheets. It's misinformation."

James ignored him. He addressed the board members. "These are lists of people whom Northwood has been supporting through bad times. You'll see that each has been unable to work because of the ailments listed, and you'll see the dates when the problems began. You'll also see the dates of the last two fires here at the mill. What you won't see is that those fires, like the one last night, were deliberately set

626

after mercury leaked from those underground drums and made people sick."

Sandy stood. "That's *enough*."

James went on. "Mercury poisoning is typically mistaken for a dozen other diseases. That was what happened. Except we knew the truth."

"Bull*shit*," Sandy roared, but James wasn't done, not by a long shot. He was actually just getting going, just finding his rhythm. He half wished Annie were in the room, but it wasn't time yet. She would be pleased, though. The board members were listening. If they didn't believe yet, they would soon.

"If you turn to page three," he said, "you'll find copies of the first of the internal memos sent at the time of each leak. They're coded, so that there was no direct mention of words like *mercury* or *illness*. But if you turn to page six," he waited through the rustle of pages, "you'll see that Aidan says it all in one memo."

Sandy turned to Aidan. "What the hell?"

Aidan seemed startled. "Not me. I didn't send this. It's a forgery."

James eyed his brother. "I have the originals in a safe place under lock and key. Your initials are right there in ink."

"I didn't send any memo."

"Your initials, Aidan. In your hand, in ink," James said with quiet confidence, and the tone served him well. Brad, who had held back, was paying close attention now. Same with Harry. Lowell, Sandy's lawyer, had his glasses on and was closely reading the pages. And Sam was sitting back, hanging on James's every word.

So James gave him more. "After Aidan's memos, you'll find ones that deal with the men who helped with the cleanup. There are invoices detailing the gear that was purchased so that they wouldn't be exposed themselves. They weren't told about any leak, by the way. They were told that wearing the gear was a precaution in case something happened while they worked. They were told that since the Gazebo, in this case, had to be rebuilt, it just made sense to get rid of the drums."

"*That* was the truth," Sandy charged. "There were no leaks."

James went on calmly, "The last two pages detail Sandy's relationship with certain people at both the local and the state level, people who may have been in a position to question the toxicity at Northwood. As you can see, he's treated them very nicely over the years. It's not surprising that they looked the other way."

"This is slander," Sandy growled in the direction of his lawyer. He took his seat, ceding responsibility for the fight.

Lowell looked over his glasses at James and said with a Brahmin air, "Your father may be right, if all you have is paper." He shook the papers, as though they weren't worth a cent. "These things can be fabricated."

Before he had finished, James was on his way to the door. He hadn't ever doubted that Ben and Annie would be there, but the sight of them warmed a cold spot in his gut. They were two of the people in his life that he most admired, albeit one for years and the other for only days. He gestured them in.

Sandy didn't like that. "This is a board meeting. They don't belong here."

"We often have guests," James said. He introduced Ben as his longtime friend and personal attorney, and Annie as the voice of the people.

"Voice of the people?" Aidan cried, sounding outraged. "Oh, come on. She's a woman wanting vengeance for something that happened years ago."

James turned on him. "And she deserves it," he said tightly, "only that's not why she's here. She's here because she has proof — listen and hear — proof that her sister Phoebe had mercury poisoning." His eyes returned to the group. "And don't anyone try to suggest that she was exposed to mercury elsewhere in town, because the very last pages of the printout you have detail the years when the mill used mercury in its chlor-alkali plant, and acknowledgment of that by the state. We used mercury, and we produced mercury waste. Those facts are a matter of public record." He drew up chairs for Annie and Ben.

Sandy was on his feet, addressing the board. "What my son hasn't told you is that Ben Birmingham is his buddy. They were roommates in college. Makes you wonder why James couldn't go to a real lawyer, and as for Anne Barnes, she's emotionally unstable. You'll get people all over town testifying to what she did here years ago."

James was undaunted. He knew just how stable Annie was. He guessed that she had as level a head on her shoulders as anyone else here.

Smiling, he looked around the room. He was his father's son. He could match the old man for grit. "Tell you what," he said with ironclad good nature, "if any of you feels that my guests have nothing valid to say and you want to leave now, go ahead. You'll miss history being made in this town." He extended a hand toward the door in invitation, raised his brows, looked from face to face.

"Well, I just might," Sandy said. "Too much hot air in here. I'd be better outside," he added with a glance at the window, but the glance stuck. He focused, frowned, craned his neck. "What is this — 'take a walk in the meadow day'? It isn't five yet. What in the hell are they doing out there?"

James looked outside, as did everyone else in the room. At first glance, it did appear that people were just walking across the grass. Second glance showed them not to be walking once they reached the point directly in front of the windows. They were turning and staring up.

James exchanged questioning looks with Annie, but she shook her head, as mystified as he.

Sandy grinned. "There. You see? Don't know how they found out about this meeting, but they're not buying what James is trying to sell." He leaned forward, hands on the table, piercing eyes going from face to face. "Because that's what he's doing — trying to sell you a bill of goods. My eldest son sees the writing on the wall. He knows his time here is limited."

James didn't reply. Nor did he back down. "Annie, please. You first." He sat down and watched her rise, and for a minute, he was startled all over again. The Annie Barnes they all remembered from the past was worlds away from the attractive and sophisticated woman who stood here now. Her clothes were perfect for the occasion, her hair was perfect, her face was perfect. Even her tone of voice, with its tentative start, was perfect. Had she come on too strong too soon, people would have called her arrogant. Starting this way, she seemed more committed than seasoned and therein genuine.

He loved her honesty. He truly did.

She began with mention of her mother's death, but gained strength as she mentioned the people in town with whom she had talked, the physical problems they faced, their reluctance to blame the mill, and their reasons for it. She brought a personal touch to the less personal lists he had produced, and grew even more impassioned when she began speaking of Phoebe. And that was the thing that worked best — the passion. James knew everything she was going to say, but found himself rapt. He loved that passion. He couldn't doubt that she cared for the people in town or that she valued her family. She told of the Middle River Women in Business, ran through dates of their meetings at the Clubhouse prior to the fire, and gave an update of the subsequent decline in health of each attendee. She produced her mother's notebook, read the entry telling of Phoebe's presence at that one fateful meeting, spoke of miscarriages and recent illness. By the time she finished telling of Phoebe's tests in New York, the first of the treatments here in Middle River, and the latest lab results, the room was silent.

By then, the crowd outside had swelled. James didn't know if this was good or bad.

Sandy didn't seem to notice the crowd. He was too busy being smug. "Well, we certainly know why she sells books. She tells a good tale."

James came to his feet. "No tale," he said, impassioned himself now. "It's the truth, which brings us full circle." He shot a thumb toward the window. "We can't do a goddamned thing about the people from th'other side who eat fish from the river after they've been told not to, but when we let people send their children daily to a building that we know sits on a powder keg, that's immoral. When we let people suffer without the medical care they could have if only they had a clue to what's wrong, *that's* immoral. Some of it can't be fixed. We can't do anything about the McCreedys' autistic son. That kind of *in utero* damage is permanent, but we can help with his education and set up a fund to help support him —"

"We're doing that!" Sandy said.

"— and we can let Emily McCreedy know that her asthma's from chronic mercury poisoning, and that maybe, just maybe, there's a treatment for it."

"Ah, *Christ,* James," Sandy cried, throwing a hand up in exasperation. "What're you going to do — tell the world the truth and have panic here and downriver and everywhere else that people want something to blame for their being sick?"

"If I have to, I will," James vowed. "We can either do this thoroughly but quietly, or we can open it up and make a big noise. Your choice."

"*My* choice? Forget mercury. The *truth* can kill people. Tell them the truth in this case, and that'll be the end of the mill. Don't you care about that? Doesn't it matter? Or are you just as happy to pack up that little girl, who isn't going to fit in here anyway, and move on?"

James was livid. "That little girl is my daughter."

"Your adopted daughter," Sandy clarified coolly.

"No," James stated and looked slowly away from his father and toward the others in the room. "Mia is my daughter. Her mother is a woman I was with for six years —"

Sandy cut in. "Did any of us ever *see* this woman he was with for six years?" He rolled his eyes.

"Oh, she was here," James said, still speaking to the board. "She was here on three different occasions, and on each she was made to feel like such a non-person by my good father that she swore she would never return." His gaze locked with Sam Winchell's. "I'm Mia's biological father. I have sole custody, because April wouldn't live here and I couldn't leave, which tells you what I feel for this town. So go ahead. Print any or all of the above in the *Times*. I'm tired of playing Sandy's game. And while you're at it —"

"James . . ." Sandy warned.

But James was beyond restraint. "—

while you're at it, you can print the fact that my mother is alive and well and happily married to a far better man than the one at the head of this table. And *that*," he said, oblivious to the reaction of those listening, "brings me to the reason why my college roommate is here. Ben happens to be one of the best legal specialists in the country when it comes to family businesses. His work involves psychology as much as it does law, and he's been talking to me for a while, counseling me on how to try to get my father to understand how bad this whole mercury thing is, but Sandy refuses to see. It's my way or the highway, he says, and that would be fine, if hundreds of people in this town weren't in need of help. So we're going to help them."

"Like hell we are," Sandy said, though with less force than before. He was looking out the window, seeming confused.

James remained focused on the board. "We're going down through our lists, making sure that the people who can be helped will be helped, that the others are compensated, and that every last bit of mercury waste is removed."

"You'll have lawsuits," Lowell warned.

"Not if we do this right," James said, "and we have the money for it, with plenty to spare for future growth of the mill. Don't you see," he asked now of the others, "that it's the right thing to do? The mill has a moral obligation to come clean."

"Over my dead body," Sandy vowed, but he sounded tired. He was still looking out the window.

Now James turned to look. He must have reacted somehow, because suddenly everyone else was looking, too, including those on the far side of the table, now rising to see what was out on the lawn.

The crowd had grown. It covered most of the immediate area, stretching from side to side, but even more striking was the sign they had raised. There was only one. It, too, stretched from side to side, with letters large enough to be read from the boardroom with ease.

WE WANT A CLEAN MIDDLE RIVER, it said.

Annie was clutching James's arm. "Do you see who's there?" she asked softly, excitedly.

James nodded. Front and center, he saw Sabina and Phoebe. But he also saw the McCreedys. He saw the Albans and the Dahills. He saw Ian Bourque, John De-Voux, and Caleb Keene. He saw people from both sides of the river, sick ones, well ones, ones who worked at the mill and ones who did not. The implication, of course, was that if push came to shove, these people would fight the mill.

Looking back at his father, he saw that Sandy understood it, too. In that handful of minutes, he had grown smaller and paler. And suddenly James was saddened. He disagreed with Sandy on most everything important, but the man was still his father.

"I don't want this done over your dead body," he said as though he and Sandy were alone in the room. "What I want is a clearheaded transition, with everyone's needs respected." He reached over to take the folder Ben held. Opening it, he pushed it to the center of the table. "These papers specify that you'll stay on as chairman of the board, but that I'll be named president and CEO."

Sandy looked stunned. "Christ," he murmured, "that gives you all the power."

James remained silent.

Aidan had been looking at his father, clearly waiting for him to say more. When he didn't, he turned on James. "What about *me?*"

"What about you?" James replied.

"I'm in line for what you're taking."

"You'll stay where you are," James said. "You're a good front man."

"But you're taking what's mine."

James might have pointed out that he was only taking *back* what had been *his*. But it was beside the point. "This is for the good of the mill. We need a change in leadership, if for credibility alone. Those people out there? Look at them. They have power by dint of sheer numbers, and they're right — we have to clean up the mess we made. This isn't about you or me, Aidan, and it isn't about Sandy. It's about Middle River. As the mill goes, so goes the town. It's as simple as that."

Chapter 29

My heart was chock-full. I don't know how else to describe what I felt when I saw all those people with their sign. Not only had I *not* been expecting them, but, sitting in that anteroom and wondering if Phoebe's case alone could do it, I had been thinking that Grace was right, that small-town people were small-*minded* people who were just stubborn enough to keep their ugly little secrets even when it went against their own self-interest.

Yet there they were out there on the lawn, people who had no idea what James had planned but who were putting their jobs at stake nonetheless. In all the running around I had done Saturday and Sunday, visiting dear friends and favorite haunts in Washington, I hadn't felt the sheer joy I felt now.

So there was the sign on the lawn — literally and figuratively, the writing on the wall for Sandy Meade. And here on the table were the agreements James would in-

sist Sandy sign. And in their elegant upholstered chairs were the board members, alternately looking subdued, cautious, or, in
Sam's case, barely restrained. And Aidan
was clearly dying.

I wanted to stay. I wanted to see Sandy
sign those agreements with my own two
eyes. I wanted to watch Aidan swallow the
bitter pill he deserved. I wanted to throw
my arms around James, give him a hug
(maybe even a kiss, if he was amenable to
that in front of others), and tell him how
good this all felt.

I did none of the above, because James
asked me to leave. He did it politely —
"Annie, we need privacy now" — and I understood. The tone he set in his first few
moments at the helm was crucial. There
was no place here for a nonlawyer, non–
board member, non–Middle Riverite. There
was no place here for a novelist, much less
the protégée of Grace Metalious.

That was the bad news. The good news
was that I didn't have to wait in the anteroom like a good little girl. I got to go outside.

That was where things got really weird. I
had been calm through my presentation to
the board. I had no illusions about the
men in that room. Other than James and

Sam (and Ben, whom I'd only just met), I had no friends here. Nor did I wish to. I could present the facts as I saw them, with the emotion that I felt, and that was that. It was like when I stood at a podium, a successful author talking to hundreds of people at a charity dinner, I could keep my cool because my audience was largely nameless.

Out here was something else. I went out the front door of the handsome redbrick Cape and walked around to the back on a paved path. But when the people came into sight — actually, when I came into *their* sight — I felt a qualm. This was their victory, far more than mine. I had come here simply to find out why my mother had been sick.

I had already stopped. Now I took several steps back. That was when Sabina spotted me. She was with Phoebe — had an arm around her waist in support, because Phoebe was still far from well. Moving as a pair under Sabina's guidance, they broke from the crowd and came toward me. Their faces held a look of victory, even defiance, but it went only so far. Only then did it occur to me that they didn't have the foggiest idea of what had gone on upstairs.

Taking a deep breath, I raised my brows, pressed my lips together, and nodded.

Two sisters, two relieved sighs, one grand whoop of delight (this, from Sabina). Then it seemed they were running, though I know Phoebe barely had the strength, but in the next instant we were hugging, all three of us, sharing victory for what I do believe was the very first time in our lives.

"Sharing" was the operative word here, of course. We'd each had victorious moments in our lives — weddings for my sisters, childbirth for Sabina, best-sellerdom for me, to name a few. But we had never "shared" a victory, in the sense of feeling it equally with each other — in fact, feeling it all the *more* because we were *with* each other.

To this day, we've never talked about it. As close as we became in the months following the takeover of the mill, some things remained unsaid. I think we simply wanted to enjoy the closeness without analyzing it to death.

But back to that afternoon. The three of us had barely had our moment when others were beside us, asking about the meeting, giving joyous shouts of their own. I was hugged by more people in that short time, many of whose names I didn't even know, than I had been hugged by even during the last breast cancer walk that I did. Have you ever done one of those? I can't begin to describe the feeling of solidarity. Hugging is its outward show.

Well, solidarity was what we had there in Middle River that afternoon. We felt the heat of the air, smelled the warmth of the grass, the dampness of the river, the sweetness of the leaves on the trees on its banks. The smell of the fire lingered, but it had fallen behind those other, more potent and heavenly smells.

And the neat thing was that the men in that conference room didn't know any of it. All they knew was that the crowd had dispersed. They were embroiled in signing their papers and agreeing to change. By the time the meeting adjourned, we were gone.

Well. I say *we* in the communal sense. I didn't leave. I couldn't. I just sat in my car while the last of the Middle Riverites returned to their lives, just sat there with the top down and the sun, no longer oppressive, listing toward the treetops to the west of my car. I pulled the pins from my hair and let my fingers be a brush.

Annie.

Shhhh.

Putting on sunglasses, I waited and watched and wondered who would be first to leave and what his mood would be.

Ben was the first. He had a plane to catch, but he saw me in the car behind his, trotted back, and gave me a peck on the cheek. He was pleased about the meeting's outcome. No doubts about that.

Annie.

Not now, I insisted.

Sam was next. One step out the door and he lit a cigar. I suspected he was as relieved by that as by what had happened inside. He was in his car, backing out of his parking place, before he spotted me. Then he drove right over and stopped, door to door.

"That was something," he said around the cigar.

"Good, don't you think?" I asked.

"Good, I do think." He looked at me with affection. "If your mother could have seen you today, she'd have been proud."

My throat closed up. I couldn't answer. Glassy-eyed, I smiled my thanks. His remark meant more than he could know.

"I have copy to write," he said on a lighter note. "Want to help?"

I shook my head.

"Didn't think so," he said. He winked at

me, put his car in gear, and stepped on the gas.

Yes, my mother would have been proud. I was a minute in recovering from that realization. It helped that Aidan and Sandy were the next to leave the building. They kept me from having to hear Grace. Aidan strode out in obvious anger, slammed into that bold black SUV, and left rubber on the road. It was juvenile, but not at all surprising. Aidan was used to getting his way. For perhaps the first time in his life, he had not.

Sandy was more restrained, but his disappointment was no less marked. His shoulders were slack, his steps were slower, his movements — hand on the sedan door, body folding into the seat, head bowing once he was inside — were tired. I knew that had things gone just a hair differently, he would have been inside at this very moment, as determined as ever to keep Middle River in the dark about what ailed it.

I could never feel for this man, as I knew James did. But I could acknowledge the passing of an era.

Sandy drove off. Eyes on the door, I waited.

Annie.

I tried to ignore her.

Why won't you let me speak? We're friends.

You're my past, maybe even my present, but this is about the future.

I just want you to know . . . just want you to know . . .

I was distracted then, because Cyrus and Harry left. Looking somber, they exchanged several words before each disappeared in his own car and drove away. It was another five minutes before Brad left, and then another five before Lowell left. Not long after that, Marshall Greenwood came from the back of the building. Deep in thought, he eased himself into the cruiser and drove off without ever seeing me there.

And still I waited — waited and wondered — until James finally emerged.

Chapter 30

Nicole had taken a sick day. She was still trying to process what had happened between Aidan and her, was trying to figure out how she felt about it and what it meant for her job. Aidan had been calling all morning, alternately angry and apologetic, but she had no desire to see him. She did go to a friend's house for lunch, though, and once word spread that she wasn't working, her home phone rang off the hook. So she knew exactly what was about to happen at Northwood, and even *then* she had no intention of going anywhere near the place.

But she kept looking at her watch through the afternoon, and when four o'clock neared, she was in her car and on her way. She didn't make a conscious decision to take part in the protest. But something caught her up and kept her there.

It wasn't until the whole front of the meadow was filled and the sign had been raised — wasn't until they had all stood there in silence looking up at the windows behind which the fate of Middle River was being decided — wasn't until Annie Barnes came around the corner of the building and was mobbed first by her sisters, then by everyone else — that Nicole knew what the something was that had caught her up and kept her there, and it had nothing to do with mercury.

It was her daughter, likely not even aware Nicole was there but looking totally comfortable — and totally *right* — in that group surrounding Annie. It was her daughter, looking totally *attractive* with these people, certainly accepted by them and clearly happy. Her daughter. *Her* daughter. Was this Kaitlin? Grown? Independent? Perhaps acting more on what she believed than Nicole did herself?

Nicole couldn't stop staring at her. Inevitably, Kaitlin glanced her way, did a startled double-take, and stood looking back.

Nicole tried to smile, but failed miserably. She was too confused.

That must have come across, because when the others around Kaitlin started to head for their cars, the girl held back. She seemed as confused as her mother.

At last Nicole approached her. "I didn't know you'd be here."

Even in confusion, there was a touch of

defiance. "We closed the store early. I thought you were sick."

Nicole might have said that she had been sick that morning but was feeling better now, only that wasn't true, and suddenly she was tired of making excuses. "I needed a break from the office. When I found out about this, it just seemed like the best place to be."

"Does he know you're here?"

Nicole knew she meant Aidan. She thought of the possibilities — his getting a call from the guard at the gate, seeing her out the window, hearing it through the grapevine after the fact. Did he know at that moment?

She shrugged. She had no idea.

"What about your job?" Kaitlin asked. "He fired Sabina for daring to mention the word *mercury* to someone, and, like, here you are, taking part in a protest? He'll fire you if he finds out."

"If he does, he does."

Kaitlin seemed shocked. "I can't believe you're so calm. Your job means the world to you."

"It did. Maybe it doesn't anymore. I just don't know."

The girl was suddenly nervous. Her expression changed in the space of a breath.

"Has something happened? You and Dad . . . ?"

Nicole shook her head. She smiled sadly. "No. Everything's the same. I'm not even sure your father knows anything about this." It was pathetic, truly. Anton was a nonplayer in her life. They passed in the house like ships in the night. It wasn't much fun. And was it reparable? She just didn't know. But Kaitlin was waiting for her to say something. "So," she said, "you like working at the store."

"Yes."

"They're your friends, the Barneses?"

"They like me," Kaitlin said, defiant again.

"So do I," Nicole argued. "You're my *daughter*, for God's sake."

"You think I'm a loser. They don't."

"I *never* said you were a loser."

"You don't have to say it to make the point, Mom." Her chin came up in an ominous way. "I have a boyfriend. You didn't even know that, did you?"

No. She hadn't. A boyfriend? What did that mean?

"His name is Kevin Stark," Kaitlin hurried on, "and he's from th'other side, and before you get all hot and bothered and tell me that you'll have Aidan fire his dad, you

651

need to know that I *know* what I'm doing. I am not marrying Kevin. He is my boyfriend right now. That's all. I'm going to college, so I can get out of Middle River, and I'll get married after I have a career, so that it'll never matter again whether I'm ugly or fat, because people will see me for who I am," she thumped her chest, "*me*, first."

Nicole didn't know where to begin. She wanted to know about the boyfriend part, but this was paving new ground. So she said meekly, "You're not ugly or fat."

"The thing is, Kevin doesn't care. And my friends at school think it's really cool that I'm with someone."

"*With*. What does *with* mean?"

"*With*. You know, Mom."

"Are you sleeping with him?" Nicole asked.

Kaitlin didn't blink. "Are you sleeping with Aidan?"

"Hold on, there. I'm an adult. I know how to take care of myself. You're a *child*."

"I am not!" Kaitlin cried. Her body had gone rigid, but there were tears in her eyes. "That's the problem with you and me. I am not a child. Why can't you see that? I'm more than able to *have* a child, which is what *three* of my classmates in school are doing, but you probably don't know that, because you'd look at the loose clothes they wear and just think they're fat. I know how to protect myself, Mom. And I know what I want. Kevin treats me like a someone. Same with the people at Miss Lissy's Closet. I *want* to be with people who treat me like a someone."

Abruptly she stopped. It was as though she had reached the heart of the matter and had nothing more to say.

The ball was in Nicole's court. The problem was, she had never been good at sports. So she tried to clear her head and distance herself from the emotional tangle that had always tripped up Kaitlin and her. She tried to think of what she would say if Kaitlin were the daughter of a friend.

"I would like to treat you like a someone," she said quietly.

"So *do* it," Kaitlin begged.

And Nicole wanted to. "But I can't do anything if I don't know what you're thinking and feeling. Maybe I still see you as a child because you don't share your feelings and thoughts."

"It's my fault?" Kaitlin asked in dismay.

Quickly, Nicole said, "No. Mine. I don't ask. So maybe I can change that." She was the one who stopped this time. She had hit on the heart of the matter.

Kaitlin must have sensed it, too, because the chin came down and there was suddenly such a look of wanting in her eyes that Nicole was touched. Without another word, she closed the space between them and wrapped her arms around her daughter, and it felt good, felt *really* good. She didn't know what to do about her husband and didn't have a clue what to do about Aidan. But Kaitlin was different. Here was something to save.

Sabina felt victorious as she left Northwood. She was proud to be a Barnes and the sister of Annie — was proud to be a Middle Riverite and a friend to all those who had come out to the mill. She was even humbled to be the mother of Lisa and Timmy, who had seen all there was to like in Annie long before she had.

Victory. Pride. Humility. Beyond it all, though, was a hollowness. It didn't take a name or a face until she pulled in at the pale blue Cape on Randolph Road and the embodiment was there in the flesh, leaning against the trunk of his car with his arms folded and his ankles crossed, looking for all the world like he was waiting for her.

Ron.

He didn't look angry, exactly. She couldn't quite gauge his mood.

She parked and went forward, stopping just beyond arm's reach. "Hi," she said tentatively.

"Hi," he said in kind, then, "I guess there was quite a show?"

She nodded. "Did you hear about James?"

"Yes. Word spread through shipping in no time. People are pleased."

"Are you?"

He nodded. "The change will be good for the mill. Sandy deserves a rest, and Aidan, well, maybe James will rein him in." He nodded again, more slowly this time, seeming to not know what to say.

Sabina knew what he needed to say, certainly knew what she needed to hear. What he proceeded to ask wasn't it.

"Do you think you'll get your job back?"

"I have no idea!" she burst out. "That wasn't the point of the protest. The people who came to the mill today did it knowing that they were risking retaliation by the Meades, and still they came. This was about something bigger than my job or your job, Ron. It was about right and wrong. It's about the world we leave for our kids."

"I know," he said, sounding duly chastised.

"I'm not sorry for anything I did, Ron, certainly not for talking to Toni even if she *did* go to Aidan. What happened today would have happened whether I'd lost my job or not, because one person in this town took on the cause. Annie has more courage than the whole of us on this block combined!"

"I know."

"I sold her short. I'm ashamed of that."

"I sold you short. I'm sorry for that."

Hearing the words, it struck her that what she had seen on his face earlier was remorse. She hadn't recognized it, because it was new. Ron had never before had cause for remorse. This was the first real blow-out they'd ever had. That was really quite remarkable.

He reached out with arms that were longer than hers, snagged her wrists, and pulled her close. "You've been a better person than me in all this. Can you live with me, knowing that?"

The hollowness in Sabina dissolved. She smiled. "I think I can."

James didn't breathe freely until the last of the board had left. That last member was Lowell. His father's lawyer, longtime friend and confidant, he held tremendous sway when it came to helping Sandy accept defeat.

"Not defeat," James had suggested to Lowell. "Can't we call it semi-retirement?"

But Lowell knew Sandy well. "He'll call it defeat. You definitely trumped him, James."

"That wasn't my bottom line. If he'd agreed to clean things up, I'd have stayed where I was."

"This is fine. It's time. Your papers are duly signed and witnessed. I'll add my resignation in the morning."

"No, Lowell. There's no need for that."

"I'm old-school. You'll want your own team."

"But this team is good. A change in quarterback may be enough. I want you to stay. I'll need your help. Let's not throw out the baby with the bathwater."

"Speaking of which —"

James held up a hand. "Mia's for another time." He extended the hand. Lowell shook it, lifted his briefcase, and left — which was when James went to the window and took a long, relieved breath. Triumph, smugness, and certainly satisfaction were mixed in. Plus excitement. That was there, too. Mostly, though, it was about relief. He had been fighting his father for too long. Finally it was done.

A movement off by one of the trees caught his eye. It was Marshall Greenwood, in his denim shirt, jeans, and brown boots, looking up at the window.

James gestured for him to come inside and pointed toward the back door. He was waiting at the top of the stairs when Marshall labored up.

"You were waiting for me," James surmised.

One step short of the top, the chief of police put a supporting hand on the banister. His breath was short and his voice raspy. "We know your father's out. I'm wondering if I am, too."

"Not unless that's what you want."

"No matter what I want. You're the boss now."

"Only of the mill. I won't be controlling the town manager like my father did. I have enough work to do without that."

Marshall seemed dubious. "You won't fire me just because . . . because . . ."

"Because you were hard on Annie? You backed off. That's done. But what you have to do next is to make it so that you aren't afraid of people finding you out."

Marshall stared at him. "What do you mean?"

James didn't say. He simply stared right back.

Marshall was the first to blink. "And how do you suggest I do that?"

James went to the table, took a piece of paper from the cube in the middle, and jotted down the name of a treatment center. He handed the paper to Marshall. "It's in Massachusetts. You and Edna can take a 'vacation.' No one'll even know you're there."

"Is this a requirement if I want to keep my job?"

James shook his head. "Just a suggestion from a caring party."

Marshall stared at him a minute longer, then turned and plodded down the stairs. James had no idea whether the man would take his advice, but he had given it. That was all he could do.

Besides, he was suddenly eager to leave. Back in the conference room, he gathered up his things. He didn't know where Annie had gone, but he needed to find her. They had to talk.

Chapter 31

I was instantly alert when he appeared, and I have to say, he was something. In a business suit, he was as dignified as any Washington luminary I had seen. The slim build, chiseled features, and salt-and-pepper hair only augmented the image. Eyes on the SUV parked in the lot, he was striding forward when he glanced to the side and saw my car. Ours were the only two in sight.

His features lifted — and, oh my, what that did to me. I actually put a hand to my chest to calm my traitorous heart lest it take off and run on its own.

As he strode my way now, he loosened his tie and took off his jacket. He was grinning by the time he reached me. Leaving the jacket on the hood of the car, he opened the passenger door and slid in. He sat at an angle to face me, then put a hand on the back of my seat.

I saw triumph on his features and was fully expecting him to remark on the victory that had just been won for the mill and the town, when he said, "You were re-markable."

I think I blushed — I think, because I hadn't had much cause to do that when I was growing up, and when I was an adult, well, blushing wasn't particularly cool. "I just talked about what I knew," I said.

His smile vanished. "I'm sorry I had to be secretive beforehand, but I've been wanting to do this for a while. When the opening came, I knew I had one shot. If something went wrong, there wouldn't be a second chance. So I was paranoid. I didn't trust that they wouldn't find out and sabotage our efforts. My father is very good at that. Money talks. I was afraid."

"I understand."

"But I was wrong. Relationships, capital *R*, imply trust."

Capital R? I was suddenly feeling equal amounts of wanting and fear. The wanting was pure heart, the fear the better part of the rest, and that had to take precedence, didn't it? My fear involved practicality. It involved reality. It involved fact.

I shrugged. It was my best shot at being casual. "Ours is so new. We barely know each other."

James's eyes were midnight brown and intense. "Then if I asked you to stay here and move in with me, you wouldn't?"

Forget casual. My breath totally left me for a minute. That hand went back to my chest. "James," I protested, "don't *say* things like that."

"I mean every word."

"But we *do* barely know each other. You haven't a clue what happens to a writer when she's in the throes of writing a book."

"Is it like being in the throes of orgasm?" he asked, straight-faced.

"No," I replied. "Absolutely not. It's like you're living with someone who isn't there."

"Greg has managed."

"Greg isn't — he doesn't — it's just *different*, James. But there's one basic fact. I live in Washington. I own a condo and I have a life. For another, I'm a Barnes and you're a Meade. Barneses and Meades don't — don't cohabitate. For a third, there's Mia. If I were to move in, find that you and I hated each other, and move out, Mia would be hurt."

"I don't think that will happen."

"What, Mia being hurt?"

"Your moving out. I think this is good, Annie. I haven't felt this way about any woman. Ever."

"But I'm *Annie Barnes!*" I cried, saying the name with a teenager's pique.

"Yes, you're Annie Barnes," he repeated, but instead of the pique, there was reverence.

Reverence? For real? What woman didn't want to be revered by a man? What woman didn't *dream* of it? But dreaming didn't make it so.

"What about April?" I asked, grasping at straws. "You were with her for six years before you realized it wouldn't work."

James was shaking his head even before I finished. "I was with April that long *because* I realized it wouldn't work. At least, deep down I realized it. I never asked her to marry me."

I held up both hands. "Don't *say* that word. It's terrifying right now." Prior to dropping my hands, I used one to swat at a fly that buzzed around my head. "Truly, James," I said in earnest. "Look what you have ahead of you. However you look at it, you have just taken on a major headache. You have the whole mill to head now, not just product development, and then there's the work involved in finding out who all was affected by those spills and making arrangements for their care. This is not the time for you to make a major change at home."

"I disagree. It's the best time," he reasoned. "I'm going to want to come home to someone."

"Mia."

His look said it wasn't the same.

"Okay," I said, "but the three arguments I made before still fit. We're adults. We have to be sensible." The fly was buzzing around his head now. I watched him swat at it. "I think that's Grace, by the way."

James snorted. "It isn't grace. It's annoyance."

"Grace Metalious. She takes various forms. A cat purring. A fly buzzing."

He seemed both curious and amused. "Grace Metalious has been dead for years."

I looked him in the eye. "I have conversations with her."

"Do you?" he asked indulgently.

I nodded, daring him to laugh at me. "We started talking when I was a kid."

He was suddenly as serious as I was. "If you're trying to scare me away by suggesting you're nuts, it won't work. You're a novelist. Having an imagination goes with that. I'd also guess that when you were a kid you needed a friend. I can't imagine it was easy for you growing up here. So tell me what she said."

He had pegged the situation so well that I couldn't help but answer. "She told me I was a good writer and that I'd be someone someday. She was like an older sister."

"An imaginary friend."

"She gave me encouragement."

"And now?"

I had to think about that. The answer wasn't as simple. "We argue a lot now," I said. "It's like she's pushing me to do things for the wrong reasons. She wants me to be angry."

"Angry?"

"About every little thing that's wrong with Middle River. Omie said Grace was using me as a vehicle for fulfillment, but if fulfillment means revenge, I can't *do* that, because there are things wrong with *every* town, if you dig deep enough. And there's another thing: being angry is *exhausting*. I don't want to be that way for the next twenty years. Nothing is perfect. No *man* is perfect." I paused, realizing I was arguing with Grace. "By the way, she thinks you're gorgeous. She was telling me that way back when I first saw you running."

"She was, was she?" James asked, pleased in a very male sort of way. "What else did she say about me?"

"She asked questions — where did you

live, were you married, that kind of thing. She kept telling me to run faster to catch up."

"Good advice."

"She also called you Archenemy Number One. She liked the drama of that. She still thinks I should be writing a book about what's happened here. That's mostly what we argue about."

James was silent. A frown crossed his brow. Finally he said, "It would make a good book."

"I told you I wouldn't," I said in a fierce burst. "I told her I wouldn't. I told my sisters I wouldn't."

"But you've earned the right —"

"I don't *want* to write a book about this, James. I've *lived* it. Why would I want to *relive* it?"

"Isn't that what authors do?"

"Some. But not me. And certainly not in this case. Besides, the story isn't *over*. It remains to be seen what finally happens to the mill, once word about this is fully out."

"I know that," James said with a return of gravity. "But that brings us full circle. Whatever does happen, I want you with me."

Exasperated, I tossed a hand in the air. "How can you tell?"

"I can tell. I know. You're different from any woman I've known."

"Uh-huh. Different, bizarre, prickly — oh, and what was it your dad said before — unbalanced?"

"He was dead wrong."

"But how do you know?" I asked, suddenly distracted. He was unbuttoning that pale blue shirt. "What are you doing?"

"I want you to feel something."

"James," I said in a half whisper and with a glance around. The day was definitely winding down, but it still had a ways to go. *"Here?"*

Catching my hand, he slipped it inside his shirt. "Feel that?"

I did. Omigod. I did. I felt the roughness of chest hair on warm, firm skin, but that wasn't what he meant. It was his heart, beating strongly against my palm.

"That is what happens to me when I'm with you. It's like I'm more alive than I was the minute before."

I wanted to cry and say, *Yes! Yes! That's how it is!* But I was frightened. Too much was happening too soon. Even aside from the three very logical reasons I had listed earlier, there was the one about love.

Love — yikes! I hadn't come to Middle River for love. Moreover, had I known that first night that I would find love *here*, I might have turned right around and driven back to Washington.

Did I love James? How could I possibly know that? I hadn't seen him in the life situations that a couple faced.

My parents had loved each other. I wanted what they had. And yes, I wanted the perfect Adam that Grace had sought. Maybe James was it. But could I tell now, when we were riding an adrenaline rush after beating Sandy and Aidan? How many people do *you* know who came together in unusual circumstances and thought they were madly in love, only to find that when they got into the nitty-gritty of living together, they were incompatible?

Besides, James hadn't said the word love. Had he. I don't ask that. I *say* it. It is fact.

Leaving that hand on his heart, I touched his face with my free one, put my soul in my voice, and begged, "I need time, James. Can you give me that?"

It took four months, during which I vacillated between falling more and more deeply in love and fighting what I felt. It was scary. I had liked people before. I had even loved people. But nothing compared with my feelings for James. They crept into every aspect of my life, from running to eating to reading to sleeping to working to being with friends. And to sex. Can't forget that. It kept getting better. Can you believe that?

Oh, we discovered differences. I like my coffee black, he likes his light. I like mine in a ceramic mug, he likes his in a travel mug. I like Starbucks, he prefers Dunkin' Donuts. And that's only coffee. There were other differences — like his taking jelly beans over chocolate any day — but they were trivial when it came to the Big Picture.

First, Mia. By early fall she was walking, and let me tell you, there was *nothing* better than returning to Middle River after a week or two in D.C. and having Mia make a bee-line for me with her little arms raised for a lift and a hug. I suspect that she and I bonded over James, but bond we did — and if you're thinking how convenient it was now for James to have someone to take care of Mia when he was late at work or preoccupied or tired, don't. I happily took care of her, because I loved the child, but he rarely missed time with her. He genuinely enjoyed feeding and playing and bathing, and if there was a bad diaper — I mean, a really *bad* diaper — he never asked me to do it, he just did it himself. And I let him. Hey, I'm no glutton for punishment. But my point here is that we shared the chores. Never once did I feel used.

Second, work. To this day I'm in awe of the way James addressed the mercury problem. He did it — really did it — used profits from the mill to provide for the people who had been hurt, and he did it in a way that made lawsuits unnecessary. He was generous to a fault. Naturally, neither Sandy nor Aidan was pleased. They accused him of stealing the guts from the mill, but James stuck to his guns. He brought in experts to handle the legal and economic angles, and they got it right.

As for my work, it didn't matter where I lived. I actually did all of the proofing for my book in James's home office because even with Mia and the nanny around, it was quieter there than in my city condo.

Third, family. James's was difficult, the proverbial thorn in his side, because neither Sandy nor Aidan took defeat lightly. Once they got their second wind after the takeover, they pushed and prodded, strong-armed Cyrus and Harry to their side, and generally did their best to sabotage what James had planned. In theory, it would have worked. With eight on the board, there was no tie-breaker. One had never been needed before. Now, though, James outfoxed his father by naming a representative from Middle River as the ninth member, and he did it in headlines on the front page of the *Middle River Times*. Once that happened, it was too late. Middle River would have raised holy hell if Sandy had nullified the appointment.

And my family? Unbelievable. Sabina got her job back. And Phoebe very slowly recovered, though that process continues as I write this. How did they take to James as my significant other? Easily. Like they weren't at all surprised. Like the new light in which they viewed me was perfectly compatible with how they viewed James. Like they loved the idea of adding a Meade to the family.

The last took me most by surprise. I had assumed that they felt the Meade-Barnes antipathy as strongly as I did. I had assumed that the whole town felt it. But it was me. My mind. My anger. When I let go of that anger, I could see **TRUTH #10: What's in a name? Not a helluva lot. It isn't the name that matters. It's the person.**

Speaking of persons, want to know what

my sister Sabina did? She convinced James to let her take Mia for a weekend (this, in mid October) so that he could surprise me in Washington. And was I ever surprised! James was deep into the mercury settlements at the time, and might have used the weekend I was gone to crash. Yet there he was at the door of the condo, replete with chocolate pennies and the warmest brown eyes. He wanted to meet Greg, he said. He wanted to meet Berri, Jocelyn, and Amanda. He wanted to see where I slept when I wasn't with him, wanted to see what it was that I loved about Washington.

Naturally, everything in Washington was better with James there.

I want to tell you about that, but first, let me add one more thing about Sabina. What she and I had found in each other, in those few days between her firing and James's coup, continued to grow. She actually became one of my closest friends, which made it easier for me to make the break.

So. Washington.

I love Washington. I always will. But even back in August, when I returned to be with Greg and his broken leg that one weekend, something had changed. Run as I might all over the city, as I had done that weekend and continued to do during the time I spent there in the fall, trying to remind myself of all that I loved and convince myself that there was absolutely no other place on earth where I could live, it didn't work. Yes, I had friends in D.C. But they had frequent-flyer numbers, too. And New Hampshire welcomed visitors. After he met James (and likely saw where my heart was leaning), Greg came. So did Berri. And each week that I spent in Middle River, I made another friend.

So the good news was that **now I had two homes, rather than one**. Do we count this as **TRUTH #11?**

Why not? Because I was wrong in this instance, too. When James asked me to live with him, I assumed it meant giving up my Washington life. The truth is that between phone, fax, FedEx, digital cameras, and the Internet, geography has been redefined. Isolationists can babble all they want about the evils of globalism, but the world has become a smaller place. My Washington life goes on, though I have now sold my share of the condo to Greg and moved north.

Which brings me to Middle River. It's a fabulous town. But you're not surprised to hear me say that, are you? And I'll be honest. It helps to be in love with one of the leaders of the town and know that even if I never wrote another book, I wouldn't have a financial worry in the world. Folks on th'other side may not be as bullish on Middle River as I am, but they would agree with me about one thing: Middle River is home.

And that was what I told Grace. It was a flurrying day in December. I was home for the holidays (yes, home — it rolls off the tongue like honey), and I had been thinking about Grace a lot. We hadn't talked since that day in August when I had shut her out. I was feeling guilty for that, was feeling that there was unfinished business between us. Since she wouldn't come to me, I went to her.

Grace Metalious is buried in Gilmanton, the small town where she lived for longer stretches of her adult life than anywhere else. The town is south of the Lakes Region, which makes it a good drive from Middle River. James knew I was planning to go. I had been talking about it, had printed directions from MapQuest, had Xed out the date on the calendar. When the weather that day dawned iffy, he insisted on driving me there himself.

It was a bleak winter day. The trees were

bare, their once colorful leaves now faded and dry at their feet, covered with a blanket of snow that was thin but growing. Once we passed under the iron arch that marked the cemetery's entrance, we had no trouble finding her stone. It stood alone in an open patch, but there were evergreens nearby and a gentle slope with trees that would be green again come spring, and beyond the trees the peaceful water of Meetinghouse Pond, near frozen now and still.

The setting was one Grace might have described in a book to be read by ten million people. But she was here all alone, her name the only one on the stone.

James parked. He stayed in the car while I pulled up my hood and walked over that frail covering of snow. I had brought gerbera daisies; of all the flowers I had considered at the McCreedys' store, these seemed to best suit Grace. They were wildly vivid, a mix of reds, oranges, yellows, and pinks, but they were simple in form. A contradiction? No more so than Grace.

I propped the flowers in the snow so that they rested against the protruding base of the large granite stone. The name Metalious was printed in block letters high on that stone and, beneath the surname, a smaller Grace. Beneath that were the years of her birth and death, nothing else.

"I'm sorry," I said softly. "I was not nice last time we talked. I cut you off. But you deserved better. You were a good friend to me when I needed one."

I paused. A red squirrel cheeped away somewhere in the trees, and though the lightly falling snow muted the woods, the breeze caused a creak now and again. My parka rustled when I drew it tighter around me. But I didn't hear Grace.

"I've learned so much," I went on in that same quiet voice. "Mostly it's about me and how bullheaded I've been about certain things. I'm good at writing books. So are you. But we trip up when it comes to personal gripes."

I paused again. Still Grace didn't reply.

"Remember when we had that last big argument? It was after the fire, after I'd spent the night with James. You said I loved him, and I denied it, and you kept badgering, goading me to say what it was I wanted in life, and I just didn't know. I know now. A lot of what I want is what you had. I want books, and I want children, and I want James. But there's something else I want, and maybe it's what you never had. You wrote about Peyton Place, and I lived Peyton Place, and the two of us kept coming *back* to Peyton Place, even though we swore we hated it. So what is its appeal? It's home, Grace, *home*."

The breeze whipped a handful of snowflakes at my face, and for a minute I wondered if that was Grace's way of telling me to pack up my brilliant insights and leave. But there was something soothing in the aftermath of that brush with cold. I felt cleansed.

"You had started to say something to me that day. You know, the last time we talked. It was after the meeting at the mill. I was sitting in my car waiting for James to come out, and you kept saying, *I just want you to know . . . just want you to know . . .* What did you want me to know?"

I waited, but she didn't answer.

So I whispered, "Can you hear me, Grace?"

After another minute, I smiled sadly and let out a misty breath. Grace was dead.

And still I stood looking at her stone, though the cold seeped in and I started to shiver. In time, I looked at the trees, then the pond, then the stone again. This time my eyes were drawn to the daisies I had brought. I was glad I had chosen these.

They were so bright, they fairly glowed in the snow.

Releasing a final misty breath, I turned and looked back. There at the end of the boxy track in the snow left by my Uggs, like so many crumbs leading me home, was the big, warm SUV with James inside.

"I just want you to know . . ." I whispered a final time, because my boots wouldn't move yet, "just want you to know . . ." I paused. What to say? That I would miss her? That she would forever be part of me? That I wouldn't have been who I am today without her, and that I loved her for that?

I didn't say any of it. I didn't need to. If the spirit of Grace was anywhere near this place, she would know.

With that realization, my boots came unglued and I started back toward the car. The walking was easier than it should have been, because I had been relieved of a weight. I had needed to come here. Now I could move on.

Lighthearted and more eager with each step, I was halfway to James when it came to me. *He's the one.* That was what Grace had wanted to say. I could hear it now. *He's the perfect one.*

I don't know about perfect. There was

the thing about drinking coffee from a travel mug in the comfort of his own kitchen. But I could forgive him that.

Smiling at the thought, I jogged over the snow. When the door opened, I slipped inside.

"I saw the starry tree Eternity, put forth the blossom Time, she thought, and remembered Matthew Swain and the many, many friends who were part of Peyton Place. I lose my sense of proportion too easily, she admitted to herself. I let everything get too big, too important and world shaking. Only here do I realize the littleness of the things that can touch me."

From *Peyton Place*,
by Grace Metalious

A Note from
the Publisher

Afterword

When we hear the words "Peyton Place," certain images come to mind: debauchery in small-town America, the pent-up passions that lurk behind white-picket fences, and sensational scandal. Banned across the globe and denounced as "moral filth," coveted by curious teenagers and hidden under the pillows of desperate housewives, Grace Metalious's *Peyton Place* was nothing less than a bombshell of a book at the time of its publication in 1956. Its provocative energy has since permeated our whole culture, touching everything from art and politics to gender relations and the role of women in society. Its enduring impact can still be felt today. As film director John Waters put it, *Peyton Place* was "the first dirty book the baby-boom generation ever read; the 'shocker' they never got over."

But in the beginning, the bombshell had trouble getting off the ground. Turned down by five publishers, the book finally found a champion in Kitty Messner, a straight-shooting feminist and one of the only women to serve as president of a major publishing house. Messner knew a good thing when she saw it.

With an unprecedented first printing of a million copies, the book went on to sell well over 10 million, making *Peyton Place* the biggest bestseller of its time — and still one of the top bestsellers of the twentieth century. No matter how hard the obscenity police tried to block its path, the book just bulldozed on through, delighting and titillating its countless devoted readers. But *Peyton Place* was much more than just its notorious reputation as a "dirty" book. It was a revolution.

"Sinclair Lewis would no doubt have hailed Grace Metalious as a sister-in-arms against the false fronts and bourgeois pretensions of allegedly respectable communities."
— Carlos Baker,
The New York Times Book Review

The book's author, Grace Metalious, was a thirty-two-year-old stay-at-home mother of three. Truly a desperate housewife herself, she wrote *Peyton Place* in the hopes that it would lift her out of the "cage of poverty and mediocrity" in which she felt trapped. Driven and passionate, she neglected her wifely duties to write ten hours a day, leaving dishes to pile up in the sink and dust to accumulate throughout her ramshackle home. Independent and single-minded, she was not a typical woman of her time.

In the famous 1956 photo of the author, Metalious is shown dressed in rolled-up blue jeans, a man's flannel shirt, and sneakers. Her hair is unceremoniously pulled back in a practical ponytail, her cigarette is burning in a nearby ashtray, and her typewriter sits before her, waiting to pound out the next steamy scene to emerge from her uncensored mind. The photo is entitled *Pandora in Blue Jeans*. It is an appropriate title. Like her mythological namesake, Metalious lifted the lid off the box of repressive 1950s society, unleashing the demons of adultery, abortion, incest, rape, and the unbridled yearnings of female sexuality. A controversial figure, to say the least, she became an instant celebrity, both applauded and reviled, as some readers deluged her with fan letters while others hurled stones and obscenities. She was, for a while, the most talked about woman in America. Soon the pressure of fame became too much for Metalious, and she turned to alcohol, losing her fortune and eventually her life before she would reach her fortieth birthday.

Today, though the talk about Metalious has long since quieted down, she is often hailed as one of the first liberated modern women and a courageous predecessor of the feminist movement. However she is remembered, as popular heroine or hellbound pornographer, one fact is undeniable: It took tremendous courage for a wife and mother, in the 1950s, to write and publish a book like *Peyton Place*.

"A vivid, vigorous story of a small town and an expert examination of the lives of its people — their drives and vices, their ambitions and defeats, their passivity or violence, secret hopes and kindnesses, their cohesiveness and rigidity, their struggles, and oftentimes their courage."

— *Boston Herald*

The story begins in a picturesque New England town, where Indian summer has come to heat up the chilly autumn landscape. "Indian summer," wrote Metalious in her famous first line, "is like a woman. Ripe, hotly passionate, but fickle, she comes and goes as she pleases so that one is never sure whether she will come at all, nor for how long she will stay." The author walks us down the leafy streets of this seemingly peaceful suburb, introducing us to the players in her drama. On one side of the tracks, there are the wealthy Leslie Harrington and his spoiled son Rodney, as well as the good-hearted doctor Matthew Swain. On the other side, living in a tar-paper shack, is young Selena Cross and her wretched family. And in the middle class stand the book's two central characters, single mother Constance McKenzie and her teenage daughter, Allison.

On its surface, Peyton Place looks picture-perfect, but, as Metalious herself once put it, "if you go beneath that picture it's like turning over a rock with your foot. All kinds of strange things crawl out." And that's exactly what Metalious does next; she turns over that rock and lets the dark truths of the American small town come crawling.

Overprotected Allison McKenzie, desperate for a friend, grows close to Selena Cross, who is just as desperate to escape poverty and the clutches of her violent and sexually abusive stepfather, Lucas. Selena works in Constance McKenzie's dress shop, seeking maternal love at a time when Allison pushes her own mother away. Constance, rigid and cool, forbids her daughter to run around with boys, especially boys like Rodney Harrington, who knocks up the town's bad girl. Constance, once a bad girl herself, is terrified that Allison will end up like her — a single woman with a child born out of wedlock, forever hiding from scandal. This truth about her daughter's birth is a carefully guarded secret, until Constance begins to thaw in the arms of the new school principal, Tom Makris. Arguing with Allison, she blurts out the secret, wounding her daughter, who flees the small town, running away to be a writer in New York City.

After four years pass, smarting from a disastrous affair with her literary agent, Allison returns to Peyton Place to attend the murder trial of her old friend, Selena Cross. The girl admits to killing her stepfather and burying him in the sheep pen, claiming self-defense. But she doesn't specify what she was defending herself against, ashamed and afraid of losing her fiancé, Ted Carter. The trial turns around when Doc Swain testifies that he performed an illegal abortion for Selena, who was raped by her stepfather. This shocking admission blows Peyton Place wide open. Unable to hide from their secrets anymore, the townspeople must stand in the harsh light of truth. For Constance and Allison, two fiercely independent women fighting to make it in a man's world, this means reconciliation and a sense of peace.

"Captures a real sense of the tempo, texture and tensions in the social anatomy of a small town."

— *Time*

Sensational and unstoppable, after publication *Peyton Place* expanded into an Academy Award–nominated film, a best-selling sequel, and a wildly popular television series. Starring Ryan O'Neal and Mia Farrow, the 1960s TV show was the first primetime soap opera, paving the way for future hits like *Dallas*, *Twin Peaks*, and, most recently, *Desperate Housewives* — where Wisteria Lane is truly an extension of Elm Street and Maple, the thorough-

689

fares that crisscrossed the town of Peyton Place.

When asked in a television interview if she thought her creation would be remembered, Grace Metalious, without a moment's hesitation, responded, "I doubt it very much." Luckily for us, Grace was wrong. Half a century after its publication, *Peyton Place* lives on, still influencing popular culture. As we approach its fiftieth anniversary in 2006, there is renewed interest in the book and its groundbreaking author. Actress Sandra Bullock is planning a major motion picture based on Metalious's biography, and writers like Barbara Delinsky are finding new inspiration from the pioneering woman writer. Metalious, says Delinsky, "was a free-thinker who was way ahead of her times where the plight of women — indeed women's rights — was concerned." In *Looking for Peyton Place*, Delinsky has crafted a creative homage to this almost-forgotten heroine, the Pandora who helped to liberate women's hidden desires and domestic sorrows, to free them from the darkness and bring them out into the light, where shame has no place. For Grace Metalious, it was just something that had to be done. "I don't know what all the screaming is about," she said in an interview soon after publication. "*Peyton Place* isn't sexy at all. Sex is something everybody lives with — why make such a big deal about it?"

A Reading Group Guide for *Looking for Peyton Place* that explores the similarities between Barbara Delinsky's novel and Grace Metalious's book is available at

www.barbaradelinsky.com
and at
www.simonsaysauthors.com/barbaradelinsky.

3 1333 03423 1140